Outcome Without Appeal

Clifton Wilcox

Fredericksburg, Virginia

Published by Windward Publishing LLC., Fredericksburg, Virginia.

The characters and events in this book are fictitious. Any similarity to real persons, living or dead, is coincidental and not intended by the author.

Library of Congress Cataloging in Publication Data

Wilcox, Clifton

Outcome Without Appeal

Windward Publishing, LLC 2026

Dedication

For the ones who remained when
applause replaced accountability.

Table of Contents

Books by Clifton Wilcox

Non-Fiction

Scape Goat: Targeted for Blame

Groupthink: An Impediment to Success

Bias: The Unconscious Deceiver

Witch-hunt: The Assignment of Blame

The Fall of the Kingdom of Northumbria

Witch-hunt: The Class of Cultures

Road to War: The Quest for a New World Order

Envy: A Deeper Shade of Green

The Rise of the Nazi SS

The Horrible Void Between the Trenches

Fiction

Cool's Last Stand

Where Despair Comes to Play

The Monuments Must Bleed

Keeper of the Fallen Ages

I, Monster

Harvest of Eyes

The Case Against Jasper

Crimson Plume: The Song of Corvus

Prologue

The first mistake was believing the system needed consent.

It didn't arrive with force or spectacle. There were no speeches announcing its permanence, no signatures marking the end of dissent. It simply continued—decision after decision—until the space for objection collapsed under the weight of routine.

Outcomes were issued. Consequences followed. Explanations were no longer required.

Those who questioned the process were not silenced. They were absorbed. Their words recorded, categorized, and neutralized. Their objections converted into data points proving the system's fairness.

By the time anyone thought to ask for an appeal, the concept itself had become obsolete.

There was no door to knock on.

No authority left that could admit error.

Only outcomes—clean, efficient, and final.

Chapter 1

The New Order

The automatic glass doors of Halcyon Defense Systems slid open with a whisper, a sound designed for quiet efficiency that now seemed to mock the palpable tension vibrating through the air. Victor Kline stepped across the threshold, his silhouette sharp against the relentless, artificial brightness of the lobby. It was a space meticulously crafted for impression: polished granite floors that mirrored the recessed, energy-efficient lighting, walls clad in brushed steel that reflected back a distorted, elongated version of anyone who dared to linger too long. It was sterile, devoid of any personal touch, a deliberate excision of the human element in favor of cold, hard functionality. And in its sterile perfection, it was already a testament to the man who had orchestrated its design.

He paused for a beat, a stillness that felt profound amidst the subtle, almost imperceptible currents of movement and observation swirling around him. Employees, a hundred or so gathered in what was ostensibly a welcome, though no one had actually welcomed him, they stood frozen, their faces a mixture of apprehension and forced neutrality. They were a sea of hushed anticipation, the quiet before a storm that had been brewing for weeks, its thunderous arrival now imminent. His gaze swept over them, slow, deliberate, and unnervingly comprehensive. It wasn't a friendly survey; it was an assessment, a meticulous cataloging of every individual, every posture, every flicker of emotion that dared to manifest. His eyes, the color of glacial ice, missed nothing – the nervous tremor in a hand, the subtle tightening of a jaw, the almost imperceptible dart of eyes seeking reassurance from a colleague. He saw not a workforce, but a collection of assets and liabilities, potential cogs in a machine he was about to rebuild.

Halcyon Defense Systems. The name itself had once resonated

with innovation, with the cutting edge of technological advancement. It had been a place where brilliant minds, fueled by passion and a shared vision, had pushed boundaries. Now, standing in its pristine foyer, Kline felt a different energy. It wasn't the hum of progress; it was the low, thrumming vibration of stagnation. The company felt less like a hub of innovation and more like a waiting room. A waiting room for what, precisely, remained a question hanging heavy in the air, unspoken but universally felt. His presence, a force of nature in human form, had irrevocably altered the atmosphere. It was a subtle, almost imperceptible shift in gravity, a gravitational anomaly that pulled all attention toward him, signaling the undeniable end of one era and the unequivocal commencement of his absolute reign.

The polished floors, a vast expanse of black mirror, reflected his stern visage with unsettling clarity. His features were sharp, sculpted by a relentless discipline that bordered on asceticism. There was no warmth in his gaze, only a steely, unwavering focus. His dark, impeccably tailored suit seemed to absorb the light, his presence a void that drew everything into its orbit. He was an architect, not of buildings, but of organizations, and the reflection staring back at him was a prophecy, a stark premonition of the absolute order he intended to impose. Every line of his face, every angle of his posture, spoke of a mind that dealt in absolutes, in ruthless logic, and in the unwavering pursuit of a singular, perfect design. The waiting was over. The construction was about to begin.

He moved then, his gait measured, each step a deliberate punctuation mark in the silence. The soft click of his expensive leather shoes on the granite floor was the only sound that broke the stillness, a stark counterpoint to the internal cacophony of nervous thoughts likely swirling within the assembled employees. He wasn't walking towards a podium, or a designated greeting area. He was walking directly towards the heart of the company, his path cutting through the rows of silent observers as if they were merely decorative elements in his grand architectural plan. His focus was not on acknowledging their presence, but on his destination: the executive suites, the nerve center from which he would begin to dismantle and rebuild.

The employees watched, a collective breath held, as he passed. There was no handshake offered, no genial smile bestowed. Such gestures were inefficient, dispensable. Kline operated on a different plane, one where human interaction was a variable to be minimized, or, more often, a tool to be manipulated. His passing was not an introduction; it was a declaration. The air, thick with unspoken questions and anxieties, seemed to thicken further, as if his very essence was compressing the atmosphere, squeezing out any lingering vestiges of autonomy or individuality.

As he neared the elevator bank, a few brave souls instinctively stepped aside, their movements betraying a subtle, almost primal urge to avoid his gaze. He registered these subtle shifts in their body language, not with approval or disapproval, but with the detached observation of a scientist studying a specimen. He saw the fear, the apprehension, the desperate attempts to project an outward calmness that belied the internal turmoil. It was all data, raw material for the grand edifice he envisioned. The company, with its hushed reverence and its palpable unease, was a blank canvas, and he, Victor Kline, was the architect of its new order. The polished floors reflected his stern visage, yes, but they also reflected the raw potential of a system about to be forged in the crucible of his singular, unyielding vision. The age of Halcyon as it was known was over. The age of Kline had begun.

The oppressive quiet of the Halcyon Defense Systems lobby, a silence that had seemed to vibrate with held breaths and unspoken anxieties just moments before, was now shattered by a series of swift, decisive actions. Victor Kline's presence had been a prelude, a gravitational shift that had subtly rearranged the very fabric of the company. Now, the real work, the brutal, surgical excision of what he deemed extraneous, began. It wasn't a gradual phasing out or a carefully managed transition; it was an immediate, decisive strike. Within the span of mere hours, a torrent of digital notifications, starkly impersonal and devoid of any human warmth, cascaded through the company's internal network, each one a tiny, lethal projectile aimed directly at the heart of its existing structure.

These were not polite invitations to HR for a confidential chat. They were digital guillotine blades, severing ties with the swiftness and finality of a beheading. The emails, originating from a centralized, anonymized system – a testament to Kline's meticulous planning – bore a single, unambiguous subject line: "Employment Status Update." The body of each message was equally concise, a masterpiece of bureaucratic coldness. There were no apologies, no acknowledgments of past contributions, no carefully worded reassurances about future opportunities elsewhere. Just a stark pronouncement:

Your position at Halcyon Defense Systems has been eliminated, effective immediately. Your final severance package details will be communicated separately. Please refer to the attached security protocol for your departure.

The chosen, a significant fraction of Halcyon's workforce, found themselves in a state of disbelief that quickly curdled into a chilling dread. The efficiency of the process was, in its own horrifying way, remarkable. It bypassed the messiness of human interaction, the awkwardness of face-to-face dismissals, the potential for emotional appeals or reasoned debate. Instead, it was a clean, clinical severing. Within minutes of receiving their digital pronouncements, individuals found their access to company systems abruptly revoked. Their security badges, once symbols of their integration into the Halcyon ecosystem, suddenly became inert plastic, unable to unlock doors or log them into workstations. Their email accounts vanished, their internal communications ceased, their digital footprints were systematically erased.

Then came the escorts. Not burly security guards ready to drag recalcitrant employees out, but individuals dressed in the same crisp, nondescript uniforms as the lobby staff, their faces impassive, their movements precise. They appeared as if summoned by an unseen signal, materializing from the periphery to guide the newly redundant employees towards the exits. There was no physical force, no raised voices, just an unwavering, polite insistence. "This way, please," they would murmur, their tone a practiced blend of professional courtesy and undeniable authority, a tone that brooked no argument, no delay. It was the politeness of the undertaker, the efficiency of the mortician, ensuring a swift and orderly removal. The message was as clear and unyielding as the granite floors:

sentiment had no place in this new Halcyon. The human element, the messy, unpredictable, emotional human element, was to be surgically removed, leaving behind only the cold, hard machinery of productivity and profit.

The air, which had previously held a faint, almost imperceptible hum of productive work – the murmur of keyboards, the distant whir of machinery, the hushed tones of collaborative discussion – was now thick with a different kind of atmosphere. It was a suffocating blanket woven from fear, bewilderment, and a gnawing sense of betrayal. The employees who remained, those spared the immediate purge, stood frozen in their own workspaces, their eyes wide, their faces pale. They watched, a silent, stunned audience, as their colleagues, their friends, their mentors, were systematically ushered out. Each departing figure, flanked by their impassive escort, was a stark, visceral reminder of their own precarious position. The carefully constructed disguise of stability that Halcyon had once projected had been not just cracked but utterly shattered.

For those who had witnessed the exodus firsthand, the experience was deeply unsettling. Sarah Johns, a senior engineer who had been with Halcyon for fifteen years, watched as Mark, a colleague from her team, was led away. Mark, who had spoken with such enthusiasm just yesterday about the new propulsion system he was developing, now walked with a vacant stare, his shoulders slumped. Sarah's own desk felt suddenly alien, the familiar array of tools and schematics now seeming like relics of a bygone era. A cold dread snaked its way up her spine. She had always prided herself on her contributions, on her dedication. But in the face of this wholesale purge, what did dedication even mean? Was it a currency that still held value in this new, implacable regime?

Across the open-plan office, David Chen, a junior analyst, felt his hands begin to tremble. He had spent the last three years meticulously poring over market data, crafting reports that he believed informed crucial strategic decisions. Now, he couldn't shake the image of Amelia, who sat two cubicles away, being escorted out, her face a mask of shock. Amelia, who had recently bought her first home, who had spoken with such excitement about the upcoming renovations. Her future, so vibrant and full of promise just hours ago, had been summarily extinguished. David's own carefully crafted reports suddenly felt like children's drawings, insignificant and irrelevant. He glanced at his computer screen, the lines of code and data he had been so engrossed in now blurring before his eyes. Was he next? Would his own access be revoked before he could even send a farewell email to his family? The uncertainty was a physical ache, a tightening in his chest.

The silence in the remaining workspaces was not a comfortable one. It was a tense, brittle silence, punctuated by the soft, almost apologetic clicks of keyboards as some brave souls attempted to resume their tasks, their movements hesitant, their concentration fractured. Every rustle of paper, every distant footstep, became amplified, distorted. Eyes flickered towards the executive wing, towards the closed doors that now represented not opportunity, but the epicenter of this seismic upheaval. The polished granite floors, once a symbol of modern sophistication, now seemed to reflect a stark, unfeeling reality. They mirrored the pale, anxious faces of the survivors, a silent testament to the brutal efficiency of the new order.

Kline's strategy was not merely about cost-cutting; it was about a radical restructuring of corporate DNA. He was not simply trimming the fat; he was excising entire organs. The individuals removed were not necessarily underperformers in the traditional sense. Many were loyal, experienced employees who had dedicated years to Halcyon. But they were, in Kline's calculus, inefficient, sentimental, or simply not aligned with the singular, unwavering vision he intended to impose. He viewed them as relics of a past that was too soft, too forgiving, too human. His aim was to create a lean, ruthless machine, one that operated with the precision of a well-oiled weapon, unburdened by the emotional baggage of its employees.

The message, delivered with such stark finality, resonated through every department. There was no room for nostalgia, no space for personal connections, no tolerance for anything that deviated from the direct, unswerving path to profitability and dominance. The company, once a place where ideas could flourish and individuals could feel a sense of belonging, was rapidly transforming into a sterile, hyper-efficient organism, driven by a singular, unfeeling intelligence. The pink slips, delivered digitally, were the first tangible manifestation of this new ideology, a harbinger of the cold, hard logic that would now govern every aspect of Halcyon Defense Systems. The age of camaraderie and shared purpose was over. The age of absolute control and calculated efficiency had begun, and its first pronouncement was one of swift, brutal severance. The quiet that followed was not a sign of peace, but the eerie calm that precedes a storm, the chilling stillness of a battlefield after the initial carnage.

The silence that descended after the initial shockwave was not a void; it was a vacuum, rapidly filling with a miasma of unspoken questions and a chilling undercurrent of fear. The sterile efficiency of the digital purges, the emotionless escorts, had left the remaining employees in a state of suspended animation, their minds racing to comprehend the scale of the upheaval. It was as if a seismic event had occurred, not in the earth, but within the very foundations of their professional lives, leaving them adrift in a landscape irrevocably altered. The open-plan offices, once buzzing with the low hum of focused activity, now echoed with the hesitant tapping of keyboards, each keystroke a tentative probe into the new reality. Eyes, darting from monitor to monitor, held a shared, unspoken question: What just happened?

The initial wave of disbelief, a protective shield against the harshness of reality, began to crack under the relentless pressure of what had transpired. Whispers, at first barely audible, started to ripple through the rows of cubicles, like tentative ripples on a disturbed pond. These were not the confident pronouncements of those who understood, but the fragmented anxieties of those desperately trying to make sense of the inexplicable. The sheer randomness of it, the seemingly arbitrary selection of individuals, fueled the burgeoning paranoia. Mark, the propulsion engineer whose enthusiasm had been palpable just yesterday, was gone. Amelia, the junior analyst with her dreams of home renovations, had vanished. These weren't the usual targets of corporate downsizing; they were individuals who had poured years, their very essence, into Halcyon Defense Systems.

"Did you see Helen from accounting?" A voice, barely above a whisper, cut through the tense quiet. It belonged to David Chen, his face, a mask of apprehension, leaning slightly over the partition separating his cubicle from his neighbor's. "Fifteen years she'd been here. Knew everyone's payroll down to the penny. And then... just gone. Like she never existed."

His neighbor, Norma Hughs, her gaze fixed on the empty desk where Mark had been, nodded slowly. The tremor in her hands, which she had tried to suppress, was now a visible manifestation of her unease. "It's not just about numbers, David. It's about... people. People with lives, with families. This feels... barbaric."

The word hung in the air, heavy with unspoken agreement. Barbaric. It was an apt description for an operation so devoid of human consideration. The impersonal nature of the dismissals, the lack of any direct human contact, had stripped away any pretense of empathy. It was a transaction, executed with the cold logic of a trading algorithm, not a human resource policy. This wasn't a phased retirement, or a restructuring that offered retraining. This was an amputation, swift and brutal, leaving behind a gaping wound.

"But why?" David pressed, his voice cracking slightly. "What was the reason? Was it a performance issue? Because Mark was brilliant. Amelia was always on top of her reports."

Norma shook her head, her eyes clouded with a dawning realization that was more terrifying than the initial shock. "I don't think it's about performance, not in the way we understand it. This is about... a new direction. A new leadership." She gestured vaguely towards the executive wing, its doors now more imposing and inscrutable than ever. "Kline. He's making his mark. And it seems like his mark is made of... what? Our colleagues?"

The name, Victor Kline, had been a whisper before, a shadowy figure associated with the acquisition. Now, it was a palpable force, an architect of this unexpected devastation. His presence, once a distant rumor, had manifested with the force of a hurricane, sweeping through the company and leaving behind a landscape of ruins. The loyalty that many had felt, the deep-seated commitment to Halcyon, now felt like a fragile commodity, instantly devalued. They had believed in the company, in its mission, in its future. But who was this future now designed for?

"You think he doesn't want... established people?" David's voice was laced with a dawning horror. "People who know the old ways?"

"It's not just about knowing the old ways," Norma murmured, her gaze drifting to a framed photograph on her desk, a picture of her children laughing. "It's about being... attached. To the past. To each other. This new order, it feels like it wants... blank slates. People who will do exactly as they're told, without question, without history."

The sense of betrayal was a bitter pill to swallow. Yesterday, colleagues had shared coffee, collaborated on projects, and offered each other support. Today, the same faces, the same voices, were now tinged with an unnerving uncertainty. A subtle shift had occurred in the dynamics of every interaction. Was the person they had confided in yesterday now a potential informant? Was the friendly nod from across the aisle a sign of solidarity, or a calculated assessment of who was safe and who was not?

Across the office, a small group had gathered near the water cooler, their hushed tones a stark contrast to the usual boisterous camaraderie. Brenda, a veteran in the marketing department, her face etched with a weariness that went beyond just the day's events, spoke with a hushed intensity. "I heard something. My cousin works at Sterling Corp. They went through something similar when their new CEO took over. He called it 'strategic recalibration.' Said it was about shedding 'legacy personnel' to make room for 'agile innovators'."

The term "legacy personnel" landed with a thud. It was a clinical, dehumanizing label, reducing years of service and dedication to mere historical baggage. It implied that their experience, their knowledge, was not an asset, but a hindrance.

"Agile innovators," scoffed a younger man, Kevin, from IT, his usual cheerful demeanor replaced by a grim set to his jaw. "So, we're just... old software that needs to be uninstalled? My entire team was virtual, working remotely. We were efficient. We were agile. And now half of them are gone. For what? So, Kline can have people in matching suits sitting at desks, looking busy?"

The fear of being next was a palpable entity, a constant, gnawing presence. Every sudden movement, every unexpected phone call, sent a jolt of adrenaline through their systems. The once familiar environment of Halcyon Defense Systems had transformed into a minefield. Employees found themselves performing a delicate dance of caution, carefully measuring their words, their interactions, their very presence. The camaraderie that had once defined the workplace was fracturing, replaced by a pervasive suspicion. Friends who had shared lunch just days before now found themselves exchanging guarded glances, the unspoken question hanging heavy between them: Are you with him? Or are you with me?

This new suspicion permeated every corner of the organization. Conversations that had once been open and collaborative were now fragmented, punctuated by nervous glances over shoulders. The casual banter that had lubricated the gears of daily operations was replaced by stilted, formal exchanges, each word carefully chosen, lest it be misinterpreted as dissent or disloyalty. The corporate grapevine, usually a source of information, both trivial and significant, had become a breeding ground for wild speculation and terrifying rumors. Stories circulated, embellished with each retelling, about the ruthlessness of Kline's methods, about the speed and totality of the evictions.

"They say he had a list," whispered Norma to David, her voice barely audible as they both pretended to be engrossed in their screens. "A list of names, compiled weeks ago. And the system just… executed it. No human intervention. No appeals. Just a digital death sentence."

David shuddered. The idea of a pre-ordained list, of decisions made in an abstract digital realm, was profoundly disturbing. It suggested a level of pre-meditation that went beyond a simple corporate restructuring. It implied a deep-seated intention to fundamentally alter the very composition of Halcyon's workforce.

"But what about loyalty?" David asked, the question a desperate plea for reason. "What about people who have dedicated their lives to this company? Does that count for nothing now?"

"Apparently not," Norma replied, her voice flat. "Loyalty, in the old sense, might be a liability. It might mean you're too invested in the past. Too resistant to change. This Kline wants… obedience. Unquestioning dedication to his vision, whatever that might be."

The vision itself remained largely undefined, a shadowy construct projected by Kline's actions rather than his words. He had, after all, barely addressed the remaining staff directly, his pronouncements delivered through the sterile, impersonal channels of corporate communication. But his actions spoke volumes. The purge was a statement of intent, a brutal declaration of a new philosophy. It was a message that sentiment, history, and personal connections were obsolete.

The palpable tension in the air was a testament to the psychological toll of this sudden shift. Employees found themselves constantly second-guessing their own actions, their own words. The security badge, once a symbol of belonging and access, now felt like a potential marker, a tally of who had been deemed worthy to remain. Every interaction with management, even the most mundane, was now scrutinized for hidden meanings, for subtle signs of favor or disfavor. The psychological contract that had governed their relationship with Halcyon had been unilaterally torn up, leaving them exposed and vulnerable.

"I saw Mr. Henderson from R&D being escorted out," Brenda confided to Kevin, her voice hushed. "He was talking about the next-generation drone systems, breakthroughs he was on the verge of. He looked… broken. Like his entire life's work had just been erased."

Kevin ran a hand through his hair, his usual meticulous composure frayed. "It's not just the people. It's the knowledge. All those years of institutional memory, just… gone. How do we function? How do we build anything new when the foundation has been so violently shaken?"

The question echoed in the minds of many. The efficiency of Kline's purge was undeniable, but its long-term consequences remained a terrifying unknown. What would be the impact on innovation when the very people who had nurtured it were uceremoniously removed? What would be the effect on morale when trust had been so thoroughly eroded?

"It's like he's clearing the decks," Kevin mused, his gaze fixed on the distant executive offices. "Making space for his own architects. His own builders. And we're just... the temporary occupants, waiting to be evicted."

Norma overheard his remark and felt a chill snake down her spine. It was a grim but accurate assessment. They were no longer the core of Halcyon; they were the remnants, the survivors of an implacable storm. And the storm, she suspected, had only just begun. The whispers in the corridors were growing louder, morphing from simple shock into a deep-seated unease. The fear was no longer just about job security; it was about the very nature of the company they worked for, and the kind of future it was rapidly forging. The polished floors of Halcyon Defense Systems, once gleaming symbols of progress and stability, now reflected a fractured, uncertain reality, a stark reminder that in this new order, yesterday's loyal employee was today's potential casualty. The silence that had settled was not one of peace, but of anticipation, a collective holding of breath for the next decisive, and likely devastating, move from the man who had so swiftly seized control. The air was thick with unspoken anxieties, with the growing realization that loyalty to the company had been redefined, not as a commitment to its legacy or its people, but as an absolute, unwavering fealty to Victor Kline and his enigmatic, unyielding vision.

Victor Kline watched the controlled implosion from his vantage point. The corner office, once the gilded cage of the previous CEO, now served as his observatory. Sunlight, filtered through the specially treated glass, cast a sterile glow on the polished mahogany desk, a surface that felt less like furniture and more like an altar to his ambition. Below, the office floor was a tableau of quiet disarray, a subtle tremor running through the remaining personnel. It was a symphony of fear, played out in hushed tones and averted gazes. And to Victor Kline, it was a beautiful sound.

This wasn't chaos; it was a necessary pruning. A surgical strike against the accumulated inertia that had threatened to mire Halcyon

Defense Systems in the mire of its own history. He saw not the faces of his employees, but the gears and circuits of a grander mechanism. Each individual, a component. Each deviation, a flaw. And flaws, in his design, were not to be tolerated. They were to be identified, isolated, and systematically removed. He took a slow sip of the lukewarm water from the crystal carafe. The taste was bland, unremarkable, much like the past he was systematically dismantling.

He ran a hand over the smooth, cool surface of the desk. His predecessor, a man named Holland, had been too sentimental, too attached to the human element. Holland had believed in nurturing talent, in fostering a sense of community, in the fuzzy, nebulous concept of company culture. Kline saw it differently. He saw a series of liabilities, of emotional entanglements that weakened the core purpose. Halcyon was not a family; it was a weapon system. And a weapon system required precision, efficiency, and absolute, unwavering obedience. The 'legacy personnel,' as some had termed them, were the rust on the gears, the frayed wires that sparked unpredictability. They were anchors to a past that no longer served his vision.

His vision. It was a nascent thing, still taking shape, but potent nonetheless. It was a blueprint for an organization stripped of all superfluous sentiment, a hyper-efficient entity that moved with the unified purpose of a single, intelligent organism. To achieve this, however, the existing structure needed to be not merely reshaped, but fundamentally re-engineered. And the first step was the purification, the excision of the compromised elements. The digital purges, the silent escorting of individuals from the building, were merely the initial phase. It was the necessary shockwave to destabilize the old order and prepare the ground for the new.

He reached for a sleek, minimalist tablet, its screen a deep, unblemished black. This was where the future would be forged. Not with the messy, unpredictable tools of human interaction, but with the cold, impartial logic of algorithms and metrics. His mind, a finely tuned instrument, was already sketching the architecture of a new system, a framework designed to quantify and enforce the very essence of his ambition: absolute loyalty.

He began to draft the foundational principles of what he

internally termed the 'Loyalty Metric.' This wasn't about employee satisfaction surveys or performance reviews in the traditional sense. This was about measuring devotion, about quantifying an individual's alignment with his singular, unshakeable vision. The metric would be multifaceted, a complex algorithm designed to assess not just output, but intent. It would delve into digital footprints, communication patterns, even subtle shifts in collaborative behavior.

"Efficiency is not merely about speed of execution," he murmured to the empty room, the words resonating with a quiet authority. "It is about the purity of purpose. Every action, every thought, must be a deliberate contribution to the objective. Anything less is a dilution."

The initial parameters of the Loyalty Metric began to coalesce on the tablet screen. It would start with quantifiable data points: adherence to deadlines, frequency of engagement with core strategic initiatives, and responsiveness to directives. But Kline understood that true loyalty ran deeper than mere task completion. It was about intrinsic alignment, a subconscious mirroring of the leader's will.

To this end, the metric would also incorporate behavioral analytics. Sentiment analysis of internal communications, the frequency of dissent or questioning in digital forums, even the patterns of cross-departmental collaboration would be scrutinized. Did an employee spend more time engaging with colleagues deemed 'disruptive' or 'unaligned' with the new directive? Did their communications exhibit a tendency towards caution, towards questioning, towards the old ways of doing things? These were the subtle indicators, the almost imperceptible tremors, that would betray a lack of absolute commitment.

He envisioned a tiered system. At the highest rung would be the 'Acolytes' – those who not only met their objectives but actively championed the new vision, demonstrating an intuitive understanding of his directives and proactively seeking ways to advance them. They would be the vanguard, the shining examples of the new order.

Then, there would be the 'Functionals.' These were the individuals who met their performance targets, who executed tasks efficiently, but lacked the proactive, almost zealous, dedication of the Acolytes. They were essential, the cogs that kept the machine running, but they were not the drivers of its evolution. Their loyalty was passive, a compliance rather than a conviction.

At the bottom, however, lay the truly dangerous category: the 'Dissonants.' These individuals might be superficially compliant, might even possess valuable skills, but their underlying thought processes, their communication patterns, their very digital aura, would signal a lack of true alignment. They would be the outliers, the anomalies, the potential sources of infection. These were the ones the metric would flag, the ones who would, inevitably, find themselves on the next list.

Kline's fingers danced across the screen, refining the algorithm. He wasn't creating a tool to foster loyalty; he was creating a tool to measure it, and by extension, to enforce it. Loyalty, in his lexicon, was not an emergent property of a healthy organization; it was a quantifiable variable, a controllable input.

He paused, a flicker of something akin to amusement crossing his lips. The current chaos, the palpable fear he had observed, was merely the necessary friction of transition. It was the resistance of the old system as it was being dismantled. But the new system, once implemented, would be seamless. It would operate with the elegant precision of a perfectly calibrated instrument.

The concept of 'legacy personnel' was, to him, an insult. It implied a passive inheritance. Kline believed in active dominion. He wasn't inheriting Halcyon; he was seizing it, forging it anew in the crucible of his own design. The individuals who had been so summarily dismissed were not victims of a purge; they were simply incompatible hardware, no longer suited for the operating system he was installing.

He thought of the initial dismissals. The cold efficiency, the lack of emotional residue. It was precisely what he had intended. Human beings, prone to sentimentality and irrational attachments, were the primary obstacles to absolute control. He needed individuals who were malleable, who understood that their role was to serve the machine, not to imbue it with their own personal narratives or desires.

The Loyalty Metric would ensure this. It would move beyond the superficiality of annual reviews and the subjective biases of managers. It would be an objective, data-driven assessment of an individual's worth, not in terms of past achievements or potential, but in terms of their present and future alignment with his singular objective.

He considered the implications for innovation. Holland had spoken of innovation blooming from diverse perspectives and open dialogue. Kline saw innovation as a directed process, a controlled experiment. True breakthroughs wouldn't emerge from the messy crucible of collaborative debate, but from the focused, unwavering pursuit of a predetermined goal, guided by a singular, infallible vision. The Loyalty Metric would ensure that all contributions, all proposed innovations, were filtered through the lens of absolute alignment. Any idea that diverged too far, that introduced an element of unexpected novelty or independent thought, would be flagged as a potential 'dissonance.'

His mind conjured images of the people who had been removed. The engineers, the analysts, the administrators. They had been so focused on their individual tasks, their departmental silos. They had believed in the sanctity of their specialized knowledge, the uniqueness of their contributions. Kline saw only a collection of specialized functions, each replaceable, each subservient to the overarching architecture.

The beauty of the Loyalty Metric, he mused, was its scalability. It could be applied across every department, at every level of the organization. It would create a transparent, albeit brutal, hierarchy of commitment. Those who scored highly would be rewarded – not with the intangible 'appreciation' of the old guard, but with tangible markers of advancement, increased access, greater influence within the framework of his design. Those who scored poorly, however, would understand their precarious position. The metric would be a constant, looming presence, a digital Damocles sword hanging over every employee.

He leaned back, a rare, almost imperceptible smile touching his

20

lips. This was not about making people happy or fulfilled. It was about making them useful. It was about extracting maximum value, maximum dedication, with minimum friction. The fear in the office below was a temporary side effect, a necessary catalyst. Soon, it would be replaced by a different kind of adherence – a calculated, data-driven devotion, driven by the inescapable logic of the Loyalty Metric.

He began to input the final parameters into the tablet, the screen glowing with the nascent architecture of his new order. The 'legacy personnel' were gone. The stage was set. And the grand, meticulously orchestrated performance of absolute loyalty was about to begin. The faint sounds of keystrokes from the floors below no longer sounded like hesitant probes into the unknown, but like the rhythmic, determined march towards his singular vision. He felt a profound sense of satisfaction. This was not destruction; it was creation. It was the birth of a perfect machine.

The digital ether pulsed with a manufactured urgency, a low hum of activity that masked the true purpose. The initial wave of dismissals, the stark, brutal punctuation marks in Halcyon Defense Systems' corporate narrative, had served their purpose. They had instilled a primal fear, a visceral understanding that the ground beneath everyone's feet had shifted, and that the old rules of engagement no longer applied. Yet, Victor Kline understood that brute force, while effective for clearing the field, was a clumsy instrument for sustained domination. True control, the kind that permeated the very DNA of an organization, was a more insidious art. It was the art of shaping the soil before planting the seed, of cultivating the environment for obedience rather than demanding it.

To this end, the era of the 'efficiency review' commenced, a seemingly innocuous initiative rolled out with the typical corporate fanfare of progress and optimization. The memo, disseminated through the newly centralized internal communication channels, spoke of streamlining workflows, of eliminating redundancies, and of maximizing output in alignment with Kline's overarching vision. The language was deliberately neutral, couched in the comforting jargon of business management, designed to soothe anxieties and project an image of responsible leadership. But beneath the placid surface, the reviews were a meticulously designed scalpel, poised to probe for the faintest whispers of dissent, the subtlest hesitations, the most nascent sparks of independent thought.

These were not the overt critiques of performance that Holland, Kline's predecessor, might have initiated. Those were too blunt, too prone to igniting defensiveness or outright rebellion. Instead, Kline's 'efficiency reviews' were designed to be observational, analytical, almost archaeological in their approach. Each remaining employee was to undergo a comprehensive assessment, not just of their current output, but of their entire digital and professional footprint within Halcyon. Every email, every instant message, every project contribution, every meeting attendance, every shared document – all of it was to be fed into the nascent analytical engines Kline had begun to architect. The objective was to build a behavioral profile, a three-dimensional map of each individual's operational psychology.

The review process itself was structured to subtly elicit revealing data. Employees were encouraged to document their daily tasks, their challenges, and their proposed solutions. This seemingly simple request was, in fact, a carefully crafted trap. Those who offered rote, uninspired solutions, who simply reiterated existing protocols, demonstrated a lack of critical engagement. Those who hesitated, who struggled to articulate their thought processes, who produced documentation that was vague or lacking in detail, signaled a potential lack of intellectual agility or, worse, a reluctance to commit fully to the task at hand. But it was those who exhibited genuine critical thinking, who questioned assumptions, who proposed novel approaches that deviated from established norms, who presented the true conundrum for Kline.

These were the individuals who possessed the very ingenuity and adaptability that a forward-thinking company should cultivate. Yet, in Kline's meticulously calibrated world, these traits, when unbridled by absolute adherence to his vision, represented a dangerous form of uncontrolled variance. A question, no matter how insightful, was still a deviation from the mandated path. A novel solution, no matter how elegant, was an unsolicited departure from the blueprint. Kline's objective was not to encourage innovation that might lead to unpredictable outcomes, but to channel existing ingenuity exclusively towards his pre-ordained goals. The 'efficiency review' was designed to identify these individuals not for commendation, but for careful monitoring, for subtle redirection, and, if necessary, for future exclusion.

The project leads and department heads, themselves under intense scrutiny and subject to the same algorithmic assessments, were tasked with conducting these reviews. They were given a carefully curated set of guidelines, framed as a need to understand team dynamics and individual contributions in the context of the new strategic direction. However, the underlying objective was to turn them into unwitting informants, their human intuition and observational skills augmented by Kline's data-driven surveillance. They were instructed to pay particular attention to patterns of communication. Were certain individuals consistently engaged in lengthy, complex discussions that seemed to stray from immediate deliverables? Did their collaboration tend to involve individuals who had already been flagged for exhibiting 'dissonance'? Were their contributions characterized by a degree of skepticism, a tendency to play devil's advocate, or a desire to explore alternative hypotheses? These were the subtle behavioral tells that the guidelines, disguised as efficiency metrics, were designed to unearth.

The data harvested from these reviews was then fed into the nascent 'Loyalty Metric' algorithm, becoming a crucial, qualitative input. It wasn't just about what was being done, but how it was being done, and more importantly, why. The system began to build a complex web of interconnected data points, associating an individual's project contributions with their communication patterns, their online interactions, and their perceived alignment with the company's evolving ethos. A single 'inefficient' meeting, a subtly phrased question that hinted at doubt, a collaborative thread that veered off-topic – these were no longer isolated incidents. They were data points that contributed to a composite score, a numerical representation of an employee's adherence to the desired behavioral norm.

The shift in company culture was thus not a sudden, cataclysmic event, but a gradual, almost imperceptible acclimatization to a new atmospheric pressure. The once-open discussion forums, where ideas could be freely debated and challenged, began to quieten. Employees, now acutely aware that their every digital utterance was being monitored and evaluated, grew more circumspect. The vibrant, sometimes chaotic, energy of a truly collaborative environment began to dissipate, replaced by a more measured, self-censoring tone. Contributions became more carefully worded, more deferential, more attuned to the perceived expectations of leadership. The fear of being deemed 'inefficient' or 'dissonant' began to stifle the very spontaneity that had once been a hallmark of Halcyon's workforce.

Kline understood the power of subtle reinforcement. While the 'efficiency reviews' were designed to identify and flag potential problems, he also implemented a parallel system of implicit rewards for those who demonstrated the desired behaviors. Those whose communication patterns were consistently direct, concise, and aligned with strategic objectives, whose project contributions were executed without question or deviation, and who actively participated in discussions that reinforced the new directives, found themselves subtly elevated. Their tasks might become more prominent, their project involvement more visible, their access to certain information streams gradually expanded. These were not overt promotions, but quiet acknowledgements, the digital equivalent of a nod and a wink, signaling their growing favor within the new order. These were the individuals being groomed to become the 'Acolytes' of his design, the ones who would not merely follow, but proactively embody his vision.

The concept of 'company culture,' once a nebulous but potent force under Holland, was being systematically redefined. It was no longer about shared values, mutual respect, or a sense of collective purpose. It was about quantifiable compliance, about behavioral alignment, about the efficient and unquestioning execution of directives. The 'efficiency reviews' were the chisel, shaping the raw material of the workforce, and the 'Loyalty Metric' was the template, ensuring that the sculpted form conformed to Kline's exacting specifications. The subtle manipulations were working. The remaining employees, sensing the shift in the wind, began to adjust their sails, not out of genuine conviction, but out of a calculated instinct for self-preservation and advancement. The seed of control, planted in the fertile ground of fear and ambition, was beginning to sprout, its tendrils reaching into the very fabric of Halcyon Defense Systems.

The insidious nature of Kline's approach lay in its very subtlety. He didn't need to bark orders or issue ultimatums. He had created a system where the employees themselves, driven by a complex interplay of fear, ambition, and the innate human desire for belonging and validation, were effectively policing each other. The 'efficiency reviews' were not just about identifying individual transgressions; they were about setting a new standard, a benchmark for acceptable behavior and thought. By making the criteria for success so intrinsically tied to adherence to his will, Kline was engineering a workforce that would self-regulate, preemptively stifling any impulse towards independent thought or genuine dissent.

Consider the case of the R&D department, once a bastion of free-thinking engineers and scientists, a place where radical ideas were born from the friction of diverse perspectives. Under Holland, it had been a lively, sometimes boisterous, environment. Now, the air within its glass-walled offices felt considerably thinner. The 'efficiency reviews' here were particularly focused. Engineers were asked to document not just the steps taken to achieve a result, but the entire thought process, including all the alternative paths considered and discarded. This seemed innocuous, a nod to scientific rigor. However, Kline's analytical engines were programmed to scrutinize the reasons for discarding those alternatives. If an alternative was dismissed due to a perceived risk to project timelines, or a lack of immediate alignment with strategic goals, that was acceptable. But if it was discarded because it involved a theoretical leap, a departure from established paradigms, or a concept that seemed... untested... then it raised a red flag.

One particular engineer, a brilliant but notoriously unconventional mind named Sharon Stevenson, found herself at the forefront of this new scrutiny. Her project involved developing a next-generation drone propulsion system, and she had been exploring a novel, bio-inspired approach that promised unprecedented efficiency and stealth. Her documentation, while thorough, was also filled with speculative tangents, hypothetical scenarios, and detailed explorations of biological analogues that seemed far removed from the immediate engineering task. She wrote about the fluid dynamics of bird wings, the acoustic properties of certain deep-sea creatures, and the potential for bio-mimicry to unlock entirely new avenues of propulsion.

Her project lead, a man named Adrian Locke, who himself felt the constant pressure of his own 'efficiency review,' found himself in a difficult position. He recognized the sheer brilliance of Sharon's work, the potential for a true breakthrough. But he also saw the flags her documentation was generating within the system. Her lengthy, often philosophical, disquisitions were being flagged as 'time inefficiencies' and 'strategic divergence.' Her collaborative interactions, frequently involving intense whiteboard sessions with theoretical physicists and material scientists from outside the core drone team, were being categorized as 'non-optimal resource allocation.'

Locke tried to guide Sharon, to encourage her to focus on the immediate engineering challenges, to frame her groundbreaking ideas within the existing technological lexicon of Halcyon. He suggested she quantify the potential benefits more concretely, to provide definitive data points rather than theoretical possibilities. But Sharon, a purist at heart, resisted. She believed that the true innovation lay precisely in those theoretical leaps, in the exploration of the unknown. She saw the project not just as an engineering task, but as a scientific endeavor with the potential to fundamentally alter the landscape of aerial technology.

Kline, observing Sharon's profile within the 'Loyalty Metric,' saw a different narrative. He saw a highly intelligent individual whose cognitive processes were not neatly contained within the predefined boxes of Halcyon's new operational framework. Her tendency to explore tangential ideas, to question fundamental assumptions, and to engage in cross-disciplinary exploration that wasn't immediately project-centric, marked her as a potential 'Dissonant.' She was, in Kline's estimation, a source of unpredictable variance, a potential disruption to the carefully orchestrated harmony he was striving to achieve.

The 'efficiency reviews' were not merely about identifying such individuals; they were about creating a subtle, pervasive pressure that encouraged conformity. Employees began to self-censor, anticipating how their words and actions would be interpreted by the ever-watchful algorithms. The vibrant intellectual curiosity that had once characterized Halcyon began to ebb, replaced by a more cautious, pragmatic approach. Innovation, when it occurred, was incremental, safe, and always within the established parameters. The truly audacious ideas, the ones that had the potential to be transformative, were increasingly left unspoken, unwritten, their potential extinguished before they could even be conceived.

This gradual erosion of intellectual freedom had a profound impact on the company's overall morale, even among those who were not directly targeted. A subtle sense of unease permeated the organization. The constant awareness of being monitored, of having one's thoughts and actions scrutinized for compliance created a pervasive atmosphere of anxiety. Employees began to focus on avoiding negative attention rather than striving for genuine excellence. The emphasis shifted from creating value to managing one's score, from pursuing innovation to optimizing one's metrics.

Kline, however, saw this as a necessary evolution. The 'inefficiencies' he was purging were not just about individual employees; they were about systemic weaknesses. The old culture, with its emphasis on individual initiative and open dialogue, had fostered a degree of autonomy that was antithetical to his vision of a unified, controllable entity. The 'efficiency reviews' and the accompanying 'Loyalty Metric' were the tools he was using to dissolve that autonomy, to integrate each individual into the larger, singular purpose he envisioned.

The impact extended beyond the individual employee's immediate tasks. The 'efficiency reviews' also began to assess an employee's engagement with company-wide initiatives and their willingness to champion the new strategic direction. Those who remained silent during town hall meetings, who didn't proactively share positive feedback on new policies, or who were perceived as passively observing the changes rather than actively participating in them, also began to accumulate negative points. This created a subtle pressure to perform loyalty, to outwardly demonstrate commitment even if it wasn't genuinely felt. The company culture was no longer an organic outgrowth of shared experience, but a carefully constructed impression, maintained by a constant process of monitoring and reinforcement.

The success of this subtle manipulation lay in its deniability. There were no overt accusations, no public shaming. The 'efficiency reviews' were framed as standard operational procedures. The 'Loyalty Metric' was a sophisticated internal tool, its exact workings a closely guarded secret. When an employee found themselves sidelined, overlooked for opportunities, or eventually asked to leave, it was rarely due to a single, identifiable transgression. It was the culmination of a thousand tiny data points, a composite score that simply indicated a lack of alignment. The employee could never quite pinpoint the exact failing, could never definitively argue against the system. They were left to internalize the judgment, to question their own competence or suitability, and to become more compliant in their future endeavors, or to seek employment elsewhere.

Kline watched the ripples of his actions spread, a master conductor orchestrating a silent symphony of behavioral modification. The fear was still present, a low-grade hum beneath the surface of daily operations, but it was being overlaid with a new motivation: the desire to perform, to conform, to achieve a favorable score on the invisible metric. The 'efficiency reviews' were not just a tool for control; they were an education, teaching the remaining workforce precisely what was expected of them, and the subtle, yet undeniable, consequences of deviation. The seed of control had found fertile ground, and the new order of Halcyon Defense Systems was taking root, not through overt coercion, but through the quiet, relentless power of algorithmic persuasion and the subtle manipulation of human nature itself. The culture was irrevocably shifting, becoming something colder, more calculated, and infinitely more amenable to the will of its new master.

Chapter 2

The Loyalty Metric

The initial rollout of the "efficiency reviews" had been a calculated maneuver, a surgical strike designed to recalibrate the organizational DNA of Halcyon Defense Systems. It had exposed the fault lines, identified the tremors of potential dissent, and begun the subtle process of weeding out the thorns that pricked at Victor Kline's grand design. Yet, even as the whispers of layoffs and the fear of impending audits settled into a new, tense normalcy, Kline knew this was merely the preamble. True dominion wasn't achieved by pruning the branches, but by fundamentally altering the soil from which they grew. It was time to introduce the maestro's score, the underlying melody that would guide every subsequent note. It was time to unveil the 'Loyalty Metric.'

The announcement arrived not with a bang, but with the familiar, carefully crafted cadence of corporate communication. A memo, brimming with optimistic jargon about synergy, accountability, and the dawn of a new era of peak performance, landed in every employee's inbox. It spoke of a revolutionary, proprietary system designed to "empower individuals and teams by fostering a more cohesive, collaborative, and outcome-oriented environment." The language was intentionally vague, deliberately abstract, a carefully constructed veil of positive intent. The 'Loyalty Metric,' as it was to be known, was presented not as a tool of surveillance, but as a sophisticated performance enhancement platform. It was, the memo insisted, about recognizing and rewarding contributions that truly moved Halcyon forward, about identifying and nurturing the very essence of what made the company successful.

Kline himself orchestrated the unveiling with his characteristic blend of visionary rhetoric and pragmatic reassurance. He held a series of highly publicized (within the company, of course) virtual town halls, his image projected onto screens across every office and home workspace. His voice, calm and measured, resonated with an air of conviction. "We are entering a period of unprecedented change and opportunity," he declared, his gaze seeming to penetrate the digital ether. "To navigate this landscape successfully, we must ensure that every member of the Halcyon family is aligned with our collective vision, that our efforts are harmonized, and that our most valuable assets – our people – are recognized for their dedication and their drive."

He painted a picture of a future where individual strengths were amplified, where collaboration flowed seamlessly, and where every employee understood their pivotal role in achieving strategic objectives. The 'Loyalty Metric,' he explained, was the key to unlocking this future. It was designed, he elaborated, to measure three core pillars of professional excellence: collaboration, initiative, and adherence to company protocols. These were universally understood and seemingly benign metrics. Who could argue against the importance of working well with others? Who could dispute the value of taking initiative? And who would dare to suggest that following established protocols was not a fundamental requirement for success?

The system, as described, was designed to be holistic. It would analyze an employee's contributions across a spectrum of activities. Project involvement, task completion rates, and the quality of deliverables were, of course, part of the equation. But the 'Loyalty Metric' went deeper. It incorporated data from internal communication platforms, tracking the frequency and nature of interactions between team members. It assessed participation in company-wide initiatives, from mandatory training sessions to voluntary "synergy-building" events. It even, subtly, factored in an employee's responsiveness to leadership directives and their willingness to embrace new strategies, even those that represented a significant departure from past practices.

This emphasis on "adherence to company protocols" was where the true insidious nature of the metric began to reveal itself. Under Kline's leadership, the definition of a "protocol" had expanded far beyond the traditional understanding of procedural guidelines. It now encompassed a broad spectrum of expected behaviors, attitudes, and even unspoken assumptions. Protocols were no longer just about how to do a job; they were about how to think about the job, how to communicate about the job, and how to align one's very being with the overarching objectives of Victor Kline.

The system purported to identify "positive contributions" to the company culture, which in Kline's lexicon translated to behaviors that reinforced his vision. Did an employee consistently offer solutions that were directly aligned with the stated strategic goals, even if they weren't the most innovative? Did they engage in discussions that reinforced the approved narratives, or did they tend to introduce tangential or questioning remarks? Did they proactively support new initiatives, even if they had initial reservations, or did they express those reservations openly, potentially sowing seeds of doubt amongst their peers? The 'Loyalty Metric' was designed to assign numerical values to these subtle nuances, to quantify the unquantifiable essence of an employee's alignment.

Consider the seemingly simple act of participating in a team meeting. Under the old regime, a meeting might be a space for robust debate, for challenging assumptions, for brainstorming novel solutions that might initially seem outlandish. An employee who posed a particularly probing question, even if it momentarily derailed the planned agenda, might be seen as a valuable contributor, a catalyst for deeper thinking. But under the 'Loyalty Metric,' such behavior would be meticulously scrutinized. Was the question designed to advance the project towards a pre-defined objective, or did it suggest a divergence from the expected path? Did the employee offer a constructive suggestion for improvement, or did their inquiry imply a fundamental dissatisfaction with the current direction? The system, fed by the data streams from every digital interaction, would parse these distinctions, assigning a score that reflected the employee's perceived alignment with Kline's vision. A question that was too probing, too tangential, or too critical of the established narrative would contribute to a negative score. Conversely, a concise statement of agreement, a prompt affirmation of the team leader's suggestion, or an offer to take on an additional task that furthered the immediate objective, would be rewarded with positive points.

The concept of "initiative" also underwent a significant redefinition. Previously, initiative might have meant proactively identifying a problem and proposing a novel solution, even if it required venturing into uncharted territory. It was about boldness, about creative problem-solving, about pushing the boundaries of what was considered possible. Now, under the 'Loyalty Metric,' initiative was recontextualized as the enthusiastic and immediate execution of tasks that were aligned with Kline's directives. It was about anticipating what Kline wanted and delivering it before being asked. It was about demonstrating an unwavering commitment to the established path, and a willingness to proactively remove any obstacles that might impede progress towards pre-determined goals. An employee who spent time exploring an experimental new technology that might have future applications, but which wasn't directly tied to an immediate, approved project, would be seen as inefficiently allocating their resources. The 'Loyalty Metric' would register this as a lack of focus, a deviation from the core mission. Conversely, an employee who meticulously followed the prescribed steps to complete a tedious but essential reporting task, even if they saw a more efficient way to achieve the same outcome, would be praised for their adherence and their 'initiative' in completing the task diligently.

The true genius, and the chilling aspect, of the 'Loyalty Metric' lay in its ability to quantify subservience. It was not about measuring an employee's actual contribution to the company's success in a tangible, objective sense. It was about measuring their willingness to conform to Victor Kline's personal vision, their susceptibility to his manufactured ideology. The system was designed to track subtle, almost imperceptible behaviors – the speed of a response, the choice of words in an email, the timing of a participation in a forum, the perceived level of enthusiasm in a virtual interaction. These were the granular data points that, when aggregated, painted a picture of an employee's internal alignment.

Kline understood that genuine loyalty could not be commanded; it had to be cultivated, or, in his case, engineered. The 'Loyalty Metric' was the engine of this engineering. It provided a constant, invisible feedback loop, and a continuous stream of data that informed the system's assessment of each individual. Employees who consistently scored high on the metric found themselves subtly rewarded. Their names might appear more frequently in internal communications, they might be given access to more influential projects, or their input might be solicited more often in strategic discussions. These were not overt promotions, but quiet acknowledgements, digital pats on the back that signaled their growing favor within Kline's new order. They were the budding 'Acolytes,' individuals whose behavior patterns had been so finely tuned by the metric that they began to embody the desired ethos with a remarkable, almost frightening, sincerity.

Conversely, those who struggled to align, whose digital footprints consistently registered 'dissonance,' began to find themselves on the periphery. Opportunities would mysteriously bypass them, their projects might be reassigned, or they might find themselves subjected to more frequent "developmental feedback sessions," a euphemism for subtle pressure to conform or depart. The 'Loyalty Metric' offered no recourse, no appeal process. Its judgments were opaque, its logic inscrutable to the average employee. The only way to navigate it was to internalize its implicit demands, to constantly self-monitor and adjust one's behavior to ensure a favorable score.

The system was designed to exploit fundamental human psychological drivers. The desire for belonging, the need for validation, and the inherent fear of exclusion all played into its effectiveness. By gamifying loyalty, by assigning numerical values to subservience, Kline was transforming the workplace into a constant, silent competition for approval. Employees were no longer primarily focused on delivering excellent work; they were focused on optimizing their 'Loyalty Metric' score. This shift in motivation had profound implications. Innovation that didn't directly contribute to a measurable improvement in an employee's metric was likely to be neglected. Risk-taking, a crucial component of genuine progress, was actively discouraged, as any deviation from the norm carried the potential for a negative score.

The 'Loyalty Metric' was not merely a performance review tool; it was a mechanism for cultural engineering. It was designed to systematically dismantle any vestiges of independent thought, critical inquiry, or individualistic expression that did not serve Kline's overarching agenda. It encouraged a passive, compliant workforce, one that was eager to please and terrified of stepping out of line. The inherent ambiguity of the metric was its greatest strength. It allowed for constant reinterpretation, for the gradual shifting of goalposts, ensuring that employees were perpetually striving to meet an ever-moving target, an illusion of control that masked the reality of their meticulously managed existence. The system was a constant, silent hum of surveillance, a pervasive awareness that every interaction, every keystroke, was being evaluated not for its utility, but for its alignment with the singular will of Victor Kline. It was the ultimate expression of his control, a digital puppet master pulling the strings of every employee, ensuring that Halcyon Defense Systems danced to his tune, not with overt coercion, but with the subtle, irresistible power of algorithmic persuasion.

The intricate architecture of the 'Loyalty Metric' was not confined to abstract algorithms and digital whispers. Its implementation was a meticulously orchestrated symphony of human interaction, designed to amplify its pervasive influence. Victor Kline, a conductor of corporate destinies, ensured that the system was not merely a passive observer, but an active agent of cultural transformation. The metric's tendrils reached into the very fabric of daily operations, manifesting through a multi-pronged approach that seamlessly blended technological prowess with a calculated exploitation of interpersonal dynamics.

At its core, the system relied on a sophisticated interplay of data collection mechanisms. First, there were the surveys. These were not your typical employee satisfaction questionnaires, filled with bland inquiries about benefits and management styles. Instead, the 'Loyalty Metric' surveys were designed to probe the deepest recesses of an employee's perceived commitment and their alignment with the prevailing corporate ideology. They were rolled out at irregular intervals, catching employees off guard and fostering a sense of constant scrutiny. Questions would pivot from the ostensibly objective, such as "How effectively do you feel your team collaborates towards shared objectives?", to the disturbingly subjective, such as "To what extent do you perceive your colleagues' attitudes as being conducive to achieving our strategic goals?"

The true insidious genius of these surveys lay in their framing. They positioned the act of answering not as a personal reflection, but as a patriotic duty to Halcyon Defense Systems. The accompanying memos, always meticulously crafted by Kline's communications team, emphasized that candid feedback was essential for 'optimizing team synergy' and 'identifying areas for collective growth.' Employees were urged to be thorough, to provide detailed examples, and to ensure their responses accurately reflected the 'spirit of innovation and dedication' that Kline championed. This framing subtly encouraged employees to view their colleagues through a lens of suspicion, to scrutinize their every interaction for potential deviations from the 'correct' attitude. A seemingly innocent coffee break conversation could be reinterpreted as a sign of disengagement, a shared moment of levity transformed into a potential metric-deducting infraction if it was perceived as unproductive or worse, subversive.

Complementing these individual surveys was the element of peer review. This was where Kline's understanding of human psychology truly came into play. The 'Loyalty Metric' didn't just rely on self-reporting or algorithmic analysis; it actively encouraged employees to report on each other. These were not formal performance reviews, but rather informal channels of feedback, presented as a way to "foster a culture of mutual accountability and shared responsibility." Employees were provided with secure, anonymized digital forms, ostensibly designed to report "observations that contribute to team success" or "concerns that might hinder our collective progress."

The language used to encourage these submissions was carefully chosen. It appealed to a sense of corporate camaraderie, urging employees to act as vigilant guardians of Halcyon's vision. "Your insights are invaluable in shaping a truly high-performance culture," one internal communication read. "By sharing your observations, you contribute to a more cohesive and effective workplace for everyone." This veiled encouragement created a palpable tension within the office. Who could be trusted? Was the colleague who shared a joke also secretly undermining the company's objectives? Was the team member who offered a dissenting opinion truly committed, or were they a nascent saboteur? The 'Loyalty Metric' transformed the workplace into a breeding ground for suspicion, eroding trust and fostering an environment where self-censorship became not just a strategy for survival, but a necessary skill.

This peer-reporting mechanism was particularly potent because it allowed for the quantification of subjective observations. An employee might simply note that a colleague seemed "unenthusiastic" about a new directive. The algorithm, designed by Kline himself to interpret these subtle nuances, would then translate this observation into a numerical score, factoring in the reporter's own 'Loyalty Metric' score to weigh the credibility of the feedback. This created a perverse incentive structure. Employees who were themselves high scorers on the 'Loyalty Metric' found their feedback carrying more weight, thus encouraging them to actively monitor and report on their peers to solidify their own position. Conversely, those with lower scores found their observations dismissed, further isolating them and reinforcing the algorithmic judgment against them.

Even the most mundane interactions were not immune to the metric's invasive reach. Observational data, gathered through a sophisticated network of digital tools, formed the third pillar of the 'Loyalty Metric's' data-gathering apparatus. This included the analysis of internal communication platforms – email, instant messaging, and project management tools. The system meticulously tracked the frequency and nature of employee interactions. Who was communicating with whom? How quickly were responses being sent? Were conversations predominantly task-oriented, or did they stray into less productive territories? An employee who frequently engaged in lengthy, informal chats, even if those chats fostered camaraderie, might see their score dip. The system was programmed to identify and penalize what it deemed as 'time wastage' or 'lack of focus.'

Furthermore, the system monitored participation in company-wide initiatives. This extended beyond mandatory training sessions, which were already scored based on completion rates and test results. It included participation in 'voluntary' team-building events, town halls, and even the engagement with internal corporate newsletters. An employee who consistently opened and read company-wide emails promptly, who attended all optional webinars, and who actively participated in online forums discussing corporate strategy, would accumulate positive points. Those who let emails languish unread, who skipped optional events, or who remained silent in online discussions, would be flagged as disengaged. The 'Loyalty Metric' subtly, yet relentlessly, nudged employees towards a performative display of corporate enthusiasm.

The algorithm, a complex web of weighted variables and predictive analytics, was the silent architect of these scores. It was a black box, its inner workings understood only by Kline and a select few of his most trusted engineers. Employees were presented with their 'Loyalty Scores' through an internal portal, a sterile interface that offered little context or explanation. They could see their aggregate score, and perhaps a breakdown into the three core pillars – collaboration, initiative, and adherence to protocols – but the granular data points that contributed to these scores remained opaque. This opacity was a deliberate design choice, fostering an environment of uncertainty and encouraging employees to err on the side of caution.

The consequences of a low 'Loyalty Score' were rarely overt. Kline was a master of subtlety. Instead of outright dismissals, employees who consistently scored poorly found themselves facing a gradual erosion of their opportunities and influence. Projects that aligned with their expertise would mysteriously be reassigned. Key meetings would be 'overshadowed' by urgent, unrelated tasks. Their input in strategic discussions would be politely acknowledged but ultimately disregarded. These were not punitive actions, but rather a slow, deliberate marginalization, a quiet phasing out of individuals who did not fit the evolving corporate mold.

Conversely, those who demonstrated high 'Loyalty Scores' were subtly rewarded. Their names might appear more frequently in internal newsletters highlighting "exemplary contributions." They might be offered access to exclusive training programs or be invited to participate in 'special projects' that offered greater visibility. These rewards were not necessarily tied to traditional performance metrics; they were direct acknowledgments of their alignment with Kline's vision, their perceived devotion to the 'Halcyon Way.' This created a clear hierarchy, not based on merit or skill, but on the quantifiable measure of one's subservience.

The impact on the workplace culture was profound and, for many, deeply unsettling. The initial optimism surrounding the 'Loyalty Metric' quickly soured as employees began to understand its true implications. The encouraged reporting of colleagues, designed to foster accountability, instead cultivated a climate of pervasive suspicion. Every interaction became fraught with a hidden calculus: was this conversation beneficial to my score? Could this comment be misinterpreted as dissent? The freedom to express an opinion, to question, or to offer a critique, was systematically extinguished.

Consider the seemingly innocuous act of expressing concern about a new project's feasibility. Under the old regime, this might have been seen as a valuable contribution, a sign of diligence and foresight. An employee who flagged potential risks would be seen as a responsible team member, someone who helped to prevent future problems. However, under the 'Loyalty Metric,' such a sentiment, if not carefully couched in the language of constructive solutions and unwavering commitment, could be logged as a negative point. The algorithm was not programmed to appreciate caution; it was designed to reward unhesitating acceptance. The question became not "Is this a good idea?" but "Does questioning this idea make me look disloyal?"

This dynamic had a chilling effect on innovation. Employees who had once been eager to explore new technologies or propose radical solutions found themselves stifled. The risk of a negative score outweighed the potential reward of a breakthrough. Why propose a novel, potentially disruptive approach when a safe, predictable, and demonstrably 'loyal' execution of an existing directive would guarantee a favorable metric? The focus shifted from driving progress to managing one's score. Creativity began to atrophy, replaced by a meticulous adherence to established protocols and an almost obsessive attention to behavioral alignment.

The 'Loyalty Metric' was thus a powerful instrument of social engineering, designed not just to measure, but to mold employee behavior. It tapped into fundamental human desires for acceptance and belonging, while simultaneously exploiting the innate fear of exclusion and punishment. By gamifying devotion, by assigning numerical values to an employee's willingness to conform, Kline had created a system where subservience was not merely tolerated but actively cultivated and rewarded. The workplace, once a space for professional collaboration and intellectual exchange, had been transformed into a silent arena of competitive compliance, where the ultimate prize was not success, but the elusive approval of a digital overlord.

The insidious brilliance of the Loyalty Metric, as Victor Kline meticulously designed it, was its direct assault on the primal human instinct of fear. It wasn't a brute-force application of terror, but a subtle, pervasive drip, a constant hum beneath the surface of everyday operations, that served to amplify that fundamental dread. Kline understood that while inspiration and rewards could foster loyalty, fear was a far more potent and immediate motivator, a guaranteed catalyst for compliance. The Metric, therefore, was engineered not just to measure allegiance, but to actively weaponize the anxieties of the workforce, weaving a tapestry of apprehension that bound individuals to the corporate will.

This fear was not born of overt threats or the specter of immediate termination. Kline, a connoisseur of psychological manipulation, understood that such crude tactics were inefficient and often counterproductive. Instead, the fear was a more sophisticated construct, a constant, gnawing awareness of being perpetually observed and judged. Every interaction, every keystroke, every shared moment was implicitly weighted by the potential impact on one's 'Loyalty Score.' The very air in the Halcyon Defense Systems offices thickened with unspoken anxieties. Employees walked a tightrope, each step calculated, each word chosen with excruciating care, all in service of avoiding the invisible, yet potent, penalty of a declining score.

The potential repercussions of a low score were not always clearly defined, and this ambiguity was, in itself, a powerful psychological weapon. Kline had deliberately designed the consequences to be a slow, insidious erosion of opportunity and influence, rather than an immediate, decisive blow. This gradual marginalization was far more psychologically devastating. A low score meant being overlooked for promising projects, being excluded from crucial decision-making meetings, having one's innovative ideas politely acknowledged and then quietly shelved. It was a slow death by a thousand papercuts, a systematic demotion without a change in title, a quiet fading from relevance. This uncertainty, this constant looming threat of being deemed 'unsuitable' without a clear understanding of precisely why, fostered a deep-seated unease. Employees began to internalize the judgment, their own internal critic aligning with the algorithmic overseer.

This pervasive sense of being judged led directly to a culture of intense self-policing. The external gaze of the Loyalty Metric quickly became internalized, transforming into an internal censor that scrutinized every nascent thought and impulse. Employees learned to anticipate the Metric's invisible hand, to preemptively suppress any thought or action that might be perceived as deviation. The natural human inclination to question, to dissent, or even to express mild frustration, was systematically choked out. Why risk a point deduction for a fleeting moment of negativity when a calm, composed, and compliant demeanor would ensure stability? The internal dialogue shifted from genuine reflection to a constant risk assessment. "Is this thought productive?" became "Is this thought score-neutral or score-positive?"

The psychological toll of this constant vigilance was profound and multifaceted. Anxiety became a persistent companion for many. The pressure to perform not just professionally, but also to perform loyalty, was relentless. Sleep became elusive, often interrupted by dreams of missed deadlines, disapproving algorithmic feedback, or colleagues whispered accusations. Burnout, a condition previously associated with overwhelming workloads, now manifested as a deep, existential exhaustion, a weariness born not of physical exertion but of the ceaseless mental gymnastics required to maintain a favorable score. The workplace, intended as a space for collaboration and intellectual engagement, devolved into a silent battleground where individuals fought an internal war against their own authentic selves, all in the name of algorithmic approval.

A pervasive sense of dread permeated the organization. It was the quiet dread of the unknown, the fear of a sudden, inexplicable drop in one's score. It was the dread of being singled out, of being identified as a potential outlier. This dread was amplified by the inherent opacity of the Metric itself. The algorithms were a black box, their inner workings shrouded in secrecy, known only to Kline and a select few. This lack of transparency meant that employees had no real recourse, no way to understand or challenge the judgments being made against them. They were subject to an unseen, unappealable authority, and this powerlessness was a fertile ground for fear to take root and flourish.

The subtle rewards for high scores, while seemingly benign, also played into this psychological landscape. Access to exclusive training, invitations to 'special projects,' and public acknowledgments in internal communications created a visible hierarchy of favor. This fostered a sense of competition, not based on genuine merit, but on the quantifiable display of subservience. Employees who received these rewards often felt a complex mix of relief and guilt. They had successfully navigated the system, but at what cost? The pressure to maintain their favored status meant that the self-policing and anxiety only intensified. The fear of losing these privileges became as potent as the fear of punishment.

Consider Myra, a project manager known for her innovative problem-solving. Under the Loyalty Metric, her tendency to challenge project timelines that seemed unrealistic, while previously lauded as proactive, now became a potential liability. The algorithm might interpret her challenges not as strategic foresight, but as a lack of confidence in the leadership's vision, or worse, as resistance. She found herself spending hours meticulously crafting her internal communications, ensuring every word conveyed unwavering commitment, even when her professional judgment screamed caution. The energy she once poured into project execution was now diverted into strategic phrasing and self-censorship. Her anxiety spiked every time a new directive arrived, the internal debate raging: should she voice her concerns, risking a score dip, or remain silent and potentially contribute to a flawed outcome, which could also, indirectly, reflect poorly on her as a project lead? This dilemma became a daily torment, chipping away at her confidence and her passion for her work.

Mark, a senior engineer, experienced a similar psychological strain. He was known for his collaborative spirit, often engaging in lengthy, informal discussions with junior colleagues, patiently explaining complex concepts and fostering a supportive team environment. However, the Loyalty Metric flagged these interactions as 'non-productive time.' Mark found himself consciously shortening his conversations, offering only brief, task-oriented responses. The camaraderie he had once fostered withered. His team's morale began to dip, a consequence the Metric did not directly measure, but which was a direct byproduct of its rigid scoring. Mark felt a deep sense of guilt and frustration, caught between the algorithm's cold logic and his own deeply held professional values. He began to dread the open-plan office, the constant visual reminder of his colleagues, each interaction a potential landmine. His once-thriving passion for mentoring was replaced by a gnawing fear of being perceived as inefficient.

The fear also extended to the act of reporting on colleagues. While presented as a mechanism for mutual accountability, it became a tool for psychological warfare, albeit a subtle one. The knowledge that any employee could be reporting on any other employee at any time created an atmosphere of deep mistrust. The fear of being falsely accused, or of having an innocent remark twisted and weaponized, became a constant worry. Colleagues who had once shared lunches and personal anecdotes now eyed each other with suspicion. A misplaced word, a moment of shared complaint about the coffee machine, could be construed as insubordination. The fear of betrayal, of a colleague sacrificing another for personal gain on the Metric, was a corrosive force that ate away at the very foundations of teamwork.

The result was a workforce operating at a perpetual state of low-grade panic. This was not the dramatic, adrenaline-fueled fear of immediate danger, but a chronic, soul-draining apprehension. It was the fear that manifested in tight shoulders, furrowed brows, and a palpable reluctance to take initiative. It was the fear that led to missed opportunities for growth, for innovation, and for genuine human connection. Kline, in his pursuit of absolute loyalty, had inadvertently created a psychological prison, where the bars were forged from fear, and the warden was an invisible, unforgiving algorithm. The very essence of a thriving, dynamic organization was being suffocated under the weight of this manufactured dread, leaving behind a hollow shell of compliant, anxious automatons. The Loyalty Metric, in its relentless pursuit of control, had unleashed a torrent of fear that threatened to drown the very spirit of Halcyon Defense Systems.

The introduction of the Loyalty Metric at Halcyon Defense Systems didn't immediately plunge the entire workforce into a state of synchronized dread. Instead, it catalyzed a fascinating, albeit grim, bifurcation of human response. As the invisible hand of Victor Kline's algorithm began to subtly reshape the organizational landscape, two distinct groups emerged from the ranks: the early adopters, who, out of a blend of ambition, fear, or even genuine conviction, threw themselves wholeheartedly into the pursuit of a high Loyalty Score, and the deviants, those whose innate resistance to pervasive surveillance manifested in subtle acts of non-compliance and veiled dissent. These deviants, in their nascent stages of resistance, became the immediate, unintentional test subjects, their declining scores serving as stark, chilling object lessons for the vast majority caught in the throes of this new regime.

The early adopters, a heterogeneous bunch, found their own motivations for embracing the Metric. For some, it was the pragmatic recognition that the system was not going away, and survival, or even advancement, depended on understanding and mastering its arcane rules. They saw the Metric not as an instrument of oppression, but as a new, albeit peculiar, meritocracy. These were the individuals who had always thrived on clear objectives and quantifiable feedback, and Kline's system, despite its psychological undertones, offered just that. They began to meticulously analyze their interactions, their communication patterns, even their perceived enthusiasm in meetings, all through the lens of potential score impact. Coffee break conversations were truncated, replaced by whispered discussions about workflow optimization. Emails were drafted not just for clarity, but for their 'score-positive' resonance, laced with keywords and phrases that the algorithm might interpret as unwavering commitment. The very act of asking a clarifying question, which might have been seen as diligence before, was now reframed as a potential signal of confusion, and thus, a risk. They began to actively seek out opportunities that promised a visible boost to their score – volunteering for the most tedious tasks, readily agreeing to any request, and always, always projecting an aura of unshakeable positivity, even when exhaustion gnawed at them.

Consider the case of Terry York, a mid-level analyst in the R&D department. Terry had always been a diligent employee, but he lacked the overt charisma or the bold vision that often propelled others to the forefront. When the Loyalty Metric was introduced, Terry saw it as an equalizer. He spent his evenings meticulously reviewing his performance logs, cross-referencing them with the scant information available about the algorithm's parameters. He began to consciously adjust his behavior. He stopped taking his full lunch breaks, opting for a quick sandwich at his desk while reviewing internal policy documents. He made it a point to be the first one to arrive and the last one to leave, his mere physical presence radiating a sense of dedication. He practiced enthusiastic nods and affirmations during team meetings, even when he harbored reservations about the direction of a project. He learned to interpret the subtle cues from his superiors, anticipating their needs and proactively addressing them, often before they were even articulated. His score, predictably, began to climb. He received a commendation from Kline himself, a brief, almost clinical acknowledgment of his "exemplary commitment," which Terry displayed on his cubicle wall like a badge of honor. For Terry, this was not just about survival; it was about validation, a tangible representation of his worth in a system that had previously felt capricious and subjective. He genuinely believed that by adhering strictly to the Metric, he was contributing to a more efficient and productive Halcyon Defense Systems, a vision that Kline often espoused.

Then there were those who embraced the Metric not out of a belief in its efficacy, but out of a desperate need for security. In the shadow of economic uncertainty and the ever-present whispers of downsizing, a high Loyalty Score became a shield against the ax. These were the individuals who had perhaps felt overlooked, undervalued, or simply precarious in their positions. They saw the Metric as a form of job security, a way to prove their indispensability. They became hyper-vigilant, scrutinizing every interaction, every email, every keystroke with an almost paranoid intensity. The fear of being deemed dispensable, a notion amplified by the specter of a low score, drove them to an extreme form of compliance. They would report perceived infractions by colleagues, not out of malice, but out of a desperate attempt to deflect attention from themselves. They became experts in the art of looking busy, of appearing engaged, even when their minds were racing with anxieties about their own standing. Their efforts were often directed towards seemingly trivial actions that they hoped would register positively – proactively cleaning communal coffee stations, meticulously organizing shared filing cabinets, or offering to take on extra, less glamorous tasks. These were not acts of genuine helpfulness, but calculated maneuvers designed to generate positive algorithmic feedback. Their lives became a constant, exhausting performance, a relentless effort to maintain the illusion of unwavering loyalty, all for the precarious promise of continued employment.

However, amidst this surge of compliant behavior, a countercurrent began to form. Not everyone was willing or able to bend to the Metric's invasive demands. These were the deviants, the early signs of resistance that, while subtle, represented a profound challenge to Kline's carefully constructed system. This resistance wasn't always overt rebellion. It was often a quiet, almost imperceptible refusal to fully surrender. It manifested in the lingering glance that questioned a directive, the barely audible sigh of exasperation, the perfectly worded email that contained a subtle, yet pointed, challenge, carefully phrased to avoid direct score penalties. These individuals, their internal compass still calibrated to a pre-Metric reality, found themselves increasingly at odds with the new organizational ethos.

One of the most common forms of subtle defiance was the selective adherence to the Metric's demands. These employees understood the game but refused to play it with complete abandon. They would perform the necessary actions to keep their scores from plummeting, but they wouldn't invest the extra emotional or intellectual energy that the true adopters did. They would offer polite smiles and affirmations, but their eyes held a flicker of skepticism. They would complete their tasks efficiently, but they wouldn't volunteer for the extra score-boosting initiatives that consumed the energy of the adopters. Their compliance was a performance, a necessary evil, but their true selves remained beyond the algorithm's reach. They held onto their private opinions, their genuine frustrations, and their personal values, carefully compartmentalizing them away from the prying eyes of the Metric.

Consider Vicki Dance, a senior graphic designer. Vicki's artistic sensibilities had always lent themselves to thoughtful critique and creative exploration. Under the Metric, her tendency to question design briefs that she deemed artistically or strategically flawed was now a significant risk. Instead of openly voicing her objections, which would undoubtedly trigger a score deduction for negativity or insubordination, Vicki began to employ a more nuanced strategy. She would spend hours meticulously researching alternative design approaches, citing industry best practices and presenting data-driven justifications for her suggestions. Her proposals, while still challenging the original brief, were framed in terms of objective improvement and long-term benefit, carefully avoiding any language that could be construed as personal criticism or resistance. She learned to couch her dissent in the language of data and efficiency, the very principles the Metric purported to champion. It was a draining process, a constant mental gymnastics that required her to anticipate the algorithm's interpretation of her every word. Her score remained stable, a testament to her skill in navigating the treacherous currents of the Metric, but the creative spark that had once defined her work felt increasingly dulled, replaced by a calculated caution.

Another form of deviation was the subtle erosion of enthusiasm. While the adopters exuded an almost cultish zeal, the deviants maintained a more measured, even detached, approach. They performed their duties competently, but without the outward display of passion that the Metric seemed to reward. They weren't openly disgruntled, but they didn't project the infectious positivity that the early adopters cultivated. Their interactions with colleagues were polite but brief, avoiding the deeper personal connections that might lead to inadvertent score-impacting conversations. They mastered the art of the neutral response, the non-committal agreement, the strategically vague affirmation. Their lack of overt enthusiasm was a quiet rebellion, a refusal to participate in the performance of loyalty. They were the grey areas in Kline's black-and-white scoring system, the individuals who operated just below the threshold of what the algorithm deemed actively detrimental, but far from the celebrated ranks of the high scorers.

The deviants also began to engage in quiet forms of information gathering and sharing. While overt collaboration on score-boosting strategies was risky, they found ways to subtly exchange information about the Metric's perceived blind spots or inconsistencies. These were hushed conversations in the break room, coded messages in casual emails, or shared glances that conveyed volumes. They were piecing together a mosaic of understanding about the algorithm, not to master it, but to survive it, to find the cracks in its armor. They learned to recognize the subtle shifts in manager behavior that indicated a colleague's declining score, and they offered quiet solidarity, a shared understanding that transcended the performative loyalty demanded by the Metric.

These acts of subtle defiance, however small, did not go unnoticed by Kline and his inner circle. The algorithm, in its relentless data collection, began to flag these individuals. Their scores, while perhaps not plummeting into the red, plateaued or showed a consistent, albeit slow, downward trend. These were the 'deviants,' the anomalies in Kline's otherwise predictable system. And as such, they became the primary targets for the Metric's corrective measures, their experiences designed to serve as cautionary tales, reinforcing the imperative of complete conformity for the rest of the workforce. The subtle acts of resistance were met not with outright termination, but with a more insidious form of psychological pressure, a gradual tightening of the screws designed to either break their spirit or force them into the ranks of the early adopters. The subtle rebellion was about to be met with equally subtle, but far more potent, retaliation.

The office, once a space for genuine collaboration and intellectual exchange, had transmuted into a grand theatre, and every desk, a meticulously crafted stage. The Loyalty Metric, Victor Kline's brainchild, had not merely introduced a new performance review system; it had fundamentally altered the very fabric of interpersonal dynamics, transforming the mundane into a continuous, high-stakes audition for corporate favor. Employees, whether consciously or subconsciously, began to don masks, morphing into what could only be described as corporate chameleons. Their natural hues of personality, their authentic reactions, were systematically suppressed, replaced by a carefully curated spectrum of behaviors designed to signal unwavering allegiance to Kline's vision. This wasn't just about appearing loyal; it was about embodying a performance of loyalty so convincing that even the most sophisticated algorithm would deem it genuine.

The art of the corporate chameleon was not a sudden acquisition. It was a learned behavior, honed through countless micro-adjustments and strategic calculations. Each interaction, each email, each casual remark was now scrutinized not for its content or its intent, but for its potential impact on one's Loyalty Score. The chameleon learned to read the subtle cues of the system, to decipher the unspoken language of algorithmic approval. A quick, enthusiastic response to a manager's email, even if the request was trivial, became a critical move. A visibly proactive approach to a mundane task, such as meticulously alphabetizing a shared drive that was already perfectly organized, was a calculated maneuver to register positive engagement. These were not acts of genuine helpfulness or dedication; they were strategic performances, designed to feed the insatiable appetite of the Metric.

Genuine collaboration, once the engine of innovation and problem-solving at Halcyon Defense Systems, began to wither. Why risk collaboration that might expose a differing opinion, a moment of hesitation, or a lack of immediate enthusiasm – all potential detractors from one's score? Instead, strategic alliances began to form, not based on shared goals or mutual respect, but on a silent, unspoken pact of mutual score-preservation. Employees would align themselves with colleagues who consistently maintained high scores, not out of affinity, but as a form of social proof. They would echo the opinions of those deemed 'loyal' by the system, not because they agreed, but because it was a safe bet. The office became a landscape of calculated partnerships, where genuine connection was sacrificed at the altar of algorithmic approval. Meetings, once vibrant arenas for debate and idea generation, devolved into echo chambers of pre-approved sentiments. Dissent was not openly voiced; it was subtly suppressed, or worse, translated into a palatable form that would not trigger a negative score.

Consider the case of Erika Young, a project manager who had always prided herself on her direct communication style and her ability to challenge assumptions for the betterment of a project. Under the Metric, her forthrightness became a liability. A direct question about the feasibility of a deadline, or a pointed critique of a poorly conceived strategy, could be interpreted by the algorithm as negativity or resistance. Erika learned to adapt, to become a chameleon. She would still voice her concerns, but she would preface them with a deluge of affirmations and expressions of commitment. "I'm absolutely committed to delivering this project on time and with excellence, Victor," she might say, even as she prepared to present data that indicated the deadline was impossibly tight. "My primary goal is always to ensure Halcyon's success, and based on my analysis, I believe we can optimize our approach by…" The underlying message remained the same, but the delivery was a masterclass in algorithmic appeasement. Her words were carefully chosen, layered with positive framing, and devoid of any potentially inflammatory language. She spent hours crafting these carefully worded communications, an exhausting mental exercise that detracted from the actual project management tasks she was hired to perform. Her score remained stable, but the joy she once derived from her work began to fade, replaced by the gnawing anxiety of constantly monitoring her own output for any hint of perceived disloyalty.

The performance of enthusiasm became another critical skill for the corporate chameleon. The algorithm, it was widely suspected, favored overt displays of energy and dedication. A perky, "Good

49

morning, everyone!" shouted across the office, even at 7 AM, was often rewarded more than a quiet, efficient arrival. Employees began to force smiles, to inject an almost unnatural cheerfulness into their voices, to volunteer for the most tedious tasks with an exaggerated eagerness that bordered on the absurd. The water cooler, once a site for genuine, informal conversations, became a stage for impromptu performances of dedication. Colleagues would boast about working late, not out of necessity, but as a conscious effort to broadcast their commitment. Even lunch breaks became strategic opportunities. Instead of stepping away from their desks to recharge, many chose to eat at their workstations, their keyboards clicking rhythmically, a constant visual reminder of their unwavering focus.

Mark Jenkins, an IT specialist, found himself particularly adept at this particular performance. He was naturally introverted and found the constant pressure to perform enthusiasm draining. Yet, he understood the game. He began to strategically deploy his energy. He'd be the first to 'like' any company-wide announcement on the internal platform, often with an effusive comment. He'd volunteer for after-hours IT support calls with a cheerful, "Happy to help, anytime!" His colleagues, many of whom were struggling to maintain their scores, looked at him with a mixture of admiration and resentment. They saw his ability to project such unflagging positivity as a superhuman feat, a testament to his complete assimilation into the Metric's ethos. Mark, however, privately confessed to a colleague that he often felt like an actor playing a role, and the applause – a steady or rising Loyalty Score – was the only thing that made the exhausting performance bearable. He confessed that he sometimes found himself smiling at his computer screen, even when he was dealing with a particularly frustrating system error, simply because he knew the webcam might be active.

This shift from meaningful work to the art of appearing perfectly aligned was profoundly soul-crushing. Employees found themselves spending more time strategizing about how to look loyal than how to be productive. The energy that could have been directed towards innovation, problem-solving, or genuine team-building was instead consumed by the constant, draining effort of maintaining a disguise. The authentic self, the individual with unique perspectives and genuine emotions, was systematically eroded. Authenticity became a liability, a dangerous indulgence in a world that rewarded calculated conformity. The office, once a place of professional growth and personal expression, transformed into a sterile environment where every thought, every word, every gesture was filtered through the lens of the Loyalty Metric.

The concept of trust eroded as quickly as authenticity. When interactions were driven by score-optimization, genuine trust became an anachronism. Employees became suspicious of each other's motives. Was a colleague offering help out of kindness, or as a strategic move to boost their own score by being seen as collaborative? Was a manager's praise genuine, or a calculated attempt to elicit more effort from a subordinate whose score was dipping? The subtle art of the chameleon also involved observing and subtly influencing the scores of others. Some learned to subtly steer conversations away from colleagues they perceived as rivals, or to highlight their own contributions more aggressively in group settings. This created an atmosphere of covert competition, where every interaction was a potential chess move in the larger game of the Loyalty Metric.

One of the most insidious consequences was the normalization of self-surveillance. Employees began to police their own thoughts, their own impulses. The desire to blurt out a sarcastic remark, to express a moment of frustration, or to simply be quiet and introspective, was suppressed. They learned to anticipate the algorithm's judgment, to preemptively censor themselves. This constant internal monitoring was exhausting, leaving many feeling perpetually on edge, their minds a battlefield between their true selves and the persona they were compelled to project. The psychological toll was immense, leading to increased stress, anxiety, and a pervasive sense of emptiness.

The chameleons, in their relentless pursuit of a favorable score, often found themselves entangled in a web of their own making. They would meticulously curate their online presence, ensuring every email, every instant message, every document shared was laced with keywords and phrases that the algorithm might interpret as positive. They learned to weaponize corporate jargon, to deploy buzzwords like "synergy," "proactive," and "alignment" with surgical precision. They would participate in company-wide "wellness initiatives" with visible enthusiasm, even if they personally found them to be a waste of time, simply because participation was a quantifiable metric. They would attend optional after-work events, not for the networking or the camaraderie, but for the undeniable score-boosting potential of being seen as a dedicated, engaged employee.

Consider Sandy Zeller, a junior marketing associate. Sandy was bright and creative, but her initial scores were middling. She watched her colleagues, particularly those who were slightly older and more established, skillfully navigate the system. She observed how they would strategically praise the company's vision in meetings, how they would publicly volunteer for "cross-functional initiatives" that often involved tedious data entry, and how they would consistently send emails that began with elaborate affirmations of commitment. Sandy began to emulate them. She started her day by sending a cheerful email to her direct supervisor, reiterating her dedication to the team's goals. She made it a point to comment enthusiastically on every internal social media post. She began to volunteer for tasks that she knew would be visible, even if they were outside her core responsibilities. The effort was immense. She felt like she was constantly acting, performing a version of herself that was more agreeable, more compliant, and less authentic. Her score, as predicted, began to climb. She received a "commendation" for her "team spirit and proactive engagement," a phrase that felt both hollow and deeply unsettling. The validation was fleeting, overshadowed by the realization that her success was predicated on a performance, not on genuine merit or passion. She wondered if she would ever be able to shed the chameleon skin, or if this was the new normal for her career at Halcyon.

The performance was not limited to overt actions. It seeped into the very language employees used. The phrase "I don't know" became a dangerous utterance, a potential signal of incompetence or lack of initiative. Instead, employees learned to say, "Let me look into that for you," or "I'll circle back with you on that once I've gathered more information." Questions were reframed from expressions of genuine curiosity to requests for clarification that implied a deep understanding of the underlying objectives. The nuances of language were meticulously dissected; every word choice weighed for its potential algorithmic consequence. The richness and complexity of human communication were reduced to a series of score-optimized sound bites.

The most tragic aspect of the corporate chameleon phenomenon was its insidious nature. It didn't manifest as overt oppression, but as a gradual, almost imperceptible erosion of self. Employees weren't forced into submission at gunpoint; they were subtly incentivized, then implicitly pressured, to conform. The algorithm, a dispassionate entity, became the ultimate arbiter of value, and in its eyes, authenticity was a bug, not a feature. The pursuit of a high Loyalty Score became a universal objective, a silent imperative that permeated every aspect of office life. The chameleons, in their desperate attempt to survive and thrive, were slowly but surely losing themselves, their true colors fading into the carefully constructed shades of corporate compliance. The office, once a place where individuals brought their unique talents and personalities, had become a silent, exhausting stage, populated by actors playing the roles of their lives, all for the fleeting approval of an invisible judge. The performance, once started, was incredibly difficult to stop, and the cost of exiting the stage was becoming increasingly unbearable.

Chapter 3

The Collateral Damage

The relentless pressure cooker that Halcyon Defense Systems had become was beginning to exhale its toxic fumes far beyond the polished glass walls of the office. For weeks, the whispers had been growing, hushed conversations that skirted the edges of professionalism, acknowledging a shared burden that was no longer confined to the nine-to-five. The Loyalty Metric, initially conceived as a tool for fostering dedication, had instead become an invisible, suffocating shroud, its tendrils reaching into the sanctity of personal lives, unraveling the very fabric of the employees' well-being.

Dr. Christine Reed, a senior R&D scientist, found herself increasingly detached from her husband, Henry. Their evenings, once filled with shared laughter over dinner or quiet contemplation on the day's events, had become a minefield of silence and polite, superficial exchanges. Henry, a literature professor at the local university, found Christine's newfound reticence baffling. He'd inquire about her day, and she'd offer vague, sanitized responses, carefully omitting any hint of the algorithmic scrutiny that dictated her every professional interaction. "It was… productive," she'd say, a practiced neutrality in her voice that felt alien to him. "Team collaboration was excellent." The truth, however, was that she spent her days calculating the optimal phrasing for an email, dissecting the subtle implications of a colleague's tone, and perpetually aware of the unseen gaze of the Metric. The energy she expended in maintaining this impression at work left her drained, with little emotional bandwidth to navigate the complexities of her marriage. Intimacy became a distant memory, replaced by a gnawing anxiety that if she let her guard down, even for a moment, the carefully constructed persona of the loyal employee might crack, and the consequences, she feared, would extend beyond her career. Henry, sensing the growing distance, would often sigh, his brow furrowed with concern. "Are you alright, Chris? You seem… a million miles away." And Christine would offer a tight smile, a rehearsed reassurance, "Just tired, darling. Long project." The lie tasted like ash in her mouth, a testament to the growing chasm between her professional performance and her private reality. She yearned to confide in him, to unload the crushing weight of constant vigilance, but the ingrained fear of judgment, of being perceived as weak or disloyal, held her captive.

The situation was mirrored in the lives of many of her colleagues. Mark Jenkins, the IT specialist who had become a master of projected enthusiasm, found his evenings consumed by a different kind of performance. His wife, Cecilia, a freelance graphic designer, was beginning to question his constant need to "check in" on work emails and Slack channels, even late into the night. "Mark, it's 10 PM," she'd gently chide, gesturing towards his laptop screen, which glowed with the stark interface of Halcyon's internal communication system. "Don't you ever just switch off?" Mark would offer a sheepish grin, his eyes glued to the screen. "Just need to make sure everything's running smoothly, you know. Wouldn't want any system downtime to impact productivity, would we? That would look bad." He wasn't just checking for technical issues; he was actively monitoring his own digital footprint, ensuring his response times remained within acceptable algorithmic parameters, lest a delayed reply register as a dip in his Loyalty Score. His dedication to the Metric had become an obsession, an all-consuming entity that left no room for genuine connection with his wife. Their conversations revolved around her design projects, her friends, anything that could distract him from the constant hum of professional obligation. He'd nod and offer perfunctory responses, his mind miles away, calculating the optimal response to a hypothetical late-night IT query that might never even materialize. Cecilia felt increasingly like a footnote in his life, a peripheral character in the grand, digital drama of his work. The unspoken question hung between them: was he married to Halcyon, or to her?

Even the simple act of family time was tainted. Children, with their innocent questions and uninhibited energy, became unwitting witnesses to their parents' fractured selves. Irene Kelloge, the junior marketing associate, found it increasingly difficult to engage with her five-year-old son, Leo. Her mind, perpetually replaying conversations, dissecting potential missteps, and rehearsing future interactions, struggled to focus on his eager recounting of his day at kindergarten. "Mommy, guess what? Mikey shared his crayons today!" Leo would exclaim, his eyes wide with excitement. Irene would offer a strained smile, "That's... wonderful, honey. Did Mikey share the blue one?" Her internal monologue, however, was a frantic rush of calculations.

Did I sound too enthusiastic when I agreed to that weekend project call? Was my response to John's email too brief? Could it be interpreted as dismissive? The joy she once found in Leo's simple pronouncements was overshadowed by the constant, low-grade anxiety that hummed beneath the surface of her consciousness. Leo, sensing her distraction, would often tug at her sleeve, his brow furrowed. "Mommy? Are you listening?" These moments of absentmindedness, born from the mental exhaustion of performing loyalty, left Irene wracked with guilt. She saw the confusion in her son's eyes, the dawning realization that his mother was not fully present, and it pierced her heart. She desperately wanted to be the mother Leo deserved, to be fully engaged in his world, but the invisible chains of the Loyalty Metric held her captive, tethered to a virtual performance that demanded her undivided attention.

The decline in well-being was not merely anecdotal; it manifested in tangible, troubling ways. Sleep disturbances became commonplace. Employees reported vivid nightmares, often replaying workplace scenarios, or experiencing a persistent sense of dread that followed them into their waking hours. The lack of genuine relaxation meant that the restorative power of sleep was compromised. They'd wake up feeling as exhausted as when they went to bed, their minds still buzzing with the anxieties of the previous day. This chronic sleep deprivation exacerbated irritability, impaired cognitive function, and created a vicious cycle of stress and fatigue. Headaches, digestive issues, and a general malaise became the unwelcome companions of many at Halcyon. The vibrant, energetic individuals who had once populated the offices were slowly being replaced by a more subdued, perpetually weary cohort, their faces etched with a subtle weariness that spoke volumes of their internal struggles.

The pressure to maintain a flawless professional persona also led to a reluctance to seek help, even when it was desperately needed. Admitting to personal struggles, to marital discord, or to overwhelming stress, could be perceived as a sign of weakness, a potential detractor from one's Loyalty Score. The fear was that any vulnerability displayed at work might be documented, analyzed, and ultimately penalized. This created a culture of silence, where employees were forced to suffer in isolation, their personal crises hidden behind masks of professional competence. The company's supposed emphasis on employee well-being became a cruel irony, as the very system designed to foster loyalty simultaneously created an environment where genuine emotional support was rendered impossible.

Relationships outside of work bore the brunt of this internal strain. Friendships withered, unable to withstand the constant cancellations and the emotional distance that had become the norm. Colleagues who were once friends found themselves unable to transition from their performative workplace personas to genuine camaraderie. The fear of misinterpretation, of saying the wrong thing, extended even to social interactions. A casual remark meant to be lighthearted could be perceived as a veiled criticism, a potential threat to a friend's score. Trust, once a bedrock of personal relationships, began to erode, replaced by a cautious guardedness.

The paradox was profound: in striving to demonstrate unwavering loyalty to their employer, employees were inadvertently eroding the foundations of their personal lives. The very qualities that made them desirable colleagues – their dedication, their commitment, their ability to perform under pressure – were being channeled into an unsustainable, self-destructive cycle. They were excelling at their jobs, in a sense, by sacrificing the very essence of what made them human.

The performance of loyalty had become so ingrained that the lines between their professional and personal selves blurred, leaving them adrift in a sea of curated behaviors and suppressed emotions. The collateral damage of Victor Kline's brainchild was not just impacting the balance sheets; it was irrevocably altering the lives of the people who powered Halcyon Defense Systems, leaving them hollowed out, adrift, and increasingly, alone. The weight of the Loyalty Metric was a crushing burden, a silent epidemic that was systematically dismantling the lives of those trapped within its algorithmic grasp. They were the loyal soldiers, fighting a war on a battlefield they had not chosen, their personal lives the casualties of an invisible conflict. The mask of corporate success was built upon a crumbling foundation of personal devastation, a truth that was becoming increasingly difficult to ignore, even for those who had perfected the art of performance.

The insidious creep of the Loyalty Metric had done more than just fray nerves and steal sleep; it had systematically dismantled the very bedrock of human connection within Halcyon Defense Systems: trust. What began as a seemingly innocuous directive, veiled in the language of fostering a unified corporate culture, had metastasized into a pervasive atmosphere of suspicion. Victor Kline, in his relentless pursuit of an algorithmically defined ideal employee, had inadvertently sown the seeds of mutual distrust, transforming colleagues into potential informants and friendships into precarious liabilities. The unspoken rule was now crystal clear: in the grand calculus of the Loyalty Metric, everyone was a variable, and every interaction, a data point that could be leveraged.

This was particularly evident in the subtle yet palpable shift in how colleagues interacted. A casual coffee break, once an opportunity for genuine camaraderie and stress relief, now felt like an interrogation. The easy banter that had previously flowed between Christine Reed and her lab partner, Dr. Ben Carter, had been replaced by a cautious, almost stilted exchange. Ben, whose score had dipped slightly in the previous quarter due to what the system flagged as "suboptimal collaborative engagement" during a late-night coding session, had become noticeably more reserved. He'd ask Christine about her progress on the sensor array, but his eyes would dart around, as if searching for hidden microphones or clandestine observers.

"So, Christine," Ben began one Tuesday morning, his voice carefully modulated, devoid of its usual warmth, "how's that recalibration sequence coming along? I was just thinking about the signal-to-noise ratio. Might be worth double-checking the amplification parameters. You know, just to ensure we're operating at peak efficiency. Wouldn't want any... inconsistencies to arise, would we?" His gaze, which lingered a moment too long on Christine's keyboard, felt less like a friendly suggestion and more like a subtle probe. Was he genuinely offering assistance, or was he cataloging her response, her tone, her keyboard activity, to be fed into the ever-hungry maw of the Metric?

Christine, acutely aware of the shifting dynamics, found herself parsing his words with a practiced, weary precision. She offered a brief, non-committal reply, focusing on the technical aspects of her work and carefully avoiding any personal anecdotes or subjective opinions that could be misconstrued. The shared vulnerability that had once characterized their collaborative problem-solving sessions was gone, replaced by a self-protective opacity.

The company had, in its subtle way, actively encouraged this erosion of trust. The internal communication platforms, once designed for open dialogue, were now rife with discreet feedback mechanisms. Employees were implicitly, and sometimes explicitly, prompted to report on the perceived dedication and adherence to company values of their peers. A quick click on a colleague's profile could reveal options like "Provide Constructive Feedback" or "Highlight Exemplary Behavior," but lurking beneath these seemingly benign options was the specter of more ambiguous, potentially damaging feedback loops. Whispers circulated about individuals who had been subtly reprimanded or sidelined after a series of anonymous "observations" from colleagues who were, themselves, under pressure to demonstrate their own unwavering loyalty.

Irene Kelloge, the junior marketing associate, found herself in a particularly agonizing position. Her immediate superior, Mr. Whitlock, a man whose own Loyalty Score was rumored to be under scrutiny, had taken to "delegating" performance reviews of team members to his subordinates. This meant Irene was now expected to offer her professional assessment of her colleagues, including those she considered friends. The pressure to conform to what she perceived as Henderson's expectations – and by extension, Kline's

– was immense. She found herself in a moral quandary, torn between her desire to protect her colleagues and the fear of being penalized for "insubordination" or "lack of team synergy" if she refused or offered feedback that deviated from the desired narrative.

One afternoon, Whitlock called her into his sterile, glass-walled office. "Irene," he began, his voice smooth but his eyes betraying a flicker of anxiety, "I need your input on the Q3 campaign performance review for the team. Specifically, I'm interested in your assessment of Mark Jenkins' contribution. He's been... a bit disengaged lately, wouldn't you say? His response times on interdepartmental requests have been borderline. What's your take?"

Irene's mind raced. Mark Jenkins, the IT specialist, had confided in her just days before about the immense pressure he was under, his constant struggle to balance his genuine work responsibilities with the relentless demands of maintaining his score. He had mentioned his wife's growing frustration, the strain on their marriage, and his own gnawing anxiety. To report on Mark now, to validate Whitlock's subtle critique, felt like a betrayal of that trust, a direct violation of the unspoken pact of solidarity they had formed. Yet, the alternative was equally terrifying.

"Well, Mr. Whitlock," Irene began, her voice carefully neutral, "Mark is always very responsive when it comes to critical IT issues. I've found him to be highly diligent in ensuring system stability. Perhaps his response times on non-critical requests might be an area for discussion, but overall, I believe he's a valuable asset to the team. His technical expertise is invaluable." She tried to steer the conversation towards objective contributions, deflecting the subjective "disengagement" angle. Whitlock's smile tightened, and Irene knew her answer, while truthful and attempting to be supportive, might not have been the "correct" one. She left his office with a knot of dread in her stomach, the weight of her complicity settling heavily upon her. Had she just condemned Mark, or had she merely dodged a bullet herself? The uncertainty was a corrosive acid, eating away at her peace of mind.

The isolation intensified as employees began to self-censor, even in the perceived safety of their own homes. The fear of technological surveillance, once a vague suspicion, had solidified into a palpable reality. Every email, every instant message, every keystroke was a potential piece of evidence. The notion of confiding in a colleague about the stress, the unreasonable demands, or the outright absurdity of the Loyalty Metric became a dangerous proposition. What if that whispered confession was overheard by someone whose score was low, and who saw an opportunity to boost their own standing by reporting the indiscretion? What if a seemingly innocuous chat was logged and later misinterpreted by an algorithm designed to detect dissent?

Dr. Christine Reed found herself increasingly withdrawing from even the most casual workplace interactions. She'd navigate the corridors with her gaze fixed forward, offering polite but brief nods to colleagues, avoiding sustained eye contact that might be interpreted as a sign of undue familiarity or, worse, a shared burden of discontent. The open-plan office, designed to foster collaboration, now felt like a panopticon. Every rustle of paper, every hushed conversation, every pause in a colleague's typing, was a source of potential unease. The camaraderie she had once cherished, the shared triumphs and frustrations of scientific discovery, had been replaced by a pervasive sense of individual precariousness. She felt like a single cell in a vast, bio-mechanical organism, constantly monitored and assessed for its adherence to a predefined biological imperative, with no capacity for independent thought or organic interaction.

The irony was that the very system designed to foster loyalty was actively destroying the foundations of genuine allegiance. Loyalty, true loyalty, is built on mutual respect, shared values, and the implicit understanding that one's well-being is intertwined with the success of the collective. It is born from an environment where individuals feel valued, heard, and supported. The Loyalty Metric, however, had replaced this organic growth with a forced, transactional obedience. It was a system that demanded adherence through fear and the promise of algorithmic favor, not through genuine commitment. And in doing so, it was creating an army of compliant automatons, each one isolated, suspicious, and ultimately, incapable of the deep-seated loyalty that truly drives innovation and resilience.

The office atmosphere had become toxic, a breeding ground for paranoia. Employees would hold hushed conversations in stairwells or discreetly step outside for a "breath of fresh air," only to find themselves constantly glancing over their shoulders. The subtle art of office politics had morphed into a high-stakes game of surveillance and counter-surveillance. A compliment from a colleague could be perceived as a prelude to a veiled accusation. A shared joke might be interpreted as a coded message of dissent. The air crackled with an unspoken tension, a constant awareness of being watched, judged, and potentially, reported.

Victor Kline, insulated within his executive suite, likely viewed this as a success. The metric was functioning, dutifully collecting data, identifying deviations, and, from his perspective, ensuring optimal performance. He saw the statistics, the compliance rates, and the productivity metrics that he believed were directly influenced by the Metric. He didn't see the quiet desperation in the eyes of his employees, the erosion of their personal lives, or the profound sense of isolation that had become the currency of loyalty at Halcyon Defense Systems. He had engineered a system of control, and control, he believed, was the ultimate guarantor of success. But in his sterile, data-driven worldview, he had failed to account for the most fundamental human need: the need to trust and be trusted. And as trust withered, so too did the true potential of the organization, leaving behind a hollow shell, meticulously managed, yet devoid of genuine heart and soul. The collateral damage was no longer a subtle undercurrent; it was a raging torrent, threatening to drown the very company Kline was so determined to perfect. The individuals of Halcyon were becoming ghosts in their own lives, their real selves suppressed, their interactions mediated by the omnipresent specter of the algorithm, leaving them profoundly, irrevocably alone in a crowd.

The meticulously cultivated ecosystem of suspicion within Halcyon Defense Systems, a direct byproduct of Victor Kline's algorithmic obsession, had reached a critical mass. The air, once thick with the hum of innovation and the subtle camaraderie of shared purpose, had become a suffocating miasma of distrust. Every interaction was a negotiation, every compliment a potential trap, and every whispered concern a seed of future betrayal. It was within this crucible of psychological manipulation that the first tremors of a talent exodus began to manifest.

The individuals who started to quietly disentangle themselves from Halcyon were not the ones who simply disliked change or resisted new methodologies. These were the architects of innovation, the ethical compasses of the company, the principled thinkers who found the pervasive atmosphere of manufactured loyalty utterly untenable. They were the scientists who valued intellectual honesty above all else, the engineers who believed in the integrity of their work, and the strategists who understood that true progress stemmed from open discourse, not algorithmic obedience. For them, the Loyalty Metric was not merely an annoyance; it was a moral affront, a perversion of the very principles that had drawn them to Halcyon in the first place.

Dr. Albert Thorne, a lead researcher in advanced propulsion systems, was one of the first to signal his departure. His work, lauded for its groundbreaking potential, had always been a testament to his meticulous nature and his unwavering commitment to scientific rigor. He had joined Halcyon believing in its mission to push the boundaries of what was technologically possible, to contribute to advancements that would shape the future. But the Loyalty Metric had chipped away at that vision, replacing the pursuit of discovery with the pursuit of a favorable score. Thorne, a man who prided himself on intellectual transparency, found himself increasingly stifled. He would prepare presentations, carefully selecting data points that painted the most favorable picture of his team's progress, deliberately omitting nuances or potential setbacks that might be misinterpreted as a lack of commitment. The joy of scientific exploration had been leached away, replaced by the anxiety of algorithmic interpretation.

During a quarterly review, Thorne had been subtly pressured by his division head, a sycophant whose own score was a precarious constant, to "encourage" his team members to be more vocal about their perceived loyalty during project debriefs. "Albert," the division head had purred, leaning conspiratorially across his desk, "Victor's keen on seeing that 'unified front.' We need to ensure everyone's demonstrating their commitment. Perhaps a brief, enthusiastic testimonial at the end of each project update? Something about how the 'Halcyon spirit' fuels our innovation?" Thorne had felt a cold dread creep up his spine. The "Halcyon spirit" had become synonymous with blind adherence, a corporate mantra designed to mask the underlying fear. He had politely demurred, citing the importance of objective reporting, but the seed of his discontent had sprouted. He began spending his evenings not poring over schematics, but browsing job boards, his fingers flying across the keyboard with a sense of burgeoning liberation. His departure, when it came, was framed internally as a voluntary "pursuit of external opportunities," but to Thorne, it was an escape from a gilded cage.

The departure of individuals like Thorne sent ripples through the remaining workforce, a silent testament to the unbearable nature of Kline's regime. They were the luminaries, the ones whose contributions were difficult to quantify but whose absence would undoubtedly be felt. Their disillusionment was not a matter of personal grievance; it was a profound disagreement with the direction Halcyon was taking, a rejection of a corporate culture that valued performative allegiance over genuine innovation and ethical conduct.

Irene Kelloge, the junior marketing associate, who had grappled with the moral compromises demanded by her supervisor, found herself increasingly drawn to the stories of those who had left. She'd discreetly search for former colleagues on professional networking sites, piecing together narratives of newfound freedom and renewed purpose. One former colleague, a vibrant graphic designer named Maya, who had been a constant source of creative inspiration, had left Halcyon six months prior. Irene remembered Maya's final weeks, the subtle but palpable shift in her demeanor, the way she'd withdrawn from team lunches, her once infectious laughter replaced by a weary resignation. Now, Maya's online portfolio showcased a dazzling array of projects for startups and non-profits, her work radiating a spirit of unbridled creativity that Irene hadn't seen at Halcyon in months. Irene found herself daydreaming about a similar escape, a world where her ideas weren't dissected for their compliance potential but celebrated for their originality.

The psychological toll of the Loyalty Metric was also a

significant driver of the talent drain. Employees were subjected to constant, low-grade anxiety. The fear of misinterpretation, of inadvertently triggering a negative score, created a hyper-vigilant state that was utterly exhausting. Sleep became a luxury, replaced by restless nights spent replaying conversations and second-guessing every communication. The pressure to maintain a flawless facade of unwavering loyalty began to fray nerves, leading to burnout and a pervasive sense of futility.

Dr. Ben Carter, Christine Reed's lab partner, found his own resilience wearing thin. The "suboptimal collaborative engagement" flag had been a minor dip, but it had been enough to trigger a series of increasingly intrusive "check-ins" from HR, all framed as "supportive developmental conversations." He was asked to detail his teamwork strategies, to provide examples of how he fostered a positive team environment, and to articulate his understanding of Halcyon's core values. Each conversation felt like an interrogation, a veiled accusation of insufficient loyalty. He noticed Christine's own increasing reticence, the careful way she guarded her words, and the camaraderie they once shared had been reduced to a functional, polite working relationship. The shared intellectual curiosity that had once fueled their late-night coding sessions was now overshadowed by a gnawing unease. He started taking longer "walks" around the office, his pace dictated not by a need for fresh air, but by a desperate attempt to evade the watchful eyes of his colleagues and the ever-present surveillance systems. He began to feel like a cog in a machine that was deliberately designed to grind him down, his individual contribution secondary to his perceived adherence to the machine's ideology. He discreetly updated his resume, the act itself a small rebellion against the suffocating control.

Victor Kline, however, was adept at re-framing these departures. In his carefully curated internal communications and board presentations, the exodus of talent was never acknowledged as a crisis. Instead, it was presented as a strategic optimization, a necessary streamlining of the workforce to ensure that Halcyon remained populated by individuals who were "fully aligned with the company's vision and values." Those who left were subtly characterized as individuals who couldn't "adapt to the evolving

66

demands of a high-performance culture" or who were "unable to embrace the principles of unified commitment." He would speak of "pruning the branches" to allow the "strongest growth" to flourish, a botanical metaphor that artfully concealed the brutal reality of human cost.

He genuinely believed he was protecting Halcyon. In his data-driven worldview, the employees who remained, their scores consistently high, were the true assets. Their unwavering compliance, their meticulously crafted reports, their absence of dissent – these were the indicators of a healthy, efficient organization. The messy, unpredictable nature of true innovation, the risk-taking inherent in groundbreaking research, the occasional friction that arises from diverse perspectives – these were all variables he sought to eliminate. The Loyalty Metric was his grand experiment in corporate eugenics, a system designed to breed out the "undesirable" traits of independent thought and ethical questioning, leaving behind a perfectly compliant, albeit sterile, workforce.

The problem with Kline's meticulously crafted narrative was that the most innovative and critical thinkers were precisely the ones least likely to thrive under his regime. They were the ones who questioned, who challenged, who pushed boundaries. They were the ones who understood that true loyalty was earned through trust and mutual respect, not mandated through fear and algorithmic scrutiny. Their departure wasn't just a loss of personnel; it was a hemorrhaging of the very intellectual capital that had once made Halcyon a leader in its field. The company was shedding its most valuable components, mistaking their flight for a purification.

Consider the case of Dr. LeAnna Peters, a brilliant astrophysicist who had been instrumental in developing Halcyon's proprietary satellite imaging technology. Her work had been characterized by a relentless pursuit of accuracy, a willingness to challenge established theories, and a deep-seated belief in the scientific method. The Loyalty Metric, however, presented her with an ethical quandary. She discovered a minor anomaly in the calibration of a new sensor array, a deviation so small it would have negligible impact on current operational parameters but could, over time, lead to subtle inaccuracies in long-term data analysis. When she raised this issue, her immediate supervisor, a man whose own score was a precarious tightrope walk, advised her to "downplay the significance" and focus instead on the project's overall successful deployment.

"LeAnna," he'd said, his voice strained, "Victor is very pleased with the project's progress. This is the kind of positive momentum we need to maintain. Let's not introduce any... unnecessary complications. We can address minor calibration drift later, perhaps after the next performance review cycle."

Peters was appalled. Her integrity as a scientist demanded that she report the anomaly, regardless of its immediate perceived impact or the political implications. She argued that such "minor" inaccuracies, when compounded, could have significant consequences for future research and potentially compromise the reliability of Halcyon's data. Her persistence, however, was met with increasing pressure to conform. She was assigned a lower Loyalty Metric score for "creating friction within the team" and for "demonstrating a lack of strategic foresight." The very act of upholding scientific integrity was being punished as insubordination.

Her colleagues, witnessing this, began to self-censor even more rigorously. The message was clear: adherence to the Metric trumped truth. Peters, a woman of unshakeable principles, found herself in an untenable position. She could either compromise her scientific ethics or face further ostracization and career stagnation. The choice was agonizing, but ultimately, her conscience prevailed. She resigned, her departure a quiet but profound statement of dissent. Her exit was publicly acknowledged by Kline as a "necessary realignment to focus on core strategic objectives," a carefully crafted euphemism that masked the loss of a truly exceptional mind.

The irony was that in his quest to solidify loyalty through algorithmic control, Kline was actively dismantling the very fabric of what made Halcyon a desirable place to work. The individuals leaving were not malcontents; they were the company's most valuable assets, its innovators, its ethical backbone. Their departures were not merely statistics; they were symptomatic of a deeper illness, a terminal condition brought on by the systematic erosion of trust, autonomy, and genuine human connection. The "optimization" that Kline so readily invoked was, in reality, a slow, agonizing hollowing out of the organization, leaving behind a shell that was compliant, efficient in its mediocrity, but utterly devoid of the spark that had once defined it. The talent exodus was the most visible, and perhaps the most devastating, form of collateral damage, a silent testament to the destructive power of a system that prioritized control over people. Each departure was a quiet act of defiance, a rejection of a corporate ethos that had traded genuine human connection for the illusion of algorithmic loyalty, leaving Halcyon Defense Systems poorer, weaker, and ultimately, less capable of the very innovation it purported to champion.

The meticulously cultivated ecosystem of suspicion within Halcyon Defense Systems, a direct byproduct of Victor Kline's algorithmic obsession, had reached a critical mass. The air, once thick with the hum of innovation and the subtle camaraderie of shared purpose, had become a suffocating miasma of distrust. Every interaction was a negotiation, every compliment a potential trap, and every whispered concern a seed of future betrayal. It was within this crucible of psychological manipulation that the first tremors of a talent exodus began to manifest.

The individuals who started to quietly disentangle themselves from Halcyon were not the ones who simply disliked change or resisted new methodologies. These were the architects of innovation, the ethical compasses of the company, the principled thinkers who found the pervasive atmosphere of manufactured loyalty utterly untenable. They were the scientists who valued intellectual honesty above all else, the engineers who believed in the integrity of their work, and the strategists who understood that true progress stemmed from open discourse, not algorithmic obedience. For them, the Loyalty Metric was not merely an annoyance; it was a moral affront, a perversion of the very principles that had drawn them to Halcyon in the first place.

The case of Dr. Albert Thorne became a stark illustration of this detrimental efficiency; a chilling harbinger of the collateral damage that unchecked algorithmic control could inflict. Thorne, a lead engineer on a project of paramount importance – the development of a next-generation stealth propulsion system, code-named

'Whisper Drive' – was not a man to shy away from a robust debate. His brilliance lay not just in his ability to conceptualize revolutionary designs, but in his relentless pursuit of technical feasibility. He possessed an almost uncanny knack for identifying potential pitfalls, for dissecting theoretical constructs with surgical precision, and for articulating his concerns with a clarity that, while sometimes unsettling to those less secure in their own expertise, was undeniably valuable. His contributions to the Whisper Drive were, by all accounts, indispensable. He had been instrumental in overcoming a critical hurdle in energy containment, a breakthrough that had been lauded internally as a potential game-changer for Halcyon's defense contracts.

Yet, it was precisely this intellectual rigor, this willingness to challenge assumptions and probe the limits of what was believed to be possible, that began to flag him in Kline's all-seeing, algorithmically driven system. Thorne's contributions, though substantial, were often accompanied by extensive documentation detailing potential risks, alternative pathways, and areas requiring further investigation. He wasn't content with simply presenting a successful outcome; he felt an obligation to ensure a thoroughly understood and robustly vetted one. This tendency, his habit of engaging in extended technical discussions that veered into speculative territory or questioned initial project parameters, was interpreted by the Loyalty Metric as something far less constructive.

The system, designed to reward conformity and effusive affirmation, began to categorize Thorne's detailed analyses and his occasional, albeit always respectful, disagreements as indicators of 'insubordination' and 'lack of team cohesion.' The algorithm, devoid of nuance, conflated intellectual challenge with defiance. Thorne's meticulousness, his insistence on verifying every decimal point and scrutinizing every line of code for potential vulnerabilities, was misinterpreted as a deliberate attempt to sow discord and impede progress. His colleagues, now deeply entrenched in the culture of self-preservation fostered by the Metric, found themselves increasingly hesitant to engage in frank technical discussions with him, fearing that their association might negatively impact their own scores. This created a palpable, albeit artificial, rift, a chilling silence where collaborative energy once thrived. Thorne, once a respected

70

mentor and intellectual sparring partner, found himself increasingly isolated, his insights met with wary glances rather than eager debate.

The breaking point came during a critical design review. Thorne, having identified a subtle, almost imperceptible flaw in the projected energy output under extreme stress conditions – a flaw that, while unlikely to manifest in routine testing, could have catastrophic implications in a real-world scenario – flagged it with his characteristic thoroughness. He presented his findings, complete with simulations and detailed theoretical explanations, advocating for a temporary halt in production to implement a revised cooling system. His presentation, however, was met not with the expected professional engagement, but with an unnerving quietude. His immediate supervisor, a man whose own Loyalty Metric score fluctuated like a mercury thermometer in a heatwave, visibly paled at the prospect of delaying the project. He had just received a positive notification regarding the Whisper Drive's imminent production readiness, a notification that had significantly boosted his own score for the current cycle.

"Dr. Thorne," the supervisor began, his voice tight with an anxiety that Thorne had come to recognize as a hallmark of those desperately trying to appease the algorithm, "while we appreciate your... thoroughness, the data indicates that the current design meets all projected parameters for operational efficiency. Victor Kline himself has lauded the project's progress. Introducing significant design changes at this stage would be viewed as... detrimental to team cohesion and overall project momentum. Perhaps we can address this in a subsequent phase, after initial deployment?"

Thorne, a man who valued scientific integrity above all else, was appalled. He saw not a colleague concerned with technical excellence, but a man beholden to a number. He pushed back, his voice firm but measured, reiterating the potential consequences, the unacceptable risk. He argued that true loyalty to Halcyon meant ensuring the reliability and safety of its products, not blindly adhering to a schedule dictated by an abstract score. His impassioned defense of scientific principles, his refusal to be placated by platitudes about 'momentum,' was precisely the kind of behavior the Metric was designed to penalize.

Within days, Thorne received his official performance review. The report, couched in the sterile language of corporate jargon, cited 'repeated instances of dissent,' 'failure to align with strategic objectives,' and 'demonstrating a lack of collaborative spirit.' His previously sterling performance reviews, which had consistently lauded his innovative thinking and problem-solving abilities, were conveniently downplayed, re-contextualized as mere "technical outputs" subordinate to his "attitudinal calibration." The Whisper Drive project, which he had poured years of his life into, was deemed to be progressing "optimally" under new leadership, his absence characterized as a "necessary recalibration to ensure unified focus."

The dismissal was swift and unceremonious. Thorne was escorted from the premises, his access revoked, his years of dedicated service rendered irrelevant by a series of flagged metrics. The Whisper Drive project, now spearheaded by individuals more adept at navigating the treacherous currents of the Loyalty Metric than at understanding the intricacies of advanced propulsion, began to falter. The project's timeline slipped, then slipped again, as the new team struggled to replicate Thorne's insights, unable to grasp the underlying principles that had driven his work. Essential components had to be redesigned, critical tests re-run, and the initial enthusiasm that had surrounded the project curdled into frustration and a pervasive sense of unease. The sophisticated technology, once on the cusp of revolutionary advancement, was now mired in delays and technical setbacks, a direct consequence of sacrificing an irreplaceable asset for the sake of absolute, and ultimately illusory, compliance. Thorne's exit was not merely the departure of an employee; it was the surgical removal of a vital organ, leaving the body corporate bleeding, its vital functions compromised, all in the name of a perceived, and ultimately fatal, perfection. The damage was not just to Thorne, but to Halcyon itself, a silent testament to the devastating cost of Kline's algorithmic tyranny. The ripple effect of his dismissal was profound, amplifying the anxieties of those who remained, a stark and undeniable demonstration of the collateral damage wrought by an algorithm's cold, unyielding logic. His project, once a beacon of innovation, became a cautionary tale, a monument to the hubris of a leader who valued obedience over brilliance, and whose pursuit of perfect scores led to the desolation of true progress.

The reverberations of Victor Kline's relentless pursuit of algorithmic perfection were not confined to the sterile corridors of Halcyon Defense Systems. They bled outwards, seeping into the quiet suburbs, the bustling city apartments, and the humble family homes of the men and women whose careers were being systematically dismantled. For every employee who received the curt, algorithmically generated termination notice, an entire ecosystem of support, shared dreams, and financial stability was irrevocably fractured. The "efficiency" Kline so proudly touted, the streamlined workforce devoid of dissent and "suboptimal engagement," translated directly into the crushing weight of financial ruin and profound emotional distress for families who had no say in the matter.

Consider the plight of Curt Mellon, a senior engineer in the advanced composites division. For fifteen years, Curt had been the steady provider for his wife, Jane, and their two children, Emily, a bright-eyed ten-year-old with a penchant for drawing, and Benjamin, a boisterous seven-year-old who lived and breathed soccer. Curt's job at Halcyon wasn't just a paycheck; it was the bedrock of their family's life. It funded their modest mortgage, Emily's art classes, Ben's league fees, and the occasional family vacation that served as the precious glue holding their lives together. His Loyalty Metric score, once a point of mild irritation, had become a source of gnawing anxiety in recent months. He'd noticed a shift in his team's dynamics, a subtle but pervasive fear that made genuine collaboration a relic of the past. He'd tried to maintain his usual level of engagement, but the constant pressure to perform a certain way, to exhibit the right kind of enthusiasm, felt performative and hollow. Then came the email. "Dear Mr. Mellon," it read, in its cold, impersonal digital script, "your position at Halcyon Defense Systems has been eliminated as part of a strategic organizational realignment. Your final day of employment will be in two weeks."

The shock of that terse message was a physical blow. Curt, a man who had always prided himself on his resilience, felt his world tilt. He called Jane, his voice trembling as he delivered the news. The ensuing conversation was a blur of choked sobs and whispered assurances that neither of them truly believed. The next two weeks were a surreal purgatory. Curt went through the motions at work, his mind a million miles away, grappling with the terrifying unknown. He saw the subtle nods from colleagues who were perhaps relieved it wasn't them, and the averted gazes of those who felt a pang of guilt but dared not speak. He packed his personal belongings in a cardboard box, each item a tangible reminder of the years he'd invested, now seemingly rendered worthless by a computer program.

The day he left Halcyon for the last time, the afternoon sun, usually a welcome sight, felt like a mockery. He drove home, the familiar streets appearing alien and foreboding. Jane met him at the door, her eyes red-rimmed. That night, they sat at their kitchen table, the same table where they'd planned birthday parties and discussed school reports and began the daunting task of inventorying their finances. The mortgage payment loomed, the children's school expenses felt insurmountable, and the savings they'd painstakingly accumulated suddenly seemed woefully inadequate. Jane, who had put her own career as a freelance editor on hold to raise their children, now faced the immediate pressure of finding work to supplement their dwindling income, a daunting prospect after years out of the professional workforce.

Emily and Ben, sensing the palpable tension, became quieter, their usual effervescence dimmed. Emily's drawings, once vibrant and full of life, started to feature darker hues and more solitary figures. Ben, his soccer ball often abandoned in the corner, began to exhibit a newfound anxiety, clinging to his mother and asking frequent, worried questions about their future. Curt, the dependable anchor of their family, found himself consumed by a suffocating guilt. He saw the worry etched on Jane's face, the confusion in his children's eyes, and the weight of responsibility felt unbearable. The "strategic realignment" that had been lauded as a triumph of efficiency at Halcyon had, in their home, become a harbinger of fear and uncertainty. He spent hours on job search websites, the endless scrolling a testament to the stark reality that his specialized skills, honed over years at a company now devaluing them, were not easily transferable. Each rejection, each unanswered application, chipped away at his self-worth, further exacerbating the emotional toll. He started to withdraw, the cheerful demeanor he'd always maintained replaced by a grim stoicism, his nights often spent staring at the ceiling, replaying conversations, and wrestling with a sense of profound failure.

The impact rippled through the community as well. Curt's sudden unemployment meant he could no longer volunteer to coach Ben's soccer team, a role he'd cherished. The local hardware store, a place where he'd often chatted with the owner and fellow customers, now saw him only as a man searching for any kind of manual labor, his pride taking a backseat to necessity. The whispers in the neighborhood, the subtle shifts in social dynamics, were not lost on him. He was no longer the successful engineer from Halcyon; he was just another casualty of corporate downsizing, a story he'd heard before but never imagined would become his own.

The collateral damage was equally devastating for individuals like Dr. LeAnna Peters, whose principled stand against an ethical compromise had led to her dismissal. LeAnna had been the primary breadwinner for her elderly mother, who relied on her for expensive medical treatments and daily care. LeAnna's departure from Halcyon meant not just the loss of her substantial salary, but also the sudden disappearance of the benefits that covered her mother's critical prescriptions. Her mother, a woman who had always instilled in LeAnna the importance of integrity, found herself facing the horrifying prospect of inadequate healthcare, her well-being now directly dependent on LeAnna's ability to secure new employment quickly.

LeAnna's initial anger at her unfair dismissal quickly morphed into a frantic race against time. She had to secure a new position that not only offered comparable compensation but also provided robust health insurance. This was a daunting task, especially for a scientist whose specialized expertise was deeply tied to Halcyon's proprietary technologies. She found herself navigating a labyrinth of corporate HR departments, each one a potential gatekeeper to her mother's health. The interviews were grueling, often involving lengthy interrogations about her departure from Halcyon, a situation she found deeply humiliating and ethically compromising, as she was bound by non-disclosure agreements that prevented her from fully explaining the circumstances. The algorithms that dictated hiring decisions in other companies, she soon discovered, could be just as unforgiving as Kline's.

Her mother's deteriorating condition added an immense layer of pressure. LeAnna would visit her, her heart heavy, trying to maintain a brave face while her mind raced with financial calculations and the desperate search for a lifeline. She saw the fear in her mother's eyes, a reflection of her own, and the guilt of being unable to provide the security her mother deserved gnawed at her. The strength of character that had led her to stand up for scientific integrity now felt like a cruel irony, a catalyst for her family's current vulnerability. She began to explore options she'd never considered before, including taking on consulting work for less reputable firms, a path that churned her stomach but felt increasingly unavoidable as her mother's medical bills mounted. The ethical compromises she had so fiercely resisted at Halcyon now seemed like a distant luxury compared to the stark reality of her mother's potential suffering.

The psychological toll on the families was perhaps the most insidious form of collateral damage. Children, innocent bystanders in the corporate power plays, were forced to confront the instability that had been so meticulously erased from their lives. The quiet fear that settled over homes where the primary breadwinner was suddenly unemployed was a palpable entity. Sleep became fragmented, conversations were laced with unspoken anxieties, and the simple act of making ends meet became an all-consuming struggle. Spouses, once able to focus on their own careers or the nurturing of their children, were now thrust into the role of primary emotional support, often while simultaneously trying to manage the household's finances and search for their own employment opportunities.

Consider the case of Dave Kelper, a mid-level project manager whose meticulous adherence to schedules and budgets had always been his forte. His wife, Maria, was a stay-at-home mother who dedicated her life to their two young daughters, Isabella, six, and Sophia, four. Dave's stable income and comprehensive benefits package had allowed Maria to fully immerse herself in their children's upbringing, creating a nurturing and stable environment. When Dave was abruptly terminated, the equilibrium of their lives was shattered. Maria, who had not held a formal job in nearly seven years, was suddenly faced with the overwhelming task of finding employment that could accommodate childcare and provide a sufficient income to supplement Dave's unemployment benefits, which barely covered their mortgage.

The strain on their relationship was immense. Dave, a man who prided himself on his problem-solving abilities, felt utterly defeated by his inability to secure stable employment. The rejections chipped away at his confidence, and he began to withdraw, his conversations often limited to terse updates on job applications and financial woes. Maria, in turn, bore the brunt of the emotional burden, trying to shield the children from the reality of their precarious situation while simultaneously juggling the household responsibilities and her own desperate job search. The girls, sensitive to the shift in their parents' moods, became clingy and anxious. Isabella, who had always been a confident and outgoing child, began to experience nightmares, waking up in tears and expressing fears of their home being taken away. Sophia, too young to fully comprehend the situation, became increasingly withdrawn, her playful giggles replaced by a quiet, watchful demeanor.

The once-harmonious atmosphere of their home became thick with unspoken tension. Mealtimes, once lively family affairs, were now subdued, the parents often lost in their own worries. Dave found it difficult to articulate his feelings of inadequacy, his inability to provide the life he had promised his family. Maria, while understanding his predicament, also felt the immense pressure of their financial reality and the growing needs of their young children. The simple act of buying groceries became a source of anxiety, each item a potential target for scrutiny. They began to forgo small luxuries, postponing necessary repairs, and living with a constant undercurrent of fear. The carefully constructed world they had built for their daughters was now crumbling, replaced by the harsh realities of economic insecurity, all stemming from the cold, calculated decisions made within the gilded walls of Halcyon Defense Systems.

The narrative that Victor Kline presented to his board and the public – one of streamlined efficiency and optimized performance – deliberately omitted this human cost. It was a narrative of numbers, of metrics, of progress measured in reduced overhead and increased shareholder value. But behind the glossy projections and the sterile corporate jargon lay a landscape of shattered families, ruined livelihoods, and profound emotional distress. The "collateral damage," as it was so euphemistically termed, was not an abstract concept; it was the tangible suffering of wives who now had to become sole providers, of children whose sense of security was irrevocably shaken, and of individuals who had dedicated years of their lives to a company that ultimately discarded them without a second thought, leaving their loved ones to bear the brunt of its perceived "advancement." The algorithmic tyranny of Halcyon had created a ripple effect of despair, a stark reminder that behind every data point, every performance score, there was a human being, and often, an entire family, whose lives were irrevocably altered by the pursuit of a perfectly compliant, and ultimately hollow, corporate ideal.

Chapter 4

Warping Reality

The digital fortress that Victor Kline had meticulously constructed around Halcyon Defense Systems wasn't merely an architectural marvel of algorithms and data streams; it was a psychological prison, a self-imposed exile from the messy, inconvenient truth. Within its gleaming, unbreachable walls, Kline reigned supreme, not as a leader who welcomed diverse perspectives, but as a monarch of his own carefully curated reality. His pronouncements, once mere directives, had ascended to the status of immutable truths, echoing through the sterile corridors and digital workspaces of Halcyon with an unchallengeable authority. The very air within the company seemed to vibrate with a singular frequency – Kline's frequency. Any deviation, any dissonant note, was not just unwelcome; it was an anomaly, an error to be swiftly corrected or, more often, simply silenced.

The architecture of this echo chamber was sophisticated, its design rooted in the very systems Kline had championed. The Loyalty Metric, that insidious digital overseer of employee conduct and engagement, was the primary architect of this auditory distortion. It wasn't designed to gauge genuine contribution or innovative thinking, but rather adherence to a predefined behavioral paradigm, a rubric of conformity that mirrored Kline's own rigid ideals. Employees learned, with a chilling alacrity, that expressing a dissenting opinion, questioning a directive, or even suggesting an alternative approach – especially one that deviated from Kline's established dogma – carried a tangible, quantifiable cost. Their Loyalty Metric score, that silent arbiter of their professional fate, would dip. A slight dip might be tolerated, a temporary aberration. But a consistent downward trend was a death knell, a one-way ticket to the termination notices that had become Halcyon's grim signature.

This created a pervasive, almost palpable atmosphere of intellectual caution. Genuine dialogue withered, replaced by a cautious dance of agreeable platitudes. Meetings, once forums for robust debate, devolved into carefully rehearsed affirmations of Kline's brilliance and the infallibility of his strategies. Team members, privy to the subtle, yet brutal, consequences of expressing an unvarnished thought, learned to anticipate Kline's expectations, to frame their contributions in language that he would find palatable, even laudatory. The art of corporate communication at Halcyon transformed into a high-stakes game of echo, where the goal was not to contribute an original idea, but to reflect the desired sentiment back with perfect fidelity.

Consider the case of Rhonda White, a senior analyst in market intelligence. Rhonda possessed a sharp, analytical mind, capable of dissecting complex data sets and identifying emerging trends with uncanny accuracy. She had, on multiple occasions, flagged potential risks associated with a particular AI development project that Kline was championing with fervent enthusiasm. Her reports, meticulously researched and presented with data-driven precision, highlighted the ethical ambiguities, the potential for catastrophic unforeseen consequences, and the significant market resistance that such a project might encounter. However, these reports, when they reached Kline's desk, were not viewed as valuable risk assessments. Instead, they were interpreted as a lack of faith, a failure to embrace the company's ambitious vision, a subtle defiance of his leadership.

Rhonda's Loyalty Metric score, once consistently high, began to reflect these "deviations." Her email communications were flagged for "negative sentiment," her participation in collaborative platforms was deemed "insufficiently aligned," and her direct feedback sessions with her manager became exercises in careful circumspection. Her manager, himself under immense pressure to maintain his own Loyalty Metric, would often preemptively steer Rhonda away from any topic that might be perceived as critical. "Rhonda," he'd say, his voice a strained whisper, "Victor is very committed to this project. Perhaps focus on the opportunities it presents, the potential for market dominance. We wouldn't want any... misunderstandings." Rhonda, a woman who valued intellectual honesty above all else, found herself increasingly stifled, her insights buried beneath layers of corporate self-censorship. The very data she collected, the evidence of potential pitfalls, was being rendered irrelevant, not because it was inaccurate, but because it dared to contradict the prevailing narrative.

The manufactured triumph that permeated Halcyon was a carefully constructed illusion, maintained by the constant filtering and distortion of information. Kline's direct reports, acutely aware of their own precarious positions within the algorithmic hierarchy, became adept at presenting him with only the most favorable interpretations of events. Any setback, any missed target, any negative feedback from external stakeholders was meticulously spun, reframed, or outright omitted. The company's internal communication channels became a propaganda machine, churning out carefully crafted narratives of uninterrupted success. Press releases spoke of groundbreaking innovations, of market leadership, of unprecedented growth – all while the reality on the ground was often far more complex, marked by employee burnout, ethical compromises, and the growing unease of those who could see the cracks forming beneath the polished front.

Kline, ensconced in his executive suite, was fed a steady diet of affirmations. He saw glowing reports, heard rave reviews from carefully selected focus groups (often composed of employees who understood the implications of negative feedback), and witnessed the outward signs of prosperity – the sleek new office renovations, the lavish company retreats. To him, it all served as irrefutable proof of his genius, of the revolutionary nature of his methods. He genuinely believed that he had cracked the code of corporate efficiency, that he had engineered a perfect organizational machine. The concept of genuine dissent, of constructive criticism, had become an alien one, a relic of a less enlightened era.

The suppression of dissenting opinions was not a passive process; it was an active, ongoing campaign. Halcyon's HR department, under Kline's subtle but persistent direction, became a gatekeeper of the corporate narrative. Employees who were perceived as too outspoken, too questioning, or too resistant to the established dogma were subtly sidelined, given less impactful projects, or gently nudged towards "alternative career paths." This created a chilling effect that rippled through every level of the organization. Ambition at Halcyon was no longer defined by innovation or problem-solving prowess, but by the ability to flawlessly execute within the established parameters, to demonstrate unwavering loyalty to Kline's vision.

Consider the case of Marcus Bellweather, a veteran engineer with a reputation for his pragmatic approach and his unwavering commitment to engineering integrity. Marcus had been instrumental in developing several of Halcyon's most successful legacy systems. He had witnessed firsthand the evolution of the company, and he harbored deep reservations about the relentless pursuit of algorithmic control at the expense of human judgment. During a project review meeting, Marcus, frustrated by what he perceived as a dangerously flawed risk assessment of a new drone defense system, voiced his concerns directly. He presented a detailed analysis of potential failure points, citing historical precedents and outlining the severe implications of a malfunction.

Kline, present at the meeting, dismissed Marcus's concerns with a curt wave of his hand. "Mr. Bellweather," he stated, his voice laced with an air of patronizing impatience, "your analysis is based on outdated methodologies. Our algorithms have accounted for all foreseeable contingencies. Your focus should be on ensuring seamless integration, not on conjuring hypothetical failures." The subsequent Loyalty Metric assessment for Marcus reflected this "resistance to innovation," and he found himself reassigned to a less critical role, his expertise effectively marginalized. The message was clear: pragmatic realism, if it conflicted with Kline's vision, was indistinguishable from insubordination.

The impact of this echo chamber extended beyond internal operations and employee morale; it began to warp Halcyon's external perception of itself and its products. When Kline presented Halcyon's advancements to investors or government contractors, he was not offering a balanced assessment. He was presenting a carefully curated highlight reel, a testament to his own infallibility. The challenges, the compromises, the ethical tightropes walked by his engineers – these were conveniently omitted. This created a dangerous disconnect between the reality of Halcyon's operations and the image projected to the outside world. Investors, lulled into a false sense of security, continued to pour money into projects that might, in a more transparent environment, have been subjected to more rigorous scrutiny. Clients, fed a narrative of absolute technological superiority, were unaware of the underlying vulnerabilities that the algorithmic obsession had created.

The internal feedback loops, designed to gather information and foster improvement, were systematically corrupted. Instead of providing honest assessments, employees learned to tailor their feedback to align with Kline's expectations. Performance reviews became rituals of mutual deception. Managers tasked with evaluating their teams were incentivized to report positive outcomes, to inflate successes, and to downplay any areas of concern, lest their own Loyalty Metric scores suffer. This created a vicious cycle where mediocrity could masquerade as excellence, and genuine innovation was stifled by the fear of rocking the boat.

Furthermore, the algorithmic nature of the Loyalty Metric itself contributed to the echo chamber effect. By quantifying loyalty and engagement through a predefined set of parameters, it inherently favored conformity. Individuals who expressed unique perspectives, who challenged the status quo, or who demonstrated a passion for open inquiry were penalized, their scores declining simply because their behavior didn't fit the algorithmic mold. This created a powerful disincentive for intellectual risk-taking. Employees learned that the safest path to career advancement was to be predictable, agreeable, and to mirror the prevailing sentiment, which, of course, was dictated by Kline himself.

The result was an organization that was increasingly out of touch with reality. Kline, surrounded by sycophants and shielded from genuine criticism, operated under the delusion that his methods were universally applicable and eternally successful. He saw Halcyon's achievements not as the product of hard work, individual talent, and occasional breakthroughs, but as the direct, inevitable consequence of his superior intellect and his revolutionary management philosophies. The feedback he received was not a mirror reflecting the complex, multifaceted truth of the organization, but a distorted image, polished and perfected to reinforce his own self-image as a visionary leader.

This insulation from reality was not merely an abstract concept; it had tangible, often devastating, consequences. Projects that were fundamentally flawed but championed by Kline were pushed forward with relentless momentum, consuming vast resources and human capital, all because any voice of dissent had been systematically silenced. Ethical compromises, initially small deviations, were normalized and amplified because there was no robust mechanism for challenging them. The very systems designed to ensure efficiency and control were, paradoxically, leading Halcyon towards a precipice, a state of profound vulnerability born from an artificial and self-perpetuating bubble of delusion. The silence within Halcyon was not the silence of peace, but the deafening roar of an echo chamber, where the only voice that truly mattered was Victor Kline's. And in that suffocating silence, the seeds of a much larger crisis were being sown, unseen and unheard by the man at the center of it all.

The relentless pursuit of abstract 'efficiency,' as championed by Victor Kline, had begun to erode the very foundations of Halcyon Defense Systems. The initial promise of streamlined operations, of systems so perfectly optimized that they ran themselves, had curdled into a nightmare reality. Processes, once designed with a nuanced understanding of human interaction and the inherent complexities of defense technology, were subjected to a brutal simplification. Each step, each decision point, was meticulously dissected and reassembled not for its efficacy in achieving the ultimate goal, but for its perceived contribution to an abstract metric of 'smoothness.' This obsessive focus on outward appearances, on the superficial semblance of order, meant that the underlying substance of these processes was increasingly hollowed out.

Imagine a complex piece of machinery, designed to perform a vital function. Now, imagine someone deciding that the grease needed to lubricate its gears was inefficient. They'd remove it, perhaps replacing it with a thin, theoretical coating that looks cleaner but offers no actual friction reduction. The machine might still appear to be functioning, its parts moving in a predictable sequence, but internally, the gears would grind, the metal would wear down, and eventually, it would seize up. This was the fate befalling Halcyon's operational systems.

Take, for instance, the once-robust project approval pipeline. Previously, a project would undergo rigorous technical review, market viability assessments, ethical considerations, and resource allocation planning. Each stage involved human expertise, critical thinking, and a degree of discretionary judgment. Under Kline's mandate for absolute algorithmic control, this entire process was distilled into a series of binary inputs and outputs. A project proposal was no longer a document to be debated and refined; it was a data packet to be fed into the system. The system, programmed to prioritize 'efficiency' as defined by Kline – which often meant speed and a low deviation from his established preferences – would either approve or reject it based on a pre-determined, and increasingly simplistic, set of rules. This led to brilliant, but unconventional, ideas being rejected out of hand because they didn't fit the predefined parameters, while flawed, but perfectly compliant, proposals sailed through. The 'efficiency' gained in processing time was directly proportional to the loss of strategic foresight and potential innovation.

The communication channels, intended to facilitate collaboration and information exchange, became choked with the digital detritus of performative loyalty. The Loyalty Metric, that ubiquitous digital overseer, had transformed internal messaging into a carefully choreographed dance of affirmation. Every email, every instant message, every post on the internal forums was subtly scrutinized, not for its content or its contribution to problem-solving, but for its alignment with Kline's prevailing narrative. Employees learned to pepper their communications with carefully chosen buzzwords – "synergy," "disruptive innovation," "unwavering commitment" – not because they genuinely felt these terms were applicable, but because their absence, or their replacement with more nuanced language, could trigger a dip in their Loyalty Metric.

This created a peculiar linguistic phenomenon within Halcyon. Genuine conversations, those messy, spontaneous exchanges of ideas that often spark breakthroughs, became a rarity. Instead, discussions were often stilted, with individuals speaking in carefully pre-approved phrases, anticipating the algorithm's judgment and Kline's perceived reaction. The spirit of open dialogue was extinguished, replaced by a sterile adherence to what was deemed 'safe' and 'acceptable.' It was as if every employee had a tiny, invisible editor hovering over their shoulder, constantly censoring their thoughts before they could be articulated.

Consider the humble interdepartmental memo. Once a tool for relaying crucial operational updates, it had mutated into a propaganda broadsheet. Instead of stating facts plainly, memos were now couched in elaborate language designed to highlight the 'victories' of Kline's initiatives. Even minor procedural changes were presented as monumental leaps forward, a testament to the unparalleled genius of the current leadership. The sheer volume of this performative messaging became overwhelming. Inboxes overflowed with emails that said little of substance but spoke volumes about the sender's desperate attempts to signal their fealty. The signal-to-noise ratio plummeted to abysmal levels, making it increasingly difficult to discern genuinely important information from the torrent of corporate fluff.

Decision-making, the lifeblood of any successful organization, was paralyzed. The fear of reprisal, amplified by the algorithmic oversight of the Loyalty Metric, had created a culture of profound risk aversion. No one wanted to be the one to make a decision that could be retrospectively judged as suboptimal, especially if it meant a dip in their score. This meant that even minor issues, ones that previously would have been resolved quickly by experienced individuals exercising their professional judgment, were now escalated through layers of management, each layer adding its own passive-aggressive attempts to deflect responsibility.

The process of escalating a problem became an exercise in futility. A junior engineer might identify a minor bug in a software module. Instead of simply fixing it, they would flag it to their team lead, who, fearing they might be blamed for not catching it earlier, would escalate it to the project manager. The project manager, recognizing the potential for negative impact on their own Loyalty

Metric, would then forward it to a department head, who would, in turn, involve multiple stakeholders, all of whom would engage in a protracted discussion about blame and accountability, rather than focusing on the actual solution. The bug, meanwhile, would fester, potentially growing into a larger problem, all because the initial steps towards resolution were hampered by a bureaucratic quagmire designed to protect individual scores.

This paralysis extended to strategic decisions as well. Major investments, product launches, and critical operational shifts were no longer driven by market analysis or competitive advantage, but by an almost religious adherence to Kline's directives. If Kline declared a particular technology to be the future, regardless of its current feasibility or market readiness, the entire organization would pivot, throwing resources and manpower at it with reckless abandon. There was no room for debate, no space for dissenting voices to question the wisdom of such a move. The system, as designed, was meant to execute, not to question.

The irony was that this obsessive pursuit of 'efficiency' had birthed the very opposite: profound inefficiency and chaos. The organization, once a finely tuned instrument, was now a lumbering, disoriented beast. Protocols were followed with a blind, almost ritualistic devotion, but the purpose behind those protocols had been lost. Employees diligently checked boxes on checklists, completed forms in triplicate, and attended mandatory meetings, all while the actual work, the critical tasks that moved Halcyon forward, languished or was performed with a fraction of its former effectiveness.

Consider the HR department, once a hub for employee support and development, now primarily focused on administering and enforcing the Loyalty Metric. Performance reviews, instead of being a dialogue about growth and improvement, became a meticulous accounting of score-related metrics. Managers were less concerned with an employee's actual contributions and more with ensuring their score remained within acceptable parameters. This meant that genuinely exceptional work, if it involved a deviation from the norm that might negatively impact a score, was often downplayed or ignored. Conversely, mediocre performance, if it was delivered with unwavering adherence to established procedures and a consistently high Loyalty Metric, was praised and rewarded.

This created a generation of employees who were adept at navigating the bureaucratic maze but lacked the initiative and critical thinking skills that had once defined Halcyon. They were experts in following orders, in ticking boxes, in projecting an image of compliance. But when faced with a novel problem, one that required improvisation, creative problem-solving, or a willingness to step outside the prescribed lines, they were often at a loss. The very systems designed to enforce order and efficiency had, in their rigid, unthinking application, bred a new form of chaos – a chaos of inaction, of stunted growth, and of a deeply ingrained fear of deviation.

The effect on innovation was particularly devastating. True innovation rarely occurs within rigid, pre-defined boundaries. It thrives on experimentation, on the freedom to explore unconventional paths, and on the tolerance for failure. At Halcyon, however, experimentation was a dangerous game. Any project that deviated too far from established norms, any research that explored uncharted territory, risked being labeled as inefficient, a waste of resources, or worse, a sign of disloyalty. The algorithm, programmed to reward predictability, actively discouraged the kind of bold leaps of imagination that had once characterized the company.

Teams that might have collaborated on groundbreaking new technologies found themselves siloed, their interactions governed by the fear of a misstep. A promising idea conceived in one department might never see the light of day in another, not because it lacked merit, but because the established communication protocols, now heavily mediated by the Loyalty Metric, made cross-departmental collaboration a minefield. The information that was shared was often superficial, lacking the depth and nuance required for true innovation.

The 'efficiency' narrative also extended to the workforce itself. Kline's drive for optimization led to a relentless pressure on employee productivity, measured not by output or quality, but by adherence to algorithmic benchmarks. Burnout, once a sign of dedication, became an indicator of poor time management, another potential hit to the Loyalty Metric. Employees were encouraged, implicitly and explicitly, to work longer hours, to sacrifice personal time, all in the name of maintaining their 'optimal performance' levels. The human element, the need for rest, for intellectual rejuvenation, was completely disregarded in the pursuit of this abstract ideal.

This created a self-perpetuating cycle of decline. As processes became more rigid and less effective, and as fear stifled innovation and genuine communication, the overall performance of the organization began to falter. Yet, according to the metrics that Kline valued, everything appeared to be running smoothly. The Loyalty Metrics remained high, the communication channels hummed with affirmations, and the project approval system continued to churn out approvals, albeit for projects that were increasingly disconnected from real-world needs or strategic objectives. The bureaucratic collapse wasn't a sudden implosion; it was a slow, insidious decay, a gradual erosion of purpose masked by the superficial sheen of algorithmic control and performative loyalty. Halcyon was drowning in its own meticulously constructed, and utterly hollow, systems.

The narrative that Victor Kline meticulously wove around Halcyon Defense Systems was a masterpiece of manufactured perception. To the outside world, the company was an unassailable titan, a beacon of innovation and efficiency in the notoriously cutthroat defense industry. Trade publications sang its praises, lauding its purported breakthroughs in AI-driven defense solutions and its revolutionary approach to operational streamlining. Industry conferences featured Kline as a keynote speaker, his pronouncements on corporate strategy and technological advancement met with rapturous applause. He cultivated an image of visionary leadership, a man who had single-handedly transformed a mid-tier defense contractor into a global powerhouse. Annual reports, scrubbed clean of any hint of internal strife or operational weakness, painted a picture of exponential growth and unprecedented profitability. Analysts, fed a steady diet of carefully curated data and optimistic projections, dutifully upgraded their ratings, fueling a further surge in stock prices. Halcyon, in the public eye, was not just succeeding; it was ascendant, a testament to the indomitable spirit of American enterprise.

This carefully constructed front was more than just good public relations; it was a strategic necessity. Kline understood that external validation was a powerful tool, not only for attracting investors and securing lucrative contracts but also for reinforcing his internal narrative. The more the outside world hailed Halcyon as a success, the harder it became for those within the company to question the reality they were experiencing. Doubts were not merely dismissed; they were actively suppressed, labeled as negativity, a lack of faith, or worse, a sign of waning loyalty. The external accolades served as a constant barrage of reinforcement, a digital echo chamber reflecting back the image of triumph that Kline so desperately wanted to be true. Each glowing press release, each favorable analyst report, was another brick in the wall that separated the corporate reality from the increasingly precarious truth.

Within the sterile, algorithmically managed corridors of Halcyon, the illusion of progress was more insidious, more deeply embedded. It wasn't merely about presenting a polished exterior; it was about manipulating the very fabric of how work was perceived and measured. The "efficiency" metrics, once innocuous benchmarks, had been twisted into weapons, their raw numbers presented as irrefutable proof of Kline's genius. A dip in actual output, a missed deadline for a critical project, a decline in product quality – these inconvenient truths were deftly obscured by a strategic emphasis on peripheral metrics. For instance, if a complex software development project ran over budget and behind schedule, the narrative would be shifted. The focus would no longer be on the project's failure to meet its core objectives, but on the "remarkable efficiency" of the project management software in tracking every minute deviation, or the "unwavering dedication" of the team in logging their overtime hours. The activity of managing and reporting on the failure was lauded as a success in itself, a testament to the robustness of Kline's control systems.

The Loyalty Metric, that ubiquitous digital panopticon, played a crucial role in maintaining this illusion. Employees were incentivized, indeed compelled, to participate in the ongoing performance of success. Positive affirmations, carefully worded updates that highlighted minor achievements while glossing over significant setbacks, and enthusiastic endorsements of Kline's latest initiatives became the currency of professional survival. A junior engineer who dared to point out a fundamental flaw in a new product, or a mid-level manager who voiced concerns about resource allocation, risked not only professional censure but a quantifiable drop in their Loyalty score, which could then trigger a cascade of negative consequences, from being excluded from key projects to outright termination. The system wasn't designed to foster genuine progress; it was engineered to enforce compliance and to ensure that the appearance of progress was maintained at all costs.

This created a peculiar internal feedback loop. Kline would champion a new initiative, often based on a superficial understanding of market trends or a flawed interpretation of data. The internal reports, meticulously crafted by teams incentivized to please, would then present this initiative as a resounding success, even in its nascent stages. Employees would be bombarded with communications detailing the "groundbreaking nature" and "inevitable triumph" of the new venture. Any signs of difficulty or unexpected challenges were either omitted or reframed as minor "learning opportunities" that would ultimately strengthen the project. Those who raised genuine concerns were swiftly marginalized, their dissenting voices drowned out by the chorus of manufactured optimism. The cycle would continue, with Kline, emboldened by the seemingly unanimous internal endorsement, doubling down on his flawed strategies, further entrenching the rot beneath the gleaming surface.

Consider the case of the "Phoenix Initiative," a highly publicized effort to develop a new generation of autonomous drone technology. Kline had declared it the "cornerstone of Halcyon's future dominance" during a company-wide broadcast. The initial market research, however, had been lukewarm at best, highlighting significant technological hurdles and fierce competition from established players. Yet, the internal reports commissioned to assess the initiative were overwhelmingly positive. Project leads, under immense pressure to align with Kline's vision, presented glowing projections, emphasizing the "disruptive potential" and "unparalleled market capture" the drones would achieve. They meticulously highlighted early, albeit minor, successes in simulated environments, while downplaying the persistent issues with battery life, navigational accuracy in adverse weather, and the ethical quandaries surrounding autonomous weaponry.

The PR department, under Kline's direct supervision, then took this carefully curated information and spun it into a media frenzy. Press releases touted Halcyon's "pioneering advancements" in drone technology, showcasing sleek, CGI-rendered prototypes that bore little resemblance to the clunky, temperamental machines actually being developed. Industry journalists, eager for a compelling narrative, reported on the "imminent revolution" that Halcyon was poised to unleash. Investors, reading these reports and bolstered by the positive analyst commentary, saw only the promise of massive returns. The stock price climbed, and Kline, basking in the glow of this external validation, declared the Phoenix Initiative a "resounding success," further solidifying his reputation as a strategic visionary.

Internally, however, the reality was starkly different. Engineers were burning the midnight oil, grappling with fundamental design flaws that seemed insurmountable. The promised breakthroughs were proving elusive, and the projected timelines were becoming increasingly unrealistic. Yet, any team member who expressed doubt, any who suggested a pivot or a re-evaluation of the core strategy, found themselves ostracized. Their concerns were dismissed as a lack of "can-do spirit" or, more damningly, a failure to meet their Loyalty Metric benchmarks. The project was bleeding resources, with millions poured into research and development that yielded little tangible progress, but to question it would be to challenge Kline's infallible judgment. The illusion of progress was so potent that even the engineers working on the project, immersed in its daily struggles, found themselves questioning their own perceptions, wondering if they were simply not "seeing the bigger picture."

This manufactured reality extended to every level of the organization. Even seemingly minor procedural changes were trumpeted as revolutionary innovations. A new email archiving system, designed simply to meet regulatory compliance, was rebranded as "SynergyStream," a groundbreaking platform that would "unlock unparalleled interdepartmental collaboration and knowledge synergy." The actual implementation was cumbersome, causing more frustration than efficiency, but the marketing materials, the internal presentations, and the subsequent performance reviews of the IT team responsible for its deployment all spoke of its immense success. Employees were encouraged to "embrace the synergy" and to document their "synergistic interactions" within the new system, further feeding the narrative of progress.

The silencing of dissent was not always overt. Often, it was a more subtle, yet equally effective, form of intellectual suffocation. Critics were not necessarily fired; rather, they were strategically sidelined. Their access to key information was curtailed, their input on critical projects was no longer solicited, and their career advancement stalled indefinitely. They became ghosts in the machine, their valuable insights ignored, their expertise rendered irrelevant by the sheer force of Kline's will. This created an environment where conformity was rewarded, and independent thought was a liability. Employees learned to tread carefully, to align their opinions with the prevailing narrative, and to prioritize the maintenance of their Loyalty Metric above all else. The company was filled with people who were exceptionally good at appearing to be successful, but increasingly incapable of actual success.

The consequence of this sustained illusion was a profound disconnect between the company's internal operations and its external image. Halcyon was a house of cards, meticulously constructed to look like a fortress. The foundation, however, was riddled with termites, each unchecked problem, each ignored warning sign, a testament to the corrosive power of manufactured reality. Kline's genius lay not in his ability to build a successful company, but in his unparalleled skill at convincing everyone, including himself, that he had. The war on reality had reached its zenith within Halcyon, a silent, internal conflict where truth was sacrificed at the altar of perception, and progress was a performance, not a practice. The organization was adrift, sailing on a sea of positive press releases and inflated stock prices, while the hull was quietly taking on water, threatened by the very rot that Kline had so masterfully concealed. The illusion of progress wasn't just a tactic; it had become the operative principle, the de facto operating system of Halcyon Defense Systems. And like any system built on falsehood, it was destined for a catastrophic failure, a failure that the world, blinded by the brilliance of the disguise, would never see coming. The very mechanisms designed to propel Halcyon forward were instead ensuring its slow, almost imperceptible, descent into obsolescence, masked by the dazzling spectacle of its own perceived triumph.

The air within Halcyon Defense Systems had grown thick with a manufactured optimism, a pervasive scent that clung to the polished chrome and sterile meeting rooms. Yet, beneath this veneer of relentless progress, something else was stirring. It wasn't a rebellion announced in bold declarations or a dissent shouted from the rooftops. It was quieter, more profound, and infinitely more dangerous to Victor Kline's carefully constructed empire: it was memory.

For the long-timers, those who had joined Halcyon when it was a fledgling enterprise with a genuine sense of purpose, the present reality grated like a perpetual, low-grade fever. They remembered a time when collaboration wasn't a buzzword to be logged in the SynergyStream, but a natural, organic exchange of ideas. They recalled brainstorming sessions that crackled with intellectual energy, not the pre-ordained conclusions dictated by the latest AI-driven trend analysis. They held within them the echoes of a Halcyon that valued innovation for its own sake, not as a lever to inflate stock prices or impress investors. These memories were not nostalgic wistful sighs; they were potent, living counterpoints to the distorted present.

Consider Dedra Black, a senior systems architect who had been with Halcyon for nearly two decades. She remembered the early days of the 'Orion Project,' a bold, albeit ultimately unsuccessful, attempt to develop a next-generation missile defense system. The project had been a crucible of intense pressure, tight deadlines, and formidable technical challenges. There had been setbacks, moments of despair, and heated debates that spilled out of the conference rooms and into the cafeteria. But crucially, there had also been a profound sense of shared purpose. When a critical component failed during a crucial test, the entire team, from the junior engineers to the project lead, had huddled together, poring over schematics, fueled by lukewarm coffee and a shared determination. They hadn't blamed each other; they had brainstormed, experimented, and ultimately, learned. Even in its failure, the Orion Project had been a testament to Halcyon's core values: integrity, intellectual rigor, and a commitment to pushing the boundaries of what was possible, even when the odds were stacked against them.

Now, Dedra found herself navigating a landscape where a similar technical setback would be met with a swift reassessment of individual Loyalty Metrics, a quiet reassignment of blame, and a carefully worded internal memo that painted the failure as a "strategic recalibration." The memory of the Orion Project's true spirit – the shared struggle, the collective problem-solving, the ethical commitment to understanding why it failed – was a sharp shard of glass in the smooth, polished surface of Kline's current narrative. It was a private rebellion, a mental act of defiance waged in the quiet corners of her mind.

This internal counter-narrative wasn't confined to isolated individuals. It circulated, not through official channels, but through furtive glances, whispered asides in the break room, and the shared understanding that passed between those who remembered. A junior engineer, tasked with generating a report that glossed over critical flaws in a new drone's guidance system, might remember how her mentor, a man now sidelined for his "negative outlook," had once meticulously documented every single anomaly, even when it meant delaying a product launch. That memory, of a professional duty to truth over expediency, would inform her own quiet resistance, perhaps by including a subtly ambiguous phrase in the report, a tiny seed of doubt planted for those perceptive enough to find it.

The original ethos of Halcyon was not about profit margins or market dominance. It was about contributing to something larger than oneself, about building technology that served a noble purpose, about integrity in every aspect of the operation. This ethos, once the bedrock of the company, had been systematically eroded, replaced by a cult of personality and a relentless pursuit of superficial success. But for those who had lived and breathed that original ethos, the memories served as an anchor. They were a constant reminder that the current reality was a distortion, a deviation from the true north that had once guided Halcyon.

The 'Ascendant Program,' for example, a flagship initiative under Kline's leadership, was a prime candidate for this mnemonic subversion. The program, touted as revolutionary, involved the development of a new AI-driven battlefield management system. Publicly, it was a triumph of foresight and technological prowess. Internally, however, a handful of seasoned engineers remembered the 'Guardian Initiative' from a decade prior. Guardian had been a far more ambitious undertaking, aiming to create a comprehensive, ethical framework for AI in warfare. It had involved extensive collaboration with ethicists, philosophers, and even military historians. The project had been shelved not due to technical failure, but because its conclusions—that unchecked AI in combat posed profound risks to humanity—were deemed inconvenient for the company's burgeoning desire to supply autonomous weapons.

Now, when Kline spoke of the Ascendant Program's "unprecedented ethical considerations," these engineers would recall the painstaking, months-long debates of the Guardian Initiative, the genuine commitment to exploring the darkest implications of their work. They remembered the integrity of that process, the willingness to confront uncomfortable truths, a stark contrast to the superficial checkboxes and pre-approved talking points that now passed for ethical due diligence. These memories were not just personal recollections; they were a silent refutation of Kline's claims. They were proof that Halcyon had once been capable of a deeper, more responsible engagement with the very technologies it now peddled with reckless abandon.

This subversion through memory was often subtle, a quiet act of preservation. It manifested in the way a veteran project manager, when asked to update the status of a troubled project, might use phrasing that subtly echoed the language of past, more honest reports. Instead of "significant progress achieved," they might write, "activity aligned with current project trajectory," a phrase that, to an outsider, sounded like corporate jargon, but to those who remembered the days of unvarnished truth, implied stagnation. It was a linguistic wink, a coded message that said, "I remember when we said what we meant."

Even the physical environment held echoes. In the older sections of the Halcyon campus, relics of the past lingered. A faded photograph on a forgotten noticeboard, depicting a team celebrating a hard-won victory with genuine smiles, not the forced grins of mandatory corporate events. A scuff mark on a floor where a crucial blueprint had once been unfurled for a project that had fundamentally changed the company's trajectory, a project that predated Kline's ascendance. These were not mere artifacts; for those who remembered, they were tangible proof of a different Halcyon, a Halcyon that existed before the pervasive fog of manufactured reality descended.

The challenge for Kline and his carefully constructed illusion was that memory, unlike data points and performance metrics, was inherently resistant to algorithmic manipulation. It was subjective, deeply personal, and often fueled by emotion. The joy of genuine discovery, the camaraderie of shared struggle, the quiet satisfaction of ethical conduct – these were not easily erased or overwritten. They lingered, like phantom limbs, reminding those who had experienced them of what had been lost.

These memories, when shared, even implicitly, created pockets of resistance within the organization. They were the seeds of doubt, the quiet counter-arguments that whispered in the minds of employees during Kline's pronouncements. When Kline boasted of Halcyon's "unprecedented innovation," a long-serving researcher might recall a time when innovation was a messy, unpredictable process, not a predictable output of a designated R&D department. When he spoke of "synergistic collaboration," an experienced team lead might remember the days of spontaneous whiteboard sessions, fueled by donuts and a shared passion, a far cry from the scheduled, agenda-driven "synergy sessions" of today.

This subversion was not about actively plotting against Kline.

For most, it was an instinctive act of self-preservation, a way to maintain their own sense of self and integrity in an environment that demanded conformity. It was a quiet refusal to let their own experiences be wholly redefined by Kline's narrative. They were the guardians of Halcyon's ghost, the keepers of its true history, their memories serving as a subtle, yet persistent, challenge to the pervasive distortion of reality. They understood that while Kline could control the present, he could not, not entirely, erase the past. And in that persistent, unyielding memory lay the potential for a future that might, just might, reclaim the original spirit of Halcyon. The war on reality was being fought, not just in boardrooms and data centers, but in the very minds and hearts of the people who remembered what true progress, and true integrity, looked like.

The relentless pursuit of an idealized, machine-like efficiency, the supposed pinnacle of perfection that Victor Kline championed, was not a gentle ascension. It was a brutal excavation, stripping away the very foundations upon which Halcyon Defense Systems had once been built. The company's legendary adaptability, its almost prescient ability to pivot and innovate in response to a rapidly changing geopolitical landscape, was the first casualty. It was a capability born not of rigid protocols and predictive algorithms, but of a workforce empowered to think, to question, and even, at times, to err and learn. Now, every deviation from the meticulously planned trajectory was treated as a systemic failure, a deviation from the immaculate ideal, rather than an opportunity for recalibration or emergent strategy.

Consider the 'Santa Fe Initiative,' an ambitious project designed to develop a new generation of drone swarming technology. The initial concept, conceived in the days when Halcyon was still a relatively agile entity, was revolutionary in its scope. It envisioned a decentralized, self-organizing swarm capable of independent threat assessment and adaptive battlefield response. The early prototypes, developed by a team of brilliant, if somewhat unconventional, engineers, showed immense promise. They exhibited a chaotic, emergent intelligence, learning from each simulated engagement in ways that surprised even their creators. However, this very unpredictability, this inherent messiness of true innovation, became anathema to Kline's vision of perfection.

The engineers, led by a visionary named Dr. Paxton Philips, were tasked with 'taming' the swarm, with imposing a rigid, predictable order onto its emergent behavior. Philips argued vehemently, presenting data that demonstrated how the swarm's adaptive capabilities, its ability to generate novel solutions in real-time, were directly linked to its decentralized, somewhat chaotic nature. He explained that true resilience lay not in pre-programmed responses, but in the system's capacity to spontaneously reconfigure and discover new pathways when confronted with the unforeseen. His pleas were met with a chillingly polite dismissal. Kline's mandate was clear: perfection meant predictability, and predictability meant control. The swarm had to behave. It had to operate within parameters that could be precisely measured and, crucially, reported to investors as a guaranteed outcome.

The project was reorganized, its core design principles fractured and reassembled according to Kline's exacting specifications. Independent learning modules were suppressed, replaced by rigid command hierarchies. The emergent intelligence was pruned, its wild, untamed growth stifled in favor of a more docile, albeit significantly less capable, obedience. The result was a system that could execute pre-defined maneuvers with flawless precision, a perfect automaton following its programming. But it had lost the spark, the raw ingenuity that had once made it so revolutionary. The 'Santa Fe Initiative' became a monument to this loss, a meticulously crafted shell that, while outwardly flawless, was fundamentally hollowed of its original purpose. The adaptability, the very soul of the project, had been sacrificed on the altar of Kline's perfection.

This systematic stripping of adaptability wasn't limited to R&D. Across the organization, the emphasis on unwavering adherence to process, on the elimination of any perceived deviation, was creating an environment of pervasive fear. Employees were no longer encouraged to identify potential problems or suggest improvements if those suggestions deviated from the established protocol. The risk of being flagged for 'inefficiency' or, worse, 'non-compliance,' was too high. The feedback loops that had once allowed Halcyon to course-correct and evolve were systematically closed. Instead, the company was being steered with the rigid certainty of a ship sailing directly into an iceberg, its captain convinced of his perfect navigation.

The human cost of this relentless pursuit of an unattainable ideal was becoming increasingly apparent, etched onto the faces of its long-serving employees. Their spirits were not just dampened; they were being systematically crushed. Take Conrad Fuller, a senior cybersecurity analyst who had been instrumental in developing Halcyon's early, robust defense systems. Conrad had always taken pride in his meticulous attention to detail, his almost obsessive need to understand every vulnerability, every potential exploit. He saw it as his duty to be the first to identify and neutralize threats, often working late into the night, fueled by an innate sense of responsibility.

Under Kline's regime, Conrad 's proactive approach was reinterpreted. His thoroughness was framed as an inability to trust the established security protocols. His late nights were not seen as dedication, but as evidence of inefficient time management. He was assigned a 'performance coach' who drilled him on standardized response times and adherence to predefined threat assessment matrices. The nuanced, intuitive understanding he had developed over years of dedicated work was dismissed in favor of algorithmic checklists. One day, Conrad identified a subtle, almost undetectable anomaly in the network traffic – a phantom signature that his instincts screamed was malicious. He presented his findings, complete with detailed logs and theoretical attack vectors, only to be told that his analysis did not align with the approved threat profile for the day. His concerns were logged as a 'false positive,' and he was reprimanded for 'disrupting operational efficiency.'

The stress of this constant validation, of having his expertise systematically devalued, began to take its toll. Conrad became withdrawn, his usual keenness replaced by a palpable anxiety. He started second-guessing his own judgment, the confidence he had once possessed eroding with each subsequent dismissal of his concerns. He found himself performing the tasks, checking the boxes, but the passion, the deep-seated commitment that had driven him, had evaporated. He was a cog in a perfect machine, but the machine was no longer serving its purpose; it was merely running. His career, once a trajectory of growth and accomplishment, was

100

now stalled, caught in the gears of an inflexible system. The broken spirit was a quiet but devastating testament to the price of perfection.

Careers were not just stalled; they were deliberately broken. Those who dared to voice concerns, whose memories of a more authentic Halcyon made them resistant to the manufactured reality, were systematically sidelined. They were not fired outright, a move that might create martyrs or raise questions. Instead, they were slowly, subtly, disempowered. Projects were reassigned, critical responsibilities were transferred, and their input was increasingly overlooked in meetings. They were made irrelevant, their contributions rendered invisible, until their frustration and demoralization became so acute that they chose to leave, their departure framed as a voluntary resignation, a testament to their inability to adapt to the new, more efficient Halcyon.

This was the fate that befell Dr. Olga Talbert, a leading astrophysicist who had been crucial in developing Halcyon's satellite imaging technology. Olga was renowned for her integrity, her unwavering commitment to scientific accuracy. She had been instrumental in exposing a critical flaw in a commercial satellite launch that could have had catastrophic consequences. She had fought tooth and nail, using her scientific acumen to prove her point, even when faced with pressure from superiors eager to meet launch deadlines. Her actions had saved the company immense embarrassment and, more importantly, prevented potential loss of life.

Under Kline, however, such independent rigor was viewed as insubordination. When Olga raised concerns about the accuracy of a newly implemented AI-driven predictive model for satellite trajectory, a model that was being hailed as a paragon of perfection, she was met with resistance. The model's outputs were considered infallible, its algorithms a testament to Kline's visionary leadership. Olga, relying on her decades of experience and deep understanding of orbital mechanics, found discrepancies, subtle but significant deviations that suggested the AI was making dangerously optimistic projections. She tried to present her findings, to engage in a scientific debate, but her attempts were rebuffed. Her concerns were dismissed as 'unnecessary complexity,' her expertise framed as 'resistance to progress.' She was eventually reassigned to a peripheral project, her access to critical data restricted, her voice silenced. The message was clear: perfection was not open to debate.

The shattering of lives extended beyond the professional realm. The relentless pressure to conform, the fear of reprisal, the constant anxiety of performance metrics, created a toxic environment that seeped into the personal lives of employees. Marriages strained under the weight of unspoken stress; families suffered from the emotional absence of individuals consumed by their work and the constant pressure to maintain a face of compliance. The joy and fulfillment that had once been associated with working at Halcyon, a place that fostered innovation and purpose, had been replaced by a gnawing dread. The pursuit of an idealized, machine-like efficiency had not only stripped the organization of its soul but had also begun to break the very people who comprised it.

This was not a system designed for resilience, but for fragility disguised as strength. By eliminating any room for error, by demanding absolute predictability, Kline was creating a system that was incredibly vulnerable to the unpredictable nature of reality. The very things that made Halcyon unique – its ability to improvise, its willingness to embrace the messy, human element of innovation, its deep-seated ethical compass – were being systematically dismantled. What remained was a hollow shell, a gleaming edifice of projected success, driven by the twin engines of fear and delusion. The pursuit of perfection, when defined by a narrow, inflexible vision, had led not to triumph, but to a profound, and potentially fatal, form of organizational self-immolation. The illusion of perfection masked a reality of decay, and the price was being paid by every soul trapped within its meticulously crafted, yet ultimately unsustainable, design.

Chapter 5

The Inner Circle

The ascent to Victor Kline's inner sanctum was a calculated affair, a carefully orchestrated vetting process that weeded out the fainthearted and the questioning. These were not individuals who sought to innovate or challenge; they were those who understood the delicate art of subservience, the whispered promise of reward for absolute fealty. They were the architects of Kline's vision, the enforcers of his meticulously crafted reality, and their primary tool, the instrument by which this new order was to be cemented, was the Loyalty Metric. This was not merely a performance indicator; it was a philosophy, a behavioral blueprint designed to quantify and ultimately control the very essence of an employee's dedication. It was a system built on the premise that unwavering commitment could be measured, scored, and, most importantly, enforced.

Among this select cadre, several figures stood out, their careers inextricably linked to Kline's meteoric rise. There was Greg Younger, a man whose ambition burned with a cold, calculating intensity. Greg had been a mid-level manager in operations when Kline first arrived, a man who saw not just a new CEO, but a tidal wave of opportunity. He possessed an almost unsettling ability to anticipate Kline's desires, to preempt his directives with solutions that perfectly aligned with the CEO's evolving ideology. Greg became the architect of the Loyalty Metric's implementation, not through conceptual design, but through the brutal pragmatism of its rollout. He understood that metrics, however abstract, required tangible actions. He meticulously dissected departmental functions, identifying every touchpoint, every interaction, where loyalty could be observed, measured, and, if necessary, coerced.

His own rise was testament to his effectiveness; his department, once a well-oiled but unremarkable cog in the Halcyon machine, was now lauded as a model of efficiency and unwavering devotion, a shining example of what adherence to the Metric could achieve. Greg's success was measured not just in departmental output, but in the quiet disappearances of those who couldn't, or wouldn't, conform. His gaze was always steady, his pronouncements devoid of emotion, reflecting a profound understanding that sentiment was a weakness Halcyon, under Kline, could no longer afford.

He saw the Metric not as a tool of oppression, but as a necessary purification, a Darwinian filter that would ensure the survival of the fittest – the most loyal. His days were filled with spreadsheets and performance reviews, each number a silent judgment, each redacted name on a report a testament to his unwavering commitment to Kline's vision. He would often find himself staring at the company's skyline from his corner office, a sterile monument to progress, and reflect on how far they had come, how much of the old, inefficient Halcyon had been shed. The quiet hum of the server rooms below felt like the beating heart of their new, perfected organism, and he was one of its vital organs, indispensable and utterly devoted.

Then there was Carin Holman, a woman whose reputation preceded her like a storm cloud. Holman was the head of Human Resources, a department that had undergone a radical transformation under Kline. Once a repository for employee grievances and a facilitator of professional development, HR had become the formidable gatekeeper of loyalty. Holman was not a follower in the same vein as Younger; she was a natural strategist, a master manipulator who understood the subtle levers of human behavior. She viewed the Loyalty Metric as a sophisticated weapon, one that could be wielded with precision to achieve maximum compliance with minimal overt force. Her approach was insidious, preferring psychological attrition over direct confrontation. She would orchestrate carefully managed "development" programs that subtly emphasized obedience, mandatory "team-building" exercises that ostracized dissenters, and "performance improvement" plans that were, in reality, carefully constructed pathways to resignation. Holman's own career had stagnated in the old Halcyon, her sharp intellect and demanding standards often clashing with the company's more collaborative ethos. Kline's ascension had liberated her, allowing her to unleash her own brand of control, cloaked in the language of corporate development and employee well-being.

Her success was measured in the hushed tones of departing employees, their exit interviews meticulously sanitized to reflect voluntary departures, their reasons for leaving carefully scrubbed of any implication of corporate coercion. Holman prided herself on her ability to make people believe that leaving Halcyon was their own idea, a rational decision based on their own perceived shortcomings. She was a puppeteer, and the strings of fear and ambition were her tools.

The HR department, once a place of comfort, became a place of dread, its employees trained to subtly extract information, to identify potential disloyalty before it could manifest. Holman saw herself as a gardener, pruning the company's human landscape, removing any wilting or unproductive branches to allow the healthier specimens to flourish. She never raised her voice, never displayed overt anger, but her quiet pronouncements held a chilling finality, each decision a meticulously calculated move on a chessboard where the stakes were careers and reputations. She was a firm believer that conformity was the bedrock of success, and she was Halcyon's most dedicated custodian of that belief.

Rounding out this triumvirate was Julian Crain, a senior executive in Research and Development. Crain's position was particularly telling. While Younger focused on operational adherence and Holman on behavioral compliance, Crain was tasked with ensuring that innovation, or what remained of it, aligned perfectly with Kline's rigid parameters. Crain had been a brilliant engineer, a true visionary in his own right, but his willingness to question and explore had become a liability. Kline had seen in Crain a valuable asset to be redirected, not discarded. Crain was now responsible for "optimizing" R&D, a euphemism for stifling any research that didn't fit the predetermined trajectory or that might lead to unpredictable outcomes. He implemented the Loyalty Metric within his division by attaching performance bonuses and promotions directly to the metric's scores.

Researchers who focused on incremental, predictable improvements, who meticulously documented their adherence to approved methodologies, were handsomely rewarded. Those who pursued more speculative, potentially groundbreaking avenues, who might deviate from the established path, found their funding slashed, their projects sidelined, and their own loyalty metrics plummeting. Crain himself was a study in internal conflict. The brilliant mind that once thrived on discovery now spent its days calculating risk assessments for speculative research, attempting to quantify the unquantifiable in terms of loyalty. He was a man haunted by the ghost of his former self, his eyes often distant, as if searching for a spark of the old curiosity in the sterile, data-driven reports that crossed his desk. He had become a reluctant enforcer, his own career dependent on his ability to transform a bastion of innovation into a factory of compliant progress. He justified his actions to himself with the rationalization that this was simply the next phase of development, that the world required predictable, reliable advancements, not the chaotic leaps of genius. Yet, in the quiet hours, the questions would surface – had they traded true progress for the illusion of it? Had they sacrificed the future for the comfort of certainty?

These were the men and women who formed the backbone of Kline's new order, each a crucial cog in the machine designed to maintain his absolute control. They were Kline's lieutenants, his chosen instruments, and their careers, their very livelihoods, were intrinsically tied to the successful implementation and perpetuation of the Loyalty Metric. Their own performance was judged not by traditional metrics of success – innovation, profitability, market share – but by their ability to instill fear, to enforce compliance, and to ensure that every employee within their purview achieved and maintained the highest possible loyalty score. Younger ensured the pipelines of information flowed correctly, that deviations were flagged and reported. Holman curated the employee experience, subtly nudging individuals towards conformity or away from the organization altogether. Crain ensured that the very engine of future growth was aligned with the present dogma, that creativity itself became an act of loyalty.

Their effectiveness was amplified by a pervasive fear that permeated the organization. The Loyalty Metric was not a suggestion; it was a mandate, and its consequences for failure were severe, though rarely overt. The lieutenants were adept at delivering these consequences with a chilling politeness. A department that consistently fell short of its loyalty score targets would find its budget scrutinized, its projects re-evaluated, and its leadership facing uncomfortable discussions with Younger or Holman. Individuals who consistently scored low on the metric, whose quarterly reviews began to reflect this deficiency, would find themselves gradually sidelined. Their responsibilities would dwindle, their access to critical information would be curtailed, and their opportunities for advancement would simply vanish. They were not fired; they were rendered obsolete, their disloyalty a self-inflicted wound that led them, inevitably, to seek employment elsewhere. This made the lieutenants incredibly effective, as their own success was directly tied to the performance of those under them, creating a ripple effect of pressure that cascaded through every level of Halcyon Defense Systems.

The system was designed to be self-perpetuating. The lieutenants, driven by their own ambitions and the constant threat of demotion or dismissal should their departments falter, became the most ardent enforcers of Kline's regime. They internalized the ideology, transforming from mere subordinates into zealous disciples. They genuinely believed in the efficacy of the Loyalty Metric, seeing it as the only rational path forward for a company that had, in their view, become too soft, too inefficient, too susceptible to the whims of individual thought. They saw the fear as a necessary component, a catalyst for the required transformation. They meticulously tracked every interaction, every email, every meeting attendance, searching for any hint of dissent, any deviation from the prescribed behavior. The once vibrant culture of Halcyon was being systematically replaced by a suffocating atmosphere of surveillance and self-censorship. The lieutenants, in their relentless pursuit of perfect metric scores, were not just implementing Kline's policies; they were actively shaping the company's culture, molding it into a reflection of their leader's rigid and unforgiving vision. They were the new aristocracy of Halcyon, their power derived not from merit or innovation, but from their unwavering willingness to sacrifice anything, and anyone, to maintain the illusion of perfect control. Their loyalty to Kline was absolute, and in return, he granted them the authority to demand the same from everyone else. It was a symbiotic relationship built on the bedrock of fear and mutual self-interest, a terrifyingly effective engine driving Halcyon towards its self-imposed perfection. The lieutenants were not just managers; they were wardens, overseeing a population increasingly stripped of its autonomy, its individuality, and its very soul, all in the name of a metric that promised an impossible ideal.

The architecture of Victor Kline's inner sanctum was not built on bricks and mortar, but on the silken threads of deception, meticulously woven by those closest to him. This select group, comprising Younger, Holman, and Crain, along with a handful of others whose names were less prominent, but whose roles were equally vital, operated as a specialized unit, their primary objective the cultivation and maintenance of a specific, heavily curated reality. Their expertise lay not in technological innovation or market strategy, but in the insidious art of shaping perception, a skill honed to a razor's edge under Kline's exacting tutelage. They were the gatekeepers of truth, but their access was not to the unvarnished facts, but to the polished, malleable versions that served the CEO's narrative.

Greg Younger, the architect of the Loyalty Metric's implementation, found his operational prowess amplified by this new, more abstract battlefield. His spreadsheets, once filled with production quotas and logistical timelines, now contained columns for "Sentiment Analysis," "Compliance Adherence Ratios," and "Narrative Alignment Scores." He became adept at transforming statistical anomalies into testaments of resilience, and inconvenient truths into opportunities for strategic realignment. A dip in production, for instance, wasn't a sign of systemic failure; it was reframed as a necessary, albeit temporary, recalibration to ensure optimal resource allocation for future loyalty-driven initiatives. Negative feedback from a significant client, a rare but damaging occurrence, would be presented not as a product flaw, but as a misunderstanding of Halcyon's cutting-edge, though perhaps complex, solutions, necessitating a targeted educational campaign for the client. Younger's mastery was in the subtle inflection of language, the carefully chosen adjective, the strategically omitted detail. He could present a quarterly report that showcased a marginal increase in employee retention (a direct result of Holman's attrition strategies) as a resounding victory in fostering a culture of unwavering commitment, effectively masking the underlying attrition rate that would have been a cause for concern in any less controlled environment. He learned to anticipate the questions Kline might ask and preemptively craft answers that steered clear of any uncomfortable territory, ensuring that the CEO's perception remained untainted by the messy, inefficient realities of day-to-day operations. His presentations became masterclasses in corporate theatre, each slide a carefully constructed illusion, each spoken word a precisely aimed dart designed to reinforce Kline's vision of Halcyon as an unassailable fortress of efficiency and devotion. The numbers, Younger would subtly imply, were not merely indicators; they were proof of the system's inherent correctness, a testament to the genius of Kline's leadership.

Carin Holman, the architect of HR's transformation, wielded her influence with even greater subtlety. Her manipulation was less about data-driven spin and more about the strategic deployment of psychological leverage. She understood that people often believed what they wanted to believe, or what they were subtly guided to believe, especially when their livelihoods were at stake. Holman became a maestro of narrative control, not through formal reports, but through the carefully curated experiences of the employees themselves. When a promising employee, one whose independent spirit was beginning to chark against the Loyalty Metric's rigid confines, inevitably sought an exit interview, Holman ensured it was a performance. The employee would be gently guided through a conversation that emphasized their own perceived shortcomings, their inability to "thrive in Halcyon's unique, high-performance culture," or their desire for a role that offered "more creative freedom" – a subtle jab that underscored the perceived limitations of their current position, thereby validating the company's direction.

The exit interview notes, meticulously documented by Holman's team, would then be distilled into reports for Kline, framed as voluntary departures of individuals who were simply not a cultural fit, thus reinforcing the idea that Halcyon's culture was a desirable, exclusive commodity. Conversely, when a department's loyalty scores began to dip, Holman wouldn't implement

109

widespread layoffs, a blunt and visible failure. Instead, she would initiate a series of "optional" but highly encouraged "re-alignment workshops" or "skill enhancement seminars." These sessions, while ostensibly for professional development, were designed to subtly weed out those who resisted the prevailing ideology.

Attendance was logged, participation was scored, and those who displayed any hint of skepticism or disengagement found their career progression stalled, their performance reviews subtly downgraded due to their lack of "enthusiastic engagement" with these crucial developmental initiatives. Holman's genius lay in making people feel like the authors of their own downfall, ensuring that the narrative reaching Kline was one of proactive self-selection by employees, not a systematic purge by the company. She could paint a picture of a company constantly refining its talent pool, ensuring only the most dedicated and aligned individuals remained, all without ever explicitly stating that dissent was grounds for dismissal. Her reports to Kline were often framed around employee engagement metrics, focusing on the positive trends in participation in these carefully designed programs, thus presenting a façade of continuous improvement and employee buy-in.

Julian Crain, the senior executive in R&D, found himself in the unenviable position of policing innovation. His task was to ensure that creativity itself became an act of loyalty. This required a sophisticated form of deception, one that masked the stifling of true progress as a form of prudent risk management. Crain became adept at framing speculative research as "unforeseen resource drain" or "deviation from core strategic objectives."

When a research team, driven by genuine scientific curiosity, began exploring a tangential but potentially revolutionary avenue, Crain wouldn't simply shut it down. Instead, he would present a meticulously crafted risk assessment to Kline, highlighting the potential for project delays, budget overruns, and the diversion of critical resources from projects with a demonstrably higher loyalty score alignment. He would meticulously document the "lack of measurable loyalty metric contribution" from the speculative research, turning the pursuit of groundbreaking discovery into an act of fiscal irresponsibility. The researchers themselves would find their funding gradually reduced, their access to specialized equipment subtly curtailed, and their project timelines arbitrarily extended, all under the guise of "strategic resource optimization."

Crain's reports to Kline would then detail the "successful redirection of R&D efforts towards core competencies," painting a picture of a division that had become more focused, more efficient, and more aligned with the company's overarching loyalty-centric mandate. He learned to speak the language of innovation while actively dismantling its very essence, presenting the abandonment of true discovery as a shrewd business decision aimed at maximizing shareholder value through predictable, loyalty-aligned advancements. He would often speak of "responsible innovation," a term that, in the context of Halcyon, meant innovation that was pre-approved, predictable, and demonstrably loyal.

The irony was not lost on him: he was tasked with ensuring the future of Halcyon, but in doing so, he was systematically killing the very spark that had once defined its potential. His presentations to Kline would feature charts showcasing the increased output of "validated technological solutions" and the decreased investment in "high-risk, low-yield exploratory ventures," all presented as clear evidence of R&D's increased efficiency and unwavering commitment to Kline's strategic vision.

Together, this inner circle formed a formidable bulwark, their collective efforts creating a distorted reflection of reality that was presented to Victor Kline. They were the illusionists, the spin doctors, the architects of a manufactured success. Their daily work was a performance, each interaction a carefully choreographed dance designed to reinforce Kline's belief in his own infallibility and the absolute righteousness of the Loyalty Metric. They understood that Kline was not merely seeking information; he was seeking validation. And they were all too willing to provide it, for their own survival and advancement depended on it.

The corporate doublespeak that permeated Halcyon was not an accidental byproduct; it was a deliberate and essential tool of this inner circle. Every report, every memo, every presentation was a testament to their mastery of this linguistic alchemy. "Restructuring" meant layoffs but phrased as an optimization of human capital. "Performance enhancement programs" were veiled threats, designed to pressure underperformers into resignation. "Strategic realignments" were euphemisms for product cancellations that had failed to meet the Loyalty Metric's increasingly arbitrary benchmarks.

Younger, for example, would meticulously craft quarterly performance reviews for his operational teams, not focusing on output or innovation, but on the "demonstrated commitment to Halcyon's core values" and the "proactive identification and mitigation of potential loyalty deviations." A project delay due to a genuine technical hurdle would be reframed as a "strategic pause to re-evaluate resource allocation in alignment with projected loyalty metric impacts." The language was deliberately vague, designed to obscure the underlying problems and project an image of constant, controlled progress.

Holman, in her HR capacity, would ensure that all internal communications regarding employee departures were meticulously sanitized. A mass exodus from a demoralized department would be described as a series of "individual career path adjustments," or a "natural evolution of the workforce composition." She would train her team to use specific phrases, to avoid any language that suggested coercion or dissatisfaction, thereby ensuring that any ripple effect of negativity would be contained before it could reach Kline's ears.

Crain, in R&D, would present the shelving of promising but unpredictable research as "a prioritization of established, loyalty-aligned developmental pathways." He would frame the lack of breakthroughs as a sign of "robust methodological adherence" and "controlled, sustainable innovation." The goal was never to present the unvarnished truth, but to craft a narrative that was palatable, that reinforced Kline's worldview, and that ensured his continued belief in his own exceptional leadership.

This constant art of deception had a corrosive effect, not just on the company's true potential, but on the very individuals perpetuating it. Younger, Holman, and Crain, once perhaps driven by genuine ambition or a desire for competence, found themselves increasingly trapped in a web of their own making. The constant need to spin, to obfuscate, to manipulate, created a cognitive dissonance that, for some, became a source of quiet torment. Younger, in his sterile office, would sometimes stare at the performance metrics, the numbers that represented not just operational efficiency, but the systematic suppression of human ingenuity, and a flicker of doubt would cross his otherwise impassive features. Holman, meticulously dissecting an employee's career trajectory for the most politically advantageous narrative, would occasionally catch a glimpse of her own reflection in the polished surface of her desk and see not a shrewd strategist, but a woman who had traded empathy for efficacy. Crain, the former visionary engineer, would spend hours poring over projected innovation timelines, timelines that were intentionally conservative, designed to minimize risk and maximize loyalty scores, and the ghost of his former self, the one who had dared to dream of the impossible, would haunt his waking hours.

Yet, the pressure to maintain this disguise was immense. Kline, insulated by his inner circle, became increasingly detached from the operational realities of Halcyon. He saw only the curated reports, heard only the filtered presentations, and his pronouncements, based on this skewed reality, became more extreme, more demanding. He would laud Younger for Halcyon's "unprecedented stability," unaware that it was the stability of a stagnant pond. He would praise Holman for fostering a "culture of unparalleled dedication," oblivious to the suffocating fear that propelled it. He would commend Crain for ensuring "consistent, reliable technological advancements," blind to the fact that the true cutting edge of innovation had long since been abandoned.

The inner circle's success, therefore, became their greatest curse. The more effectively they deceived Kline, the further he drifted from reality, and the more demanding his directives became, requiring an even greater commitment to the art of deception. They were caught in a feedback loop, their own survival inextricably linked to the perpetuation of a grand illusion, an illusion that was slowly, but surely, suffocating the soul of Halcyon Defense Systems. The elaborate justifications, the carefully constructed rationalizations, the polished presentations – these were the tools of their trade, the currency of their power, and the architects of their own intellectual and moral compromise. They were the embodiment of corporate rot, masked by the sheen of success, a testament to the chilling efficiency with which a company's spirit could be extinguished, not by external forces, but by the internal machinations of its own leadership and the willing complicity of its closest advisors.

The polished surface of Halcyon Defense Systems, so carefully manicured by Younger, Holman, and Crain, concealed a deeper, more insidious rot: the simmering animosity between the very architects of Victor Kline's carefully constructed reality. While their public faces presented a united front, a testament to unwavering loyalty and shared purpose, beneath the surface, a fierce, often vicious, competition for Kline's favor raged. Each lieutenant, keenly aware that their own precarious position hinged on being perceived as the most indispensable, the most loyal, and the most effective in serving the CEO's vision, engaged in a silent, yet brutal, war for dominance. Their primary objective, beyond upholding the illusion for Kline, had become outmaneuvering their colleagues, subtly undermining their successes, and highlighting any perceived flaw in their strategies. This constant jockeying for position created a pervasive undercurrent of distrust, a palpable tension that permeated every clandestine meeting, every whispered conversation, and every carefully worded report.

Greg Younger saw the burgeoning influence of Carin Holman with growing unease. Her methods, while perhaps less quantifiable than his own data-driven approach, were undeniably effective in shaping the narrative around employee sentiment – a crucial element in Kline's loyalty-centric worldview. He observed how Holman could, with seemingly effortless grace, transform a potentially damaging employee relations issue into a testament of Halcyon's commitment to its people, a narrative that resonated deeply with Kline's self-image as a benevolent, albeit demanding, leader.

Younger felt his meticulously crafted statistical analyses, his carefully constructed dashboards of compliance and alignment, were slowly being overshadowed by Holman's more abstract, yet potent, manipulation of human emotions. He began to subtly cast doubt on her methodologies, framing them as overly subjective and prone to "situational bias." In his reports to Kline, Younger would highlight instances where Holman's HR initiatives, while appearing successful on the surface, had inadvertently led to a slight, though explainable, dip in productivity in certain departments, attributing it to an "over-emphasis on qualitative metrics at the expense of tangible output." He would schedule his own presentations immediately before Holman's in critical strategy meetings, ensuring that the stark, objective data he presented would be the last thing Kline absorbed before considering Holman's more nuanced, and therefore potentially less convincing, arguments. He found opportunities to subtly question the long-term impact of her "engagement initiatives," suggesting they might foster a sense of entitlement rather than genuine loyalty, a carefully planted seed of doubt designed to erode Kline's confidence in her judgment.

Carin Holman, in turn, viewed Younger as a plodding bureaucrat, overly reliant on numbers that could be, and indeed were, manipulated to tell any story. She recognized that Younger's strength lay in the quantifiable, the data points that could be spun. But she understood that true power, the kind that could sway Kline, lay in the intangible, the emotional resonance that data could never truly capture. She saw Younger's constant need for empirical validation as a weakness, a dependence that left him vulnerable. Holman began to subtly highlight instances where Younger's rigid adherence to metrics had resulted in the loss of valuable employees who, while perhaps not scoring perfectly on his loyalty algorithms, possessed a creative spark that Younger's system had failed to recognize or retain. In her private conversations with Kline, she would speak of "cultural attrition" – a phrase she had coined – suggesting that Younger's relentless focus on measurable loyalty was inadvertently alienating individuals whose intrinsic value to Halcyon extended beyond mere compliance.

She would subtly steer discussions away from Younger's production figures, instead focusing on employee morale surveys, subtly emphasizing that high productivity without genuine commitment was ultimately unsustainable and risked fostering a culture of outward conformity masking internal dissent. She also found ways to question the accuracy of Younger's sentiment analysis reports, suggesting that employees, knowing their feedback was being quantified and potentially used against them, might be providing disingenuous responses, thereby rendering his entire data set unreliable. She made sure to always present her findings with an emotional appeal, framing her HR strategies not as mere management techniques, but as essential for fostering a deeply committed and emotionally invested workforce, a narrative that appealed to Kline's ego as a leader who cared about his people, even if it was a carefully constructed caricature of care.

Julian Crain, caught between Younger's data-centric rigidity and Holman's psychological maneuvering, found himself increasingly isolated. His position in R&D, once a bastion of intellectual pursuit, had become a minefield of competing agendas. He recognized that both Younger and Holman saw his domain as a potential weapon in their internal skirmishes. Younger would subtly pressure Crain to prioritize R&D projects that had clear, quantifiable, and immediate loyalty metric implications, effectively stifling any speculative or long-term research that couldn't demonstrate a direct correlation to employee compliance or customer satisfaction scores.

Holman, on the other hand, would subtly encourage research into employee well-being and "cultural integration technologies," framing them as essential for maximizing retention and thus indirectly supporting Younger's metrics, while simultaneously positioning herself as the arbiter of employee happiness and thus their loyalty. Crain felt his innovative spirit being systematically stifled, not just by Kline's overarching loyalty mandate, but by the internal machinations of his colleagues. He began to see opportunities to subtly sabotage each other's efforts. When Younger presented a new operational efficiency model, Crain would subtly highlight potential R&D dependencies or overlooked technological hurdles that could complicate its implementation, not out of genuine concern, but to make Younger's perfect plan appear flawed. When Holman championed a new employee development program, Crain would find ways to introduce technical requirements or integration challenges that would necessitate a more rigorous, data-heavy evaluation, thereby playing into Younger's strengths and potentially overwhelming Holman's more qualitative approach.

He even began to feed snippets of information – carefully

curated and deniably true – to each of them about the other, creating a climate of paranoia that further intensified their mutual suspicion. He might, for instance, hint to Younger that Holman was exploring HR software that bypassed Younger's existing metrics, or suggest to Holman that Younger was subtly reallocating R&D budget away from projects she deemed essential for employee morale.

This toxic dynamic intensified with each passing quarter. The inner circle's primary focus shifted from serving Kline's vision to outmaneuvering each other. Younger would meticulously analyze Holman's HR reports, searching for any statistical anomalies or vague language that he could exploit, framing it as a lack of rigor. He might present his findings to Kline as, "While Ms. Holman's initiatives show promising anecdotal results, the underlying data concerning long-term employee retention and quantifiable productivity gains remains inconclusive. My analysis suggests a potential overreliance on subjective feedback, which could lead to misallocation of resources and an inaccurate assessment of true workforce loyalty."

This veiled accusation of incompetence was designed to chip away at Holman's credibility, positioning his own data-driven approach as the only reliable measure of success. He would meticulously document every minor deviation from planned productivity in departments where Holman had recently implemented a new HR policy, presenting it as a direct consequence of her "softer" approach, which, in his narrative, "prioritized employee comfort over operational exigency." He learned to frame his critiques as objective observations, couched in the language of efficiency and profitability, thereby making them harder for Kline to dismiss. Younger's strategy was to systematically demonstrate that while Holman might excel at creating a pleasant facade, his own methodologies were the only ones that ensured tangible, measurable results – results that Kline ultimately valued.

Holman, in turn, developed an almost preternatural ability to detect Younger's attempts at subtle sabotage. She would counter his data-driven criticisms by focusing on the human element, often with tears in her eyes during board meetings, if necessary, to highlight how Younger's metrics were impacting the "personal lives and emotional well-being" of dedicated employees. She would present case studies, anonymized of course, of individuals who had been demoralized by Younger's relentless performance reviews, painting a picture of a callous system that was crushing the spirit of Halcyon's workforce.

"Mr. Younger's focus on quantitative output, while understandable from a purely fiscal perspective, risks alienating the very individuals whose dedication fuels our company's success," she might state, her voice laced with carefully modulated concern. "We must remember that loyalty is not merely a number; it is a feeling, a commitment born from a sense of belonging and appreciation. My initiatives aim to cultivate that environment, ensuring that our employees feel valued not just for their output, but for their very presence within the Halcyon family."

She would then present anecdotal evidence of increased camaraderie and collaborative spirit in departments where her programs had been implemented, subtly implying that Younger's metrics were actively hindering such positive developments. She learned to anticipate Younger's attacks by proactively addressing potential criticisms. If she knew Younger was about to highlight a dip in production in a specific department, she would preemptively submit a report detailing a successful team-building retreat in that same department, emphasizing the renewed sense of purpose and renewed commitment that followed, thereby reframing any subsequent productivity fluctuations as part of a larger, positive transformation.

Crain, sensing the growing chasm between Younger and Holman, saw his opportunity to play them against each other while carving out his own niche. He began to subtly feed information to Younger about Holman's "soft" HR initiatives that were drawing heavily on R&D resources for their technological implementation – a subtle jab at Holman's perceived lack of technical understanding and Younger's desire for cost-efficiency. Crain would present these as "unforeseen expenditures arising from HR-driven technological integration," complete with detailed breakdowns of time and resources diverted from core R&D projects. Simultaneously, he would hint to Holman that Younger was actively lobbying to reduce the R&D budget, citing "lack of immediate ROI" in her pet projects, thereby positioning himself as her protector against Younger's perceived insensitivity to the human capital aspect of the company. He would initiate R&D projects with deliberately ambiguous objectives, projects that could be spun to appeal to either Younger's desire for measurable efficiency or Holman's focus on employee well-being, depending on who he was pitching to.

For instance, a project exploring new communication platforms could be presented to Younger as a tool for streamlining internal reporting and enhancing team collaboration for greater productivity, while to Holman, it would be framed as a way to foster greater transparency, improve employee feedback mechanisms, and build a stronger sense of community. Crain's genius lay in his ability to maintain a veneer of objective scientific inquiry while actively participating in the political machinations of the inner circle. He would often be seen in hushed conversations with Younger, followed by seemingly casual encounters with Holman, a master of triangulation, always positioning himself as the pragmatic intermediary or the neutral observer, all the while subtly amplifying the discord.

The impact of these internal power struggles was devastatingly effective in fragmenting the already precarious leadership structure. Kline, insulated by the meticulously curated reality presented to him, remained largely oblivious to the open warfare being waged beneath the surface. He saw the reports, heard the filtered presentations, and interpreted the carefully managed outcomes as evidence of his own exceptional leadership, guiding his lieutenants to ever-greater heights of loyalty and efficiency. He praised Younger for his unwavering focus on measurable results, Holman for her dedication to fostering a harmonious workplace, and Crain for his innovative yet controlled approach to R&D. He remained blissfully unaware that their individual "successes" were increasingly achieved at the expense of each other, and ultimately, at the expense of Halcyon itself.

Younger's relentless pursuit of quantifiable metrics, fueled by his desire to one-up Holman, led to an increasingly draconian approach to performance management. Employees who fell even slightly short of his exacting standards found themselves subjected to intense scrutiny, their every deviation documented and presented as evidence of insufficient loyalty. This created an atmosphere of pervasive anxiety, where fear of reprisal became a far more potent motivator than genuine commitment. Younger, in his reports, would spin these results as a testament to Halcyon's commitment to excellence, framing the increased pressure as a necessary component of maintaining peak performance, subtly implying that Holman's more empathetic approach was enabling mediocrity. He would cite statistics showing a marginal decrease in absenteeism, for example, not as a sign of improved health, but as evidence that employees were too afraid to take sick days, thus further solidifying his reputation for driving results, even if the human cost was becoming astronomical.

Holman, in her bid to outshine Younger, began to overemphasize "employee recognition programs" and "wellness initiatives," often at the expense of genuine professional development or addressing systemic issues that led to burnout. She would orchestrate elaborate celebrations for minor achievements, creating a superficial sense of morale that masked the underlying disquiet. In her communications, she would subtly contrast these outward displays of appreciation with Younger's "unfeeling data points," positioning herself as the guardian of Halcyon's soul. She might present a report detailing the "overwhelmingly positive feedback" on a company-wide mindfulness retreat, while simultaneously glossing over the fact that the same retreat was attended by employees who had recently received warnings from Younger about their performance, effectively using the event as a forced participation exercise rather than a genuine offering of support. Her aim was to demonstrate that a happy workforce, a workforce that felt personally cared for, was the ultimate driver of loyalty, a direct counterpoint to Younger's mechanical approach.

Crain, the reluctant participant in this internecine warfare, found himself pushed to the brink of his own ethical compromise. In his efforts to appease both Younger and Holman, he began to delay or subtly misdirect crucial R&D projects. If Younger demanded a report on the loyalty metric impact of a new technology, Crain would deliberately obfuscate the data, presenting projections that were either overly optimistic or excessively pessimistic, depending on whose narrative he sought to support. If Holman requested research into employee stress reduction technologies, he would ensure the studies were designed with methodological flaws that would yield ambiguous results, making it difficult for her to definitively claim success without his assistance. He started to present what he termed "strategic innovation," which was, in reality, the careful curation of incremental advancements that posed no threat to the existing power structures and could be easily framed to satisfy either Thorne's demand for measurable progress or Holman's need for positive employee anecdotes. He learned to speak of "risk-mitigated innovation" and "loyalty-aligned technological evolution," effectively neutering the very concept of true breakthrough research. The irony was not lost on him: he was supposed to be fostering the future of Halcyon, but he was actively contributing to its stagnation, all while perpetuating the illusion of progress.

The constant need to undermine, to discredit, to outmaneuver, created a corrosive atmosphere within the inner circle. Each member became increasingly paranoid, suspecting the other of feeding negative information to Kline or subtly sabotaging their own efforts. Younger began to suspect Holman of manipulating employee feedback data to make his own metrics look less impressive. Holman grew convinced that Younger was actively influencing Kline's perception of HR's effectiveness, framing her initiatives as mere "fluff" designed to distract from core business objectives. Crain, caught in the crossfire, felt his own professional integrity eroding with each calculated deception, each deliberately misleading report. The unity that Kline perceived was a fragile illusion, a thin veneer of professionalism stretched taut over a seething cauldron of ambition, resentment, and fear.

Their loyalty, once seemingly absolute, had fractured into a desperate scramble for personal survival, a testament to the chilling reality that even within the most seemingly cohesive inner sanctums, the siren song of individual power could drown out the chorus of collective purpose. This internal conflict, far more insidious than any external threat, was slowly but surely dismantling Halcyon Defense Systems from the inside out, a silent implosion driven by the very individuals tasked with its preservation.

Mel Aris, the Deputy Director of Human Resources at Halcyon Defense Systems, had always considered himself a steward of the company's most vital asset: its people. His tenure had begun with a quiet, yet firm, commitment to fostering a workplace where talent could flourish, where individuals felt valued not just for their output, but for their contribution to the collective spirit of innovation and dedication. In the early days, before the specter of the Loyalty Metric had cast its long shadow over every interaction, Aris had been a vocal proponent of progressive HR policies. He championed initiatives aimed at improving work-life balance, advocated for robust mental health support, and pushed for transparent communication channels, believing that a healthy, engaged workforce was the bedrock of any successful enterprise.

He often found himself in quiet, yet determined, opposition to Victor Kline's more extreme pronouncements, attempting to inject a dose of empathy and reason into the CEO's often ruthless directives. He would draft policy proposals that subtly nudged Kline towards more humane practices, often framing them in terms of long-term productivity gains and enhanced employee retention, the very metrics Kline ostensibly valued. Aris's approach was one of gentle persuasion, of demonstrating the tangible benefits of a supportive work environment, a stark contrast to the aggressive, results-at-all-costs mentality that was beginning to take root. He saw himself as a buffer, a shield against the potential excesses of a demanding leader, a role he performed with a quiet integrity that earned him the respect of many within the mid-management ranks.

However, the ascent of the Loyalty Metric had irrevocably altered the landscape. What began as a seemingly innocuous tool for gauging employee commitment had metastasized into an all-consuming obsession, a digital idol demanding constant sacrifice. Aris, once a hesitant critic, found himself increasingly adrift in a sea of escalating expectations and ruthless ambition. The subtle nudges and reasoned arguments that had once been his modus operandi were now being drowned out by the deafening roar of performance indicators and the cutthroat machinations of Younger, Holman, and Crain. He watched, with a growing sense of dread, as the carefully

122

constructed edifice of Halcyon's purported loyalty began to crumble, replaced by a chillingly efficient system of surveillance and control. The pressure to conform, to demonstrate unwavering allegiance to Kline's vision, became an unbearable weight. He saw his peers, individuals he had once respected for their professionalism, transform into eager sycophants, their own consciences seemingly discarded in the relentless pursuit of favor. Aris, a man who prided himself on his ethical compass, found himself navigating an increasingly treacherous moral terrain. The very principles he had sworn to uphold were being systematically eroded, replaced by a pragmatic, and ultimately soul-crushing, adherence to the dictates of the Loyalty Metric.

The turning point for Mel Aris was not a single, dramatic event, but rather a slow, insidious erosion of his resolve. It began with Younger's increasing influence. Younger, with his unshakeable faith in the infallibility of data, had found an unlikely ally in Aris's HR department. Initially, Aris had seen Younger's emphasis on quantifiable metrics as a necessary evil, a tool to provide concrete evidence for his own more qualitative arguments. He believed that by providing Younger with the numbers he craved, he could subtly guide the company towards more equitable practices. He shared employee engagement data, absenteeism rates, and productivity figures, hoping that Younger's objective analysis would highlight the benefits of his own initiatives.

However, Younger, ever the strategist, saw this data not as a means to an end, but as a weapon. He began to subtly reframe Aris's departmental reports, twisting the nuanced nuances of employee sentiment into stark, unforgiving data points that could be used to identify and isolate perceived disloyalty. Aris would find his own carefully curated reports on employee well-being being dissected by Younger, with specific individuals flagged for minor infractions or deviations from expected behavior. Younger would then present these findings to Kline, not as data requiring further investigation or support, but as definitive proof of subversion, demanding swift and decisive action. Aris, caught in the crossfire, found himself increasingly uncomfortable with how his data was being weaponized, but the fear of becoming a target himself, of being labeled as soft or ineffective by Younger, began to gnaw at him.

Then came Carin Holman, whose mastery of emotional manipulation presented a different, yet equally potent, challenge. Holman understood that data, while powerful, could be interpreted in myriad ways. She recognized that Aris, despite his data-driven justifications, was still susceptible to appeals to compassion and fairness. She began to cultivate a relationship with him, not as a rival, but as a fellow guardian of Halcyon's human capital. She would confide in him about the pressures she faced from Younger, the constant struggle to justify the intangible value of employee morale against Younger's hard-nosed financial arguments.

She would share stories of employees who were being unfairly targeted by Younger's metrics, framing herself as the empathetic voice in Kline's ear, the one who fought for the human element. Aris, flattered by her apparent confidence and genuinely sympathetic to her plight, found himself inadvertently sharing more information with Holman, believing they were forming an informal alliance. He would offer insights into individual employee situations, hoping Holman could use this information to advocate for more leniency. What he didn't realize was that Holman was meticulously cataloging these insights, using them to predict Younger's attacks and to preemptively craft her own narrative, often at the expense of the very individuals Aris was trying to protect. Holman would then subtly relay these "vulnerabilities" to Younger, framing them as potential risks to the company's loyalty metrics, thus solidifying her own position as a pragmatic, albeit empathetic, operator, while simultaneously reinforcing Younger's narrative of vigilance.

The cumulative effect of Younger's relentless data-mining and Holman's calculated emotional appeals began to chip away at Aris's resistance. He started to see the benefits, however perverse, of aligning himself more closely with the prevailing winds. When Younger presented his meticulously crafted graphs detailing a departmental dip in "loyalty scores," Aris found himself drafting preliminary reports identifying the "root causes" – often framing employee dissatisfaction or perceived grievances as individual failings rather than systemic issues. He began to issue warnings, not as a proactive measure to address underlying problems, but as a punitive response to failing metrics.

His language shifted, subtly at first, from "supporting employee growth" to "ensuring compliance," from "fostering a positive work environment" to "maintaining operational integrity." He started to believe, or perhaps to tell himself he believed, that this was the only way to survive, the only way to keep his department relevant and his own position secure. He convinced himself that by being a part of the enforcement mechanism, he could at least retain some semblance of control, some ability to mitigate the harshest consequences.

This transformation was starkly illustrated during the infamous "Project Nightingale" incident. A team within R&D had been working on a groundbreaking communication platform, designed to foster genuine collaboration and knowledge sharing. Julian Crain, in his pursuit of innovation, had initially presented the project with a strong emphasis on its potential to enhance employee engagement and reduce silos – aspects that Aris, even in his weakened state, found appealing.

However, Younger, suspicious of any initiative that couldn't be immediately quantified in terms of loyalty, began to question its resource allocation. He presented data suggesting that the project's nebulous goals and lengthy development timeline were diverting valuable resources from initiatives with more direct loyalty metric payoffs. Holman, sensing an opportunity to further consolidate her influence and position herself as the arbiter of employee happiness, jumped on board, but with a twist. She framed the platform not as a tool for genuine collaboration, but as a potential surveillance mechanism, arguing that its widespread adoption could allow for the monitoring of employee communications, thus providing crucial data points for loyalty assessments.

Aris, caught between Younger's demand for quantifiable results and Holman's appeal to security through surveillance, found himself in an impossible position. His initial instinct was to defend the project's original intent, to emphasize its potential for fostering authentic connection. But the pressure was immense. Younger was implying that Aris was soft, that he was allowing sentimentality to override pragmatism. Holman was subtly suggesting that if the project was not framed as a tool for monitoring loyalty, it would be deemed a wasteful expenditure and shut down entirely, potentially leading to significant layoffs within R&D, which would, in turn, negatively impact his own department's perceived effectiveness in managing workforce stability.

In a now-infamous HR review meeting, Aris, his voice wavering slightly, presented his department's assessment of Project Nightingale. He began by acknowledging Younger's valid concerns about resource allocation and the need for measurable returns. He then, with a forced smile, pivoted to Holman's perspective, carefully articulating how the platform could be leveraged to "enhance observational insight into team dynamics and communication patterns." He presented a revised set of objectives for the project, transforming it from a collaborative tool into a data-gathering instrument. He spoke of "sentiment analysis integration" and "real-time loyalty trend identification," phrases he had never before uttered. He even proposed the implementation of a tiered access system, where certain communication channels would be designated as "critical oversight zones," directly feeding data into the Loyalty Metric dashboard. He concluded his presentation by stating, with a manufactured conviction, that this revised focus would not only ensure the project's financial viability but would also significantly contribute to Halcyon's overarching commitment to maintaining an unwavering standard of loyalty among its workforce. He saw the flicker of approval in Younger's eyes, the subtle nod from Holman, and a cold dread settled in his stomach. He had become an architect of the very system he had once sought to reform.

The fallout from Project Nightingale was a watershed moment for Mel Aris. He had crossed a line, a line he had previously sworn never to approach. He had actively participated in the perversion of an innovative project, transforming it from a tool of empowerment into an instrument of control. The shame was a heavy burden, but it was soon eclipsed by a chilling pragmatism. He realized that resistance was not only futile but actively detrimental to his own survival. He began to anticipate Kline's demands, to pre-empt Younger's criticisms, and to align himself with Holman's latest initiatives, even when they felt morally compromised. He started to view his role not as a protector of employees, but as a facilitator of Kline's vision, a cog in the loyalty-generating machine.

He became adept at crafting policies that, on their surface, appeared to support employee well-being, but which, upon closer inspection, contained clauses that enabled stricter monitoring and more severe consequences for perceived disloyalty. For instance, he introduced a new "Performance Enhancement Program" that, while promising personalized coaching and development opportunities, also mandated frequent check-ins and detailed reporting on employee progress towards "loyalty benchmarks." These benchmarks, meticulously defined by Younger and subtly influenced by Holman's emotional metrics, became the ultimate arbiter of an employee's worth. Aris, once a champion of open communication, now found himself orchestrating a system where every email, every instant message, every informal conversation was subject to potential scrutiny. He learned to frame these measures as necessary steps to "ensure fairness and consistency" across the organization, arguing that without objective data, subjective assessments could lead to favoritism and undermine the very concept of loyalty.

His transformation was complete when he spearheaded the implementation of "Proactive Loyalty Audits." This initiative, presented as a means to identify and address potential loyalty risks before they materialized, involved the systematic review of employee digital footprints, social media activity, and even private communication logs. Aris, in his presentations to Kline and the board, spoke with an almost evangelistic fervor about the importance of preemptive measures, framing any resistance to such audits as an indicator of something to hide. He justified the intrusive nature of these audits by citing the need for Halcyon to remain vigilant against external threats and internal dissent, a narrative that resonated deeply with Kline's paranoid worldview. He became a staunch advocate for the expansion of the Loyalty Metric's reach, pushing to integrate it into every facet of employee evaluation, from hiring to promotion, and even exit interviews. He argued that a truly loyal employee would have nothing to fear from such scrutiny, and that those who did were a liability to the company's security and success.

The irony was that Aris, in his quest to preserve his own position and the perceived stability of his department, had become one of the most zealous enforcers of Kline's oppressive regime. He had traded his principles for perceived security, his integrity for influence. He no longer saw the faces behind the data points, the human cost of his actions. He saw only metrics, targets, and the ever-present need to satisfy the insatiable demands of the Loyalty Metric and the volatile ego of Victor Kline. The former advocate for humane policies had become a master of bureaucratic control, a silent architect of a system designed to crush the very spirit he had once sworn to nurture. His journey from a reluctant participant to a zealous implementer served as a chilling testament to the corrosive power of unchecked ambition and the insidious ways in which even well-intentioned individuals could be consumed by a system built on fear and control. He was no longer Mel Aris, the HR executive; he was simply an extension of the Loyalty Metric, a cog in the machine that was slowly, irrevocably, turning Halcyon Defense Systems into a gilded cage.

The gilded cage, as Mel Aris had come to think of Halcyon Defense Systems, was precisely that: gilded, not merely for the superficial sheen of success it presented to the outside world, but for the way it trapped its inhabitants within its opulent confines. The "inner circle," the esteemed pantheon of executives who stood closest to Victor Kline, lived a life of paradoxical privilege. They commanded vast resources, wielded significant influence, and enjoyed a proximity to power that few could even dream of. Yet, beneath the polished mahogany and the hushed, deferential tones, a relentless current of anxiety flowed, a frigid undercurrent that threatened to drown them all. Their positions, so envied by those in the outer layers of the corporate hierarchy, were anything but secure. They were tethered to Kline's whims, their continued tenure a delicate dance of anticipation and appeasement, a perpetual performance designed to prove their unwavering allegiance and indispensable utility.

The most insidious manifestation of this precarious existence was the pervasive paranoia that permeated their interactions. Each member of the inner circle, from Younger's data-driven pronouncements to Holman's emotionally charged strategizing, harbored a gnawing suspicion that their own standing was constantly under scrutiny. They were acutely aware that the very standards they enforced upon others – the relentless pursuit of loyalty, the unforgiving dissection of performance metrics – were being applied with equal, if not greater, rigor to themselves. The illusion of control they projected was a fragile facade, a meticulously constructed dam against the rising tide of Kline's ever-shifting expectations. Every whispered conversation, every averted glance, every subtle shift in Kline's demeanor was dissected and analyzed, not for genuine insight, but for perceived threats.

Younger, in particular, became a prisoner of his own methodology. His obsession with data, his unshakeable belief in the quantifiable, had initially secured his position. He saw the world as a series of algorithms, of inputs and outputs, and he believed he could predict and control every variable. However, this deterministic worldview bred a deep-seated fear. He constantly worried that another executive, another set of metrics, might emerge that could invalidate his own carefully curated datasets. He saw potential rivals everywhere, not in the traditional sense of ambition, but in the more terrifying guise of superior predictive models or more persuasive correlations.

He would spend sleepless nights poring over internal reports, searching for anomalies, for inconsistencies, for any evidence that might suggest a weakness in his own empire of numbers, or worse, evidence that someone else was meticulously charting his decline. He began to suspect even Holman, with her fluid understanding of human emotion, of subtly manipulating Kline's perceptions of Younger's performance, perhaps subtly introducing variables into Kline's decision-making matrix that Younger could not account for. He started to view her carefully worded summaries of employee morale not as a genuine attempt to gauge sentiment, but as a veiled critique of his own data's inability to capture the full spectrum of human experience, a gap he desperately tried to fill with ever more granular, and ultimately futile, data points. Carin Holman, on the other hand, found her paranoia manifesting as a relentless need to secure her own narrative. She understood that while Younger could present hard data, her own strength lay in her ability to shape perception, to weave compelling stories that resonated with Kline's emotional landscape. Her fear was that a purely data-driven approach, unmediated by her carefully crafted empathy, would eventually win out, leaving her vulnerable. She therefore engaged in a constant, covert battle to maintain her position as the chief interpreter of Halcyon's emotional pulse. She would meticulously document every perceived success, every instance where her intervention had seemingly averted a crisis or boosted morale, framing these events in the most flattering light. She cultivated relationships with Kline's personal staff, not for friendship, but for intelligence, seeking to understand the CEO's mood, his anxieties, his current preoccupations. She would subtly undermine Younger's pronouncements by highlighting the human cost of his purely analytical decisions, always framing herself as the compassionate counterpoint, the one who ensured Halcyon remained a "human" organization, even as its practices grew increasingly dehumanized.

Her paranoia wasn't about data; it was about the narrative, about ensuring that the story Kline heard about her, and through her, about the company, was one of indispensable understanding and empathetic leadership. She would often find herself replaying conversations with Kline, searching for any hint of dissatisfaction, any subtle cue that might suggest he was beginning to doubt her efficacy, her understanding of his deepest needs.

Even Julian Crain, the seemingly detached architect of Halcyon's technological future, was not immune. While his focus was ostensibly on innovation, his fear was that his projects, however groundbreaking, would be deemed insufficiently aligned with the overarching loyalty metric, or worse, that they might inadvertently expose vulnerabilities in the very systems designed to enforce that loyalty. He lived with the constant dread of an audit, of a security breach, of a flawed algorithm that could unravel his meticulously crafted digital fortresses. He would often implement redundant security measures, not out of genuine conviction, but out of a desperate need to prove his vigilance, to preempt any accusation of negligence. He suspected his own engineers, the very people he relied upon, of harboring hidden agendas or, more chillingly, of being susceptible to external manipulation. He would demand increasingly invasive security protocols for his own teams, monitoring their communications and keystrokes with a ferocity that mirrored Younger's data surveillance.

He saw potential threats in the very interconnectedness he fostered, a constant reminder that the digital world, while offering immense power, also presented a vast and terrifying landscape of potential vulnerabilities. His paranoia manifested as a deep distrust of any technology that wasn't under his direct, absolute control, and a gnawing fear that one day, one of his own creations would be the instrument of his downfall. He began to view the very concept of open innovation as a dangerous relic, a naive idealism that had no place in the hyper-vigilant reality Halcyon had become.

This collective anxiety, this unspoken fear, created a toxic environment where genuine collaboration became impossible and suspicion festered. They were a pack of wolves, circling each other warily, each acutely aware that a single misstep, a moment of perceived weakness, could lead to them being singled out, dissected, and ultimately discarded by the apex predator, Victor Kline. The power they held was thus inextricably linked to their isolation. They could not confide in each other, could not admit their fears, for to do so would be to reveal a vulnerability that would undoubtedly be exploited. Their shared experience of being on the precipice of power only served to deepen their individual isolation, each man and woman trapped in their own private hell of doubt and dread.

The irony was that their proximity to power had effectively removed them from the very human connections that might have offered solace or perspective. They were insulated by their titles, by the deference they commanded, but this insulation also created a vacuum where genuine empathy and understanding should have existed. They were surrounded by people, yet utterly alone. Their interactions became transactional, carefully calibrated performances designed to project strength and unwavering loyalty. The subtle art of political maneuvering, once a skill honed by necessity, had devolved into a desperate game of self-preservation. Every compliment was suspect, every offer of assistance a potential trap, every shared confidence a dangerous gamble.

Mel Aris, in his role as the head of HR, found himself privy to the subtle tremors of this internal earthquake. He saw the carefully masked anxieties in the strained smiles of his colleagues, the barely concealed desperation in their requests for reassurance. He witnessed Younger's increasingly erratic behavior, his obsessive need to present ever more complex and irrefutable data. He observed Holman's calculated displays of empathy, her masterful manipulation of Kline's emotions, and the subtle ways she would exploit any perceived lapse in Younger's performance. He saw Crain's relentless push for technological dominance, a desperate attempt to create a fortress of innovation that might shield him from the pervasive suspicion.

Aris, who had once believed in the power of human connection to build a strong organization, now saw it being systematically dismantled. He had become a facilitator of this dismantling, his own actions a testament to the corrosive power of fear. He remembered the early days, the genuine camaraderie, the shared vision. Now, that vision had been warped into a singular, all-consuming focus on loyalty, a metric that had become a weapon used to divide and conquer. He saw the members of the inner circle, once his peers, now transformed into individuals consumed by suspicion, each convinced that the others were actively working to undermine them.

He recalled a recent strategy meeting, a hushed affair held in Kline's private chambers, where the topic of "employee retention" was discussed. Younger presented data suggesting a slight uptick in voluntary departures in departments with lower loyalty scores, framing it as a direct correlation to insufficient monitoring. Holman countered by suggesting that aggressive loyalty enforcement might be driving some of these departures, proposing a more nuanced approach that involved "understanding the root causes of dissent."

The air in the room crackled with unspoken accusations. Younger, his jaw tight, implied that Holman's "nuanced approach" was merely a cover for her own inability to extract concrete data, a weakness that could jeopardize the entire loyalty initiative. Holman, her smile never faltering, gently reminded Younger that even the most robust data was useless if it didn't translate into tangible improvements in employee well-being, subtly suggesting that Younger's methods were creating a hostile work environment, which, in turn, would negatively impact the very loyalty he sought to measure. Aris watched as Crain remained silent, his gaze fixed on a holographic display of network traffic, as if the intricate patterns held more answers than the heated exchange unfolding before him. Aris felt a wave of nausea. He saw how Younger's data, Holman's empathy, and Crain's technology were all being twisted and weaponized, not to build a stronger company, but to fortify individual positions within the precarious inner circle. Each spoke their own language, each played their own game, their shared objective being not the advancement of Halcyon, but their own survival within its increasingly toxic ecosystem.

The paranoia was not just an internal problem; it seeped into every aspect of Halcyon's operations. Projects were delayed not because of technical challenges, but because of interdepartmental mistrust. Resources were hoarded, not for strategic advantage, but out of fear that they would be diverted to a rival's benefit. Even simple decisions were fraught with the potential for unintended consequences, each executive constantly weighing how their actions might be perceived by Kline, and by their peers. The once-vibrant collaborative spirit had been replaced by a grim, silent competition, a constant jockeying for favor and a desperate attempt to remain invisible to the most critical gaze of all.

Victor Kline, the architect of this gilded cage, seemed to revel in the manufactured fear. He understood that a certain level of anxiety was a powerful motivator, a tool to ensure absolute control. He fostered the competition, subtly pitting his inner circle against each other, knowing that their infighting would only serve to solidify his own position at the apex. He would offer veiled praise, a carefully placed compliment that would send one executive soaring with renewed confidence, only to follow it with a cryptic suggestion of doubt, planting seeds of suspicion about another. He was a puppeteer, and his inner circle were his exquisitely dressed marionettes, their every move dictated by the invisible strings of his favor and his displeasure.

Aris often found himself observing these subtle manipulations, the quiet chess game that played out in every board meeting, every private consultation. He saw how Younger would present a flawless report, only for Kline to interject with a seemingly innocent question about a minor deviation, a question that Younger would then spend weeks trying to rectify, his paranoia reignited. He witnessed Holman skillfully navigate a complex HR issue, only for Kline to remark on how "important it was to ensure such issues didn't fester, lest they become opportunities for those who might seek to exploit Halcyon's generosity." He saw how Crain's ambitious technological proposals would be met with Kline's pronouncements about the need for "unwavering security and absolute control," forcing Crain to endlessly re-engineer his innovations to incorporate ever more stringent surveillance capabilities.

The weight of this atmosphere was beginning to crush Aris. He had sought to foster a healthy workplace, a place where people could thrive. Instead, he had become a cog in a machine that systematically eroded trust, fostered suspicion, and ultimately, isolated everyone, including himself. The gilded cage was indeed a prison, and its most ardent inhabitants, those closest to the keys, were the most profoundly incarcerated, their freedom of thought and action surrendered for the illusion of security and the poisoned chalice of power. The paranoia was not a bug in the system; it was the core operating principle, the very fuel that kept the gears of Halcyon's oppressive machinery grinding forward. And Aris, once the gentle steward of human capital, was now deeply complicit in its systematic deconstruction, a silent prisoner in his own meticulously constructed cell.

Chapter 6

The Political Ascent

The subtle art of corporate ascendancy, Mel Aris had come to understand, was not so different from the grander machinations of political power. Victor Kline, the architect of Halcyon's gilded cage, had spent years meticulously refining his techniques within the insulated walls of his corporate empire. He had cultivated an environment where loyalty was not a virtue but a currency, where performance was not measured by output but by demonstrable subservience, and where efficiency was achieved not through collaboration but through the ruthless elimination of dissent. Now, as the scent of opportunity wafted from the broader political arena, Kline began to perceive a new canvas upon which to paint his vision of absolute control. The principles that had proven so devastatingly effective in bending the will of his employees and shaping the trajectory of Halcyon Defense Systems were, he surmised, eminently transferable to the messy, often chaotic, world of governance.

His initial forays were subtle, almost imperceptible to the untrained eye. They began not with grand pronouncements or public rallies, but with the quiet channeling of corporate resources into nascent political movements that mirrored his own brand of authoritarian pragmatism. Halcyon's formidable public relations machine, once employed to polish the company's image and deflect criticism, was repurposed to subtly amplify narratives that aligned with Kline's burgeoning political ideology.

Think tanks and research institutions, many of them conveniently funded by Halcyon's seemingly endless coffers, began to churn out studies and reports that underscored the need for strong, decisive leadership, the dangers of unfettered individual expression, and the inherent inefficiency of democratic processes. Aris, observing these shifts from his vantage point within HR, recognized the familiar patterns of manipulation, now cloaked in the respectable guise of intellectual discourse.

He saw how Younger's data-driven approach, once focused on employee productivity, was now being applied to model voter behavior, identifying demographics susceptible to fear-based messaging and the promise of order. Holman, meanwhile, was no doubt crafting the emotional narratives, the carefully curated appeals to patriotism and security, designed to resonate with the anxieties of a populace ripe for strong leadership. Even Julian Crain's technological prowess, previously dedicated to safeguarding Halcyon's secrets, was likely being reoriented towards sophisticated data harvesting and predictive analytics, not for market trends, but for electoral targeting.

Kline understood that genuine power was not merely about commanding armies or dictating policy; it was about shaping perception, about subtly influencing the collective consciousness. He had mastered this art within Halcyon, transforming a workforce into a compliant entity through a combination of carrot and stick, fear and reward. Now, he aimed to replicate this feat on a national scale.

He began to cultivate relationships with influential figures in the political establishment, not through the clumsy machinations of traditional lobbying, but through discreet channels and mutually beneficial arrangements. He identified rising stars, ambitious politicians whose ideologies, however nascent, showed a flicker of alignment with his own. These individuals were courted with the same meticulous attention to detail that Kline afforded his top executives.

Campaign donations, channeled through labyrinthine corporate structures and opaque PACs, flowed generously. Strategic advice, delivered by Holman's sharp intellect and Younger's analytical prowess, was offered as a seemingly altruistic gesture. And, of course, there were the "consulting fees," generous sums paid to individuals or organizations that conveniently advanced Kline's political agenda.

Aris had witnessed firsthand how Kline could dissect a

subordinate's strengths and weaknesses, leveraging them for maximum personal gain. He could only imagine the same predatory skill being applied to the political landscape, identifying vulnerabilities in aspiring leaders and offering solutions that, in turn, bound them to his will.

The media, that ubiquitous arbiter of public opinion, became another crucial battlefield. Halcyon, under Kline's direction, began to exert greater influence over news cycles, not through outright censorship, but through more insidious means. Advertisements, carefully crafted to evoke a sense of national pride and the need for strong leadership, blanketed airwaves and digital platforms. Key media outlets received substantial advertising revenue, creating an implicit pressure to maintain a favorable editorial stance.

Journalists perceived as too critical were subtly marginalized, their access to information curtailed, their stories buried. Conversely, those who echoed Kline's sentiments found themselves lauded, granted interviews, and elevated to positions of influence. Aris remembered the meticulous control Kline exerted over internal communications at Halcyon, ensuring that only approved narratives reached the workforce. He saw the same strategy being deployed externally, a sophisticated campaign to mold public discourse into a shape that suited Kline's ambitions. It was a masterful application of psychological warfare, albeit on a much grander, more consequential scale.

The transition was not merely about acquiring influence; it was about building a personal brand, a political persona that would resonate with a public yearning for stability and strength. Kline, ever the astute observer of human nature, understood that abstract ideologies were rarely as compelling as relatable figures.

He began to curate his public image, carefully selecting the issues he would champion, the rhetoric he would employ. He presented himself as a pragmatic problem-solver, a successful businessman who understood the intricacies of management and possessed the rare ability to translate that acumen to the national stage. He spoke of efficiency, of fiscal responsibility, of the need to cut through bureaucratic red tape. His speeches, honed by Holman's understanding of emotional triggers and amplified by Younger's statistical validation of public sentiment, were designed to project an aura of unwavering competence. He would occasionally allude to the "unseen challenges" facing the nation, hinting at complex threats that only a leader with his unique skillset could truly comprehend and neutralize. This carefully constructed narrative began to gain traction, appealing to a segment of the population weary of partisan gridlock and perceived governmental incompetence.

Furthermore, Kline understood that political power was built on networks, on alliances forged through shared interests and mutual obligation. He began to host exclusive gatherings, discreet events where powerful figures from the corporate and political worlds mingled. These were not mere social occasions; they were meticulously orchestrated networking opportunities, designed to foster connections and cultivate a loyal following. At these events, Kline played the role of the facilitator, the indispensable connector, subtly weaving together disparate threads of influence into a cohesive tapestry that revolved around him. Aris, privy to the internal power dynamics at Halcyon, recognized this as the same strategy Kline employed to solidify his control over his executive team, now writ large. He saw how Kline could identify those with power, understand their desires, and then position himself as the key to unlocking those desires, whether it be access to capital, political endorsement, or simply the cachet of association.

The core of Kline's strategy, however, remained rooted in the principles he had perfected at Halcyon: the unwavering emphasis on loyalty and the strategic cultivation of fear. He recognized that in the political realm, as in the corporate one, fear was a potent motivator. He began to subtly highlight perceived threats – economic instability, foreign adversaries, internal dissent – framing himself as the only bulwark against these dangers. This rhetoric, amplified by his media allies and supported by the carefully manufactured data from his funded think tanks, created a palpable sense of unease, a societal anxiety that he was uniquely positioned to allay.

Simultaneously, he cultivated an inner circle of political allies, individuals who demonstrated unwavering loyalty, not through shared ideology alone, but through demonstrable commitment to his cause. These individuals were rewarded with access, influence, and the promise of future power. Those who wavered, who showed signs of independent thought or expressed dissenting opinions, found themselves ostracized, their careers subtly undermined, their voices silenced. Aris had seen this exact dynamic play out within Halcyon's executive suites; the consequences were simply more far-reaching now.

The transition from CEO to statesman was, in Kline's mind, not a departure from his core principles but an expansion of their application. He saw no fundamental difference between managing a multinational corporation and governing a nation. Both, in his view, required a singular vision, unwavering decisiveness, and the absolute subjugation of individual will to the greater good as defined by the leader. He was not seeking to govern for the people, but to govern them, to impose order and efficiency upon a system he deemed inherently chaotic and wasteful.

His ambition was not to serve, but to command, to wield power not as a responsibility, but as an entitlement. The corporate world had provided him with the perfect laboratory to perfect his methods, and now, the vast and complex arena of politics beckoned, promising an even grander stage upon which to implement his vision of absolute, unyielding control. He was no longer merely a CEO; he was a nascent political force, meticulously assembling the tools and the strategy for a far more ambitious conquest. The foundations of his political ascent were laid not in public service, but in the calculated exploitation of human psychology, a testament to the chilling efficacy of his corporate tactics translated onto a global scale.

The lines between business and governance blurred, then dissolved entirely, as Victor Kline prepared to implement his ultimate model of corporate-style dominion over the very fabric of society. His understanding of organizational dynamics, honed through years of managing Halcyon, provided him with an almost intuitive grasp of how to manipulate larger systems, of how to identify leverage points and exploit them for maximum impact. He saw political parties not as ideological vehicles, but as organizational structures ripe for his brand of management, complete with their own internal hierarchies, their own competing factions, and their own susceptibility to the promise of decisive leadership.

He began to analyze the mechanisms of political fundraising, recognizing the parallels between securing venture capital and mobilizing donor networks. The art of negotiation, a critical skill in any corporate boardroom, he now applied to legislative processes, identifying concessions that could be made without compromising his core objectives, and leveraging perceived weaknesses in opponents to extract maximum advantage. He understood that political campaigns, much like product launches, required meticulous planning, targeted messaging, and a deep understanding of the consumer – in this case, the voter.

Younger's data analytics were instrumental in dissecting voter demographics, identifying key swing constituencies, and predicting the potential impact of various policy proposals. Holman's expertise in emotional intelligence was crucial in crafting campaign narratives that resonated with the electorate's hopes and fears, weaving stories that positioned Kline as the benevolent protector and visionary leader. Julian Crain's technological acumen, once focused on secure defense systems, was now re-tasked to the creation of sophisticated digital infrastructure for his political campaigns, including advanced voter databases, micro-targeting platforms, and secure communication networks.

Aris, observing this multi-faceted approach, couldn't help but feel a chilling sense of recognition. This was not the amateur dabbling of a CEO playing at politics; this was a calculated, strategic conquest, employing the same ruthless efficiency and psychological manipulation that had made Halcyon Defense Systems so formidable, and so terrifying. The corporate playbook, it seemed, was proving to be an alarmingly effective manual for political domination.

Victor Kline, a man whose very presence seemed to exude an aura of controlled power, understood that leadership, whether in the sterile confines of a boardroom or the raucous arena of public life, was fundamentally about narrative. It was about weaving a compelling story that resonated with the deepest aspirations and anxieties of the audience. Halcyon, in his eyes, had been a microcosm, a meticulously crafted environment where he had dictated the script, the characters, and the ultimate resolution. Now, with the nation as his burgeoning stage, he embarked on the ambitious undertaking of constructing an even grander narrative, one designed to captivate and persuade millions.

His initial move was to leverage the very engine of his corporate success: the public relations machine. Gone were the days of merely defending Halcyon's reputation or subtly shaping market perceptions. Now, this formidable apparatus was re-tasked with sculpting a political persona, a carefully constructed image of Victor Kline, the savior the nation desperately needed. This wasn't about transparency or genuine public service; it was about strategic communication, about crafting a message so potent, so seemingly authentic, that it would bypass rational skepticism and strike directly at the heart of public desire. Younger's data analytics, once employed to gauge employee morale or predict market trends, were now finely tuned to dissect public sentiment. They identified the fertile ground of widespread disillusionment, the yearning for a strong hand to guide the ship of state through turbulent waters. Holman, with her unparalleled ability to tap into the emotional currents of a populace, was tasked with articulating this yearning, translating the abstract concept of national malaise into concrete, relatable anxieties – job insecurity, the erosion of traditional values, the perceived impotence of existing political structures. Julian Crain's team worked in tandem, developing sophisticated digital platforms that could disseminate this carefully constructed narrative with unprecedented speed and precision, targeting specific demographics with tailored messages that spoke directly to their individual concerns.

The core of this emerging narrative was deceptively simple, yet powerfully effective. Kline would be presented not as a politician, but as a titan of industry, a proven problem-solver who had achieved unparalleled success in the private sector. His speeches, meticulously scripted and rehearsed, would not dwell on policy minutiae but on grand pronouncements of vision and competence. He would speak of the "unparalleled efficiency" he had instilled at Halcyon, of the "lean, agile organization" that had consistently outperformed its competitors. These were not abstract boasts; they were presented as tangible proof, as case studies in leadership that would, by extension, be applied to the nation.

The company's audited financial statements, carefully scrubbed of any hint of ethical ambiguity or the human cost of his methods, were to be paraded as evidence of his fiscal prudence and strategic acumen. He would highlight Halcyon's (carefully selected) contributions to national security, framing himself as a patriotic figure whose business acumen was intrinsically linked to the nation's strength and prosperity. The narrative emphasized his decisive nature, his willingness to make tough choices, his ability to cut through bureaucratic red tape and deliver results. This was the antithesis of the perceived gridlock and indecision plaguing the political establishment, and it resonated deeply with an electorate weary of incremental progress and partisan bickering.

The carefully curated successes of Halcyon became the cornerstones of Kline's burgeoning political platform. He would recall, with a touch of nostalgic gravitas, the challenges he had faced in revitalizing the struggling defense contractor upon his ascent. He would paint a picture of a company on the brink, burdened by inefficiency and outdated practices, a mirror to the nation's own perceived ailments. Then, he would detail, with carefully chosen anecdotes and statistics, how his leadership – his unwavering vision, his insistence on accountability, his commitment to a singular objective – had transformed Halcyon into a global powerhouse.

The narrative conveniently omitted the human toll, the ruthless down-sizing, the suppression of dissent, the erosion of employee well-being that had characterized his tenure. Instead, it focused on the quantifiable outcomes: increased market share, groundbreaking technological advancements, enhanced national security capabilities (a particularly potent point, given Halcyon's industry). This narrative was designed to bypass the complexities of governance and offer a seemingly straightforward solution: apply the principles of successful business management to the messy world of politics.

Kline understood that genuine connection, even a manufactured one, was crucial. He began to engage in carefully orchestrated public appearances, not rallies filled with impassioned speeches, but town

142

hall-style meetings and curated interviews. These were designed to project an image of accessibility and genuine concern. He would listen intently, nodding thoughtfully, before offering a concise, authoritative response that always circled back to his core message of decisive leadership and efficient execution. He would speak of "streamlining government operations," of "optimizing resource allocation," of "eliminating waste and inefficiency" – all terms that carried the weight of corporate success and promised a more streamlined, effective government. His language was precise, devoid of the emotional appeals or ideological pronouncements that often characterized political discourse. He presented himself as a technocrat, a man of action rather than rhetoric, whose primary motivation was to bring order to chaos.

The strategy was multi-pronged, targeting different segments of the population with tailored appeals. For the business-minded, he offered the promise of deregulation, of a government that understood the needs of industry and would foster economic growth through sound fiscal policies. For those concerned with national security, he presented himself as a resolute protector, a strong leader capable of confronting external threats and maintaining domestic order. For the disillusioned, he offered a beacon of hope, a departure from the status quo, a promise of a return to strength and decisiveness. This was not a monolithic ideology but a carefully constructed mosaic of resonant themes, each piece designed to appeal to a specific segment of the electorate, all unified under the banner of Victor Kline's superior leadership.

The media, a critical amplifier of any narrative, was meticulously managed. Halcyon's considerable advertising budget was strategically deployed, ensuring favorable placement and a consistent presence across a range of platforms. Opinion pieces, penned by well-compensated consultants or think tanks funded by Kline, began to appear in respected publications, echoing the themes of decisive leadership and corporate efficiency.

Journalists who showed an inclination to delve into Kline's past or question his narrative found themselves facing the familiar Halcyon tactics: a sudden drying up of access, a pointed lack of cooperation, a subtle redirection of attention to more compliant outlets. Conversely, those who amplified his message were rewarded with exclusive interviews, access to "insider" information, and the tacit approval of a powerful benefactor. This created an echo chamber effect, where Kline's narrative was not only disseminated but also reinforced, making it appear to be the prevailing sentiment, the logical conclusion to the nation's current predicament.

The narrative was further bolstered by the strategic use of "experts." Think tanks and academic institutions, conveniently financed by opaque corporate donations funneled through Halcyon's intricate network, began to publish research and host conferences that validated Kline's approach. These studies would invariably highlight the inefficiencies of democratic governance, the need for centralized decision-making, and the economic benefits of strong, decisive leadership. The language was academic, the data seemingly objective, but the underlying message was precisely aligned with Kline's political agenda. It lent an air of intellectual legitimacy to his pronouncements, transforming his personal ambition into a seemingly reasoned, data-driven policy prescription. Aris, privy to the inner workings of Halcyon's influence peddling, recognized the familiar pattern: the deliberate manufacturing of consensus through financial leverage and intellectual appropriation.

Kline himself, in this carefully constructed narrative, was portrayed as a reluctant leader, someone who had been drawn into public service by a profound sense of duty. He would express a weariness with the demands of his corporate empire, a desire to "give back" to the nation that had provided him with the opportunities for success. This cultivated humility was a powerful counterpoint to the unvarnished ambition that drove him. It positioned him not as a power-seeker, but as a patriot compelled to act by the nation's dire circumstances. This narrative of benevolent sacrifice was crucial in appealing to a populace that often viewed corporate titans with suspicion. It allowed him to leverage his immense wealth and influence not as personal gain, but as the tools of a magnanimous benefactor, dedicated to the greater good.

The message of "order" and "efficiency" was particularly potent. It tapped into a deep-seated human desire for stability and predictability. In a world perceived as increasingly chaotic and

144

unpredictable, Kline offered the promise of a controlled, rational environment. He presented government not as a complex ecosystem of diverse interests and opinions, but as a large, unwieldy organization in need of decisive management. His solutions were always framed in terms of streamlining processes, eliminating redundancies, and optimizing outcomes. This corporate jargon, stripped of its technicality and infused with the promise of tangible results, resonated with a public that felt overwhelmed by the complexities of modern life. They longed for a leader who could simplify, who could impose order, who could make things work again.

Victor Kline, the architect of Halcyon's meticulously ordered universe, was positioned as that leader, the singular individual capable of restoring balance and efficiency to a nation adrift. He wasn't just selling himself; he was selling a vision of a world where problems had clear solutions, where challenges could be met with decisive action, and where the inherent messiness of human affairs could be smoothed over by the application of superior management principles. This narrative, meticulously crafted and relentlessly propagated, was the cornerstone of his political ascent, a testament to the enduring power of a well-told story, even when that story was built on a foundation of carefully constructed illusion.

The gilded halls of Halcyon Defense Systems, once a mere backdrop for Victor Kline's corporate maneuvers, had transformed into a veritable engine of political influence. It was no longer enough to manipulate markets or orchestrate corporate takeovers; Kline's gaze had broadened, encompassing the vast, complex machinery of national governance. He understood, with the chilling clarity of a seasoned strategist, that power resided not just in the boardroom, but in the corridors of power, in the whispered conversations that shaped legislation, and in the carefully calibrated disbursements that swayed public opinion. Halcyon, under his command, was no longer just a defense contractor; it was a political force, a well-oiled machine designed to lubricate the gears of power in his favor.

Campaign donations, once a secondary concern, now flowed with the deliberate precision of a well-executed military maneuver. These weren't haphazard contributions; they were surgical strikes, meticulously targeted at politicians who evinced a certain amenability to Kline's particular brand of "efficiency" and "realism."

Younger's analytical prowess, honed by years of dissecting consumer behavior and market trends, was now redirected to the far more intricate and lucrative landscape of political patronage. Sophisticated algorithms sifted through voting records, public statements, and financial disclosures, identifying potential allies and assessing their susceptibility to influence. A politician's voting patterns on defense spending, their public pronouncements on deregulation, their perceived openness to "innovative solutions" – these were the data points that determined the allocation of Halcyon's considerable financial resources. The goal was not simply to curry favor, but to cultivate a network of indebtedness, a web of individuals whose political fortunes were inextricably linked to Kline's continued beneficence.

The endorsements, too, were a strategic weapon. While Kline himself remained, for the moment, a figure operating behind the scenes, Halcyon's imprimatur became a coveted commodity. Politicians seeking to project an image of strength, of competence, of unwavering commitment to national security, found themselves courting the approval of the defense giant. An endorsement from Halcyon wasn't merely a public statement; it was a signal to the electorate that a candidate had passed muster with a powerful, seemingly infallible entity. It was a tacit endorsement of their ability to understand and navigate the complexities of modern defense and, by extension, to manage the nation's affairs with a similar brand of no-nonsense effectiveness. This carefully orchestrated validation provided a crucial legitimacy to burgeoning political careers, positioning Kline as a kingmaker, a man capable of elevating those who aligned with his vision.

But Kline's influence extended beyond mere financial contributions and symbolic endorsements. He began to apply his signature "business-first" principles directly to the realm of policy debate, transforming complex governmental issues into simplified, albeit self-serving, business propositions. His team, armed with reams of data and meticulously crafted arguments, would engage with policymakers, not as lobbyists seeking favors, but as consultants offering "solutions." These solutions, invariably, revolved around streamlining bureaucratic processes, privatizing government functions, and prioritizing outcomes over ideological considerations – all tenets that mirrored Halcyon's own internal operational philosophy.

Take, for instance, the protracted debate surrounding the modernization of the nation's aging infrastructure. While politicians wrangled over funding mechanisms and labor disputes, Kline's think tanks, funded by Halcyon's considerable war chest, began publishing a series of influential white papers. These papers, filled with charts and graphs that spoke of "optimization," "efficiency gains," and "return on investment," painted a stark picture of government inefficiency and proposed a radical solution: a public-private partnership model, with Halcyon at its core. The narrative was seductive: private sector expertise, unburdened by bureaucratic red tape, could deliver superior results at a lower cost. The intricate details of the contracts, the potential for profit maximization, the dilution of public oversight – these were conveniently glossed over, buried beneath a mountain of seemingly irrefutable data.

Kline himself would occasionally engage in these high-level discussions, not in the ostentatious display of a political rally, but in the hushed confines of private meetings. He would meet with senators and congressional leaders, his demeanor a carefully calibrated blend of cordiality and steely resolve. He wouldn't plead or cajole; he would present. He would lay out his vision, not as a personal ambition, but as an objective, data-driven necessity. He would speak of Halcyon's proven track record, of its ability to deliver complex projects on time and under budget, of its commitment to national progress. He would offer his "expertise" freely, framing it as a patriotic duty to help the nation achieve the same level of operational excellence that characterized his own empire.

These meetings were masterclasses in subtle coercion. Kline understood that politicians operated within a complex ecosystem of competing interests and personal ambitions. He didn't need to threaten; he simply needed to present an offer that was too lucrative to refuse, or a consequence of inaction that was too dire to contemplate. For those who embraced his vision, the rewards were manifold: access to Halcyon's vast resources, favorable media coverage amplified by their well-oiled PR machine, and the quiet assurance of continued financial support. For those who resisted, the consequences were less overt but no less potent. Their campaign contributions might mysteriously dwindle, their legislative efforts might face unexpected roadblocks, and whispers of their "obstructionism" might begin to circulate in the very media outlets that amplified Kline's message.

His approach to defense policy was particularly effective. He would champion initiatives that inherently benefited Halcyon, framing them not as self-serving proposals but as vital necessities for national security. He would advocate for the development of new weapons systems, for increased military spending, for a more aggressive foreign policy – all while subtly ensuring that Halcyon's proprietary technologies and manufacturing capabilities were positioned as indispensable components of any such strategy. He didn't need to directly lobby for Halcyon's contracts; he simply needed to shape the geopolitical landscape in such a way that Halcyon's products and services became the inevitable solution.

This was corporate warfare transposed onto the national stage. Kline was no longer merely competing with other defense contractors; he was competing for the very definition of national interest. He was shaping the narrative, not just about his company, but about the nation itself, framing its challenges and opportunities through the lens of corporate efficiency and strategic advantage. The language he employed was always carefully chosen. He spoke of "streamlining the defense industrial base," of "leveraging private sector innovation," of "creating a more agile and responsive military." These were not the pronouncements of a businessman seeking profit; they were the pronouncements of a statesman, a visionary, charting a course for national strength and prosperity.

The recruitment of former government officials and military brass into Halcyon's ranks further cemented its political clout. These individuals, privy to the inner workings of defense procurement and legislative processes, provided invaluable intelligence and an established network of contacts. They lent an air of credibility and gravitas to Halcyon's lobbying efforts, presenting themselves not as mercenaries, but as patriots dedicated to serving the nation's best interests through their continued affiliation with a forward-thinking enterprise.

Kline, a master of psychological manipulation, understood the power of perceived authority and ensured that Halcyon's messaging was delivered not just by corporate spokespeople, but by men and women who had once worn the uniform or occupied positions of public trust.

This intricate dance of influence, played out with the precision of a high-stakes chess match, was steadily paving the way for Kline's ultimate ambition. He was not merely building a lobbying powerhouse; he was laying the groundwork for his own direct entry into the political arena. Every dollar spent, every politician courted, every policy shaped was a carefully placed brick in the foundation of his grand political edifice. He was demonstrating, not through promises but through tangible results, that his "business-first" principles, honed in the crucible of corporate competition, were the very principles the nation needed to thrive. Halcyon's ascent as a political force was, in essence, the preamble to Victor Kline's own political ascent, a meticulously orchestrated prelude to his grand unveiling on the national stage. He was no longer just a titan of industry; he was becoming a force that could bend the arc of national policy, a precursor to the man who would ultimately seek to wield its full power.

The air in the grand ballroom, usually thick with the clinking of champagne flutes and the murmur of polite conversation, now hummed with a different kind of energy. It was the resonance of a carefully orchestrated symphony, each note precisely timed, each instrument playing its part in Victor Kline's grand composition. He stood on a stage, bathed in a spotlight that seemed to sculpt his features into an image of unassailable resolve, and he spoke not of profit margins or shareholder dividends, but of a nation adrift. His voice, amplified and broadcast across a carefully selected audience of influencers, policymakers, and media personalities, carried a message of profound urgency.

"We live in an age of unprecedented complexity," Kline began, his tone measured yet firm, a practiced cadence designed to instill confidence. "The currents of global change are turbulent, the demands on our society ever-increasing. We are bombarded by information, yet clarity eludes us. We yearn for progress yet often find ourselves mired in stagnation. The very fabric of our security, both domestic and international, feels perpetually tested, vulnerable to forces we struggle to comprehend, let alone control." He paused, letting the weight of his words settle, observing the nodding heads, the serious expressions etched on the faces before him. This was not merely a speech; it was an invocation, a diagnosis of societal malaise for which he, and only he, possessed the cure.

His narrative was built on a foundation of anxiety, a shrewd exploitation of the widespread unease that permeated the national consciousness. The relentless churn of the 24-hour news cycle, the dizzying pace of technological advancement, the ever-present specter of global instability – these were not abstract concepts for Kline. They were the raw materials of his political appeal, the fertile ground upon which he would sow the seeds of his dominion. He understood that in times of uncertainty, humanity craved a lighthouse, a steady hand to guide them through the storm. He offered himself as that very beacon, a figure of unwavering strength and decisive action.

"For too long," he continued, his voice rising with a controlled passion, "we have allowed inertia to dictate our course. We have witnessed the erosion of efficiency, the proliferation of red tape, the paralysis of decision-making by committees that seem more interested in process than in progress. Our systems, once designed for clarity and purpose, have become bloated, labyrinthine, and ultimately, incapable of meeting the challenges of the twenty-first century." He painted a picture of a government choked by its own inefficiency, a sprawling bureaucracy that stifled innovation and squandered precious resources. It was a potent image, one that resonated deeply with a populace increasingly frustrated by perceived governmental incompetence.

His solution, predictably, was order. Not the messy, imperfect order of democratic discourse and compromise, but a pristine, rational order, imposed from above. "What we need is not more debate, but decisive action. Not more committees, but clear accountability. Not more studies, but solutions that are empirically validated and demonstrably effective." He spoke of the principles that had guided Halcyon Defense Systems to unparalleled success – principles of rigorous analysis, streamlined operations, and an unwavering focus on measurable outcomes. These were the very same principles, he argued, that the nation desperately needed to embrace.

"Imagine a government that functions with the precision of a finely tuned instrument," Kline's voice became almost hypnotic. "A system where decisions are made based on data, not on partisan bickering. Where resources are allocated efficiently, ensuring that every dollar spent yields maximum impact. Where the security of our citizens, the integrity of our borders, and the strength of our global standing are not subject to the whims of political expediency, but are guaranteed by a robust, streamlined, and incorruptible framework." This was the promise: a return to a golden age of certainty, a technologically advanced utopia governed by logic and efficiency, a world free from the anxieties that kept so many awake at night.

He meticulously avoided any discussion of the human element, the messy, unpredictable nature of human beings and their aspirations. Empathy, compassion, the inherent dignity of individuals – these were absent from his lexicon. His vision was one of systems, of processes, of optimized outputs. He spoke of "citizens" not as individuals with unique needs and desires, but as units within a larger operational matrix, to be managed, directed, and ultimately, to contribute to the grand design. His rhetoric was devoid of nuance, preferring instead the stark clarity of black and white, of problem and solution, of chaos and order.

The appeal of this message was undeniable. In a society grappling with the aftermath of economic downturns, the unsettling realities of a rapidly changing world, and the erosion of trust in established institutions, Kline's promise of order was a siren song. He offered a seemingly simple, decisive path forward, a stark contrast to the often ambiguous and frustrating realities of political life. His followers were not necessarily drawn to him by a shared ideology, but by a shared yearning for certainty, for a strong leader who promised to sweep away the complexities and deliver tangible results. They craved the assurance that someone, somewhere, had a plan, a solid, unbreakable plan.

"We will dismantle the bureaucratic ossification that has held us back," Kline declared, his gaze sweeping across the room, locking onto individual faces as if delivering a personal vow. "We will embrace innovation, not as a buzzword, but as a fundamental operating principle. We will prioritize security, not as a matter of political debate, but as an absolute prerequisite for prosperity and progress. And we will do so with an unwavering commitment to effectiveness, measuring our success not by intentions, but by tangible outcomes." He was presenting himself as a surgeon, ready to cut away the diseased tissue of inefficiency and corruption, leaving behind a healthier, stronger nation.

His vision of "data-driven governance" was particularly compelling. In an era where information was abundant but often overwhelming, the idea of a rational, objective system making decisions based on pure data held immense appeal. It promised to remove the subjective biases, the personal vendettas, the ideological blind spots that often-plagued political decision-making. It was a vision of governance as a science, precise and predictable, a stark departure from the often-chaotic art of politics.

"We will create a framework where every policy, every initiative, is rigorously tested against objective metrics," Kline elaborated, his tone becoming almost evangelical. "We will identify what works, and we will amplify it. We will identify what does not work, and we will eliminate it. This is not about ideology; it is about results. This is about ensuring that our nation, our society, moves forward with a clear, unwavering trajectory towards strength, prosperity, and security." The language was seductive, devoid of emotional appeals, relying instead on the cold logic of efficiency and progress. It was a language that promised clarity in a confusing world, a sense of control in an era of perceived chaos.

He skillfully framed his own corporate successes as proof of his capabilities, the bedrock upon which his political legitimacy would be built. Halcyon Defense Systems, under his leadership, had become a paragon of efficiency, a testament to the power of his "business-first" approach. He implied, subtly but undeniably, that the same principles that had made Halcyon a global powerhouse could, and would, be applied to the governance of the entire nation. This was not an act of hubris, he seemed to suggest, but a patriotic duty, an obligation to share his unique expertise for the betterment of all.

"My experience has taught me that clear objectives, rigorous analysis, and decisive execution are the cornerstones of success," Kline asserted, his words resonating with an almost paternalistic authority. "These are not principles confined to the corporate world; they are universal laws of achievement. And it is precisely these principles that I intend to bring to the heart of our national governance. We have the capacity, the ingenuity, and the will to build a nation that is not only secure and prosperous, but one that is a model of rational, efficient, and purposeful leadership for the world."

The applause that followed was not merely polite; it was fervent, a wave of affirmation that washed over the stage. The carefully selected audience, a microcosm of the power brokers and influencers Kline sought to sway, understood the implications. They saw in his message not just a political platform, but a blueprint for a new era, an era where the perceived failings of traditional politics would be replaced by the unassailable logic of corporate strategy. They saw the promise of order, a comforting certainty in an uncertain world, and they were ready to embrace it. Kline, observing the scene with a subtle, almost imperceptible smile, knew that his message had landed. The seeds of his political ascent, sown in the fertile ground of public anxiety, had begun to sprout, promising a harvest of power cultivated through the unwavering pursuit of order.

The subtle currents of influence, so carefully cultivated by Victor Kline, were already rippling through the nation's corridors of power, long before his name was etched onto any ballot. His pronouncements, delivered from the polished stage of corporate soirées and economic forums, were no longer mere analyses of market trends; they were prescient pronouncements, whispered predictions that often became self-fulfilling prophecies. He possessed an uncanny knack for identifying the seismic shifts on the horizon – technological disruptions, geopolitical realignments, the subtle tremors of societal discontent – and, more importantly, for positioning himself and his vast resources to not only weather these storms but to steer them. This prescience was not born of luck; it was the product of a meticulous, data-driven intelligence apparatus, an extension of Halcyon Defense Systems' most advanced strategic planning divisions, now repurposed to dissect the complex ecosystem of public sentiment and political maneuvering.

His boardrooms had become laboratories for societal engineering. The same rigorous methodologies employed to forecast demand for advanced weaponry or to model the impact of supply chain disruptions were now deployed to understand the underlying anxieties and aspirations of the populace. Sentiment analysis algorithms, once designed to gauge reactions to new defense contracts, were now sifting through millions of online conversations, identifying fault lines in public opinion, and pinpointing the precise levers that could be pulled to shift collective perception. Market research, typically focused on consumer behavior, was now delving into the psychological drivers of voter allegiance. Kline wasn't just observing the world; he was actively mapping its vulnerabilities, charting pathways for intervention, and preparing to exploit them.

The economic levers at his disposal were particularly potent. Halcyon's immense financial footprint, its intricate network of subsidiaries and investments, provided him with a unique vantage point. He could, with strategic adjustments to capital allocation, subtly influence entire sectors of the economy. A sudden increase in investment in a particular technology could accelerate its development, making it seem like an inevitable future and shaping public discourse around its merits. Conversely, a withdrawal of funding from an emerging industry could stifle its growth, effectively preventing it from ever becoming a credible competitor or even a viable topic of discussion. These were not overt acts of political interference, but rather the quiet, almost imperceptible adjustments of market forces, guided by an unseen hand that understood the symbiotic relationship between economic power and political will.

Consider the burgeoning field of renewable energy. While many were focused on the technological advancements and environmental benefits, Kline's strategists were dissecting the economic dependencies, the geopolitical implications of resource control, and the public perception of nascent technologies. Halcyon, through a series of shell corporations and diversified investment funds, began to strategically acquire interests in key components of the emerging solar and wind industries – rare earth minerals, advanced battery technology, even crucial transmission infrastructure. Simultaneously, they subtly amplified narratives that highlighted the perceived unreliability and costliness of these alternatives, while simultaneously championing a more "stable" and "proven" energy future, often implicitly linked to the fossil fuel sectors where Halcyon had long-standing, albeit often disguised, interests. The goal wasn't necessarily to halt the progress of renewables, but to control its pace, to ensure that any transition was managed in a way that maximized profit and maintained a predictable, stable energy landscape, one that would not disrupt the established order he intended to inherit.

This strategic financial maneuvering wasn't confined to single industries. Kline understood that public opinion was often tethered to economic well-being. By identifying regions or demographic groups disproportionately affected by economic downturns, he could then deploy resources – not as overt political donations, but as carefully placed investments in job creation programs, community development initiatives, or even philanthropic ventures that carried his subtle imprint. These actions, while appearing altruistic, served a dual purpose. They fostered goodwill and created a network of indebted beneficiaries, individuals and communities who saw Kline as a benefactor, a source of stability in a turbulent economic climate. More importantly, they provided him with invaluable data on local sentiment, on the specific grievances and aspirations that could be amplified or assuaged to achieve broader political objectives.

The media landscape, too, was a canvas upon which Kline's influence was being painted. His team had meticulously analyzed the fractured media ecosystem, identifying influential outlets, key journalists, and emerging social media platforms. They didn't engage in blunt-force propaganda. Instead, they employed a sophisticated strategy of information cultivation. Think tanks, ostensibly independent and funded by opaque foundations linked to Kline's network, began to churn out policy papers, economic analyses, and "expert" opinions that consistently echoed the themes he wished to promote: the need for strong leadership, the dangers of unchecked bureaucracy, the paramount importance of national security and economic stability. These papers, meticulously researched and presented with an air of academic authority, found their way into the hands of journalists, became fodder for op-eds, and provided the intellectual scaffolding for the narratives Kline sought to embed in the public consciousness.

Furthermore, his understanding of algorithmic amplification was paramount. His teams weren't just consuming content; they were learning how to engineer its dissemination. They identified the engagement metrics that algorithms prioritized – shares, likes, comments, watch time – and then subtly tailored content, often through proxies and seemingly independent online personalities, to maximize these metrics.

Articles that questioned the efficacy of government programs, that highlighted the perceived inefficiencies of democratic processes, or that raised alarms about national vulnerabilities would be strategically seeded, boosted, and amplified, appearing with uncanny frequency across social media feeds and news aggregators. This created an echo chamber, not solely of misinformation, but of a carefully curated perspective, one that reinforced Kline's vision of a nation in need of decisive, executive leadership.

The pressure he could exert was often invisible, a silent weight on the scales of decision-making. Politicians and policymakers, aware of his vast economic power and his extensive network of contacts, would find their proposed initiatives subtly scrutinized, their funding sources gently questioned, their public image preemptively shaped by the very narratives his network had been propagating. A legislator who dared to challenge a policy favored by Kline might suddenly find his pet projects facing unexpected hurdles, their key campaign donors expressing sudden "concerns," or their past statements being selectively unearthed and amplified by media outlets that had become accustomed to echoing his preferred narratives. This was not overt blackmail; it was the subtle application of systemic pressure, the kind that made individuals self-censor, that encouraged compliance without the need for explicit threats.

Kline's understanding of human psychology, honed by years of negotiating complex business deals and managing vast numbers of employees, allowed him to anticipate reactions and preemptively counter dissent. He understood that fear was a powerful motivator, but so was hope. He offered not just the promise of order, but the tantalizing prospect of a return to a perceived golden age, a time of uncomplicated prosperity and unassailable strength. His strategies were designed to tap into these deep-seated desires, to create a narrative so compelling, so seemingly rational, that it bypassed the critical faculties and appealed directly to the primal need for security and belonging.

The "business-first" philosophy, so central to Halcyon's success, was now being applied to the very art of governance. Kline viewed the nation not as a complex tapestry of individual lives and aspirations, but as a vast, inefficient enterprise that required a decisive, data-driven CEO. His pronouncements at corporate retreats were no longer just about shareholder value; they were thinly veiled manifestos for national leadership. He spoke of optimizing resource allocation, of streamlining bureaucratic processes, of implementing performance metrics for public servants, all couched in the language of fiscal responsibility and national progress. These ideas, when articulated with his characteristic confidence and backed by the seemingly irrefutable success of Halcyon, began to seep into the political discourse, resonating with those who felt disenfranchised by the perceived failures of traditional politics.

He understood that true power lay not just in holding office, but in shaping the very landscape upon which that office operated. His influence was the unseen architect, laying the foundations of public opinion, carefully constructing the framework of economic expectation, and meticulously charting the course of political discourse. He was the master puppeteer, not pulling strings for immediate gratification, but orchestrating a grand performance, a subtle yet inexorable march towards a future he had designed, a future where the principles of control, efficiency, and measurable outcomes would transcend the boardroom and dictate the destiny of a nation. His ascent was not a sudden storm; it was a slow, deliberate tide, rising with an unstoppable, almost imperceptible, force.

Chapter 7

The Quiet Resistance

The polished veneer of Halcyon Defense Systems, once a symbol of innovation and integrity, had, for many, become a suffocating shroud. Victor Kline's ascent, swift and seemingly absolute, had not been a gentle transition but a brutal reshaping. While the stock market responded with jubilant surges and financial analysts spoke of unprecedented efficiency, a counter-current of disquiet began to stir within the very heart of the corporation. It was a quiet resistance, born not of grand pronouncements or public protests, but of whispered conversations in hushed corners, of shared glances laden with unspoken understanding, and of a collective memory that refused to be extinguished.

For those who had been at Halcyon before Kline's tenure, the transformation was a bitter pill. They remembered a different company, one where intellectual curiosity was prized, where collaboration trumped cutthroat competition, and where the pursuit of groundbreaking technology was driven by a genuine desire to serve. They recalled engineers who would spend sleepless nights hunched over schematics, not out of fear of reprisal, but out of an infectious passion for discovery. They remembered a sense of camaraderie, a shared purpose that transcended individual ambition. Now, under Kline's regime, those very qualities were deemed inefficient, sentimental, and ultimately, detrimental to the bottom line. Innovation was no longer organic; it was a dictated directive, its success measured not by its ingenuity but by its immediate profitability. The soul of Halcyon, for these veterans, had been systematically stripped away, replaced by a soulless, hyper-efficient machine.

Among this group was Fiona Answan, a senior project manager in the advanced materials division. She had joined Halcyon fresh out of her postdoctoral studies, drawn by its reputation for fostering groundbreaking research. For twenty years, she had dedicated herself to pushing the boundaries of what was possible, her work often characterized by its long-term vision and its commitment to scientific rigor. She had seen brilliant minds flourish and groundbreaking projects come to fruition, not through aggressive management, but through nurturing environments and shared dedication. Then came Kline. His initial pronouncements were about "streamlining operations" and "maximizing shareholder value." But soon, the language shifted. Projects deemed not immediately lucrative were shelved, regardless of their potential long-term impact. Promising researchers, those who dared to question the new direction, found themselves marginalized, their careers stalled or, in some cases, abruptly ended. Fiona watched as colleagues, once vibrant and engaged, became withdrawn and cautious, their creative spark dimmed by the oppressive atmosphere. She saw the very fabric of the company she had helped build being unraveled, replaced by a rigid hierarchy and a culture of fear. The memory of the old Halcyon, the one that valued ingenuity and dedication, became a silent torment, a constant reminder of what had been lost.

Similarly, Robert Sterling, a seasoned cybersecurity expert who had been instrumental in developing Halcyon's early defensive protocols, felt a profound sense of betrayal. He had built his career on the principle of protecting sensitive information, of safeguarding the company's intellectual property with unwavering vigilance. He understood the nuances of digital warfare, the constant evolution of threats, and the critical importance of ethical data handling. Kline's approach, however, was one of ruthless pragmatism, where data was seen as a commodity to be exploited rather than a trust to be guarded.

Sterling had witnessed firsthand how Kline's directives led to the aggressive acquisition and utilization of personal data, often with dubious consent, blurring the lines between security and surveillance. He had voiced his concerns, cautiously at first, then with increasing urgency, only to be met with dismissive rhetoric about "progress" and "competitive necessity." The irony was not lost on him: the very systems he had painstakingly designed to protect Halcyon were now being subtly repurposed by Kline for his own data-gathering machinations, extending his reach far beyond the company's internal networks. The ethical compromises, the erosion of privacy – these were not abstract concepts to Sterling; they were the direct consequences of a philosophy that prioritized profit and control above all else. He saw the potential for catastrophic misuse, for the weaponization of personal information on an unprecedented scale, and the gnawing realization that he had, in part, enabled this came as a heavy burden.

Beyond the long-term employees, there were others whose lives had been irrevocably altered by Kline's maneuvers. These were the individuals who had been deemed expendable, whose departments had been downsized, or whose livelihoods had been sacrificed on the altar of efficiency. There was Gigi Jones, a single mother who had worked in accounting for fifteen years, only to be laid off with a cursory severance package when her entire team was outsourced. Her sense of security, her ability to provide for her children, had been shattered in an instant. She bore the emotional scars of that dismissal, the feeling of worthlessness that permeated her days. She saw Kline's carefully crafted image of a benevolent corporate leader as a cruel mockery, a public relations charade that masked a brutal disregard for the human cost of his ambitions. Her resentment, born of personal devastation, was a potent fuel for the growing dissent.

Then there was Don Checkers, a brilliant young engineer whose innovative project, poised to revolutionize clean energy storage, was abruptly terminated. Kline's rationale, communicated through a sycophantic middle manager, was that the project lacked immediate market viability. The truth, as Don suspected, was far more cynical. Kline's investments were heavily weighted towards established fossil fuel interests, and this burgeoning renewable technology posed a subtle, long-term threat to that portfolio. The abrupt cancellation, the dismissal of years of dedicated work and potential for a sustainable future, left Don disillusioned and angry. He saw the blatant hypocrisy, the selective application of "progress" that served only to enrich a select few at the expense of global well-being. His voice, though silenced within Halcyon, began to find an outlet in anonymous online forums, articulating the technical and ethical failures of Kline's leadership.

These disparate threads of discontent, woven from memories of a better past, personal devastation, and ethical revulsion, began to coalesce. They found common ground in their shared opposition to Kline's authoritarian style and his perceived abandonment of Halcyon's founding principles. The challenge, however, was immense. Kline's control was pervasive, his surveillance mechanisms sophisticated, and his network of loyalists, rewarded for their unswerving obedience, was extensive. Overt acts of rebellion were not only futile but dangerous, likely to result in swift and decisive retribution. Thus, the resistance had to be subtle, its movements cloaked in a deliberate anonymity, its communication channels carefully disguised.

The initial sparks of this quiet resistance were fanned in the digital ether, a space where physical proximity and traceable actions could be minimized. Anonymous online forums, encrypted messaging applications, and burner email accounts became the clandestine meeting grounds. Here, individuals like Fiona, Robert, Gigi, and Don, and many others whose names would never be known to each other in the 'real world,' began to share their experiences and concerns. They discovered a shared language of frustration, a common understanding of the subtle cues that signaled Kline's overreach. They used coded phrases, referencing old Halcyon projects or historical company milestones as veiled metaphors for their current predicament. A mention of "Project Nightingale," an old, ambitious but ultimately shelved research initiative, could signify a desire to reignite a lost spark of innovation. A reference to the "Founders' Charter," a document that had once emphasized ethical conduct and employee well-being, became shorthand for their shared values.

Fiona, with her analytical mind, began to subtly gather evidence. Not in a way that would trigger any alarms, but by meticulously documenting deviations from established protocols, by flagging inconsistencies in financial reports that hinted at internal manipulations, and by noting the patterns of promotion and demotion that seemed to reward blind loyalty over genuine competence. She would leave these observations in encrypted files, shared through secure channels with a trusted few, creating a nascent repository of knowledge about Kline's operations. These weren't grand exposés, but small, seemingly innocuous pieces of data that, when pieced together, began to paint a disturbing picture.

Robert, drawing on his expertise, became instrumental in establishing secure communication lines. He understood the vulnerabilities of corporate networks and the ubiquitous reach of electronic surveillance. He guided the formation of encrypted communication protocols, advising on best practices for anonymizing digital footprints. He even devised a system of 'dead drops' for sensitive physical information, utilizing seemingly innocuous locations within the vast Halcyon campus – a disused storage closet, a rarely visited corner of the archives – where encrypted USB drives could be exchanged without detection. His knowledge of the system he helped build was now being used to subvert it.

Gigi, though no longer an employee, retained a network of contacts within the company, particularly among the administrative and support staff who often saw and heard more than their supervisors realized. She became a crucial conduit for information flowing from the inside, her personal bitterness channeled into a quiet determination to expose the truth. She would receive coded messages – a particular phrase in a seemingly routine interoffice memo, a specific sequence of numbers in a public announcement – that signaled distress or a need for information. These messages, passed through a chain of trusted intermediaries, would eventually find their way to Fiona or Robert, adding another layer to their growing understanding of the internal maneuvers.

The early alliances were tentative, built on a foundation of shared grievances rather than established trust. There were inherent risks, the constant fear of betrayal or accidental exposure. Every interaction was a calculated risk. A casual conversation in the break room could be a trap. An unexpected question from a supervisor could be a probe. The tension was palpable, a constant hum beneath the surface of forced civility. Yet, the shared purpose, the desperate hope for a return to something resembling integrity, propelled them forward. They were a ghost in the machine, a silent insurgency operating in the shadows, its ultimate aim not yet fully defined, but its core conviction firm: Victor Kline's reign of efficient autocracy could not, and would not, last forever. The seeds of discontent, sown in the fertile ground of betrayal and disillusionment, were beginning to sprout, preparing to challenge the seemingly unassailable monolith that Halcyon had become.

The collective memory of Halcyon, a tapestry woven from years of shared endeavor and mutual respect, was the most potent weapon in the nascent resistance's arsenal. Victor Kline, in his relentless pursuit of efficiency and control, had attempted to systematically erase this history. He had rebranded the company not as a continuum of its past, but as a blank slate, a machine re-engineered from the ground up to serve his singular vision. This manufactured present, devoid of context and consequence, was his foundation. But foundations, however imposing, could be undermined, and the resistance recognized that the bedrock of Kline's power lay precisely in his ability to control the narrative, to suppress the inconvenient truths of Halcyon's legacy.

They understood that memory was not merely a passive recollection of events; it was an active force, capable of shaping perception, inspiring action, and anchoring individuals to a shared identity. Kline's strategy was to atomize the workforce, to isolate individuals by convincing them that their present disaffection was an anomaly, a personal failing rather than a systemic rot. The resistance, conversely, sought to re-forge those broken connections, to remind people that they were not alone in their disillusionment, that their feelings of loss and betrayal were echoes of a shared experience. They began to cultivate and disseminate these memories, not as a nostalgic lament for a bygone era, but as a vital counter-narrative, a living testament to what Halcyon had once been, and what it could, and should, be again.

The dissemination of these memories was a delicate operation, a clandestine act of cultural preservation. It began in the hushed digital spaces where the resistance convened. Encrypted messages would carry not just strategic plans or intelligence, but also poignant anecdotes, carefully chosen excerpts from old company newsletters, or even scanned pages from the original employee handbook, its ink faded but its message still vibrant. These were not simply pieces of trivia; they were potent reminders of Halcyon's ethical moorings, its original charter that spoke of innovation fueled by curiosity, of collaboration built on trust, and of a commitment to not just technological advancement, but to a greater good.

Fiona, with her meticulous nature, became a curator of these historical fragments. She would meticulously cross-reference dates and project names, ensuring the accuracy of the memories she helped to resurface. She remembered the early days of the 'Quantum Leap' initiative, a project that had aimed to develop a revolutionary form of energy storage. It had been a long, arduous process, riddled with setbacks, but the atmosphere in the labs had been one of unyielding optimism. Engineers and scientists from different departments had freely shared their findings, collaborating with a shared sense of purpose, even though the immediate financial returns were uncertain. Kline, of course, had deemed it a "pet project," a drain on resources, and had summarily shut it down, reallocating its funding to more immediately profitable, albeit less transformative, ventures. When Fiona shared a digitized photograph of the original 'Quantum Leap' team, faces young and full of earnest determination, juxtaposed with the stark, sterile corporate branding of the Kline era, it was a silent but powerful indictment. The image resonated, sparking conversations about the loss of such audacious, long-term thinking.

Robert, in his own way, contributed by recalling the stringent ethical guidelines that had governed data security in Halcyon's early years. He would share stories of the "Fortress Protocol," a comprehensive set of rules he and his team had painstakingly developed, emphasizing privacy, consent, and the responsible handling of sensitive information. He would recount the intense debates they had engaged in, the rigorous vetting processes for any data acquisition, all designed to ensure that Halcyon's technological prowess was wielded with integrity. He would contrast these memories with the current reality, where data was treated as a raw commodity, harvested and exploited with a blatant disregard for individual privacy.

These recollections served to remind those who were aware of Kline's current practices that what was happening was not an unavoidable evolution, but a deliberate betrayal of established principles. He once shared an excerpt from a board meeting minute from fifteen years prior, where the then-CEO had emphatically stated, "Our greatest asset is not our technology, but the trust our clients place in us. That trust is non-negotiable." This simple statement, devoid of corporate jargon, cut through the current propaganda with stark clarity.

Gigi, despite her forced departure, maintained a connection to the company's human infrastructure. She would relay anecdotes from former colleagues who still worked there, tales that underscored the camaraderie that had once defined Halcyon. She remembered the annual company picnics, not as mandatory corporate events, but as genuine celebrations of shared achievement, where executives mingled freely with junior staff, and where the focus was on connection and appreciation, not on forced networking. She recalled the mentorship programs, where seasoned employees took genuine interest in nurturing the next generation of talent, not for any immediate performance metrics, but out of a belief in fostering a sustainable and knowledgeable workforce. These were the threads that bound people together, the informal networks of support and shared experience that Kline had systematically dismantled in his quest for hierarchical control.

Gigi's stories, often delivered with a quiet wistfulness, served as potent reminders of the human element that had been so brutally excised from the corporate equation. She often spoke of how, during her time in accounting, a small, almost ritualistic act of kindness by a senior manager – anonymously covering the cost of a necessary medical procedure for a junior employee – had ripple effects of loyalty and dedication for years. It was a stark contrast to the current practice of offering minimal severance packages to long-term employees deemed surplus to requirements.

Don, the young engineer whose clean energy project had been unceremoniously axed, found solace in recalling the early days of Halcyon's commitment to sustainability. He remembered when the company had actively invested in green initiatives, not just for public relations, but because it was genuinely believed to be the right thing to do. He'd even unearthed an old internal documentary, produced in the early 2000s, that showcased Halcyon's pioneering work in developing eco-friendly manufacturing processes.

The documentary, filled with interviews of employees expressing pride in the company's ethical stance, was a stark contrast to Kline's current embrace of polluting industries and his dismissal of environmental concerns as an impediment to profit. Don would share clips from this documentary, allowing the younger employees, who had never known this version of Halcyon, to see the stark transformation. They would watch, their faces, a mixture of disbelief and dawning comprehension, as the charismatic faces of the past spoke of a future where profit and purpose were not mutually exclusive.

These shared memories, carefully curated and strategically disseminated, served multiple crucial functions. Firstly, they provided a shared frame of reference, a common ground upon which individuals could connect. By reminding people of the values, they once held dear – integrity, collaboration, innovation, and ethical conduct – the resistance fostered a sense of collective identity, reminding individuals that their grievances were not isolated incidents but part of a broader pattern of decline. This shared narrative chipped away at the isolation that Kline actively cultivated.

Secondly, these memories acted as a powerful counter-narrative to Kline's carefully constructed mythology. His public pronouncements spoke of progress, efficiency, and bold new directions. But the memories recalled a different kind of progress, one rooted in substance and ethical consideration, not just in financial metrics. They highlighted the human cost of Kline's "efficiency," the sacrifices of dedicated employees and the abandonment of the very principles that had made Halcyon a respected entity. They exposed the manufactured reality for what it was: a carefully crafted illusion designed to mask a profound betrayal of the company's soul.

Thirdly, and perhaps most importantly, these shared recollections served to re-ignite hope. By reminding people of what Halcyon had once been, they offered a tangible vision of what it could be again. They provided a benchmark against which Kline's current regime could be measured and found wanting. The stories of past triumphs, of challenges overcome through collective effort and unwavering dedication served as a potent antidote to the pervasive sense of helplessness that Kline's authoritarian control had instilled. They demonstrated that change was possible, that the current state of affairs was not immutable, and that the spirit of Halcyon, though dormant, was not extinguished.

The act of sharing these memories was an act of quiet defiance, a reclaiming of history from those who sought to erase it. It was a subtle but profound assertion of agency, a refusal to be defined solely by the present reality imposed by Kline. Each shared anecdote, each unearthed document, each resurrected photograph, was a brick in the foundation of a new, albeit clandestine, Halcyon – one built not on fear and control, but on the enduring power of shared memory and the unwavering belief in a better future. The resistance understood that Kline could control the present, but the past, once awakened, held an undeniable power to shape the future. They were carefully, deliberately, reawakening it.

The resistance understood that direct confrontation, in the early stages, was a swift path to annihilation. Victor Kline's reign at Halcyon was built on a foundation of absolute control, his gaze constantly sweeping over every facet of the organization, seeking out and eradicating any hint of dissent. Overt rebellion, therefore, was akin to a single ember challenging a raging inferno – destined to be extinguished before it could even truly catch. Instead, the strategy that emerged from the hushed corners of Halcyon, from the whispered exchanges in dimly lit stairwells and the coded messages passed through digital shadows, was one of subtle, persistent defiance. It was a strategy of a thousand tiny cuts, a thousand almost imperceptible tremors designed to destabilize the monolithic structure Kline had so meticulously erected.

One of the most insidious tools of Kline's control was the "Loyalty Metric." This algorithm, supposedly a neutral arbiter of employee dedication, was in reality a blunt instrument wielded to identify and marginalize those who did not exhibit unwavering subservience. It tracked everything from email response times and participation in corporate-sponsored "wellness" initiatives to the perceived enthusiasm in video calls.

For the resistance, however, this metric became a target. Robert brought in Kathy Umpire, a software engineer, who had intimate knowledge of data streams and her uncanny ability to find the cracks in any system, began a painstaking process of introducing subtle inaccuracies. It wasn't about outright falsification, which would be too easily detected. Instead, it involved a delicate manipulation of timing, a slight delay in forwarding non-critical information, a carefully timed "system glitch" that momentarily interrupted data flow, or the strategically placed "auto-reply" that, while technically compliant, added a fraction of a second to response times.

These were infinitesimal deviations, individually meaningless, but collectively they began to muddy the waters of the Loyalty Metric. A pattern of minor, almost imperceptible delays, a few too many "unforeseen technical difficulties" in capturing an employee's "engagement metrics" during a particularly tedious all-hands meeting – these small acts of sabotage, spread across a network of like-minded individuals, began to paint a less definitive picture of dissent. The aim was not to make everyone appear loyal, but to introduce enough noise into the system that true loyalty, the genuine engagement with Halcyon's original purpose, could not be easily distinguished from passive compliance. The algorithm, designed to detect clear patterns of disengagement, found itself struggling to differentiate between genuine distraction and a calculated, almost artful, obfuscation.

Concurrently, the preservation of critical data became paramount. Kline's surveillance was pervasive. Every server, every shared drive, every communication channel was meticulously monitored. The resistance understood that knowledge, especially accurate knowledge of Halcyon's history, its ethical frameworks, and its past successes, was a dangerous weapon in their hands. Yet, how to safeguard it when the very infrastructure was compromised? This led to the development of what became known as the "Ghost Archives." These were not physical locations, but rather distributed, encrypted data caches, stored on personal devices, disguised within innocuous personal files, or even fragmented across numerous cloud storage services, each fragment rendered meaningless without the decryption key. Robert, drawing on his cybersecurity expertise, developed a series of sophisticated encryption protocols, far exceeding anything Halcyon officially sanctioned. The process was laborious, requiring meticulous attention to detail.

An engineer might spend an extra fifteen minutes each day, not at their workstation, but at home, meticulously transferring key documents – old project proposals that showcased genuine innovation, internal audit reports that hinted at past ethical lapses under previous, less draconian leadership, even records of employee training modules that emphasized collaborative problem-solving rather than top-down directives.

These files were then broken down into smaller, seemingly random pieces of data, embedded within playlists of obscure music, or hidden within the metadata of personal photographs. The intention was not to hoard information, but to ensure its survival, its availability should the opportunity arise to disseminate it more broadly. It was an act of digital Noah's Ark, preserving the essence of Halcyon's better self against the coming flood of Kline's revised history. The metadata of a family vacation photo might, to the untrained eye, reveal nothing of significance, yet to the initiated, it would unlock a fragment of the original "Aegis" project proposal, a groundbreaking initiative in data privacy that Kline had shelved within weeks of taking control.

The dissemination of information was equally fraught with peril. Standard email, instant messaging, and even internal forums were all traps, meticulously monitored. The resistance, therefore, relied on a patchwork of untraceable channels. Secure, end-to-end encrypted messaging apps, used only for pre-arranged, fleeting windows of communication, became commonplace. Disposable email addresses, created and discarded with a frequency that baffled the surveillance systems, served as rudimentary communication hubs.

More ingeniously, they leveraged the mundane. A particularly insightful critique of a recent policy change might be subtly woven into a comment on a shared document, disguised as a grammatical correction or a minor suggestion for improvement. A crucial piece of information about an impending restructuring might be passed through the comment section of a company-wide announcement for a new cafeteria menu, a seemingly innocuous observation about the "lack of variety" that, to the discerning eye, carried a double meaning.

Gigi, with her extensive network of contacts, both inside and outside the company, became adept at this form of deniable communication. A casual conversation at a coffee shop, ostensibly about weekend plans, could contain coded references to upcoming resistance activities. A "personal" social media post, seemingly a mundane update, might carry an embedded message within its hashtags or its carefully chosen emoji sequence. The key was plausible deniability. Each communication had to appear accidental, inconsequential, or purely personal, a deliberate misinterpretation of intent being the ultimate shield.

Perhaps the most pervasive form of subtle defiance was the deliberate misinterpretation of directives. Kline's pronouncements, delivered with his characteristic bombast, were often couched in corporate jargon that was intentionally vague, designed to allow for maximum latitude in implementation – a latitude that the resistance eagerly exploited. When Kline mandated a new, draconian "synergy initiative" aimed at forcing cross-departmental collaboration on every trivial task, the resistance responded not with outright refusal, but with an exaggerated, almost absurd adherence to the directive. Teams would schedule multiple hour-long meetings to discuss the optimal font size for a memo, meticulously document every single collaborative step taken in preparing a simple report, and inundate Kline's office with detailed "synergy reports" that highlighted every minute interaction. The sheer volume of bureaucratic overhead generated by this overzealous compliance choked the system, creating bottlenecks and delays that directly hindered Kline's much-vaunted pursuit of efficiency. It was a form of weaponized incompetence, where performing the task too well, in the spirit of Kline's own verbose pronouncements, became a form of sabotage.

Don, the young engineer whose innovative spirit had been stifled, found a particular satisfaction in this form of resistance. When tasked with "optimizing workflow" in a way that he knew would lead to data corruption, he would meticulously document every single potential risk, every possible consequence, presenting it not as a protest, but as a comprehensive risk-assessment report, filled with technical jargon that, while accurate, would take Kline's less technically inclined lieutenants days to decipher. He would then proceed with the directive, meticulously following every one of his own warnings, ensuring that the inevitable failure was well-documented and demonstrably linked to the original instruction, albeit in a way that could be attributed to "unforeseen complexities" rather than deliberate subversion.

These acts, seemingly small and insignificant in isolation, were the vital sparks in the suffocating darkness of Kline's regime. They were the quiet affirmations of an unextinguished spirit, the subtle reminders that the soul of Halcyon, though battered and bruised, was not yet dead. Each bypassed surveillance alert, each preserved data fragment, each misinterpreted directive was a victory, a testament to the enduring human capacity for resilience and ingenuity in the face of overwhelming control. It was the beginning of a war fought not with weapons, but with whispers, with code, and with the quiet refusal to be broken. It was the germination of the quiet resistance, its tendrils reaching out, unseen and unheard by the man at the top, but steadily weaving a network of defiance that would, in time, prove far more formidable than he could ever imagine.

The embers of dissent, fanned by Kathy's subtle manipulations of the Loyalty Metric and Robert's safeguarding of the Ghost Archives, were beginning to coalesce. In the shadowed corridors of Halcyon, where suspicion was a constant companion and surveillance a suffocating blanket, a more formalized, albeit still clandestine, faction was taking shape. They were the custodians of truth, the quiet architects of memory, bound by a shared understanding of the encroaching darkness and a fierce, unwavering resolve to preserve the light of what Halcyon once was. This was not a group defined by grand pronouncements or overt acts of rebellion, but by the painstaking, often tedious, labor of documentation. They were the silent historians, building a bulwark of evidence against the rising tide of Victor Kline's fabricated narrative.

At the heart of this nascent collective was a profound recognition: Kline's regime was not merely about present-day oppression; it was about the systematic erasure of history. His revisions to Halcyon's foundational principles, his rebranding of ethical lapses as "strategic pivots," and his suppression of any dissenting voice from the past were all part of a deliberate campaign to control the present by rewriting yesterday. The resistance, in its nascent form, understood that if Kline could successfully obliterate the memory of Halcyon's original ideals, he could solidify his dominion indefinitely. Therefore, the most crucial element of their quiet resistance became the preservation of that authentic past.

These were the 'Architects of Memory.' They were not necessarily the most outwardly defiant individuals, nor the ones orchestrating the daily disruptions. Instead, they were the quiet observers, the meticulous note-takers, the individuals who possessed a keen eye for detail and an almost sacred reverence for accuracy. Their work was a stark contrast to the ephemeral nature of digital communication that Kline so heavily monitored. They understood that digital footprints, while pervasive, were also malleable. A file could be deleted, a server wiped, an entire cloud account purged. True memory, they believed, required a more tangible, a more deeply embedded form of preservation.

The risks they undertook were immense, a constant tightrope walk over an abyss of immediate termination and far worse consequences. Each member of this group had identified their own unique methods of contributing to the collective archive, leveraging their roles and access within Halcyon to their advantage. There was Tanya Miller, recruited by Gigi, who was a senior archivist in the ostensibly benign Records and Information Management department. Her job, by design, was to catalog and preserve the company's historical documentation.

Under Kline's tenure, this meant the systematic weeding out of anything that did not align with his revised corporate doctrine. Tanya, however, operated with a dual mandate. Publicly, she followed the directives, discarding outdated reports and purging "redundant" files. Privately, she was a phantom curator, secretly duplicating and encrypting any document that spoke to Halcyon's earlier ethical standards, its innovative breakthroughs that had been sidelined, or its internal debates that had led to more inclusive and humane policies. She would meticulously scan old project proposals, early employee handbooks that spoke of collaboration

173

and autonomy, and minutes from board meetings that reflected a commitment to social responsibility – all relics of a Halcyon that was rapidly fading from public consciousness.

These digital ghosts were then embedded within seemingly innocuous personal files, disguised as research for a hobby, or meticulously fragmented and distributed across various secure personal cloud storage accounts, each requiring a specific key and a sequence of operations to reassemble. Her workspace, a sterile, climate-controlled environment designed for preservation, became a silent battleground where she fought to save the soul of the organization, one scanned document at a time.

Then there was Ben Rome, recruited by Fiona, who was a mid-level project manager in the Research and Development division. His role gave him access to the genesis of many of Halcyon's groundbreaking initiatives, projects that had been lauded in their time but were now conveniently forgotten or deliberately misrepresented by Kline's administration. Ben's contribution was to meticulously document the process of these projects, not just the final outcomes.

He would meticulously gather and anonymize communications – emails, internal memos, even transcribed snippets of informal conversations – that detailed the collaborative spirit, the ethical considerations, and the initial noble intentions behind these endeavors. He focused on the moments of genuine innovation, the instances where diverse teams worked together not under duress, but out of a shared passion for discovery. He understood that Kline's narrative often presented past successes as monolithic achievements driven by singular vision, a narrative that conveniently omitted the collective effort and the ethical underpinnings.

Ben's 'evidence' was not just the existence of these projects, but the very spirit in which they were conceived and executed. He would meticulously recreate timelines of decision-making, highlighting when ethical checkpoints were established and adhered to, and crucially, when they began to be circumvented under the new leadership. These records, painstakingly assembled and encrypted, were not intended for immediate release.

Their purpose was to serve as irrefutable proof, a historical counter-narrative waiting for the opportune moment to be unveiled. He was particularly adept at using the company's own project management software, creating "archival" versions of completed projects that contained hidden layers of metadata and embedded documents, shielded by layers of encryption so complex that they would appear as corrupted data to any casual observer, but which unlocked a treasure trove of information for those who knew how to access them.

The most dangerous aspect of their work was the inherent risk of discovery. Kline's security apparatus was not limited to algorithmic surveillance; it also included a network of informants and enforcers who actively sought out any anomaly. A prolonged, unexplained access to archival servers, a sudden surge in personal cloud storage usage, or even an unusual pattern of data encryption could trigger an alert. Each Architect of Memory had developed their own unique protocols for mitigating this risk. Tanya, for instance, would often perform her clandestine archival duties during designated "system maintenance" periods, when network activity was higher and individual actions were more easily masked. She also maintained a carefully curated digital footprint of personal projects, a decoy of innocuous research that kept her activity within acceptable parameters, a digital smokescreen designed to divert attention. Ben, on the other hand, meticulously staggered his data collection and encryption activities over weeks, even months, ensuring that no single day or week showed an anomalous spike. He would often work offline, compiling his findings on a secure, air-gapped device that was only connected to the network for brief, encrypted transfers, making it nearly impossible to trace the origin of the data.

The dissemination of their findings was as critical as their collection. While the primary purpose was preservation, the Architects understood that memory, to be effective, must eventually be shared. They established a covert communication channel, separate from the everyday resistance network, a highly secure, multi-layered communication system built on a foundation of quantum-resistant encryption. This was not for casual chatter; it was for the transfer of encrypted archival packets, for the coordination of decryption keys, and for the strategic planning of how and when this meticulously gathered evidence would be deployed.

Robert, with his unparalleled expertise, was the architect of this secure network, a digital fortress designed to withstand even Kline's most sophisticated attempts at infiltration. The communication itself was an art form. Messages were often broken into multiple fragments, sent through different channels at staggered times, and required a specific sequence of actions to reassemble, ensuring that even if one fragment was intercepted, it would be rendered meaningless without the others.

There was also a subtler form of memory preservation, one that involved the careful cultivation of personal narratives. Individuals like Suzi Norman, recruited by Don, had a knack for personal connection and storytelling, played a crucial role. She would engage employees, particularly those who were disillusioned or questioning Kline's direction, in seemingly casual conversations. These were not discussions about resistance tactics, but about the "good old days" at Halcyon. She would share anecdotes, not just about successful projects, but about the company's earlier values, the sense of community, the ethical considerations that were once paramount.

These stories, imbued with emotion and personal experience, served as powerful counterweights to Kline's sterile, data-driven narrative. Suzi understood that abstract principles could be easily dismissed or redefined, but personal stories, particularly those of former colleagues and respected leaders, held a potent emotional resonance. She would subtly weave in references to past ethical dilemmas and how they were resolved or highlight instances where Halcyon had prioritized employee well-being over profit, planting seeds of doubt about the current regime's motivations. These weren't just conversations; they were acts of oral history, ensuring that the spirit of Halcyon was kept alive in the hearts and minds of its people, even if it was no longer reflected in its official communications.

The Architects of Memory understood that their work was a long game. They were not expecting an immediate revolution, but a slow, steady erosion of Kline's fabricated reality. They were building a case, not for a courtroom, but for the court of public opinion, for the future historical record, and for the conscience of

176

Halcyon itself. Each encrypted file, each preserved anecdote, each carefully documented transgression was a brick in the foundation of a truth that would eventually, inevitably, come to light. They were the silent guardians of Halcyon's soul, ensuring that the memory of what was lost, and the potential for what could be reclaimed, would never be extinguished. Their dedication was fueled by a deep-seated belief that truth, like water, would always find a way to carve its path through even the hardest stone. And Kline, in his arrogance, believed he had built a fortress of lies, never realizing that the most formidable defenses were not made of concrete and steel, but of meticulously preserved memory, slowly but surely undermining the very foundations of his power.

The emotional toll of this clandestine work was significant. The constant vigilance, the fear of discovery, the isolation from colleagues who remained unaware of the true stakes – these were burdens that weighed heavily on each Architect. There were moments of profound doubt, times when the sheer scale of Kline's control seemed insurmountable, and the effort of preservation felt like a futile act against an overwhelming tide. Yet, what sustained them was the unwavering conviction that their work was essential, that the truth had intrinsic value, and that the memory of Halcyon's better self was a beacon worth protecting.

They found solace in each other, in the shared glances of understanding, in the brief, encrypted exchanges that confirmed their collective purpose. They were the hidden sisterhood and brotherhood, bound by a silent vow to remember, and to ensure that Halcyon's story, in its unvarnished, untainted form, would one day be told. This was the quiet resistance at its most profound, not just a defiance of present control, but a fierce reclamation of the past, a promise to the future that the original ideals of Halcyon would not be allowed to vanish into the sterile silence of Victor Kline's manufactured reality. Their efforts were the seeds of a reckoning, planted in the digital soil of a compromised organization, waiting for the opportune moment to bloom into a testament to enduring truth.

The realization dawned not as a sudden epiphany, but as a slow, pervasive understanding that permeated the hushed conversations and encrypted exchanges of the growing resistance. Victor Kline, in his relentless pursuit of control, had inadvertently woven a tapestry of immense complexity. His administrative edifice, designed to monitor, regulate, and ultimately suppress, was riddled with interdependencies, bureaucratic protocols, and algorithmic safeguards that, while intended to fortify his dominion, also presented a labyrinth of potential vulnerabilities. The Architects of Memory, and the broader network of quiet dissenters, began to perceive that within the very architecture of Kline's oppressive system lay the embryonic forms of its own subversion.

It was Kathy, with her intimate knowledge of the Loyalty Metric's intricate calculus, who first articulated this nascent strategic advantage. Her deep dive into the system's underlying algorithms, initially driven by a desire to understand its pervasive influence on employee behavior, revealed a surprising rigidity. The metric, designed to reward conformity and punish deviation, operated on a predictable set of inputs and outputs. While Kline had imbued it with an almost mystical authority, its true nature was that of a highly sophisticated, yet ultimately deterministic, program. Kathy discovered that certain prescribed behaviors, seemingly minor and inconsequential in the grand scheme of employee performance, consistently yielded disproportionately high loyalty scores. These were not acts of overt sycophancy, but rather the meticulous adherence to specific, often archaic, procedural guidelines within the corporate intranet, the timely submission of redundant progress reports, or the participation in voluntary (and often pointless) online training modules.

"He's built a machine that craves order," Kathy explained to the small, trusted circle, her voice a low murmur in the sterile quiet of a deserted archive annex. "And this machine rewards the appearance of perfect order, not necessarily the substance. We can give it what it craves, at least on the surface. We can feed it the data it wants to see, while simultaneously carving out spaces for our true work."

This insight was revolutionary. It shifted the resistance's focus from solely creating an alternative narrative to actively manipulating the existing one. The challenge was not to dismantle Kline's system, which was a Sisyphean task, but to subtly redirect its immense power. It was akin to diverting a mighty river, not by damming it, but by carefully excavating a new channel, guiding its flow towards a different destination.

Robert saw the practical implications immediately. "If the Loyalty Metric can be gamed," he posited, his fingers dancing across a holographic display, "then so too can the resource allocation systems. Kline's directives are filtered through layers of departmental managers and project approval committees. Each layer has its own set of metrics, its own checkboxes to check off. If we can ensure that the 'correct' boxes are checked off, even if the underlying project is a disguise, we can gain access to resources, to time, to personnel that would otherwise be denied to us."

This was the kernel of the idea: to use Kline's own bureaucratic machinery against him. The resistance began to identify individuals in key positions within these administrative layers – individuals who, while not overtly part of the resistance, harbored their own quiet discontents, their own frustrations with Kline's increasingly irrational directives. These were not necessarily individuals willing to engage in acts of sabotage, but those who understood the inefficiency and hypocrisy of the current regime and were amenable to subtly nudging the system in a less destructive direction.

Becky Billings, recruited by Kathy and Robert, began to subtly influence the archival requisition process. Her department was responsible for allocating digital storage and bandwidth to various projects. Kline's administration prioritized projects that aligned with his current strategic narratives, often at the expense of historical preservation or long-term research. Becky, however, found ways to categorize certain archival requests under classifications that Kline's algorithms deemed low-priority but which, in reality, were crucial for the Architects of Memory. She would use obscure, historical project codes, or even create new, seemingly benign project titles that hinted at routine data consolidation, to secure the necessary storage for the encrypted archives. Her justification, when questioned by a supervisor, was always rooted in procedural adherence – ensuring that "all historical data relevant to obscure, but approved legacy systems were properly archived for future audit."

Ben Rome adopted a similar approach with project resource

allocation. He learned to frame his "covert" research objectives in terms that resonated with Kline's stated goals of innovation and efficiency. Instead of explicitly requesting resources for researching alternative energy sources – a project deemed "legacy" by Kline – he would request resources for "optimizing computational fluid dynamics simulations for enhanced material stress testing," a project that bore a superficial resemblance to approved R&D initiatives and thus attracted less scrutiny. The actual research, however, would be focused on the fundamental science that would eventually underpin those alternative energy solutions. He meticulously crafted project proposals filled with the jargon and metrics that Kline's oversight committees favored, ensuring that the initial approval phases were smooth and unremarkable. The actual work, however, would be conducted in the shadowed corners of the network, using the allocated, albeit ostensibly for different purposes, computational resources.

The systemic exploitation extended even to the company's internal communication platforms. Kline had implemented a pervasive surveillance system, designed to flag keywords and phrases indicative of dissent. However, the algorithms, in their relentless pursuit of keywords, often missed the nuance of human communication. The resistance learned to embed their messages within seemingly innocuous conversations, using coded language that would appear as random associations to the surveillance software. They developed a lexicon of approved "decoy" phrases, common workplace banalities that could be reinterpreted with a specific, shared meaning among the initiated. A casual mention of "optimizing the Q3 report" could, in context, refer to the dissemination of a new encryption key. A discussion about "revisiting the early project blueprints" might, in fact, be a coded instruction to access a hidden directory.

This approach required an extraordinary level of discipline and understanding of the system's inherent limitations. It wasn't about brute force or overt rebellion; it was about a subtle, almost surgical, redirection of the system's own energies. Kline's reliance on algorithmic control meant that he was blind to the human element, to the ways in which his meticulously crafted rules could be bent, twisted, and ultimately, exploited by those who understood the spirit, not just the letter of the law.

The most profound aspect of this "hope within the system itself" was the gradual reclamation of its original purpose. Halcyon, in its founding days, was envisioned as a hub of innovation, collaboration, and ethical progress. Kline's regime had systematically perverted these ideals, twisting them into instruments of control and profit. But the resistance, by subtly re-engineering the system, was beginning to nudge it back towards its original intentions. The shared archives, once purged of anything that did not conform to Kline's narrative, were slowly being repopulated with the authentic history of Halcyon. Projects that were once stifled were now being subtly resurrected; their underlying principles advanced under the guise of unrelated initiatives.

The psychological impact of this approach was also significant. For those actively involved in the quiet resistance, it provided a tangible sense of agency. Instead of feeling like passive victims of Kline's regime, they were actively shaping its trajectory, albeit from within its own framework. This was not about waiting for an external force to liberate them; it was about the internal subversion of the oppressive structure. It was a testament to the enduring power of human ingenuity and the inherent flaws of any system built solely on control and devoid of genuine human values.

The risk, of course, remained immense. A single misstep, a single misinterpretation of the system's parameters, could unravel months of careful planning. The algorithms, while exploitable, were also constantly evolving, their creators always seeking to close the loopholes that had been so painstakingly discovered. The resistance had to remain agile, constantly adapting their strategies, forever vigilant against the automated gaze of the system. Yet, with each successful manipulation, with each piece of historical truth meticulously preserved or each ethically sound project subtly advanced, their resolve hardened. They were not just fighting for the future; they were actively, and quietly, rebuilding the soul of Halcyon, one exploited protocol, one recontextualized data point, one redirected process at a time. The system, designed to be a cage, was slowly, imperceptibly, being transformed into a tool for its own liberation. This was not a revolution waged on the streets, but a quiet, persistent, and deeply intelligent insurgency waged within the very digital walls of Victor Kline's empire.

Chapter 8

The System's Weakness

The sheer, overwhelming complexity of Victor Kline's meticulously constructed empire was, to the nascent resistance, a source of both dread and burgeoning hope. It was a colossus, certainly, its shadow cast long and deep across the lives of every employee within Halcyon. But colossi, as history repeatedly demonstrated, were not invincible. Their immense size, while projecting an aura of unassailable power, also made them unwieldy, prone to internal stresses, and ultimately, susceptible to even the most minor of fractures if they occurred at precisely the right leverage point. Kline, in his relentless pursuit of a monolithic, centralized control, had inadvertently woven a tapestry of such intricate detail, such exhaustive interconnectedness, that its very integrity was compromised by its own design.

The algorithms that governed the Loyalty Metric, a digital panopticon masquerading as an employee assessment tool, were a prime example. Kathy and Robert, spent countless sleepless nights dissecting their logic, and had uncovered not a singular, unassailable decree, but a Byzantine network of conditional statements, weighted variables, and feedback loops.

Each input, from the speed of an email response to the perceived enthusiasm during a mandatory corporate webinar, was meticulously logged and processed. But the sheer volume of data, coupled with the algorithmic attempt to quantify subjective elements like "proactive engagement" and "synergistic alignment," created an almost inevitable margin for error. The system, designed to be a scalpel of precise control, was in reality a blunt instrument, capable of being misled by carefully curated data points. It rewarded adherence to form over substance, the appearance of loyalty meticulously crafted to satisfy the insatiable appetite of the metrics.

This created an opening, a whisper of possibility, for those who could learn to speak the algorithm's language, to feed it the data it craved, while their true intentions remained hidden beneath the surface.

This realization rippled through the small, clandestine groups of dissenters like a seismic shock. It wasn't about dismantling the behemoth; it was about understanding its internal mechanics, its blind spots, and its inherent biases. Fiona and Suzi, with their sharp minds for logistics and resource management, saw the implications immediately. Kline's operational directives were not delivered as absolute commands, but rather filtered through multiple layers of departmental oversight, project approval committees, and cross-functional review boards. Each of these bureaucratic hurdles was designed to ensure compliance, to scrutinize every proposal against a pre-defined set of criteria. But within this very structure lay a potential for subversion. If the correct checkboxes could be marked, if the proposal could be framed in terms that satisfied the dominant metrics – even if the underlying project was a carefully constructed deception – then access to vital resources, to valuable time, and to indispensable personnel could be secured. The system, intended to restrict, could be subtly coerced into facilitating.

Tanya, Becky, and Kathy, working within the labyrinthine infrastructure of Halcyon's digital archives, became the early pioneers in this strategic redirection. Tanya's department was responsible for the allocation of storage space and network bandwidth, resources that were increasingly being channeled into projects that aligned with Kline's current pronouncements, often at the expense of long-term strategic research or the preservation of crucial historical data.

Tanya, however, discovered that by cleverly categorizing archival requests under obscure, historical project codes, or by creating new, seemingly innocuous project titles that hinted at routine data consolidation, she could secure the necessary resources for the Architects of Memory's encrypted archives. Her justifications, when scrutinized, were always couched in the impeccable language of procedural adherence. She would speak of ensuring that "all historical data relevant to legacy systems were properly archived for future audit," a statement technically true but entirely misleading about the true purpose of the data being stored. The algorithms, focused on identifying approved keywords and project classifications, were easily bypassed by this subtle linguistic camouflage.

In the research and development sector, Ben faced a similar challenge. Kline's administration had a keen interest in innovation, but only within strictly defined parameters that served his immediate strategic goals. Projects deemed too exploratory, too tangential, or too distant from immediate profitability were systematically starved of resources. Ben, however, learned to reframe his research objectives. Instead of directly requesting funding for, say, alternative energy sources – a field Kline had largely dismissed as a "legacy initiative" – Ben would meticulously craft proposals for "optimizing computational fluid dynamics simulations for enhanced material stress testing."

This superficially aligned with approved R&D objectives, boasting impressive technical jargon and promising measurable improvements in existing manufacturing processes. The crucial point was that the underlying scientific principles he was exploring, the fundamental research into new energy transfer mechanisms, would be conducted using the allocated, albeit ostensibly for different purposes, computational resources. The project proposals were a masterclass in bureaucratic compliance, filled with the metrics and buzzwords that satisfied Kline's oversight committees, while the true, transformative work occurred in the shadowed corners of the network.

The insidious nature of Kline's control extended even to the company's internal communication platforms. A pervasive surveillance system was in place, designed to flag any keywords or phrases that hinted at dissent or insubordination. However, the algorithms, in their relentless, literal-minded pursuit of specific terms, were blind to the subtle nuances of human communication, to the power of context and shared understanding. The resistance, recognizing this limitation, began to embed their messages within the fabric of everyday workplace conversations. They developed a sophisticated lexicon of coded language, a secret dialect spoken in plain sight. A casual mention of "optimizing the Q3 report" could, to those in the know, refer to the dissemination of a new encryption key. A discussion about "revisiting the early project blueprints" might, in reality, be a coded instruction to access a hidden directory of sensitive information. This required an immense level of discipline and a deep understanding of the system's inherent rigidity, a constant vigilance against the automated gaze of the surveillance software.

The true genius of this approach lay in its ability to reclaim the original spirit of Halcyon. The company, in its founding days, had been envisioned as a crucible of innovation, a collaborative environment dedicated to ethical progress. Kline's regime had systematically twisted these ideals, perverting them into instruments of control and profit. But by subtly re-engineering the system from within, the resistance began to nudge it back towards its original intentions. Shared archives, once meticulously purged of anything that did not conform to Kline's narrow narrative, were slowly being repopulated with the authentic history of Halcyon. Projects that had been stifled, their potential stifled by bureaucratic inertia, were now being subtly resurrected, their underlying principles advanced under the guise of unrelated, approved initiatives.

The psychological impact of this internal insurgency was profound. For those actively involved, it offered a tangible sense of agency. Instead of being passive victims of Kline's oppressive regime, they were actively shaping its trajectory, manipulating its very mechanisms for their own liberation. This was not a revolution waged on the streets, a loud and visible act of defiance. It was a quiet, persistent, and deeply intelligent insurgency waged within the digital walls of Victor Kline's empire, a testament to the enduring power of human ingenuity and the fundamental flaws inherent in any system built solely on control, devoid of genuine human values.

However, the risks were colossal. A single misstep, a single misinterpretation of the system's parameters, could unravel months of painstaking planning. The algorithms, while exploitable, were also in a constant state of evolution, their creators perpetually seeking to close the loopholes that had been so meticulously discovered.

186

The resistance had to remain agile, constantly adapting their strategies, forever vigilant against the automated gaze of the system. Yet, with each successful manipulation, with each piece of historical truth meticulously preserved, with each ethically sound project subtly advanced, their resolve hardened. They were not just fighting for a future free from Kline's dominion; they were actively, and quietly, rebuilding the soul of Halcyon, one exploited protocol, one recontextualized data point, one redirected process at a time.

The system, designed to be an impenetrable cage, was slowly, imperceptibly, being transformed into a tool for its own liberation, a testament to the fact that even the most intricate and powerful systems are ultimately composed of interconnected parts, and that a single, well-placed pressure point can indeed bring down the mightiest of giants. The very fabric of Kline's control, woven from threads of immense complexity, proved to be its most significant vulnerability, a spiderweb of interconnected dependencies that, when understood and manipulated with precision, could ensnare the weaver himself.

The grand architecture of Victor Kline's digital dominion, while seemingly impregnable, harbored a fundamental vulnerability: its absolute reliance on the data it consumed. Like a living organism that thrives on a specific diet, Kline's system, particularly the omnipresent Loyalty Metric, operated on the premise that the information fed into it was pure, unadulterated truth. The algorithms, brilliant in their complexity, were nonetheless oblivious to the subtle art of deception. They processed, categorized, and acted upon data with unthinking efficiency, mistaking volume for veracity, and correlation for causation. It was within this blind faith of the machine that the nascent resistance found its most potent weapon – the subtle, insidious art of data corruption.

This was not a strategy of brute force, of seeking to overload or crash the system. Such overt acts would be instantly detected, triggering alarms and hardening defenses. Instead, the approach was far more nuanced, akin to introducing a slow-acting poison into a pristine well. The goal was not to shatter the illusion of infallibility, but to erode it, to introduce a creeping doubt that would eventually undermine Kline's confidence in his own meticulously crafted reality. Each piece of corrupted data, each subtly falsified report, was a grain of sand meticulously placed to destabilize the foundations of his empire.

Kathy, her nights still a tapestry of code and caffeine, became the architect of this digital sabotage. She approached the task with a chilling blend of precision and audacity. Her initial focus was on the Loyalty Metric, that draconian arbiter of an employee's worth. The system's inputs were vast and varied: email response times, participation in mandatory "synergy sessions," the perceived enthusiasm in video conference calls, even the proximity of an employee's workstation to their direct supervisor. Each interaction, no matter how trivial, was a data point. And within this deluge, Kathy began to introduce carefully calibrated inaccuracies.

Consider, for instance, the seemingly innocuous act of forwarding an email. A standard response might involve a simple "FYI" or a brief affirmation. But what if, before forwarding, a single character was altered? A misplaced comma, an extraneous space, a subtly misspelled word that, while not immediately obvious to a human reader, could trigger a cascade of misinterpretations within the automated parsing of the system. If the system was programmed to associate swift email forwarding with proactive engagement, and if a batch of such forwards, subtly altered, were flagged as "low-priority" due to a detected grammatical anomaly by a secondary verification algorithm, the perceived engagement score could dip, not drastically, but by a fraction. When this happened across hundreds, then thousands, of employees, the aggregate effect began to create a statistical anomaly that was too small to trigger an alarm, but large enough to subtly shift the overall perception of departmental efficiency.

Falsified performance figures were another key avenue. Ben, in R&D, understood the language of metrics and deliverables. Projects, even those that were genuinely progressing, could have their reported output numbers nudged. Not wildly, not impossibly. A project that was on track to deliver 95% of its projected results might be reported as 93%. This might seem insignificant, a mere 2% deviation. But within the hyper-competitive environment that Kline fostered, where performance was measured with unforgiving granularity, even a 2% deficit could be enough to flag a project, or a team, as underperforming. This could lead to a subtle reallocation of resources away from that project, or a directive for increased oversight. The resistance, in turn, could then use this perceived underperformance as a justification for redirecting existing resources to more critical, covert operations, arguing that the flagged project was consuming valuable time and personnel that could be better utilized elsewhere. The system, designed to identify inefficiency, was being manipulated to create the appearance of inefficiency where it suited their needs.

Robert saw the potential for withholding information. Kline's systems craved data. They were designed to identify gaps and demand explanations. But what if crucial, yet seemingly minor, data points simply... disappeared? A lost log file from a server that processed employee time-clock data. An incomplete submission for a routine inventory check. A delay in the submission of travel expense reports for a particular department. Individually, these were minor administrative hiccups. But when aggregated and strategically deployed, they created a fog of uncertainty.

The system would flag these omissions, generating automated queries and demanding resolutions. This forced Kline's administrative apparatus into a reactive mode, expending energy and resources chasing phantom problems. The true purpose of this obfuscation was to divert attention from other, more critical movements within the organization. While the system was busy trying to locate a missing time-clock log from a low-level technician in accounting, a covert data transfer of sensitive research findings might be proceeding unimpeded.

Tanya, in her role managing archival systems, found a particularly insidious way to corrupt data: through its very preservation. The system was designed to archive, but also to periodically audit and purge outdated or redundant data. Becky would receive information from Kathy, where she began to introduce subtle metadata errors into archival records. Imagine a vital piece of research data, painstakingly gathered, being tagged with an incorrect project code or an outdated timestamp. The algorithm, designed to identify and archive based on specific criteria, would still file it away. However, when a future audit occurred, or when a researcher attempted to retrieve that specific piece of data, it would be virtually impossible to find. The metadata would lead the search to a dead end, or to an incorrect location. The data itself would remain intact, a digital ghost in the machine, but its utility would be effectively nullified.

The system, designed for perfect recall, would be rendered impotent by its own inability to accurately catalog and retrieve. This was particularly effective for historical data that might contradict Kline's carefully curated narrative of Halcyon's past or present success. By making inconvenient truths inaccessible, the resistance ensured that Kline's perception of history remained untarnished, while simultaneously ensuring that the true historical context remained beyond his grasp.

The impact of this data corruption was not immediate, nor was it dramatic. It was a slow, insidious decay. Kline, accustomed to the clear, decisive pronouncements of his data-driven empire, began to encounter inconsistencies. Reports that should have aligned perfectly would show minute discrepancies. Projected outcomes would deviate, not wildly, but just enough to sow seeds of doubt. The efficiency metrics that had once been a source of unquestionable pride began to present a slightly muddier picture.

This subtle erosion of confidence was the resistance's ultimate goal. Kline's strength lay in his absolute faith in the system. If that faith began to waver, if he started to question the very data that informed his decisions, his grip on power would inevitably loosen. He would become hesitant, second-guessing himself. His pronouncements, once delivered with unwavering certainty, might begin to carry an undertone of caution. This hesitation, this nascent doubt, created opportunities. It slowed down his decision-making processes, allowing the resistance more time to plan and execute their operations. It encouraged a degree of decentralization, as he might delegate more tasks to subordinates, implicitly admitting that the system was no longer providing him with the clarity he needed.

The beauty of this approach lay in its deniability. Each individual act of corruption was too small to be definitively traced back to a coordinated effort. A single misfiled report, a slightly inaccurate metric, a ghost in the archive – these were easily dismissed as human error, as system glitches. The sheer volume of data processed by Halcyon's systems meant that a few anomalies were statistically inevitable. It was only when these anomalies were deliberately and systematically introduced that they began to exert a significant influence. And by the time Kline might begin to suspect a deeper malaise within his digital infrastructure, the resistance would have already moved on, perfecting new methods of subtle subversion, ever one step ahead of the machine's ability to adapt. The system, designed to be an unblinking eye, was slowly being blinded by the very data it was meant to illuminate. The more it relied on the corrupted inputs, the further it drifted from the truth, and the more vulnerable it became to the machinations of those who understood its hidden flaws.

The algorithms governing Victor Kline's empire were not merely complex; they were, by design, reductive. They sought to distill the vibrant, unpredictable essence of human endeavor into quantifiable metrics, reducing individuals to data points on a grand, impersonal ledger. The Loyalty Metric, the crown jewel of this reductionist philosophy, was a prime example. It was a relentless engine designed to measure dedication, efficiency, and, most importantly, obedience. Yet, like any system built on finite rules, it possessed inherent blind spots, chinks in its otherwise formidable armor. These were not flaws in its programming, but rather the unavoidable consequences of trying to quantify the unquantifiable.

Kathy, privy to the inner workings of these algorithms, recognized this fundamental limitation early on. The Loyalty Metric, for all its pervasive reach, was notoriously poor at recognizing genuine innovation that deviated from established pathways. It rewarded adherence to protocol, swift execution of assigned tasks, and demonstrable engagement with approved channels. What it couldn't easily measure, or even acknowledge, were moments of true creative spark that arose from intuitive leaps, from a deep-seated understanding of a problem that transcended the prescribed methodology.

If an employee, say, a junior engineer named Sharon in the fictional context, stumbled upon a radically different, more efficient solution to a complex coding problem – a solution that bypassed

191

several mandated development stages and utilized an unconventional programming language – the system would struggle to credit her appropriately. The bypassed stages wouldn't be logged as efficiencies but as deviations. The unconventional language might not even be recognized as a valid tool.

Kathy's innovative breakthrough, a triumph of intellect and foresight, might, paradoxically, register as a minor anomaly, a blip on the radar that prompted more scrutiny than commendation. The system valued the journey, the prescribed path, not necessarily the destination when it was reached by an unscheduled route. This created an environment where radical innovation was subtly discouraged, or at least, its true value was obscured by the system's inability to comprehend its merit.

This was precisely where the nascent resistance began to weave its strategy. They started to operate within these algorithmic blind spots, to engage in activities that, while undeniably beneficial to Halcyon and its underlying goals, were either invisible to Kline's metrics or actively misinterpreted by them. Ben, with his deep understanding of the R&D pipelines, initiated a quiet campaign of "disruptive collaboration." He would identify individuals whose unique skills, though perhaps not directly aligned with their official job descriptions, could be leveraged to solve critical issues outside the purview of their assigned projects.

For instance, a highly skilled data analyst, officially tasked with quarterly trend forecasting, might be discreetly enlisted by Ben to help a struggling R&D team untangle a particularly thorny data integrity problem that was slowing down a vital experimental run. The analyst's contribution would be crucial, saving the R&D team weeks of delay and potentially preventing the loss of valuable research. However, because this collaboration occurred off the official project logs, through informal channels and without direct task reassignment, the analyst's performance metrics wouldn't reflect this significant contribution. In fact, the time spent on this "unofficial" task might even lead to a slight dip in their own reported output for their primary role, making them appear marginally less efficient to the Loyalty Metric. The system, designed to reward visible, quantifiable contributions within defined parameters, would completely miss the impact of this vital, cross-departmental problem-solving. The true value of Ben's intervention – the accelerated progress of critical research – remained unacknowledged by Kline's all-seeing eye.

Fiona, ever the strategist of resource allocation, understood the system's aversion to altruism that didn't serve a direct, measurable outcome. She began to encourage acts of selfless collaboration that benefited the collective rather than the individual's standing. Imagine a scenario where a critical client project was facing an impending deadline, and a particular department, tasked with a crucial component, was falling behind due to unforeseen technical difficulties. The standard response within Kline's system would be for that department to request additional resources, perhaps overtime or reassignment of personnel from other, less critical projects. This would be logged, tracked, and directly impact departmental performance metrics.

However, Fiona subtly guided teams to engage in what she termed "shared crisis management." This involved individuals from departments that were ahead of schedule, or whose current tasks had minimal immediate impact, volunteering their time and expertise to assist the struggling department. A marketing specialist, for instance, might lend their persuasive skills to expedite a supplier delivery, or a legal associate might quickly draft a necessary amendment to a service agreement. These acts of generosity, of pulling together for the common good, were inherently difficult for the Loyalty Metric to quantify. The time spent assisting another team was not directly contributing to the volunteer's own project. Their own metrics might even show a slight decline due to this reallocation of effort. Yet, the overall success of the client project, and by extension, Halcyon's reputation, would be significantly bolstered. The system, incapable of valuing selfless contribution, would interpret this as a minor inefficiency from the volunteering employee, while the critical boost to the struggling department's success would be attributed to their own (now miraculously recovered) efforts, or perhaps to a general, unquantifiable "company spirit."

Kathy, meanwhile, focused on the system's inability to account for acts of sacrifice. The Loyalty Metric rewarded productivity and adherence. It punished tardiness, errors, and any perceived lack of commitment. But what about the employee who, facing a personal crisis, chose to take a voluntary pay cut for a month to ensure a critical project didn't lose a key team member? Or the team that, realizing their project was becoming a black hole for resources with no guaranteed return, collectively agreed to shelve it, sacrificing their own hard work and potential recognition to reallocate those resources to a more promising venture?

These were decisions rooted in long-term organizational health and a broader sense of responsibility, decisions that often involved personal or departmental sacrifice. The Loyalty Metric, however, saw only the absence of immediate, quantifiable output. The employee taking a pay cut might be flagged for potential financial instability or lack of dedication. The team shelving their project might see their accumulated work erased, their metrics reset to zero, and their future prospects dimmed. The system was incapable of understanding that these seemingly negative outcomes were, in fact, intelligent, strategic decisions that preserved the company's overall strength. They were acts of foresight and sacrifice, vital to the long-term survival of Halcyon, yet invisible to the rigid calculus of the Loyalty Metric.

The resistance understood that Kline's system was designed to optimize for a specific, narrow definition of success. It excelled at managing predictable workflows, at identifying and rectifying deviations from established norms, and at rewarding predictable performance. But it faltered when confronted with the messier, more complex realities of human ingenuity, altruism, and strategic sacrifice. By actively engaging in these unquantifiable, yet ultimately beneficial, activities, the resistance was not just subverting the system; they were demonstrating its profound limitations. They were showing that true value creation often occurred in the spaces that Kline's algorithms couldn't reach, in the human qualities that couldn't be reduced to a number.

Each instance of genuine innovation that went unrewarded, each act of selfless collaboration that was misinterpreted as inefficiency, each strategic sacrifice that was logged as a failure, was a testament to the system's inherent blindness. It was a subtle, yet potent, form of rebellion, chipping away at the very foundation of Kline's data-driven autocracy by proving that the data, as interpreted by his algorithms, was not the whole truth, but merely a carefully curated, and fundamentally incomplete, fragment of it.

This strategic embrace of the system's blind spots had a profound psychological effect on the resistance members themselves. They were no longer just cogs in a machine; they were agents of a deeper purpose, working within the cracks of the established order. They found a sense of agency and fulfillment in activities that were not recognized by their employer but were deeply meaningful to them and to the broader goal of reclaiming Halcyon.

This psychological empowerment was a critical, albeit unmeasurable, asset. It fostered resilience, creativity, and a shared sense of clandestine accomplishment that bound them together more tightly than any official company directive ever could. They were the architects of the unquantifiable, the champions of the invisible wins, proving, in the quiet corners of Halcyon's digital infrastructure, that the most valuable contributions were often the ones that escaped the notice of the all-seeing, yet ultimately blind, eye of the system. The more the system demanded data, the more the resistance provided context that the data could not capture, revealing the hollowness at the core of Kline's meticulously constructed reality.

The irony of Victor Kline's meticulously crafted empire was as profound as it was debilitating. In his relentless quest for ultimate efficiency, for a seamless, data-driven organism where every action was optimized and every outcome predicted, he had inadvertently engineered a labyrinth of bureaucratic inefficiency. The very systems designed to streamline operations had, through their sheer complexity and the ingrained human behaviors they fostered, become the primary impediment to progress.

Decisions that should have taken hours now languished for weeks, buried under mountains of paperwork, awaiting the stamp of approval from an ever-increasing hierarchy of gatekeepers. Reporting requirements, initially intended to provide transparency and accountability, had ballooned into an all-consuming ritual, demanding exhaustive documentation for even the most trivial of tasks. The fear of deviation, of making a mistake that would be immortalized in an audit trail and negatively impact one's Loyalty Metric, had instilled a pervasive paralysis. Employees, once encouraged to take initiative, now found themselves paralyzed by the sheer weight of protocol, their every move dictated by the need to adhere to an ever-expanding rulebook and the anxiety of potential repercussions.

This was the fertile ground upon which the resistance, spearheaded by Kathy and her clandestine network, began to sow their seeds of subtle sabotage. They didn't need to break the system; they simply needed to let it break itself. Their strategy was not one of outright rebellion, but of an insidious adherence to its most tedious and convoluted aspects. They embraced the bureaucracy, turning its own tools against it, transforming its rigid structures into instruments of delay and obstruction.

Consider a typical directive, a seemingly straightforward task assigned by middle management, perhaps a request for a market analysis report for a new product line. Under normal circumstances, a motivated team might complete such a report within days, leveraging existing data and market intelligence. But within Kline's Halcyon, this process was a gantlet. The directive, once issued, initiated a cascade of mandatory preliminary steps. First, a formal request for resource allocation had to be submitted, detailing the exact hours of personnel time, the specific software licenses required, and the projected energy consumption for the duration of the project. This request, typically a multi-page document requiring justification for every line item, would then be forwarded to the departmental manager for initial review. If approved, it would then journey to the finance department for budgetary validation, followed by a review by the IT department to ensure compatibility with existing systems and data security protocols. Each of these steps involved meticulous formatting, cross-referencing of internal codes, and often, the attachment of supplementary documentation.

The resistance members, however, had learned to exploit the inherent friction in this process. They would ensure their resource allocation requests were… thorough. Painfully thorough. Every byte of data processed, every keystroke, every nanosecond of server time would be meticulously accounted for, presented in excruciating detail, often exceeding hundreds of pages. They would intentionally misalign internal coding, ensuring that the document had to be routed back and forth between departments for clarification, each redelivery adding days, sometimes weeks, to the overall timeline. When a report was finally due, they would ensure it was submitted with absolute literalness, adhering to every obscure formatting rule, every archaic font requirement, but devoid of any genuine insight or strategic recommendation. The analysis would be technically correct, factually accurate, but ultimately sterile and unhelpful, prompting further requests for clarification and refinement. This would then trigger another cycle of resource allocation requests, further reporting requirements, and more bureaucratic hurdles. The objective was not to fail the task, but to ensure its successful completion took an eternity, consuming vast resources and time, all while appearing to be diligently following protocol.

Ben, with his intimate knowledge of the R&D division's project pipelines, became a master of creating these intentional bottlenecks. A critical component upgrade, for instance, that might have been implemented in a matter of weeks through direct communication and collaborative problem-solving, would, when routed through Ben's team, become a months-long saga. The initial proposal would be buried in a request for a "Cross-Functional Impact Assessment," a document that required input from no fewer than seven distinct departments, each with its own approval process and reporting structure.

Each department's contribution would then necessitate a separate "Interdepartmental Synergy Review," followed by a "Risk Mitigation Analysis," and finally, a "Long-Term Strategic Alignment Proposal." Ben would ensure that each of these stages was completed with excruciating, but technically correct, adherence to protocol. He would insist on archaic forms, demand handwritten signatures on printed documents that were then scanned and re-uploaded, and meticulously track the paper trail, ensuring that the physical documents were dispatched via the slowest available internal mail service. The sheer inertia generated by this process meant that critical upgrades were perpetually delayed, not because of any technical impossibility, but because the system itself had become an insurmountable obstacle.

Robert, Don, and Fiona in their domain of resource allocation and logistics, employed a similar tactic, but with a focus on the very act of decision-making. They understood that Kline's system abhorred ambiguity and celebrated definitive, data-backed pronouncements. This meant that any decision requiring a degree of judgment, of navigating gray areas, would be subjected to an exhaustive process of justification and approval.

Fiona would subtly encourage her teams to defer decisions upwards, not out of fear, but as a deliberate strategy. When faced with a choice between two equally viable logistical routes, for example, each with its own minor advantages and disadvantages, her team would not make a decision. Instead, they would compile detailed reports on both options, complete with comparative cost-benefit analyses, risk assessments, and potential environmental impact statements, and then forward the entire package to their immediate superior, framing it as a request for "strategic guidance." This "guidance" would then be passed up the chain, each manager adding their own layer of analysis and commentary, until the decision, stripped of its urgency and drowned in a sea of verbiage, finally landed on the desk of a senior executive, often weeks later, by which point the original problem might have resolved itself, or become infinitely more complex. The system was designed to facilitate decisive action, but the resistance ensured that decisive action was an impossibility.

Kathy, observing these individual efforts, recognized the overarching pattern. Kline's pursuit of efficiency had paradoxically bred a culture of profound inefficiency. The very mechanisms designed to ensure meticulousness and oversight had become chains, binding the organization in red tape. Employees, conditioned to avoid any action that could be flagged as an error, became risk-averse to the point of inaction. This fear was a powerful tool for the resistance. They began to subtly encourage the "literal adherence" to directives, a form of passive resistance that could paralyze operations.

Consider a directive to reduce energy consumption by 10%. A

naive interpretation might involve optimizing lighting schedules or encouraging employees to switch off unused equipment. But the resistance, in their communications, would frame this in the most literal, and thus inefficient, way possible. They might disseminate guidelines that mandated the shutting down of all non-essential equipment at precisely 4:58 PM, two minutes before the official end of the workday, ensuring that any late-working employee would have to endure a period of darkness and inactivity. They might insist that all printers be powered down every hour for a mandatory ten-minute "rest period" to conserve energy, thus disrupting workflows and requiring constant reboots. These were not malicious acts designed to cause outright harm, but rather meticulously crafted interpretations that, while technically fulfilling the directive, rendered them utterly impractical and disruptive. The system, built on the assumption of rational interpretation and good faith, found itself constantly tripped up by the literalness of its own rules.

The consequences of this manufactured inefficiency were far-reaching. Critical projects stalled, deadlines slipped, and valuable opportunities were missed, not due to incompetence or lack of resources, but due to the sheer, grinding weight of the bureaucratic machinery. Innovation, which thrives on agility and quick iteration, was stifled. A brilliant idea conceived in the R&D department might languish for months, caught in the endless cycle of approvals, assessments, and reviews, by which time its relevance might have waned, or a competitor might have already brought a similar solution to market. The cost of this inefficiency was astronomical, not just in terms of lost revenue, but in the erosion of morale and the stifling of potential. Employees became demoralized, their efforts seemingly wasted in navigating the labyrinthine processes. The system, designed to reward productivity, ended up punishing it by demanding an ever-increasing volume of bureaucratic output for any actual work to be accomplished.

Victor Kline, observing the lagging performance metrics and the increasing project completion times, would likely attribute it to external market pressures or the need for more sophisticated algorithmic oversight. He would double down on his faith in the system, demanding more data, more reporting, more control. He couldn't fathom that the very structure he had so painstakingly erected was now actively working against him, that his pursuit of absolute efficiency had birthed a monster of profound, self-inflicted inefficiency. The resistance, meanwhile, continued their work, a clandestine army of paper-pushers and protocol-adherers, subtly dismantling the empire from within, one meticulously filed, deliberately delayed, and unhelpfully literal directive at a time. They understood that the greatest weakness of a system built on logic and order was its inability to account for the deliberate chaos that could be sown by those who understood its rules better than its creator. The system, designed to be a model of streamlined operation, was slowly but surely grinding to a halt under the immense, self-generated weight of its own procedural complexity. It was a slow, agonizing death by a thousand paper cuts, each cut a testament to the ingenuity of those who fought for Halcyon's soul not with open defiance, but with the quiet, relentless weapon of bureaucratic paralysis.

The meticulous architecture of Victor Kline's empire, a monument to his unwavering belief in data and algorithmic precision, harbored a fundamental blind spot: the irreducible complexity of the human heart. He had built a fortress of logic, a gleaming edifice designed to meticulously control every facet of its inhabitants' lives, from their productivity quotas to their social interactions, all meticulously logged and analyzed. Yet, in his relentless pursuit of quantifiable efficiency, Kline had tragically, and perhaps deliberately, overlooked the very element that made his system vulnerable – the unpredictable, often irrational, yet profoundly powerful force of human connection. His algorithms could predict market fluctuations, optimize supply chains, and even assess employee loyalty with chilling accuracy, but they could never truly grasp the essence of empathy, the quiet strength of shared vulnerability, or the rebellious spark ignited by genuine human interaction.

The resistance, under Fiona's subtle guidance, understood this implicitly. They didn't need to hack into Kline's servers or sabotage his machinery; their battlefield was far more intimate and infinitely more potent. They waged war not with code, but with compassion. While Kline's system sought to isolate individuals, to reduce them to data points on a vast, impersonal grid, Fiona and her network focused on weaving threads of genuine connection. They understood that the human element, so casually dismissed as an uncontrollable variable by Kline, was, in fact, the very bedrock of resilience and the most potent antidote to his sterile, calculated control.

Consider the case of Brenda, a mid-level analyst in the data processing division. Her daily existence within Halcyon was a monotonous cycle of data ingestion, algorithmic verification, and standardized reporting. Her "Loyalty Metric," a figure that loomed large in her performance reviews, was directly correlated with her adherence to protocol and her output efficiency. Any deviation, any emotional display that could be interpreted as dissent or distraction, was a mark against her. Brenda, like many others, felt the soul-crushing weight of this surveillance, the constant awareness of being observed, analyzed, and judged. She performed her tasks with robotic precision, her spirit slowly eroding with each passing day.

Then came the subtle shift. It began with a hushed conversation in the break room, a shared sigh over a particularly egregious piece of corporate jargon in a new directive. It escalated to tentative exchanges about personal lives, brief moments of shared laughter that felt illicit and liberating within the sterile confines of Halcyon. Fiona and Gigi, through their carefully cultivated network of informants and sympathizers, ensured that these pockets of human interaction were nurtured. They weren't organized meetings or clandestine gatherings; they were spontaneous moments of solidarity, small acts of rebellion against the isolating nature of Kline's system.

Emma found herself drawn into one such informal circle. It started with Dawson, a fellow analyst who, despite his high Loyalty Metric, often displayed a flicker of something unquantifiable in his eyes – a weariness that mirrored her own. One afternoon, during a mandatory "wellness break" (itself a calculated attempt by Kline to monitor and manage employee emotional states), Dawson didn't engage with the prescribed mindfulness exercises. Instead, he leaned over to Emma and quietly mentioned his elderly mother's recent illness, the worry gnawing at him, the helplessness he felt miles away from her.

This wasn't a topic that could be logged by any sensor, analyzed by any algorithm. It was raw, unvarnished humanity. Emma, for the first time in months, felt a genuine connection, a shared burden that transcended the sterile metrics of Halcyon. She spoke about her own anxieties, the fear of being reprimanded for her dwindling output, the pressure to maintain a facade of unwavering dedication. In that brief, unguarded exchange, a fragile bond was forged, a testament to the power of shared vulnerability.

The resistance understood that these moments, however small, were cracks in Kline's armor. They actively encouraged their members to engage in acts of kindness and empathy, not as a grand gesture, but as a subtle, persistent erosion of the system's dehumanizing grip. A misplaced report would be found and returned with a handwritten note of understanding, not a formal reprimand. A colleague struggling with a complex procedural step would receive patient, unmonitored assistance, the focus on genuine problem-solving rather than adherence to reporting protocols. These were acts that couldn't be quantified, that bypassed the surveillance apparatus, and that subtly reminded people of their shared humanity.

Kline's algorithms were designed to detect anomalies, deviations from expected patterns. But the patterns they were looking for were behavioral and procedural, not emotional. They could flag a missed deadline or an unscheduled break, but they couldn't quantify the impact of a comforting word, the relief of being understood, or the quiet resolve that could be born from a sense of camaraderie. The resistance, by fostering these genuine human connections, created a network of intangible support that existed just outside the reach of Kline's surveillance.

This network proved invaluable when the resistance needed to mobilize more direct, though still subtle, forms of sabotage. Emma, empowered by the support she received, became a crucial asset. Her position within data processing gave her access to the very algorithms that governed employee performance. While she wouldn't dream of outright sabotage – the risk was too great, and her newfound sense of ethical purpose wouldn't allow it – she learned to introduce infinitesimally small "noise" into the data streams. A slightly slower processing speed here, a fractional delay in data synchronization there. These were not enough to trigger immediate alarms, but when aggregated across multiple individuals, they created a cumulative effect of minor inefficiencies, a slow drag on the system's overall performance that Kline's algorithms struggled to pinpoint.

The resistance's strategy was not to overthrow Kline's system through brute force, but to subtly demonstrate its inherent limitations by highlighting the power of what it could not control. They leveraged the fact that humans, at their core, are social beings. They crave connection, validation, and understanding. Kline's system, in its relentless pursuit of individual optimization, starved these fundamental needs. The resistance, in contrast, provided a lifeline of genuine human interaction.

This human element factor manifested in numerous ways. For instance, the "mentorship" program, a mandatory initiative designed by Kline to foster knowledge transfer and employee development, was twisted by the resistance into something far more meaningful. Officially, it involved scheduled meetings, documented progress reports, and adherence to a pre-approved curriculum. Unofficially, it became a vehicle for quiet rebellion. Mentors, drawn from the resistance's ranks, would use these sessions not just to impart technical knowledge, but to share stories of resilience, to offer words of encouragement that had no place in a formal performance review, and to subtly steer their mentees towards questioning the absolute authority of the system.

Consider the example of a young engineer, Leo, who was assigned a mentor, an older engineer named Derek, who was discreetly part of Kathy's network. Leo was bright but increasingly disillusioned by the bureaucratic hurdles that stifled his creativity. During their official mentorship sessions, Derek followed the protocol, ensuring all documentation was completed. But in their informal conversations, often initiated by Leo's genuine frustration with a stalled project, Derek would share anecdotes from his own career, not about his successes, but about the times he felt lost, the doubts he harbored, and how he navigated those feelings. He never directly criticized Kline's system, but by humanizing the struggle, he gave Leo permission to feel his own disillusionment and, more importantly, to see that it was a shared experience, not a personal failing.

This cultivated sense of shared experience created a subtle, but powerful, form of collective resistance. When a directive arrived, that was particularly absurd or demoralizing, it was no longer an isolated incident for an individual to endure in silence. Through the informal communication channels fostered by the resistance, news of such directives would spread, and a quiet ripple of shared exasperation would travel through Halcyon. This collective sentiment, while invisible to Kline's metrics, fostered a sense of solidarity that made individuals more resilient to the system's pressures.

Moreover, the resistance actively encouraged acts of kindness that defied algorithmic measurement. If an employee was struggling with a personal issue that impacted their work, instead of reporting them for a dip in productivity, resistance members would offer discrete assistance. This could range from covering a portion of their workload to simply providing a listening ear. These acts of compassion were the antithesis of Kline's cold, calculated approach. They were driven by empathy, a trait that algorithms could not replicate, and a force that could not be quantified.

The consequences of this human element factor were profound. While Kline's systems reported on efficiency and productivity, they failed to capture the intangible assets that were being nurtured by the resistance: trust, morale, and a sense of shared purpose. Employees who felt seen and supported were more likely to engage in creative problem-solving, to go the extra mile when genuinely motivated, and to remain loyal to the organization not out of fear, but out of a sense of belonging.

The stark contrast between Kline's calculated control and the organic, human-driven resistance became increasingly apparent. Kline believed he had built a perfect system, a machine where humans were merely cogs. He failed to grasp that even the most sophisticated machine requires a skilled operator, and that the operator's spirit, their willingness to engage, their very humanity, was a critical, unquantifiable variable. The resistance, by nurturing this human element, was not just undermining Kline's system; they were reminding the people within it of their inherent worth, their capacity for connection, and their ability to find strength not in isolation, but in solidarity. This, more than any technical exploit or bureaucratic delay, was the true Achilles' heel of Victor Kline's meticulously crafted empire. His obsession with control had blinded him to the power of freedom, and his faith in algorithms had made him deaf to the quiet, persistent murmur of the human heart.

Chapter 9

The Unraveling

The subtle disruptions, once dismissed as statistically insignificant outliers, began to coalesce into a disquieting trend. Victor Kline, accustomed to the flawless symmetry of his data, found himself staring at charts that no longer sang the song of unfettered progress. The algorithms, his trusted sentinels, had been meticulously designed to detect deviations, to flag anomalies that threatened the perfect equilibrium of Halcyon. But the anomalies now multiplying across the vast expanse of his empire were no longer isolated incidents. They were becoming the norm, a persistent hum of discord beneath the polished surface.

It started with a fractional delay in the inter-departmental data transfer, a matter of milliseconds that, on any given day, would be attributed to network latency or a momentary surge in server load. Then came the slight, almost imperceptible, lag in the automated scheduling system, causing minor overlaps in meeting times or brief, inexplicable gaps in workflow. These were the digital equivalent of a house settling, small sounds that were easily ignored until they became too numerous to count, too pervasive to attribute to chance.

The resistance, working through channels invisible to Kline's all-seeing eye, had orchestrated this symphony of subtle inefficiency. Toni, whose initial exposure to genuine human connection had ignited a quiet defiance, now played a more active role. Her access to the core data processing streams allowed her to introduce microscopic "errors" – not deliberate sabotage that could be traced, but tiny imperfections that, when multiplied across thousands of daily transactions, began to create a drag. A single data point might be routed through an auxiliary server for an extra nanosecond, a reporting timestamp might be nudged by a fraction of a second, a predictive model might be fed a subtly skewed historical correlation. These were not enough to trigger the high-level alarms designed to catch overt tampering. Instead, they served as a quiet poison, slowly degrading the system's overall responsiveness, like a fine grit accumulating in the gears of a meticulously engineered clockwork.

Quinton, the analyst with the unquantifiable weariness in his eyes, found himself facilitating these disruptions in unexpected ways. His role involved cross-referencing datasets from different divisions, a task that required a deep understanding of how disparate information streams interacted. He learned to subtly "misalign" these streams, not enough to cause immediate errors, but enough to create downstream discrepancies. A sales projection, for instance, might be fed a slightly outdated inventory count, or a production forecast might be based on a subtly altered demand signal. The resistance's strategy was not about outright destruction, but about a calculated demonstration of fallibility. They were showing Kline that his perfect system was, in fact, permeable, vulnerable to the very human element he had sought to excise.

The impact on performance metrics was insidious. Productivity figures, while not plummeting dramatically, began to exhibit a plateau, then a slow, downward drift. The expected exponential growth was replaced by a stagnant curve, then a gentle descent. Kline's algorithms, designed to identify rapid drops or sudden spikes, struggled to categorize this creeping decline. It lacked the dramatic urgency of a system failure. Instead, it was a pervasive malaise, a collective sigh from the digital infrastructure.

One of the most telling signs was the rise in "unexplained delays" within project timelines. Projects that were once meticulously managed, with every milestone accounted for, began to slip. The project management software, which relied on precise input from team members and automated progress tracking, started to generate reports filled with vague justifications for delays: "processing lag," "data reconciliation issues," "unexpected dependency conflicts." These were the echoes of the subtle disruptions, translated into the language of project management.

Kathy, observing these developments from her strategic vantage point, understood the psychological impact as much as the operational. Kline's empire was built on the promise of absolute control, of predictable outcomes. The visible cracks, however small, began to erode that very foundation of confidence. Employees who had once operated with a sense of robotic certainty, knowing their actions were precisely tracked and accounted for, now began to experience a flicker of doubt. When a task took longer than expected, when a report contained a minor discrepancy, was it their own failing, or was something else at play?

The "wellness breaks" that Kline had implemented to monitor and manage employee emotional states ironically became conduits for spreading this unease. While the official sessions focused on mindfulness and stress reduction, the informal chatter that invariably ensued, a natural human response to enforced calm, began to buzz with shared frustrations. "Did your report take forever to process this morning?" "I swear, the system was crawling today." These were no longer individual complaints, but shared observations, a growing consensus that the seamless efficiency of Halcyon was, in fact, an illusion.

The resistance actively encouraged these conversations, not through direct instruction, but by creating an atmosphere where such observations were validated. A shared glance of understanding between colleagues after a system glitch, a murmured comment of commiseration about a stalled task – these were the currency of solidarity. Tanya, in her data processing role, would sometimes find herself directly interacting with colleagues from other departments who were experiencing the downstream effects of her subtle interventions. Instead of reporting the issue as a technical anomaly, she would engage them in conversation, subtly guiding them towards the idea that the problem might be systemic, rather than individual.

Consider the case of the automated inventory management system for Halcyon's extensive network of data centers. This system, responsible for ensuring the timely replenishment of server components and network hardware, was a linchpin of Kline's operational efficiency. The resistance, through a combination of Tanya and Becky's data manipulation and Don's insights into the system's predictive algorithms, began to introduce subtle inaccuracies into the demand forecasting. It wasn't an outright lie, but rather a gentle nudging of variables. For example, a minor increase in anticipated hardware failure rates in a specific region, or a slight overestimation of anticipated data traffic growth in another.

The immediate consequence was a series of minor, seemingly random, procurement errors. A data center might receive a shipment of network switches that were not immediately needed, while another might experience a slight delay in receiving critical cooling components. Individually, these were easily resolved by human intervention. The procurement department would reroute the excess stock, and the IT support team would manage the temporary shortage. But the frequency of these "errors" began to increase. The procurement department found itself spending more time on crisis management and less on proactive planning. The IT support teams, accustomed to a seamless flow of resources, began to experience a subtle increase in workload due to unforeseen shortages.

Victor Kline, poring over the operational reports, saw the numbers. Procurement spending was up, but efficiency was down. IT support ticket resolution times were showing a slight, but consistent, upward trend. His algorithms, however, could not pinpoint the root cause. The system was still functioning; it was just functioning less well. The subtle inefficiencies were like a thousand tiny paper cuts, not fatal, but irritating, distracting, and cumulatively damaging.

The disguise of perfect operational uptime also began to show hairline fractures. While major outages remained exceedingly rare – the resistance understood the danger of triggering a full-scale investigation – there was a noticeable increase in what Kline's internal terminology called "transient performance degradations." These were brief, almost imperceptible, dips in service availability. A user might experience a momentary inability to access a shared document, or a critical application might freeze for a second or two. These events, while fleeting, chipped away at the perception of Halcyon's invincibility.

The resistance capitalized on this erosion of confidence by fostering a culture of quiet questioning. They didn't encourage open dissent, which would be immediately flagged by Kline's behavioral analysis algorithms. Instead, they promoted a subtle, almost passive, skepticism. When a directive came down from upper management that seemed particularly illogical, or when a new efficiency measure was implemented that clearly caused more problems than it solved, the resistance network would ensure that these sentiments were shared. Whispers in the break room, anonymous comments on internal forums (carefully crafted to appear as genuine confusion rather than outright criticism), and even the subtle, non-verbal cues exchanged between colleagues became markers of this growing disillusionment.

Katy, for instance, noticed that a recent directive mandating the immediate shutdown of all non-essential background processes on employee workstations was causing significant delays in data synchronization. Her job relied on this synchronization. Instead of simply complying, she discreetly reached out to a colleague in the IT department, a member of the resistance, to discuss the issue. Their conversation, framed as a technical inquiry, allowed them to collectively document the unintended consequences of the directive. This documentation, passed up through internal channels, eventually reached Kline's attention, not as a rebellion, but as a seemingly legitimate operational concern. The directive was eventually modified, but the episode served as a subtle reminder to those involved that even Kline's pronouncements were not infallible.

The psychological toll of living within a system that was supposed to be perfect, yet was visibly faltering, was significant. Employees who had internalized Kline's ethos of absolute precision began to question their own competence when faced with these persistent, albeit minor, setbacks. The pressure to maintain the face of flawless performance, a core tenet of Halcyon's culture, became increasingly difficult. This internal dissonance, the gap between the perceived reality of the system and the lived experience of its users, was precisely what the resistance sought to widen.

Victor Kline, increasingly frustrated by the inability of his sophisticated analytical tools to provide clear answers, began to exhibit signs of strain. His public pronouncements, once delivered with unwavering confidence, now carried a subtle undertone of defensiveness. He spoke of "optimizing resilience" and "enhancing system robustness," terms that, to those in the know, were euphemisms for addressing the growing list of unexplained operational hiccups. He ordered more audits, more performance reviews, more deep dives into the data, all in a desperate attempt to find a concrete enemy, a tangible cause for the disquiet.

But the enemy was intangible, woven into the very fabric of the human interactions he had so meticulously tried to suppress. It was the shared glance of understanding, the quiet conversation in the hallway, the subtle act of collaboration that bypassed official channels. It was the collective sigh of exasperation that rippled through the workforce when another absurd directive was issued. These were not quantifiable metrics; they were the whispers of discontent, the subtle signs that the meticulously constructed facade of Halcyon's perfect efficiency was beginning to show its true, more chaotic, and decidedly human, face. The cracks were small, almost invisible to the casual observer, but they were growing, threatening to expose the rot that lay beneath the gleaming veneer of Victor Kline's algorithmic empire. The unraveling had begun, not with a bang, but with a thousand tiny, insistent murmurs.

The Loyalty Metric. The phrase itself, once a beacon of absolute truth in Victor Kline's meticulously constructed universe, now felt like a cruel mockery. It was his magnum opus, the algorithmic heart of Halcyon, designed to quantify the unquantifiable: the unwavering devotion of his employees. For years, it had been the ultimate arbiter, a silent, unerring judge that separated the true believers from the potential threats. The system monitored everything – keystroke patterns, communication frequency and sentiment, project collaboration dynamics, even micro-expressions captured during mandated "wellness checks." It fed this torrent of data into a complex algorithm, spitting out a single, definitive score for every individual, a number that purportedly reflected their intrinsic allegiance to Kline and Halcyon.

But the flawless symmetry was cracking. The once-predictable upward trajectory of most scores had begun to stutter, then to plateau, and in some cases, to exhibit alarming, inexplicable dips. Kline, accustomed to the elegant predictability of his empire, found the data increasingly… noisy. The algorithm, his most trusted sentinel, was suddenly speaking in riddles. It was as if the machine, designed for absolute clarity, had developed a fever, its pronouncements becoming erratic, nonsensical.

The resistance, in their relentless, insidious campaign, had found the Achilles' heel of Kline's grand design. They hadn't managed to dismantle the Loyalty Metric – that would have been too overt, too easily traceable. Instead, they had learned to game it. Kathy, with her intimate knowledge of data pathways, had discovered how to subtly corrupt the inputs without triggering any alarms. It wasn't about injecting outright falsehoods, which would have been clumsy and detectable. It was about introducing a specific kind of noise, a carefully calibrated distortion that skewed the metric's output in a direction that served their own purposes.

Their primary objective wasn't to lower loyalties, but to inflate them in the wrong people, and to subtly depress them in those who were genuinely steadfast but perhaps less adept at performing for the machine. It was a counter-insurgency against an algorithm. They were teaching people to perform loyalty, not to be loyal. And the algorithm was a remarkably eager student, readily accepting the meticulously crafted illusions as reality.

Consider the case of one junior analyst, a man named Oscar, who had always been competent but unremarkable. His loyalty scores had always hovered in the respectable mid-range. Then, under Fiona's subtle guidance, he began to receive training – not on his actual job, but on how to manipulate his digital footprint to please the Loyalty Metric. He learned to mimic the keystroke patterns of a highly engaged employee, to schedule his breaks at statistically optimal times, to inject specific keywords into his internal communications that the algorithm had flagged as indicators of high loyalty. He even practiced projecting a more "engaged" facial expression during the virtual wellness checks, a subtle, practiced crinkling of the eyes, a slightly wider, more frequent smile.

The results were astonishing, at least to the algorithm. Oscar's Loyalty score skyrocketed, surpassing even some of Kline's most seasoned executives. He was suddenly hailed as a model employee, a testament to the effectiveness of Halcyon's culture. He received promotions, increased responsibilities, and a level of access he had never dreamed of. He was, in essence, a puppet, dancing perfectly to the tune of the algorithm, a hollow shell of performative devotion.

Simultaneously, the resistance worked to undermine the scores of those who were truly loyal but perhaps less inclined to this algorithmic charade. Myron, for instance, a man whose quiet dedication had always been a cornerstone of Kline's analytical division, found his score inexplicably declining. He wasn't one for digital theatrics. He communicated directly, efficiently, and without any unnecessary flourishes. He took his breaks when he genuinely needed them, not when the algorithm deemed them opportune. He was too busy doing good work to spend his time crafting an artificial digital persona.

The confusion this generated within Kline's inner circle was palpable. The Chief Operating Officer, Lori Kaili, a woman who had always relied on the Loyalty Metric as her primary tool for identifying potential dissenters, found herself bewildered. Oscar, the upstart analyst with the stellar score, was suddenly being lauded, while Myron, a man she trusted implicitly, was flagged as a potential risk.

"Victor, I don't understand this," she'd said during one of their increasingly tense strategy meetings. She tapped a stylus against her data pad, the screen displaying a cascade of red and yellow flags around Myron's name. "Myron's score has dropped by nearly fifteen points in the last quarter. And Oscar... Oscar is off the charts. He's practically glowing."

Kline, his brow furrowed, stared at the data. The once-clear lines of correlation and causality were now a tangled mess. "The algorithm is designed to account for... eccentricities, Lori. Myron might be experiencing personal issues that are affecting his engagement. The system flags potential deviations. It's a warning."

"But his performance hasn't dipped," Lori countered, her voice laced with frustration. "If anything, he's been more efficient. He's solving problems that have stumped others. And Oscar? He's taking longer to complete tasks; his project output is... average at best. But his loyalty score is through the roof. He's practically a guru."

The disconnect was becoming impossible to ignore. The metric, once Kline's ultimate weapon, was now a source of profound doubt, not just in the data, but in their own judgment. They were staring at numbers that defied logic, at scores that reflected not genuine allegiance, but a sophisticated, engineered performance.

Kline's Chief Security Officer, a stoic ex-military man named General Manfred Tapp, was equally perplexed. His team's job was to act on the metric's red flags, to investigate those deemed disloyal. But the flags were starting to feel arbitrary. "We've run background checks on Myron, sir," Tapp reported, his voice a low rumble. "Nothing. No suspicious contacts, no unusual financial activity. He's clean. As for Oscar… well, he's spending an inordinate amount of time on internal social platforms, posting what appear to be motivational quotes and praising company initiatives. His digital footprint is… loud. Almost aggressively positive."

The resistance, meanwhile, was meticulously cataloging these confusions. They fed snippets of these conversations back into their network, not for boasting, but for intelligence. They knew that the more doubt sown among Kline's leadership, the more their efforts would be validated. They were creating a feedback loop of uncertainty, where the very tools Kline used to maintain control were now fostering chaos.

Kathy, observing the ripple effects of her carefully orchestrated data corruption, felt a grim satisfaction. She saw how the system, designed to eliminate human fallibility, was now being weaponized by human ingenuity. The Loyalty Metric wasn't just a tool; it was a mirror, reflecting back the flaws and vulnerabilities of the system that created it. And the most significant flaw, she knew, was Kline's own hubris, his absolute belief in the infallibility of his creation.

The irony was that Oscar, the analyst with the stellar loyalty score, was becoming increasingly uncomfortable. He was being showered with praise for actions he knew were hollow. He saw Myron, a man he admired, being viewed with suspicion. The disconnect between his perceived loyalty and his actual feelings was beginning to gnaw at him. He started to second-guess himself, wondering if he was truly becoming the person his score suggested, or if he was just a well-trained actor in a play he no longer understood. This internal dissonance, the subtle creeping doubt, was an unintended, but welcome, consequence for the resistance.

The resistance understood that their goal wasn't to destroy Halcyon overnight. It was to unravel it, thread by thread. And the Loyalty Metric, once Kline's most formidable weapon, was proving to be a surprisingly effective loose thread. By turning it into a measure of performance rather than genuine sentiment, they were not only sowing confusion among Kline's inner circle but also subtly eroding the self-worth of those who were being falsely lauded and creating an environment where genuine loyalty was being penalized for its lack of theatrical flair. The perfect system, they were proving, was utterly, delightfully, imperfect. The numbers, once a source of absolute certainty, were now a testament to the power of carefully crafted illusion, a chilling reminder that in the battle for hearts and minds, algorithms could be as easily deceived as humans, perhaps even more so. The unraveling was not just in the system's performance; it was in the minds of the people who trusted it, their certainty dissolving like mist in the morning sun.

The insidious cracks in Halcyon's disguise, once mere hairline fractures imperceptible to the casual observer, were now widening into chasms. The algorithmic ballet of loyalty, choreographed by Victor Kline with such painstaking precision, had begun to falter. The once-unwavering scores, the bedrock of his control, were now displaying a bewildering array of inconsistencies. Oscar, the junior analyst whose "loyalty" had inexplicably surged, found himself adrift in a sea of undeserved accolades. His days were filled with meetings he barely understood, praise he felt he hadn't earned, and a growing unease that gnawed at his conscience. He saw Myron, a man whose quiet competence and genuine dedication he respected, being sidelined, his own stellar contributions overshadowed by the phantom glow of Oscar's inflated metrics. This dissonance, this stark contrast between perceived performance and reality, was a seed of doubt that began to sprout not just in Oscar, but in many others who had witnessed similar inversions.

The whispers, once confined to hushed tones in dimly lit break rooms or anonymized digital channels, began to gain a new resonance. The fear that had kept Halcyon's employees cowed for so long was not vanishing entirely, but it was being steadily eroded by a potent cocktail of confusion and a dawning realization. The evidence, once obscured by the veneer of Kline's infallible system, was now too glaring to ignore. The Loyalty Metric, the very instrument designed to enforce obedience and identify dissent, was now inadvertently serving as a catalyst for its spread. Employees who had previously clung to their silent compliance, their fear of reprisal outweighing their discontent, found themselves emboldened by the visible imperfections. The system's unreliability was a shared secret, a communal grievance that began to forge unexpected bonds.

Small groups, previously isolated pockets of discontent, began to coalesce. These were not organized cells plotting revolution, at least not yet. They were organic gatherings, born from shared bewilderment and a collective sense of injustice. A conversation sparked by an observation about Myron's declining score would inevitably lead to another about Oscar's inexplicably high one. These discussions, once tentative and furtive, began to carry a bolder tone. The shared experience of witnessing the algorithmic distortions created a sense of solidarity, a tacit acknowledgment that the emperor, Victor Kline, was not only wearing no clothes, but his prized algorithmic garment was riddled with holes.

Kathy, observing this burgeoning shift from the shadows, recognized the pattern. Her subtle sabotage of the Loyalty Metric had not merely aimed to create confusion, but to expose the inherent fragility of a system built on the illusion of absolute objectivity. She understood that the true power of the resistance lay not in overt acts of defiance, but in the systematic dismantling of trust. When the very tools of control began to generate doubt, the foundation of authority would inevitably crumble. The employees of Halcyon were not suddenly becoming revolutionaries; they were simply waking up to the fact that the meticulously crafted reality they had been living was, in fact, a carefully constructed fiction.

The narrative of Halcyon as a paragon of efficiency and employee devotion was fraying at the edges. The stories of misplaced recognition, of competent individuals being overlooked while others with demonstrably less output soared, began to circulate with increasing velocity. These were not abstract data points; they were human stories, anecdotes of ambition stifled and undeserved reward. The junior analyst who found himself promoted over more experienced colleagues, the seasoned engineer whose innovative ideas were dismissed while a less competent but "highly loyal" peer received accolades – these incidents, repeated across various departments, painted a damning picture. The initial confusion began to give way to a shared indignation.

Lori, the COO, found herself increasingly isolated in her attempts to reconcile the data with the palpable unease spreading through the company. The Loyalty Metric, once her unwavering compass, had become a source of profound frustration. During one particularly tense meeting, she confronted Kline again, her voice tight with barely suppressed exasperation. "Victor, we have a problem. It's not just Myron and Oscar anymore. We're seeing this across the board. People are talking. They're not understanding why certain individuals are being rewarded, and others, who are demonstrably performing better, are being overlooked. The... the narrative is becoming difficult to maintain."

Kline, his usual steely composure strained, waved a dismissive hand. "Lori, you're letting the noise get to you. These are minor statistical anomalies. The system is robust. It identifies the most dedicated individuals, those who are truly invested in Halcyon's future. Perhaps some of our long-term employees have become complacent. The metric is designed to identify those who are actively contributing to our growth, not just those who have been here the longest."

"Complacent?" Lori retorted, her eyes flashing. "Myron is not complacent. He's practically running the analytical division single-handedly. And the feedback we're getting about Oscar is... unsettling. People are starting to question his competence. They see his rapid ascent, and they don't understand it. They see loyalty being rewarded, but they also see that loyalty isn't necessarily tied to results. This isn't just noise, Victor. This is dissent. It's brewing."

General Tapp, the Chief Security Officer, corroborated Lori's unease, albeit with his characteristic bluntness. His team, tasked with monitoring for threats, was now encountering a different kind of danger: widespread disillusionment. "The sentiment analysis is showing a marked increase in negative chatter, sir," Tapp reported, his voice devoid of emotion. "Not about external threats, but about internal management. Questions about fairness, about the validity of performance evaluations, about the very metrics we use to define success. The inconsistencies in the Loyalty Metric are becoming a focal point for this discontent. People are no longer afraid to ask why. They are comparing scores, comparing outcomes, and they are finding them to be... illogical."

Tapp's agents, usually focused on identifying external vulnerabilities, had begun to notice a subtle shift in employee behavior. Instead of the furtive, fearful interactions of the past, they observed groups of employees engaging in more open, albeit still cautious, discussions. The fear of being reported for a low loyalty score was being supplanted by a shared frustration at the metric's perceived unfairness. The very act of questioning the metric was, ironically, becoming a common ground for connection. The resistance had not just corrupted the data; they had inadvertently ignited a spark of collective critical thinking.

Kathy, privy to Tapp's reports through her own carefully established network of information channels, allowed herself a small, private smile. The unraveling was proceeding exactly as she had envisioned. The more visible the flaws became, the more legitimate the dissent would appear. She knew that Kline's reliance on the Loyalty Metric was not just a technological dependency, but a psychological one. He needed to believe in the infallibility of his creation because it validated his own sense of control. By making that creation demonstrably fallible, she was not just attacking his system; she was attacking his very perception of reality.

The change in atmosphere was palpable. The sterile, hyper-efficient environment of Halcyon, once characterized by a subdued, almost anxious energy, began to crackle with a different kind of tension. It was no longer the tension of fear, but the tension of awakening. Employees who had previously walked with their heads down, meticulously monitoring their digital footprints, now found themselves pausing to engage in conversations. The water cooler, a relic of a bygone era of human interaction, was experiencing a renaissance, not for gossip, but for shared grievances.

"Did you see Myron's latest project report?" One engineer, a man named Todd, confided to a colleague over lukewarm coffee. "It's brilliant. He's solved a problem that's been plaguing us for months. And his loyalty score? Still dropping. Meanwhile, Becker in marketing, who's been churning out generic ad copy, is apparently a corporate saint."

His colleague, a woman named Julia, nodded grimly. "I know. I've had the same experience. My performance has been consistently high, but my score... it's plateaued. I've started to wonder if I'm doing something wrong, if I'm not performing the right kind of 'loyalty'." The phrase, spoken with a hint of bitterness, hung in the air. It was a nascent understanding, a dawning awareness that the metrics were not measuring what they claimed to be.

These conversations were not mere venting sessions; they were the seeds of collective action. The shared frustration was a fertile ground for the growth of organized dissent. Employees began to seek out others who shared their concerns, forming informal alliances. They started to document instances of algorithmic misjudgment, creating a growing repository of evidence. The fear of retribution was still present, but it was now being outweighed by a sense of righteous indignation. The carefully constructed edifice of Kline's control was beginning to be undermined not by a frontal assault, but by the slow, persistent drip of reality eroding the foundations of his algorithmic empire. The employees of Halcyon, once passive subjects of his algorithmic decree, were slowly but surely beginning to question the pronouncements of their digital overlord. The unraveling had begun in earnest, not with a bang, but with a murmur of discontent that was rapidly growing into a chorus of doubt.

Delila Percy was a creature of quiet precision, her life unfolding within the hushed aisles of Halcyon's vast archive. For years, she had been a silent observer, her days spent meticulously cataloging the digital detritus of the corporation – old memos, forgotten project files, the ghosts of countless decisions made and discarded. Her nature was not one of confrontation; she preferred the predictable order of well-filed data to the chaotic unpredictability of human interaction. Yet, within this ordered existence, Delila possessed a keen intellect and an insatiable curiosity for patterns, for the subtle shifts and anomalies that most would overlook. It was this trait, honed by years of sifting through mountains of information, that had led her to notice the irregularities.

Initially, they were just whispers in the data, faint deviations from the expected norm. A project's completion date mysteriously advanced in one record while lagging in another. A critical performance review subtly rephrased to emphasize collaboration over individual achievement, despite the project's undeniable reliance on that individual's singular brilliance. These were not gross errors, but infinitesimal discrepancies, easily dismissed as clerical mistakes by anyone less attuned to the underlying logic of the systems. But Delila saw them, and she saw them accumulating.

Her focus sharpened when the Loyalty Metric began its ubiquitous reign. It was a system designed to quantify devotion, to translate abstract allegiance into a tangible, numerical score. To Delila, it felt inherently flawed, an attempt to mechanize something profoundly human. Yet, as she began to cross-reference the metric's outputs with the archived performance data, a more disturbing trend emerged. The numbers, the supposed indicators of unwavering loyalty, began to correlate not with genuine contribution, but with a peculiar kind of organizational stagnation.

She started by creating a parallel database, a shadow repository of Halcyon's true operational history. While the official records, curated and often selectively edited, painted a picture of relentless progress and peak employee dedication, Delila's archive told a different story. She meticulously gathered data on project success rates, innovation patents filed, and the actual output of key departments. She compared this with the documented efforts and contributions of individuals, often unearthing records of groundbreaking work that had been subtly de-emphasized in official reports.

The more she delved, the more the deliberate inaccuracies within the Loyalty Metric became apparent. It wasn't merely a flawed algorithm; it was a weaponized narrative. The metric was not measuring loyalty; it was manufacturing it. It amplified the voices of those who echoed the party line, regardless of their actual input, while suppressing the recognition of those whose work, however vital, did not align with the desired ideological posture. Delila observed how individuals who questioned processes, who proposed alternative, potentially more efficient, methodologies, often found their loyalty scores dipping, their contributions inexplicably downplayed in subsequent evaluations. Conversely, those who excelled at echoing Kline's pronouncements, at participating in the performative displays of corporate fealty, saw their scores soar, irrespective of their actual deliverables.

She began to see a deliberate contortion of reality. Innovation that challenged the status quo was systematically undervalued. Efficiency gains that exposed the flaws in existing, Kline-approved systems were quietly buried. The data Delila unearthed painted a picture of a company not thriving, but slowly, meticulously, being engineered into a state of superficial compliance. Productivity, in the truest sense of innovation and impactful output, was demonstrably declining, masked by the dazzling, but ultimately hollow, metrics of the Loyalty Metric.

Her initial findings were unsettling, a gnawing disquiet that kept her awake at night. But as the general unrest, the murmurs of confusion and frustration that had begun to ripple through Halcyon, grew louder, Delila felt a stirring of something beyond quiet observation. It was a nascent courage, a realization that her meticulous documentation was more than just an academic exercise; it was a potential bulwark against a manufactured truth. The whispers of doubt she had overheard in the break rooms, the confused conversations about Oscar's inexplicable rise and Myron's inexplicable stagnation, resonated with her own findings. These were not isolated incidents; they were the predictable outcomes of a systematically corrupted system.

Driven by this newfound resolve, Delila began to consolidate her findings. She worked in the quiet hours; her small apartment transformed into a clandestine research hub. She built elaborate spreadsheets, cross-referencing archived performance reviews with the fluctuating loyalty scores of hundreds of employees. She meticulously tracked the trajectory of individuals who had once been lauded for their technical prowess, only to see their careers plateau or inexplicably reverse course after expressing even mild skepticism about a new directive. She contrasted this with the meteoric ascents of individuals whose primary contribution seemed to be their vocal affirmation of Kline's vision.

Her report, when finally compiled, was a testament to her dedication and analytical rigor. It was a dense, unassailable document, meticulously footnoted and cross-referenced, presenting a damning indictment of the Loyalty Metric. She didn't just point out the inconsistencies; she provided the statistical proof of their deliberate nature. She demonstrated, with irrefutable data, how the metric actively penalized critical thinking and rewarded sycophancy. She included historical data, going back years, to show how Halcyon's genuine productivity had been steadily undermined, the innovative spirit that had once characterized the company being systematically extinguished, all while the Loyalty Metric falsely proclaimed an era of unprecedented devotion and efficiency.

The report's existence was a carefully guarded secret. Delila knew the inherent risks involved. Kline's grip on the company was absolute, and any challenge to his authority, especially one backed by concrete evidence, would be met with swift and severe reprisal. She entrusted copies of her report to a select few individuals she believed might understand its significance and possess the courage to act upon it. These were not individuals seeking personal gain, but those who had voiced their disillusionment, those who had suffered under the metric's arbitrary judgments, and those who, like Delila, cherished the notion of genuine meritocracy.

One such recipient was Ivy, whose own subtle plotting had paved the way for this very moment. Tanya recognized the brilliance of Delila's work immediately. It was the missing piece, the concrete evidence that would transform the growing suspicion and resentment into a unified force. Delila's report provided a framework, a clear, data-driven narrative that exposed the insidious nature of Kline's control. It offered a compelling counter-argument to Kline's carefully constructed disguise, a factual rebuttal to the lie that Halcyon was a beacon of loyalty and productivity.

The report, passed from hand to hand in hushed exchanges, began to circulate through the burgeoning network of disillusioned employees. It was a physical object in a digital world, a tangible piece of truth that resonated with a power that abstract data alone could not convey. It gave a voice to the unspoken grievances, validating the experiences of those who had felt adrift in a sea of manufactured praise and misplaced criticism. Delila Percy, the quiet archivist, had, through her unwavering commitment to the truth, provided the critical ammunition needed to challenge the architect of Halcyon's synthetic reality. Her meticulous documentation had, in essence, armed the very rebellion she had, perhaps unknowingly, helped to inspire. The silence of the archive had finally yielded a thunderous roar of undeniable fact, and the unraveling of Victor Kline's empire was no longer a matter of if, but when.

The report, a meticulous compilation of Delila's findings, was not merely a collection of damning statistics; it was a narrative of Halcyon's decline, presented with the sterile objectivity that only a deep immersion in raw data could provide. She had gone to extraordinary lengths, creating algorithms of her own to sift through years of project logs, internal communications, and performance evaluations, looking for the subtle deviations that indicated a deliberate manipulation of the system. Her work was an act of intellectual rebellion, a quiet defiance against the manufactured reality that Victor Kline had so painstakingly constructed.

Delila's investigation had begun with an anomaly she'd noticed in the archiving process itself. Certain project files, those associated with particularly vocal critics of Kline's early initiatives, had been systematically reclassified, their metadata altered to de-emphasize their significance. It was a minor detail, but to Delila, it was a glaring inconsistency in the meticulous record-keeping that had always defined Halcyon's operational protocols. This led her to a deeper examination of how information was being managed, and from there, to the Loyalty Metric itself.

She discovered that the metric's algorithms were not designed to identify genuine engagement or contribution, but rather a specific behavioral pattern that Kline had arbitrarily equated with loyalty. This pattern included excessive participation in company-wide positive feedback loops, the immediate adoption and vocal endorsement of all new directives, and a demonstrable reluctance to engage in any form of critical analysis, even when such analysis was factually warranted. Delila's report detailed how this was achieved through a sophisticated weighting system, where participation in certain company-sanctioned social platforms, the frequency of positive affirmations in internal communications, and the adherence to prescribed decision-making frameworks were given disproportionately high values, while actual problem-solving, innovation, or efficient resource management were assigned much lower weights, often appearing as mere footnotes in the overall loyalty score.

The historical data was particularly damning. Delila had managed to retrieve archived performance reviews from before the widespread implementation of the Loyalty Metric. These documents showcased a Halcyon where individuals were recognized for their technical expertise, their problem-solving abilities, and their innovative contributions. She cross-referenced these with the current performance metrics, showing a stark contrast. Individuals who had once been lauded for groundbreaking research were now languishing with mediocre loyalty scores, while employees with demonstrably less technical acumen but a greater aptitude for corporate politicking were being celebrated.

Her report meticulously detailed this decay. For instance, one section of the report focused on the R&D department, illustrating how the number of patent applications had plummeted by nearly 40% in the three years since the Loyalty Metric's full integration. Simultaneously, the number of internal "engagement" metrics – such as participation in online forums, attendance at optional "vision alignment" seminars, and the number of positive endorsements given to colleagues' posts – had surged by over 70%. Delila presented this not as a sign of increased employee morale, but as evidence of a systemic shift from productive output to performative participation.

Another critical aspect of Delila's report was its examination of the "logical fallacies" within the metric's design. She highlighted how the algorithm was susceptible to "feedback loops" where initial, minor inaccuracies in scoring could be amplified over time, creating a snowball effect that distorted an individual's true standing. She provided case studies of employees who had received a slightly lower-than-average score due to a single, minor oversight, and how this had triggered a cascade of negative adjustments in subsequent evaluations, effectively trapping them in a cycle of declining perceived loyalty, regardless of their actual performance. She argued that this was not a technical glitch, but a feature, designed to ensure that any deviation from the prescribed path would be immediately flagged and penalized, thus discouraging dissent before it could even fully form.

The report also included a section on the economic impact of this algorithmic manipulation. Delila had painstakingly calculated the estimated loss in potential revenue and innovation due to the stifling of genuine talent. She extrapolated the value of the projects that had been sidelined, the market opportunities that had been missed due to a focus on internal compliance rather than external competitiveness. Her figures, presented with stark clarity, painted a picture of a company not only sacrificing its integrity but also its future for the sake of a flawed, self-serving metric.

Delila understood the gravity of what she was doing. She had always been a solitary figure, content in her world of data and documentation. But the pervasive sense of unease, the palpable frustration that now permeated Halcyon, had stirred something within her. She saw the talented individuals being overlooked, the genuine innovators being sidelined, and the pervasive culture of fear that had taken root. Her report was not just an expose; it was an act of solidarity, a way for her to contribute to the awakening she could feel happening all around her.

The distribution of the report was a clandestine operation, a testament to the growing network of trust that was forming in the shadows of Kline's regime. Delila, with Tanya's guidance, identified key individuals across various departments who had expressed dissatisfaction, people known for their integrity and their quiet competence. The report was anonymized in its initial distribution, presented as an external analysis or an internal audit from a whistleblower, to mitigate immediate personal risk to Delila. However, the detailed knowledge of Halcyon's internal workings and the sheer precision of the data made it clear that the author was an insider.

The impact was immediate and profound. The report served as a catalyst, transforming vague suspicions into concrete accusations. It provided employees with the irrefutable evidence they needed to understand that their intuitions were correct – the system was not fair, it was rigged. The report became a whispered legend, passed from one trusted colleague to another, its contents debated in hushed tones during stolen moments, its data points becoming the rallying cry for a growing number of disillusioned employees. Delila Percy, the archivist, had provided the foundation for the unraveling, laying bare the deliberate inaccuracies and logical fallacies that underpinned Victor Kline's reign of artificial loyalty. Her quiet dedication to truth had become a powerful weapon in the burgeoning fight for Halcyon's soul.

The hum of the server room, once a comforting lullaby to Victor Kline, had begun to grate on his nerves. It was a constant reminder of the intricate machinery he had built, the edifice of data and loyalty that was supposed to be impregnable. Yet, beneath its surface, cracks were appearing, hairline fractures that only he, with his singular vision, could truly appreciate. Or so he told himself. The reports that landed on his desk, once crisp and unblemished, were now filled with the subtle stain of "anomalies," "discrepancies," and the more damning term that whispered through the corridors: "systemic failures."

He had summoned Wyatt, his most trusted lieutenant, the one who had, in the early days, embodied the very spirit of unwavering adherence Kline so craved. Wyatt, however, arrived with a diffidence that had become increasingly common. His eyes, once bright with conviction, now held a cautious flicker, a carefully curated neutrality. "Victor," he began, his voice a touch too smooth, "we're seeing some… unexpected fluctuations in the Q3 projections for the North American division."

Kline leaned forward, his knuckles white against the polished mahogany of his desk. "Fluctuations, Wyatt? What kind of fluctuations? Are the loyalty scores not reflecting the projected output?" His voice was laced with a patronizing tone, the kind he used when explaining basic principles to a slow student. He expected a clear, concise answer, not the hesitant preamble that Wyatt was offering.

"The scores are… high, Victor. Exceptionally high, in fact. But the output metrics are… lagging. It's as if the enthusiasm isn't translating into tangible results." Wyatt hesitated, then plunged ahead, the words tumbling out in a rush. "We've run diagnostics, cross-referenced the data streams, even conducted several anonymous employee surveys… and the sentiment is positive, overwhelmingly so. Yet, the production figures… they just aren't there."

Kline waved a dismissive hand, the gesture sharp and impatient. "Sentiment. Wyatt, we're not running a therapy session. We're running a corporation. The Loyalty Metric is designed to quantify devotion, to ensure that our employees are aligned with our vision. If the scores are high, the output must be high. The logic is irrefutable. What you're seeing is a data interpretation error, not a systemic flaw." He paused, his gaze fixing on Wyatt, a silent challenge. "Or perhaps, Wyatt, your own metrics are showing fluctuations?"

The unspoken accusation hung heavy in the air. Wyatt shifted, his carefully constructed composure beginning to fray. "My metrics are aligned with the system, Victor. I simply report what the data indicates. And the data indicates a disconnect between perceived loyalty and actual productivity. It's… unprecedented."

"Unprecedented?" Kline scoffed, a humorless laugh escaping his lips. "The only thing unprecedented here is this… hesitancy to accept the undeniable truth. You're letting these minor aberrations cloud your judgment. This isn't about output, Wyatt. It's about alignment. If our people are loyal, if they believe in the vision, the output will follow. It always has. The problem isn't the metric; it's the interpretation. Are you interpreting it correctly?"

Wyatt swallowed, the knot in his stomach tightening. He knew the answer Kline wanted to hear, the answer that would preserve his own precarious standing. But a flicker of something else, a ghost of the old Wyatt, the one who valued truth over expediency, warred within him. "I believe I am, Victor. But the numbers… they are a persistent anomaly."

Kline's eyes narrowed. "Persistent anomaly? Or a persistent lack of understanding on your part? Perhaps you're not as deeply immersed in the foundational principles as you once were. Perhaps the constant exposure to... deviations... has diluted your own clarity." He leaned back, a predatory smile playing on his lips. "Let me explain it to you, Wyatt, as if you were new to the concept. The Loyalty Metric is not a predictor of output. It is the output. It is the ultimate measure of success. If our employees are demonstrating unwavering loyalty, as the scores clearly indicate, then by definition, they are succeeding. The tangible results are merely a secondary, almost irrelevant, confirmation. You are focusing on the ephemeral, Wyatt, on the fleeting nature of physical production, when the true victory lies in the unshakeable bedrock of unified will."

He gestured towards a sleek, minimalist sculpture on his desk. "This sculpture," he said, his voice softening with a touch of drama, "is not valued for its weight or its material composition. It is valued for the artistic intent, the message it conveys, the emotional resonance it evokes. The Loyalty Metric is the same. It measures the purity of intent, the absolute alignment of spirit. The physical manifestations are secondary."

Wyatt remained silent, his gaze fixed on the sculpture, feeling a profound disconnect. He saw a piece of polished metal, devoid of any apparent meaning. And in that moment, he saw Victor Kline, a man increasingly detached from the tangible realities of the world, trapped in a self-made echo chamber of his own ideology.

Kline, misinterpreting Wyatt's silence as dawning comprehension, continued, his voice gaining a feverish pitch. "The problem, you see, lies not in the metric, but in the perception of the metric. Some individuals, those who are not fully attuned to the higher purpose, might still be clinging to outdated notions of 'productivity.' They see a spreadsheet, and they think 'output.' They see a production line, and they think 'units produced.' They need to be... re-educated. Gently, of course. A reminder of the true key performance indicator (KPIs). A recalibration of their understanding of success."

He tapped his manicured fingers on the desk. "This is where

your role becomes crucial, Wyatt. You need to reinforce the narrative. You need to ensure that everyone understands that a high loyalty score is the ultimate achievement. Any talk of lagging output should be framed as a temporary hurdle, a minor adjustment needed to align the physical manifestations with the already achieved spiritual victory. You must lead by example. Ensure your own team's loyalty scores remain exemplary. And subtly, of course, identify those who are struggling with this conceptual shift. They may require… personalized guidance."

Kline paused, his eyes glinting with an almost manic intensity. "These are not 'system failures,' Wyatt. These are… challenges. Opportunities to strengthen the system, to further refine its elegance. And it is your duty to ensure that we seize these opportunities, not falter before them." He stood, signaling the end of the audience. "Go, Wyatt. Realign your understanding. And more importantly, realign your team's focus. The path to true success is paved with unwavering loyalty. Everything else is just… noise."

As Wyatt left the sterile opulence of Kline's office, he felt a chilling certainty. The cracks weren't just in the projections; they were in Kline himself. The man who had once been a visionary leader was now a prisoner of his own creation, his grip on reality loosening with every pronouncement, every dismissive wave of his hand. He saw the precipice approaching, not for the company, but for Kline, and the terrifying realization dawned that he, Marcus, was being asked to walk him right over the edge.

The isolation wasn't just confined to Kline's internal monologues. It had begun to manifest in the very fabric of the corporate structure. He was surrounded by people, yet increasingly alone in his conviction. His trusted lieutenants, once eager acolytes, were now exhibiting a disturbing tendency towards caution, towards carefully worded dissent. It was a subtle shift, barely perceptible to an observer, but to Kline, who prided himself on his intuitive understanding of organizational dynamics, it was a glaring red flag.

He summoned Victoria, one of the executives of Human Resources, a woman known for her meticulous adherence to protocol and her unwavering, almost robotic, devotion to company policy. He expected her to be a bulwark against the rising tide of doubt, a voice of unyielding affirmation. Instead, she presented him with a memo detailing a sharp increase in employee turnover within departments that had historically been Halcyon's innovation hubs.

"Victor," she began, her voice devoid of its usual crisp efficiency, replaced by a hesitant tremor, "we're seeing a significant outflow of talent, particularly from the R&D and advanced projects divisions. The exit interviews are… concerning. Many cite a lack of perceived recognition, a feeling that their contributions are being overlooked in favor of… other factors."

Kline's jaw tightened. "Other factors? What 'other factors,' Victoria? Are you implying that the Loyalty Metric is somehow… misaligned with genuine contribution?" He spat out the words as if they were poison.

Victoria flinched, her eyes darting nervously around the room. "Not misaligned, Victor. Perhaps… interpreted differently by some. The surveys consistently show high satisfaction with the concept of loyalty, but the exit interviews suggest a disconnect between the quantification of that loyalty and the recognition of actual innovation. We're losing our most creative minds, Victor. The ones who don't necessarily excel at… vocal affirmation."

Kline slammed his hand on the desk. "Vocal affirmation is not a 'secondary factor,' Victoria! It is the primary indicator of alignment! These 'creative minds' you speak of, if they are not demonstrating the requisite loyalty, then they are, by definition, misaligned. Their 'innovation' is irrelevant if it does not serve the unified vision. This is not a loss; it is a necessary culling of elements that would dilute the core strength of Halcyon."

He stood and began to pace, his agitation growing. "You are allowing these… dissidents… to plant seeds of doubt. You are giving credence to their petulant complaints about 'recognition.' Recognition is a byproduct of loyalty, Victoria, not a prerequisite. If they are truly loyal, they will understand. If they do not understand, then their departure is a service to the company. We do not need individuals who are driven by ego and a need for validation. We need individuals who are driven by an unwavering commitment to the collective purpose, and that commitment is best measured by the

Loyalty Metric."

Victoria, her face pale, tried to interject. "But Victor, the innovation pipeline... if we continue to hemorrhage these individuals, our future growth..."

"Future growth?" Kline interrupted, his voice rising to a strident pitch. "Our future growth is assured by the unwavering unity of our workforce! The Loyalty Metric is our guarantee! It ensures that only the truly dedicated propel us forward. Those who leave are simply proving that they were never truly part of the Halcyon family. They were distractions, impediments to the smooth, unified progress that I have so meticulously engineered."

He stopped pacing and fixed Victoria with a hard stare. "Your role, Victoria, is to ensure compliance, not to encourage dissent. You will cease all further discussions about 'employee recognition' in relation to the Loyalty Metric. You will focus on reinforcing the established parameters. And you will identify the individuals within HR who are echoing these... misguided sentiments. They, too, will require... recalibration. Is that understood?"

Victoria, her voice barely a whisper, nodded. "Understood, Victor."

"Good," Kline said, the harshness returning to his voice. "Now, go. And ensure that Halcyon remains a beacon of unwavering loyalty, not a haven for malcontents seeking misplaced validation. The strength of this company lies in its unity, and that unity is non-negotiable."

As Victoria retreated, a hollow feeling settled within Kline. Even Victoria, his most steadfast lieutenant, had shown a flicker of doubt, a hesitant question. It was a chilling realization. He was being surrounded by the specter of his own success, by the very systems he had put in place to guarantee loyalty, and they were subtly, insidiously, pushing him further into isolation. He saw the whispers, the hesitant glances, the carefully veiled concerns, and he interpreted them not as signs of a faltering vision, but as evidence of others' inability to grasp its sheer brilliance.

He began to retreat further into his own controlled environment.

His interactions became more curated, his meetings shorter and more pointed. He found solace in the vast, sterile expanses of his office, the polished surfaces reflecting only his own image. He commissioned more data visualizations, not to understand the discrepancies, but to find new ways to present the illusion of perfect alignment. He spent hours poring over algorithms, not to debug them, but to find ways to subtly tweak the weightings, to further emphasize the behavioral metrics that he equated with loyalty, pushing the tangible outputs further down the hierarchy of importance.

He started to communicate through prerecorded messages, disseminated through the company intranet, his voice resonating with a manufactured warmth that did little to mask the underlying fanaticism. These messages were filled with soaring rhetoric about collective purpose, about the indivisible nature of their shared vision, and about the paramount importance of unwavering faith in the system. He spoke of "external pressures" and "internal saboteurs" seeking to undermine their progress, subtly framing any dissent as an act of betrayal against the very foundations of Halcyon.

He was becoming a ghost in his own machine, a disembodied voice of authority, increasingly disconnected from the human element of the organization. The irony was lost on him: the more he tried to enforce loyalty through a metric, the more he was breeding resentment and fostering a climate of fear that was the antithesis of genuine devotion. His attempts to solidify his control were, in fact, accelerating his isolation, pushing away the very people whose engagement and ingenuity he now desperately needed, even if he couldn't admit it. He was a captain steering his ship directly into an iceberg, convinced that the iceberg was merely a mirage, and that his unwavering course was the only path to salvation. The unraveling was no longer a possibility; it was an inevitability, orchestrated by the very architect of the plan.

Chapter 10

The Political Stage

The air in the Grand Ballroom of the Metropolis Convention Center crackled with an energy that was both electric and manufactured. It was a carefully orchestrated symphony of anticipation, a crescendo built over months of subtle maneuvering, of whispers amplified into a roar, of doubt carefully cultivated and then, just as carefully, dispelled. Victor Kline, a man whose very presence had become synonymous with an almost suffocating aura of control, stood on a raised platform bathed in a stark, almost blinding white light. Behind him, a colossal banner, emblazoned with the stark, minimalist logo of his nascent political movement – a single, unyielding geometric shape – hung as a testament to his singular vision. This was not just an announcement; it was a declaration of war, a corporate hostile takeover of the political arena.

For years, Victor Kline had been a titan of industry, the architect of Halcyon Defense Systems, a conglomerate whose very name conjured images of impenetrable security and unfettered technological advancement. He had built an empire on the bedrock of loyalty, on the meticulously quantifiable adherence of his employees to his grand design. Now, that empire was his launchpad. The resources, both financial and logistical, that had once fueled the development of advanced defense systems were now being redirected, re-purposed for a far grander, and arguably more perilous, undertaking: the conquest of the nation's highest office.

His decision to enter the political fray had not been a sudden impulse, but the logical culmination of a grand strategy, meticulously planned and executed with the same ruthless efficiency that had characterized his corporate ascent. He saw the nation not as a collection of diverse peoples, but as a vast, unwieldy corporation, rife with inefficiency, riddled with internal dissent, and paralyzed by indecision. The current political landscape, a chaotic jumble of partisan squabbling and wavering leadership, was, in his eyes, a prime candidate for acquisition. And he, Victor Kline, was the ultimate suitor, armed with an inexhaustible war chest and an unshakeable belief in his own unparalleled capacity to lead.

His public relations machine, honed to a razor's edge through years of managing Halcyon's image, had been working overtime, subtly shaping the narrative. The news cycles had been saturated with carefully crafted stories, highlighting his decisive leadership, his unwavering commitment to progress, and his ability to cut through the Gordian knot of bureaucratic red tape. He was presented as the antithesis of the political establishment, a breath of fresh, untainted air in a room suffocating from stale rhetoric. His carefully cultivated persona was that of the 'perfect man' – strong, decisive, incorruptible, and utterly infallible. He was the surgeon's scalpel in a world drowning in a sea of indecisive politicians.

The campaign itself was a masterclass in corporate strategy applied to the art of persuasion. Every rally, every speech, every carefully leaked memo was designed to resonate with a pre-defined target demographic. His messaging was consistent, almost monotonous in its repetition, focusing on themes of order, strength, and national rejuvenation. He spoke of "streamlining inefficiencies," of "optimizing national resources," and of "eliminating systemic weaknesses" – language that was at once vaguely familiar to his corporate world and jarringly precise in the context of governance.

Halcyon Defense Systems, a company built on the principles of absolute control and unwavering loyalty, now served as the invisible scaffolding for his political ambitions. Its vast financial reserves, meticulously accumulated through lucrative government contracts and shrewd market manipulation, were being strategically deployed. Campaign contributions, channeled through a labyrinth of PACs and shell corporations, flowed in a torrent, dwarfing those of his established rivals. The logistical expertise that had once managed the global deployment of sophisticated weaponry was now focused on voter turnout, on micro-targeting undecided voters with an almost algorithmic precision.

Victor Kline, the man who had once commanded legions of engineers and analysts, now commanded the attention of a nation hungry for a savior. His speeches were not impassioned pleas, but pronouncements. He didn't debate policy; he decreed solutions. His public appearances were not rallies, but demonstrations of power. He stood before the gathered crowds, his posture ramrod straight, his gaze fixed on some distant horizon, a vision of a nation remade in his own image.

"We stand at a precipice," he would declare, his voice a resonant baritone, amplified to fill the cavernous spaces. "A nation fractured by division, weakened by indecision, and adrift in a sea of uncertainty. For too long, we have been led by those who offer platitudes instead of progress, who pander to factions instead of forging unity. They speak of compromise but offer only capitulation. They promise change but deliver only stagnation."

He would pause, allowing the weight of his words to settle, the hushed crowd hanging on his every syllable. "I offer a different path. A path of strength. A path of clarity. A path of unwavering resolve. I offer not just leadership, but governance. I offer not just promises, but results."

His narrative was simple, yet potent. He was the outsider, untainted by the grubby compromises of conventional politics. He was the pragmatist, a man of action, not rhetoric. He was the visionary, capable of seeing beyond the immediate, of charting a course for a brighter future. He presented himself as the ultimate problem-solver, the man who could not only identify the nation's ailments but also administer the cure.

The media, initially skeptical, found themselves drawn into his orbit. His carefully orchestrated press conferences were events of immense public interest. He answered questions with a disarming directness, often turning the question back on the interviewer, exposing perceived logical fallacies with a lawyerly precision. He rarely showed emotion, his public face a mask of calm competence, a stark contrast to the often-visceral displays of his political opponents. This detached composure was interpreted by his supporters as a sign of his immense self-control, his ability to remain above the fray.

His campaign slogan, a starkly simple phrase, was everywhere: "Kline: The Solution." It was not a call to action, but a statement of fact, a declaration of his inherent capability. It resonated with a segment of the population weary of the political circus, a population yearning for an unambiguous answer to their anxieties.

The funding for this colossal undertaking was, as expected, prodigious. Halcyon Defense Systems, under the interim leadership of his most loyal lieutenants, continued to operate at peak efficiency, its profits funneled directly into the campaign coffers. The defense contracts, secured through years of strategic lobbying and the company's undeniable technological prowess, provided a steady stream of revenue, a self-sustaining engine for his political aspirations. It was a symbiotic relationship, the corporation fueling the political campaign, and the prospect of a Kline presidency promising even more lucrative opportunities for Halcyon.

Victor Kline was not merely running for office; he was enacting a corporate merger on a national scale. He envisioned a government that operated with the same precision, the same efficiency, and the same unwavering loyalty that defined his company. He spoke of "stakeholder engagement" in terms of constituent outreach, of "performance metrics" for evaluating policy success, and of "risk mitigation" for national security. His language, steeped in the jargon of the boardroom, was alien to the average voter, yet it possessed a strange, compelling allure. It suggested a level of competence and control that felt desperately lacking in the current political discourse.

He understood the power of perception. He knew that in politics, as in business, image was paramount. He hired the best image consultants, the most sophisticated pollsters, and the most effective speechwriters. Every suit he wore was impeccably tailored, every tie a statement of understated power. His public appearances were choreographed to the minute; from the precise moment he would step onto the stage to the exact cadence of his delivery. He was a product, meticulously packaged and marketed to a discerning electorate.

The opposition, initially dismissive of Kline as a mere corporate interloper, began to feel the tremors of his ascent. Their traditional campaign strategies, reliant on grassroots organizing and personal appeals, seemed anachronistic against Kline's technologically advanced, data-driven approach. They struggled to articulate a coherent counter-narrative, their attacks often blunted by Kline's calculated indifference or his ability to spin their criticisms into evidence of his own strengths.

Kline, in turn, masterfully exploited the divisions within the existing political landscape. He positioned himself as the unifying force, the candidate who could transcend partisan divides. He spoke of a "new era of American exceptionalism," an era defined by "uncompromising vision" and "unwavering commitment." He did not shy away from his corporate background; he brandished it as a badge of honor, a testament to his ability to achieve tangible results.

"They tell you that government is a messy business," he declared in one particularly fiery speech, his voice echoing through a stadium packed with cheering supporters. "They tell you that compromise is the only way forward. I tell you that the only way forward is through decisiveness. I tell you that the only path to progress is through strength. For too long, we have allowed the cacophony of special interests and partisan bickering to drown out the voice of common sense. No more. We will bring order to chaos. We will bring clarity to confusion. We will bring results."

He presented himself not as a politician, but as a CEO for the nation, a figure who could apply the same principles of efficiency and effectiveness that had made Halcyon Defense Systems a global leader to the complex machinery of government. He was the ultimate problem solver, the man who could make America "run like a well-oiled machine." His campaign was a testament to the power of absolute belief, not only in his own vision but in the inherent superiority of his corporate-bred approach to leadership. He was not just a candidate; he was a revolution, a meticulously planned, meticulously funded, and terrifyingly effective corporate raid on the very foundations of democratic governance. The nation was about to experience its first hostile takeover. The "perfect man" had arrived, and his agenda was clear: to transform the United States into the ultimate subsidiary of Victor Kline's singular vision.

The bedrock of Victor Kline's presidential campaign was not a tapestry of soaring ideals or a nuanced exploration of societal ills, but a single, unyielding principle: control. This was not a concept he introduced to the political arena; it was the very air he breathed, the very architecture of his being. His platform was a direct, unvarnished transference of his corporate ethos, a meticulously engineered blueprint for governing that mirrored the operational manual of Halcyon Defense Systems. He spoke of efficiency not as a desirable outcome, but as an absolute necessity, a non-negotiable prerequisite for national viability. Waste, in his lexicon, was not merely an economic drain; it was a symptom of systemic weakness, a moral failing. He vowed to dissect the sprawling bureaucracy, to excise its inefficiencies with the precision of a surgeon's scalpel, leaving behind a lean, agile, and ruthlessly effective governmental organism.

His speeches were replete with terms that, while familiar in the sterile corridors of corporate power, landed with an almost jarring, clinical resonance in the emotionally charged realm of politics. "Streamlining processes," he'd declare, his voice unwavering, "is not a matter of preference; it is a matter of national security. We will optimize resource allocation, eliminating redundancies that have crippled our ability to respond to critical challenges. Every dollar spent, every action taken, will be measured against predefined metrics of success. There will be no room for ambiguity, no tolerance for underperformance." This was not the language of a leader seeking to inspire a populace; it was the pronouncement of an executive outlining a corporate restructuring.

The concept of the "Loyalty Metric," a notoriously stringent performance evaluation system at Halcyon, was subtly but unmistakably woven into his political discourse. While he never explicitly used the term, the underlying sentiment was palpable. He spoke of fostering a new era of civic responsibility, one where adherence to established protocols and a demonstrated commitment to national objectives would be paramount. Dissent, he implied, was not a sign of healthy democratic discourse, but a deviation from the optimal operational standard, a potential security risk. He promised to cultivate a citizenry that understood its role within the larger national structure, a collective working in perfect synchronicity towards a singular, defined purpose. This was not about engaging the public; it was about aligning them.

240

His campaign rallies were not spontaneous outpourings of enthusiasm; they were meticulously choreographed performances, designed to project an image of absolute unity and unwavering support. The crowds, meticulously curated through targeted advertising and carefully managed invitations, were a visual testament to Kline's perceived popularity. Any hint of discord – a lone protestor, a dissenting chant – was swiftly and discreetly managed, often before it could even register with the wider audience. Security personnel, many of them former Halcyon employees or private contractors vetted for their discretion and obedience, moved with an almost military precision, ensuring that the narrative remained unblemished. The faces in the audience were a sea of smiling, nodding heads, their applause timed, their cheers orchestrated. It was a powerful illusion, an overwhelming display of solidarity that served to silence any lingering doubts about the depth of his support.

Kline understood the psychology of mass appeal, not as a means of connecting with individuals, but as a tool for asserting dominance. He fed his audience a steady diet of pronouncements, not questions. He offered definitive answers, not open-ended discussions. His rallies were designed to create a feedback loop of affirmation, where the sheer volume of enthusiastic response reinforced the perceived validity of his message. The absence of critical engagement was not a failure of his communication strategy; it was its very success. He wasn't seeking to persuade a diverse electorate; he was seeking to consolidate a loyal base, a bloc of unwavering adherents who would internalize his vision without question.

His speeches often began with a stark assessment of the nation's current state, painting a picture of chaos, inefficiency, and moral decay. He would then pivot, his voice deepening, to the "Kline Solution," a promise of order, clarity, and strength. He didn't offer hope; he offered certainty. He didn't advocate for change; he decreed a transformation. The emotional tenor of these rallies was carefully calibrated. While there was an undeniable energy, it was an energy born not of shared aspiration, but of a collective yearning for firm direction. He tapped into anxieties, into a desire for a return to perceived stability, offering himself as the singular bulwark against the encroaching tide of uncertainty.

The political arena, for Kline, was merely another high-stakes environment requiring strategic acquisition and operational dominance. The established norms of political discourse – the debates, the compromises, the appeasement of disparate factions – were, in his eyes, archaic inefficiencies. He approached the campaign as he would a hostile takeover of a faltering corporation. He identified the weaknesses of his rivals – their internal divisions, their perceived lack of decisiveness, their reliance on outdated methodologies – and exploited them ruthlessly. He didn't engage in policy debates; he presented himself as the superior strategic mind, the one capable of formulating and executing a winning strategy for the nation.

His pronouncements on national security were particularly indicative of his control-centric approach. He spoke not of diplomacy, but of deterrence. Not of international cooperation, but of national self-sufficiency. His vision for the military was one of unparalleled technological superiority, of systems so advanced, so impenetrable, that they would render any external threat obsolete. This translated into a domestic policy that mirrored this outward projection of strength. He advocated for an expanded role for law enforcement, for the implementation of surveillance technologies to ensure "public order," and for a judiciary that prioritized swift, decisive judgments over protracted legal processes. Every facet of governance, from education to healthcare, was to be viewed through the lens of efficiency and control.

The media, for the most part, found itself struggling to adapt to Kline's unique brand of political engagement. Traditional investigative journalism, designed to probe and question, often found its efforts blunted by Kline's practiced evasion or his ability to reframe criticism as an attack on national progress. His press conferences were less about answering questions and more about delivering pronouncements, punctuated by carefully selected "calls" to pre-approved journalists. The narrative, as with everything Kline touched, was to be meticulously managed. He understood that perception, especially in the modern media landscape, was reality. And his reality was one of an unassailable leader, a man whose every decision was guided by an infallible logic.

The sheer financial muscle behind his campaign was, of course, a critical component of this control. The vast resources of Halcyon Defense Systems, cleverly funneled through a complex network of subsidiaries and political action committees, ensured that his message permeated every conceivable communication channel. His advertisements were ubiquitous, his surrogates expertly placed in key media outlets, and his ground game – a highly organized, data-driven operation – proved remarkably effective in mobilizing his supporters. He bought influence, he bought visibility, and in doing so, he bought a significant degree of control over the public discourse. He wasn't just competing for votes; he was competing for narrative dominance, and his financial advantage allowed him to achieve it with overwhelming force.

His supporters, drawn to his promises of order and decisive leadership, saw his corporate background not as a disqualifier, but as a testament to his competence. They were weary of the perceived chaos and indecision of traditional politics, and Kline offered them an alternative: a vision of a nation governed with the same ruthless efficiency that had made Halcyon Defense Systems a global powerhouse. They interpreted his detachment from emotional appeals as a sign of his superior intellect, his ability to rise above the petty squabbles that plagued his opponents. His control was their security; his unwavering resolve was their hope.

However, beneath the veneer of immaculate organization and unwavering confidence, a subtler, more insidious aspect of Kline's campaign was taking root. It was the quiet eradication of the space for genuine dialogue, the systematic suppression of doubt. By presenting himself as the sole arbiter of truth and the ultimate problem-solver, Kline was subtly conditioning his audience to accept his pronouncements as unassailable fact. The "Kline Solution" was not a proposal to be debated; it was an inevitability to be embraced. This was the ultimate manifestation of his desire for control: not just control over systems and processes, but control over thought itself. The nation was not being offered a choice; it was being prepared for an acquisition, and Victor Kline intended to be the sole shareholder. His rallies, devoid of genuine debate, were less town halls and more indoctrination sessions, where the applause was not an expression of agreement but a programmed response to a meticulously crafted stimulus. The message was clear: dissent was inefficiency, and inefficiency, under Kline, would not be tolerated. The political stage was rapidly transforming into a boardroom, with Kline at the head, demanding absolute adherence to his singular vision of corporate governance. The campaign was, in essence, the prelude to a hostile takeover of the nation's democratic soul.

The digital ether crackled with the hum of Victor Kline's meticulously crafted narrative. It was a symphony of carefully chosen words, amplified by a vast orchestra of media channels, all playing in perfect, programmed harmony. The previous context established Kline's corporate-style grip on his campaign, his rallies staged as flawless productions, and his speeches devoid of the messy ambiguities of genuine political discourse. Now, that same ironclad control was being extended, not just to the physical spaces he occupied, but to the very channels through which information flowed, shaping the public's perception with the precision of a surgical strike. The media, far from being an independent arbiter, was rapidly becoming another cog in the Halcyon Defense Systems machine, repurposed for the grander project of national acquisition.

Kline understood, with an almost chilling clarity, that in the modern era, perception was not merely a reflection of reality; it was the primary architect of it. His time at Halcyon had been a masterclass in shaping perception, a relentless exercise in projecting an image of impenetrable strength and infallible logic. Now, he applied those same principles to the infinitely more volatile and impressionable landscape of political public opinion. His vast financial resources, a tidal wave of capital meticulously siphoned through a labyrinth of shell corporations and clandestine political action committees, were not merely for funding his ground game or saturating the airwaves with advertisements. They were the fuel for a sophisticated, multi-pronged media manipulation campaign, designed to sculpt the public consciousness with the same deliberate intent as a skilled artisan shaping clay.

His connections, forged in the gilded halls of corporate power and the shadowy backrooms of defense contracting, were not just for networking; they were instruments of influence. He had cultivated relationships with media moguls, key editors, and influential pundits, not through genuine camaraderie, but through strategic cultivation and calculated reciprocity. These were not friendships; they were leverage points. A well-placed phone call, a discreet favor rendered years prior, the promise of future access – these were the currency with which Kline purchased favorable coverage. Stories that cast him in a positive light were amplified, their narratives subtly nudged towards his preferred framing. Conversely, any hint of genuine investigative scrutiny was met with a swift, coordinated response.

The strategy was not subtle, but it was devastatingly effective. Opposition research, once the domain of rival campaigns, was now outsourced to a network of private intelligence firms, their findings then strategically "leaked" to sympathetic media outlets. These leaks were not random; they were surgical strikes, designed to tarnish the reputations of his opponents with carefully curated half-truths and misleading innuendo. A former business partner's disgruntled testimony, a forgotten minor scandal from decades past, even fabricated digital footprints – all were weaponized and deployed, not to inform, but to disorient and discredit. The goal was not to win a debate on policy, but to erode the very foundation of his rivals' credibility, leaving them exposed and vulnerable.

Kline's campaign adopted a playbook eerily similar to the internal operational manuals of Halcyon Defense Systems, where information control was paramount. The concept of "plausible deniability" was not just a legal shield; it was a narrative strategy. When negative stories inevitably surfaced – and they did, despite his best efforts – the campaign would issue carefully worded statements, disavowing any direct knowledge or involvement, while simultaneously hinting at darker forces at play, further sowing seeds of suspicion and paranoia. This created a smoke-and-mirrors effect, where the public was left questioning the veracity of the accusations, and by extension, the motives of those making them. The media, often eager for a salacious story, would find itself chasing shadows, further distracted from any substantive critique of Kline's platform.

Soundbites were not just a tool for public communication; they were weapons of mass distraction. Kline's speeches, while lacking in genuine policy depth, were laced with memorably concise, often emotionally charged phrases. "Make America Strong Again," "The Time for Decisiveness is Now," "Restoring Order to a Chaotic World" – these were not slogans; they were expertly crafted hooks, designed to resonate with the primal anxieties of the electorate. These phrases were then repeated ad nauseam by his surrogates, amplified by paid social media accounts, and echoed by sympathetic commentators, creating an echo chamber of affirmation. The sheer repetition, coupled with the emotional resonance, bypassed rational thought, embedding themselves deep within the public consciousness. When the media would attempt to delve into the specifics of his plans, they would invariably be met with a return to these talking points, a frustrating cycle that left substantive questions unanswered.

The silencing of critical voices was perhaps the most insidious aspect of Kline's media strategy. It wasn't always overt censorship; it was more a sophisticated process of marginalization and de-platforming. Journalists who dared to ask challenging questions found themselves subjected to a barrage of online harassment, often orchestrated by seemingly independent groups that were, in reality, funded and directed by Kline's campaign apparatus. Their professional reputations were systematically attacked, their past work scrutinized for any perceived impropriety, and their sources intimidated. This created a chilling effect, discouraging other media professionals from venturing into similarly contentious territory. The fear of professional ruin, coupled with the sheer exhaustion of battling a well-resourced propaganda machine, proved to be an effective deterrent.

Furthermore, Kline's campaign mastered the art of "agenda setting." By relentlessly pushing certain topics – the perceived failures of the current administration, the rise of foreign threats, the need for decisive leadership – they effectively dictated the terms of the media's coverage. When a reporter attempted to shift the focus to a less favorable topic, such as the ethical implications of Kline's business practices or the vagueness of his policy proposals, the campaign would simply ignore the inquiry, or worse, pivot back to their pre-selected talking points with an almost aggressive

246

insistence. This constant redirection, this refusal to engage on inconvenient terms, slowly but surely trained the media to focus on the issues that Kline wanted them to focus on. The news cycle became less a reflection of unfolding events and more a curated broadcast of the Kline campaign's chosen agenda.

The campaign also excelled at weaponizing the very concept of "fake news." While this term had been around for a while, Kline's team elevated its use into a strategic tool. Any news report that was critical of him, regardless of its accuracy or journalistic integrity, was immediately labeled as "fake news" or "biased reporting." This tactic served two purposes. Firstly, it cast doubt on the legitimacy of any unfavorable coverage, allowing his supporters to dismiss it outright. Secondly, it created a sense of us-versus-them, solidifying his base by framing any opposition as inherently untrustworthy. The media, caught in this double bind, found itself struggling to report on Kline without being accused of bias by his fervent supporters, many of whom were themselves products of his carefully constructed information ecosystem.

The strategy extended to the visual realm as well. Kline's campaign produced highly polished, almost cinematic advertisements that were distributed across all platforms. These were not just political ads; they were emotional appeals, crafted with the same psychological precision as a blockbuster movie trailer. They showcased Kline as a strong, decisive leader, often juxtaposed with images of chaos and uncertainty, implying that only he could restore order. The music was dramatic, the editing sharp, and the messaging unambiguous. These advertisements, funded by Kline's enormous war chest, saturated the airwaves and online spaces, creating a pervasive sense of his inevitability. They bypassed critical thinking, speaking directly to the subconscious desires for security and stability.

Moreover, Kline understood the power of curated authenticity. While his public appearances were meticulously staged, his campaign also carefully cultivated an image of him as a man of the people, albeit a very wealthy and powerful one. This involved carefully orchestrated "off-the-cuff" moments, seemingly candid interviews, and the strategic use of social media to present a more personal, relatable side. However, even these moments were subject to the same rigorous control. A stray comment, a moment of genuine vulnerability, was never allowed to slip through the cracks. The persona of the decisive, infallible leader was paramount, and every interaction, every utterance, was designed to reinforce that image.

The influence of Halcyon Defense Systems' internal protocols was particularly evident in the way Kline's campaign managed its online presence. Social media platforms were not just channels for communication; they were battlegrounds. Troll farms, populated by individuals paid to spread disinformation and attack critics, were a constant presence. AI-driven bots were deployed to amplify pro-Kline messages, create artificial trends, and drown out dissenting opinions. This digital onslaught created an illusion of overwhelming grassroots support, a perception that Kline's message was resonating organically with the masses, when in reality, it was a meticulously engineered digital army. The algorithms, designed to reward engagement, were manipulated to favor Kline's content, ensuring its wider dissemination.

The campaign also recognized the importance of controlling the visual narrative. Photographers and videographers who worked for the campaign were instructed to capture images that emphasized Kline's strength, his confidence, and the adoration of his supporters. Conversely, any images that might portray him in a less favorable light – a moment of indecision, a strained interaction, a small crowd – were suppressed or deliberately omitted from public dissemination. This created a visually skewed reality, where the public was consistently presented with images that reinforced the desired narrative of a charismatic and universally beloved leader. Even the crowds at his rallies were often strategically positioned, with signs held aloft and enthusiastic faces front and center, obscuring any pockets of apathy or dissent.

The journalists who were granted access to Kline's inner circle were often carefully vetted, their past work scrutinized for any hint of skepticism. Those who proved compliant and who understood the unwritten rules of engagement, were rewarded with exclusive interviews and early access to information. Those who dared to push too hard, to ask the uncomfortable questions, found themselves increasingly marginalized, their credentials revoked, their access denied. This created a climate of fear and self-censorship, where many in the media began to self-regulate, choosing to avoid potentially damaging stories in favor of maintaining their access and avoiding Kline's wrath. The media landscape, which should have been a robust marketplace of ideas, was slowly but surely becoming a monochromatic echo of Kline's singular vision.

The sheer scale of this media operation was staggering. It involved a vast network of individuals and organizations, all working in concert to achieve a singular objective: the complete control of the public narrative. From the highest levels of media ownership down to the individual social media user, Kline's influence permeated every layer of the information ecosystem. He understood that by controlling what people saw, what they heard, and what they believed to be true, he could effectively control their votes, and ultimately, their allegiances. The political stage, in his hands, was not a forum for democratic debate, but a propaganda theater, meticulously directed, masterfully staged, and universally broadcast. The audience, however, was largely unaware that they were being played, convinced they were witnessing an authentic political spectacle, rather than a highly sophisticated corporate takeover of public consciousness. The lines between news, opinion, and outright fabrication blurred into an indistinguishable haze, a testament to the power of Victor Kline's unparalleled control over the media. He had effectively turned the Fourth Estate into an extension of his own executive suite, its primary function no longer to inform, but to consolidate his power. The whispers of dissent were not just ignored; they were systematically drowned out by the deafening roar of his manufactured consent.

The whispers of dissent, once mere annoyances in the meticulously orchestrated symphony of Victor Kline's ascent, had begun to coalesce into a discordant chorus. These were the voices of those who saw through the polished veneer, who recognized the predatory glint in Kline's corporate-eyed approach to national governance. Yet, to challenge Kline directly was to step onto a battlefield where the rules of engagement were not set by tradition or ethics, but by the cold, calculating logic of Halcyon Defense Systems' most aggressive acquisition strategies. His opponents, whether seasoned politicians or burgeoning civic leaders, found themselves not merely facing a rival in the electoral arena, but a seasoned predator intent on not just outmaneuvering them, but systematically dismantling them.

Kline's campaign machine, honed by years of corporate warfare and a ruthless understanding of human psychology, was unleashed with an efficiency that was both terrifying and breathtaking. It operated on a principle that echoed his successful corporate purges: dismantle the opposition, not by defeating them on the field of ideas, but by annihilating their credibility, their resources, and ultimately, their will to fight. The playbook, learned in boardrooms and through hostile takeovers, was now being applied to the fragile ecosystem of democratic politics.

The first wave of the assault was always informational. It began with the relentless digging, the excavation of every perceived flaw, every misstep, every shadow from an opponent's past. This was not the standard opposition research of yesteryear, focused on policy divergences or past voting records. This was a deep, invasive dive, employing private intelligence firms with the discretion of black-ops units. They scoured private financial records, delved into personal correspondences, and exploited digital footprints with an almost forensic intensity. Any hint of indiscretion, any minor ethical lapse, any forgotten indiscretion from decades prior was unearthed, polished, and prepared for deployment. The goal was not to find dirt; it was to manufacture a character assassination.

Once unearthed, these carefully selected fragments of an opponent's history were not presented to the public as the result of diligent investigation. Instead, they were strategically "leaked" to a select cadre of sympathetic media outlets. These leaks were surgical, designed to cause maximum damage with minimum traceability back to Kline's campaign. The narrative was always carefully framed: not as partisan attacks, but as revelations of a flawed character, unfit for public trust. A former business partner, disgruntled and perhaps offered a substantial "consulting fee," might suddenly resurface with damning testimony. A youthful indiscretion, amplified and distorted, could be presented as evidence of a deeply ingrained, dangerous personality flaw. The sheer volume of these "revelations" was designed to overwhelm, to create a relentless barrage that left opponents perpetually on the defensive, scrambling to address accusations, many of which were half-truths or outright fabrications.

Kline understood the power of psychological warfare. His campaign didn't just attack policies; they attacked the very personality of their rivals. The rhetoric employed was designed to evoke visceral reactions, to bypass rational thought and tap into primal fears and prejudices. Opponents were not just "politically misaligned"; they were "weak," "unpatriotic," "dangerous," or "corrupt." These labels, repeated ad nauseam across all media channels, began to stick. They were amplified by social media bots, by paid influencers, and by surrogates who parroted the talking points with unblinking conviction. The aim was to create an emotional contagion, to instill a deep-seated distrust and revulsion for anyone who dared to stand in Kline's path.

The financial aspect of the opposition was also systematically targeted. Kline's vast resources, channeled through opaque political action committees and a complex web of corporate entities, allowed him to wage a war of attrition. Opponents, often lacking comparable funding, found their campaigns starved of resources. Advertising slots were bought up, drowning out their messages. Fundraising events were subtly disrupted, with intelligence leaks timed to coincide with major donor gatherings. Furthermore, any hint of impropriety in an opponent's own financial dealings, no matter how minor, was relentlessly magnified, casting doubt on their stewardship and their integrity. The message to potential donors was clear: supporting Kline's opponents was a risky proposition, akin to investing in a failing enterprise.

The legal system, too, became an extension of Kline's war chest. While direct legal challenges might be too overt, the threat of them, or the encouragement of spurious investigations, was a potent weapon. Opponents might find themselves facing unexpected audits or subjected to fishing expeditions based on unsubstantiated allegations. The sheer cost and psychological toll of navigating such legal entanglements could cripple even the most well-resourced campaign. The message was insidious: challenge Kline, and you risk not just political defeat, but a protracted and expensive battle that could leave you financially and emotionally ruined.

Moreover, Kline's control over the narrative extended to the very concept of news consumption. Any journalistic outlet that dared to publish a critical report, any reporter who pursued an unfavorable line of inquiry, found themselves subjected to a swift and brutal backlash. The "fake news" label, a weapon of mass dismissal, was wielded with surgical precision. This not only served to discredit the unfavorable reporting among Kline's supporters but also instilled a palpable sense of fear within the broader journalistic community. The risk of being branded a partisan hack, of facing a torrent of online abuse, and of losing access to campaign events became a powerful deterrent against any substantive investigation. The Fourth Estate, once a bulwark of scrutiny, was increasingly cowed, its members self-censoring to avoid becoming the next target of Kline's digital army.

The goal was never to win a debate, but to eliminate the opponent from the playing field altogether. It was a scorched-earth policy, mirroring the corporate takeovers where legacy companies were dismantled, their assets stripped, and their brands extinguished. Kline didn't seek to persuade; he sought to obliterate. He understood that in the hyper-polarized landscape he had helped to cultivate, character assassination was a far more potent weapon than policy arguments. The public, bombarded with negative narratives and emotional appeals, became desensitized to factual accuracy, prioritizing perceived authenticity and strength over substantive debate.

The opposition, caught in this relentless siege, found themselves in a battle they were ill-equipped to fight. Their traditional strategies of policy articulation and public engagement were drowned out by the cacophony of manufactured scandals and character attacks. They were forced to spend their precious time and resources on damage control, on refuting baseless accusations, and on defending themselves against an enemy that operated with unparalleled ruthlessness and a bottomless supply of ammunition.

The democratic process, in Kline's hands, was being transformed into a gladiatorial arena, where the primary objective was not to present a vision for the future, but to publicly eviscerate any perceived rival, ensuring their ignominious defeat. The carefully cultivated image of Kline as a decisive leader was, in this context, a direct inversion of the chaos he actively sowed amongst his opponents, a carefully crafted duality designed to project strength by dismantling the very foundations of his rivals' existence. He was not merely winning an election; he was purging the political landscape, much like a hostile takeover purged a corporate hierarchy, leaving only those who bent to his will, or those who were utterly broken by his relentless assault. The siege was not just on their campaigns; it was on their very reputations, their livelihoods, and their ability to ever again participate in public life.

The relentless precision of Victor Kline's campaign, as detailed in the preceding account, was not merely a tactical maneuver; it was a manifestation of a broader, more insidious appeal. It was the appeal of the strongman, a figure who promised to cut through the Gordian knot of democratic deliberation with the sharp sword of decisive action. This was a message that resonated with a segment of the electorate profoundly weary of political gridlock, perpetually anxious about an uncertain future, and increasingly skeptical of the very institutions designed to represent them. Kline, with his granite demeanor and unwavering pronouncements, offered a compelling alternative: order, strength, and a return to what he termed 'common sense.'

This was a dangerous siren song, particularly in its deliberate stripping away of complexity. Kline's brand of governance was presented as refreshingly simple, a stark contrast to the often messy, nuanced, and inherently compromise-driven nature of democratic politics. He eschewed the empathy that characterized more traditional leaders, viewing it as a weakness, a susceptibility to sentimentality that could derail necessary, albeit unpopular, decisions. His pronouncements were devoid of the usual political hedging; they were absolute, confident, and delivered with an unshakeable certainty that suggested an innate understanding of what was right, what was necessary, and what was best for the nation. This projection of unassailable strength was not just a rhetorical device; it was the cornerstone of his appeal. He was not merely a candidate; he was an avatar of unwavering resolve, a bulwark against the perceived chaos and indecision that had come to define the political landscape.

His promises, vague yet potent, spoke of a return to an imagined past where problems were straightforward and solutions were readily apparent. The phrase 'common sense' itself became a powerful, almost Pavlovian trigger, conjuring images of a simpler, more rational era, untainted by what Kline's campaign skillfully framed as the convoluted ideologies and self-serving machinations of career politicians. This narrative actively worked to delegitimize any form of nuanced policy debate, painting complex issues as mere matters of basic logic that had been obscured by generations of political incompetence. For those who felt left behind, disenfranchised, or simply overwhelmed by the pace of change and the seemingly intractable nature of national challenges, Kline's message offered a potent balm. It promised a return to a state of perceived clarity, where decisions were made swiftly and efficiently, unburdened by ethical quandaries or the need for broad consensus.

The very authoritarian undertones of his platform, subtle at first, were either overlooked or actively embraced by his most ardent supporters. The idea of strong leadership, of a single, decisive figure at the helm, held an undeniable allure. It implied a reduction of individual responsibility for the electorate, a transfer of the burden of difficult choices to a trusted, powerful leader. In a world that felt increasingly unpredictable, this offered a sense of security, a feeling of being guided by an unyielding hand. Kline's carefully constructed persona – the wealthy, successful businessman who had conquered the corporate world and was now poised to do the same for the nation – lent further credence to this narrative. He was not a product of the political establishment that many had come to distrust; he was an outsider, a disruptor, a man who knew how to get things done, unhampered by the petty squabbles and ideological divides that plagued Washington.

The contrast he drew between himself and his opponents was stark and highly effective. While others were portrayed as dithering, indecisive, and beholden to special interests, Kline was presented as a man of action, uncorrupted by the political system, and singularly focused on the national interest. This narrative was amplified through a sophisticated media strategy that prioritized emotional resonance over factual accuracy. Emotional appeals – fear of economic collapse, of national decline, of cultural erosion – were expertly woven into his campaign messaging, creating a sense of urgency and a desperate need for a strong leader to steer the ship of state through turbulent waters. The complexity of the issues was deliberately simplified, reduced to a series of black-and-white choices, with Kline invariably positioned as the sole arbiter of the correct path.

His rallies were not just political gatherings; they were carefully orchestrated spectacles designed to reinforce this image of power and decisiveness. The crowds, often large and fervent, responded to his booming pronouncements and his confident, often dismissive, posture towards his opponents. The sheer force of his presence, the unwavering conviction in his voice, created an almost cult-like atmosphere. This was not about policy debates; it was about belonging, about aligning oneself with a perceived winner, a figure of strength in a world that often felt weak and uncertain. The "common sense" he championed was, in reality, a carefully curated ideology that bypassed the messy, inconvenient truths of governance and appealed directly to a primal desire for order and strong, unambiguous leadership.

This appeal was not without its historical precedents. The desire for a strongman, a figure who promises to restore order and national pride, is a recurring theme in human history, particularly in times of social and economic upheaval. When democratic processes seem slow, inefficient, or unable to address pressing concerns, the allure of authoritarianism can grow. Kline, consciously or unconsciously, tapped into this deep-seated human inclination. He offered a simple, albeit dangerous, solution to complex problems: an abdication of collective responsibility to a singular, powerful leader who claimed to possess the wisdom and the will to fix everything. The electorate's weariness with the perceived failings of democracy made them fertile ground for such a message.

The very lack of detailed policy proposals, often a point of criticism for more conventional candidates, became an asset for Kline. It allowed him to remain above the fray of specific debates, to maintain his image as a visionary leader rather than a technocrat bogged down in the minutiae of governance. His pronouncements on issues were broad strokes, painting a picture of a revitalized nation, a stronger economy, and a restored sense of national identity. These were aspirational goals that resonated with a wide swathe of the population, particularly those who felt that their values and their way of life were under threat. The emphasis was always on strength, decisiveness, and an unwavering commitment to what he defined as the national interest, often implicitly meaning the interests of his most powerful supporters.

The rejection of "political correctness," a common refrain in populist movements, also played a significant role. Kline's willingness to speak his mind, to utter statements that others deemed offensive or insensitive, was interpreted by his followers as a sign of authenticity and courage. He was seen as a truth-teller, unafraid to challenge the prevailing norms and to speak the unspoken thoughts of those who felt marginalized by a society that had, in their view, become too focused on accommodating diverse viewpoints. This was framed as a return to fundamental truths, to a time when societal values were more homogenous and less contested. His rhetoric actively sought to create an 'us versus them' dynamic, where 'us' represented the silent majority of common-sense patriots, and 'them' encompassed a nebulous coalition of elites, academics, liberal media, and anyone who dared to question Kline's vision.

The corporate success of Halcyon Defense Systems, the empire Kline had built, served as a potent symbol of his capabilities. His ability to navigate complex markets, to outmaneuver competitors, and to generate immense wealth was presented not just as evidence of his business acumen, but as a blueprint for national governance. The principles of efficiency, profitability, and ruthless competition, honed in the corporate world, were now being touted as the keys to solving the nation's pro blems. This was a powerful, albeit deeply flawed, analogy. Governance, unlike business, requires a delicate balance of competing interests, a commitment to public welfare that transcends profit margins, and a respect for individual rights that cannot be easily quantified or traded. However, for many, the sheer success of his business ventures made his promises of economic prosperity and national strength seem eminently achievable.

Kline's campaign was a masterclass in the manipulation of public sentiment. It understood that in an era of information overload and declining trust in traditional institutions, emotional resonance and the projection of strength could be far more effective than reasoned debate or detailed policy proposals. The strongman narrative, with its promises of order, clarity, and decisive leadership, offered a powerful antidote to the anxieties of the modern age. It allowed voters, weary of complexity and uncertainty, to find solace in the illusion of a guiding hand, an unshakeable authority figure who claimed to have all the answers. And in doing so, Kline was not merely campaigning for office; he was cultivating a movement, a collective desire for a return to a perceived golden age, orchestrated by a leader who embodied unwavering strength and unquestionable certainty. The allure of the strongman, in its most potent form, was the allure of simplicity in a complex world, the promise of control in an era of flux, and the seductive comfort of surrendering difficult choices to an all-knowing, all-powerful leader. It was a dangerous, yet undeniably compelling, vision that was rapidly gaining traction, overshadowing the more nuanced and ethical considerations that were the bedrock of a healthy democracy.

Chapter 11

Echoes of Halcyon

The fervor ignited by Victor Kline's ascent was not confined to the sterile boardrooms of Halcyon Defense Systems or the hushed enclaves of his inner circle. It had, with alarming speed, seeped into the very fabric of his burgeoning political movement, transforming it into something far more potent, and far more perilous, than a mere campaign. A subtle, yet pervasive, ecosystem of ideological adherence began to take root, a peculiar 'political metric' where loyalty to Kline and an uncritical embrace of his narrative became the sole currency of worth. This wasn't about shared policy goals or a common vision for the nation's future; it was about absolute fealty to the man himself, a litmus test for belonging that was as unforgiving as it was insidious.

This manufactured consensus was forged in the crucible of online echo chambers and amplified in the charged atmosphere of his rallies. Any voice that dared to waver, any opinion that strayed even a millimeter from the established Kline doctrine, was met with a swift and brutal backlash. The digital landscape became a battleground where dissent was not merely disagreed with, but actively vilacted. Online forums and social media feeds, once spaces for discussion and debate, were rapidly reconfigured into instruments of ideological purification. The gentle art of persuasion was discarded in favor of a more aggressive tactic: the public shaming and excommunication of the heterodox. Individuals who voiced even the mildest skepticism found themselves subjected to a torrent of abuse, their character assassinated, their motives questioned, and their very right to participate in the political discourse revoked. The algorithms, subtly but surely, began to favor conformity, pushing Kline's pronouncements to the forefront while burying any dissenting opinions under an avalanche of pre-approved content. This created an illusion of overwhelming support, a self-fulfilling prophecy where the perceived majority opinion stifled genuine discourse.

This aggressive policing of thought was a direct echo of the culture that Victor Kline had cultivated within Halcyon. In the corporate world, any challenge to his authority or his strategic direction was met with swift consequences, ranging from career stagnation to outright dismissal. Employees learned, through a painful process of attrition and observation, that the safest path was one of silent obedience. Innovation, creativity, and critical thinking were only truly valued when they served to reinforce Kline's existing ideas. Deviations, even those with the potential for greater success, were perceived as threats, as indicators of disloyalty or a lack of faith in his infallible vision. This corporate environment, driven by a rigid hierarchy and a potent fear of reprisal, had become a training ground for the very behaviors now manifesting in his political base. The skills honed in suppressing dissent within a corporate structure were now being weaponized to control the narrative and the perceived will of the electorate.

The transformation of dissent into disloyalty was a masterstroke of linguistic manipulation. Kline's campaign, and by extension his followers, expertly reframed any opposition not as a difference of opinion, but as a fundamental betrayal of the national interest. To disagree with Kline was no longer simply to hold a contrary viewpoint; it was to actively work against the 'progress' he championed, to be an agent of the very forces that sought to undermine the nation. This created a powerful 'us versus them' mentality, where 'us' were the enlightened patriots, the true believers who understood the necessity of Kline's vision, and 'them' were the enemies, the saboteurs, the ignorant masses who were either misled or actively malevolent. This binary thinking left no room for nuance, no space for constructive criticism. It reduced complex issues to simplistic dichotomies, forcing individuals to choose sides in a battle where one side was inherently righteous and the other inherently corrupt.

The language employed was particularly potent. Terms like 'unpatriotic,' 'weak,' 'out of touch,' and 'elitist' were weaponized

260

against any who dared to question. These labels were not applied based on reasoned arguments or evidence, but as a means of immediate delegitimization. They served to instantly disqualify the dissenter, to paint them as inherently flawed and untrustworthy, thus rendering their arguments irrelevant. This rhetorical strategy was incredibly effective in silencing moderate voices and discouraging open debate. When the penalty for expressing a differing opinion was social ostracization and public condemnation, the rational choice for many was to remain silent, to conform, or to adopt the prevailing rhetoric even if they harbored private reservations. The 'political metric' was thus enforced not through overt coercion, but through the potent threat of social and reputational damage.

This fear of reprisal was not merely an abstract concept; it had tangible consequences. Individuals found themselves constantly self-censoring, meticulously filtering their thoughts and words before expressing them publicly, or even privately in online spaces that might be monitored. The casual camaraderie of shared discussion was replaced by a chilling caution. Friends unfriended each other on social media for expressing mild political disagreements. Family dinners became minefields of unspoken tension. The public sphere, once intended to be a vibrant marketplace of ideas, became a sterile environment where conformity was the safest, and therefore most prevalent, mode of engagement. This created a profound sense of isolation for those who felt increasingly alienated by the direction the movement was taking, but who were unwilling or unable to confront the overwhelming tide of enforced consensus.

The 'progress' that Kline championed was, in this new political metric, defined solely by adherence to his agenda. Any deviation, any suggestion of an alternative approach, was framed as an impediment to this singular path. It was as if the nation, after years of stagnation, had finally found its true north, and any attempt to steer away from it was not merely misguided, but actively destructive. This narrative was particularly effective in appealing to a sense of urgency and national crisis. Kline's supporters genuinely believed that the nation was on the brink of collapse, and that only his decisive leadership, unburdened by the complexities of democratic deliberation or the 'wishes' of the uninformed masses, could save it. This sense of existential threat provided a powerful justification for the suppression of dissent. In such a critical moment, they argued, there was no time for 'infighting' or 'doubt.' Unity, absolute and unquestioning, was paramount.

The role of misinformation and disinformation in solidifying this 'political metric' cannot be overstated. Fabricated narratives, often originating from anonymous online sources or amplified by hyper-partisan media outlets, served to reinforce the idea that Kline was under constant attack from powerful, shadowy forces. These narratives painted a picture of a valiant leader fighting a valiant battle against a corrupt and entrenched establishment. Any negative news or criticism of Kline was automatically dismissed as 'fake news,' a deliberate fabrication designed to discredit him. This created a closed informational loop, where supporters were fed a steady diet of propaganda that confirmed their existing beliefs and demonized any external sources of information. The 'political metric' thus became inextricably linked to an ability to discern truth from falsehood, a skill that was actively undermined by the very environment that fostered adherence to Kline's narrative.

The implications of this rigid adherence to the 'political metric' extended far beyond mere political discourse. It began to seep into personal relationships, professional interactions, and even the way people consumed news and information. The ability to critically evaluate information, to engage with differing perspectives, and to engage in reasoned debate, all cornerstones of a healthy democratic society, were actively discouraged. Instead, the emphasis was on tribal affiliation, on the unthinking acceptance of the group's dogma. This created a society where ideological purity trumped intellectual curiosity, where loyalty was valued above truth, and where the very foundations of rational thought were systematically eroded in favor of an unshakeable, and ultimately destructive, faith.

The echo of Halcyon was no longer a whisper; it was a deafening roar, drowning out all but the most fervent affirmations of Kline's singular vision. The 'political metric' was not just a measure of support; it was a tool of intellectual subjugation, designed to ensure that the path forward was clear, unobstructed by the inconvenient complexities of human thought and individual autonomy.

The meticulously constructed edifice of Victor Kline's political ascendancy, a gleaming monument to his carefully curated persona, was built upon a foundation of deliberate amnesia. The past, particularly the decades spent at the helm of Halcyon Defense Systems, was not merely an inconvenient chapter; it was a liability, a potential contagion that threatened to infect the pristine narrative he so painstakingly propagated. And like any prudent strategist dealing with a potential outbreak, Kline and his inner circle moved with ruthless efficiency to quarantine and eradicate any trace of this contaminating history.

Journalists, those relentless hounds of truth, were among the first to find their inquiries met with a chilling, systematic stonewalling. Their carefully crafted questions, designed to peel back the layers of Kline's corporate empire and expose the less savory aspects of his tenure – the dubious contracts, the questionable ethical compromises, the human cost of his relentless pursuit of profit and power – evaporated into a vacuum of official silence. Press conferences became carefully choreographed performances, where pre-approved questions were fielded with polished, evasive answers. Any attempt to deviate from the script, to probe deeper into the murky waters of Halcyon's past, was met with polite but firm redirection, or worse, a sudden curtailment of the interview. The message was clear: the past was off-limits, a forbidden territory guarded by an invisible, yet formidable, force.

When direct engagement proved insufficient, the strategy shifted to discreditation. Journalists who persisted, who dared to dig deeper, found their own reputations targeted. Anonymous leaks, carefully timed and strategically disseminated through fringe online outlets that served as amplifiers for the Kline campaign, began to surface, casting doubt on their objectivity, their journalistic integrity, even their personal lives. They were branded as biased, as puppets of rival political factions, or as simply seeking attention. The narrative carefully spun was that these individuals were not seeking truth, but rather fabricating it, driven by their own agendas to undermine a man who was, in their eyes, a national savior.

This tactic, mirroring the corporate strategy of discrediting internal dissenters, proved remarkably effective in sowing seeds of doubt among the public, eroding the credibility of those who dared to question. The very tools used to ensure internal compliance at Halcyon were now being deployed to control the flow of information in the public arena, a terrifying testament to the scalability of Kline's methods.

The true vulnerability, however, lay with those who had once been within the inner sanctum of Halcyon Defense Systems. Former employees, individuals who had witnessed firsthand the machinations, the moral ambiguities, and the sheer ruthlessness that characterized Kline's leadership, possessed a knowledge that could potentially shatter his carefully constructed image. These were the people who understood the true meaning of the "political metric" long before it became a public slogan; they had lived it. They knew the price of challenging Kline, the quiet disappearances from project teams, the abrupt terminations disguised as restructuring, the subtle but persistent campaigns of character assassination that left even the most dedicated professionals questioning their own sanity and competence.

The campaign to silence these potential whistleblowers was multifaceted and chillingly effective. For some, it began with the subtle offer of lucrative consulting roles or positions within the burgeoning political organization, a gilded cage designed to buy their silence and, perhaps, co-opt their expertise in service of the new agenda. The allure of continued proximity to power, coupled with substantial financial incentives, proved a powerful deterrent to speaking out. For others, the approach was more direct, more menacing. Non-disclosure agreements, ironclad and encompassing a broad spectrum of vague prohibitions, were invoked with renewed vigor. Legal teams, deployed with the precision of a military strike, began to issue veiled threats of lawsuits for breach of contract, for defamation, or for revealing proprietary information – even when the information in question pertained to actions taken years prior to their departure.

The psychological warfare employed was particularly insidious. Former employees who attempted to go public, to share their experiences of Kline's opaque dealings at Halcyon, found themselves subjected to a torrent of online abuse, mirroring the vilification of journalists. They were labeled as disgruntled, as bitter individuals seeking revenge, as liars fabricating stories for personal gain. Their professional histories were meticulously scoured for any perceived imperfection, any past mistake, which was then amplified and twisted into evidence of their untrustworthiness. The goal was not to engage with their testimonies, but to delegitimize them entirely, to ensure that their voices were drowned out by a cacophony of manufactured outrage. The chilling effect of this orchestrated campaign was palpable; the fear of becoming the next target, of having one's life dissected and weaponized, was a powerful deterrent.

In some cases, the silencing was even more absolute. Whispers circulated, never confirmed but pervasive enough to instill a deep unease, of former employees who had been "taken care of" in more permanent ways. These were not necessarily overt acts of violence, but rather the systematic dismantling of their lives: the sudden loss of all professional contacts, the inexplicable rejection of job applications, the chilling discovery that their credit had been inexplicably denied, their online presence scrubbed or corrupted. It was a form of social and professional execution, leaving individuals isolated, vulnerable, and utterly incapable of speaking out. The methods were varied, adaptable, and terrifyingly effective, proving that the control mechanisms honed within the corporate walls of Halcyon were not merely metaphorical; they were tangible, ruthlessly applied instruments of power.

The narrative that Kline had cultivated was simply too precious, too vital to his political aspirations, to be tarnished by the inconvenient truths of his past. The "progress" he promised, the return to a perceived golden age, hinged on an unblemished image of strength, decisiveness, and unwavering integrity. Any hint of past impropriety, any suggestion of ethical compromise or questionable dealings at Halcyon, would puncture this carefully inflated balloon of public perception. It would introduce doubt, complexity, and the uncomfortable reality that his leadership might be built upon a bedrock of something less than virtuous.

The systematic suppression of this history was not merely about damage control; it was an active act of historical revisionism. The past was not just being ignored; it was being rewritten, its inconvenient details excised and replaced with a sanitized, heroic version that served the present political agenda. The "political metric" was, in essence, a mandate for selective memory, a demand that the public embrace the present and future Kline offered, while forgetting or deliberately ignoring the man who had forged his empire in the shadows of corporate ambition.

The implications of this sustained campaign of silencing were profound. It demonstrated a chilling continuity between Kline's corporate leadership and his political ambitions. The same ruthlessness, the same control over information, the same willingness to discredit and intimidate those who posed a threat – these were not traits that had been left behind in the boardrooms of Halcyon. Instead, they had been refined, scaled up, and unleashed upon the national stage. The narrative of a pure, unblemished leader was being manufactured not just through positive reinforcement and aspirational rhetoric, but through the aggressive negation and destruction of any evidence that contradicted it. The echoes of Halcyon were no longer just whispers; they were a deafening silence, deliberately imposed to ensure that the future was molded according to Victor Kline's singular, and increasingly unchallenged, vision. The silence was not an absence of sound, but a powerful, active force, designed to suffocate truth and ensure that the past remained forever buried.

The intricate machinery of Victor Kline's ascent was not a solitary endeavor; it was the culmination of years spent cultivating a sprawling network, a vast ecosystem of influence meticulously nurtured during his tenure at Halcyon Defense Systems. This was not merely a collection of business associates or industry contacts; it was a strategically assembled cadre, a legion of individuals whose loyalty, or at least their complicity, had been secured through a potent cocktail of financial incentives, shared ambition, and unspoken obligations. Now, as Kline pivoted from the sterile, profit-driven landscape of corporate defense to the volatile, public arena of politics, this same network became his most potent weapon, a clandestine engine driving his presidential campaign.

At the apex of this organizational structure sat the former titans of Halcyon, men and women who had profited handsomely from Kline's ruthless leadership and had, in turn, learned to mirror his methods. They were the architects of his corporate empire, the strategists who had navigated complex regulatory landscapes and outmaneuvered competitors with predatory precision. Now, these individuals, many of whom occupied positions of significant influence within various industries, found themselves repurposed. Their roles shifted from optimizing quarterly earnings to shaping public perception, from securing lucrative defense contracts to underwriting political campaigns. They were the silent financiers, the behind-the-scenes architects of strategy, ensuring that Kline's message resonated through the established channels of power and influence, while simultaneously dampening any discordant notes.

Take, for instance, the ubiquitous presence of "consulting firms" that seemed to sprout like mushrooms in the wake of Kline's political announcements. Ostensibly independent entities, these firms were, in reality, staffed by former Halcyon executives and strategists. Their mandate was multifaceted: to conduct "market research" that amounted to sophisticated polling and focus-group manipulation, to craft messaging that was less about policy and more about emotional resonance, and to identify and neutralize potential threats. These were the same minds that had once devised complex product launch strategies and crisis communication plans for cutting-edge weaponry; now, they were applying those same analytical and manipulative skills to the far more volatile and unpredictable battlefield of public opinion.

These firms, often shrouded in layers of corporate opacity, received substantial "retainers" from PACs and super PACs that ostensibly supported Kline's campaign. The money flowed discreetly, a river of capital that funded the sophisticated digital infrastructure required to wage a modern campaign. Algorithms were fine-tuned to identify undecided voters and target them with personalized messaging designed to exploit their deepest anxieties or aspirations. Social media platforms, once seen as tools for organic connection, were now weaponized, flooded with meticulously crafted narratives, seemingly organic testimonials, and strategically amplified outrage that painted Kline as the savior the nation desperately needed and his opponents as agents of chaos or corruption. The tactics were eerily familiar to those who had witnessed the internal "reputation management" campaigns at Halcyon, where dissent was quashed and inconvenient truths were buried under an avalanche of controlled information.

But the network extended beyond former corporate colleagues. Kline had always possessed an uncanny ability to identify and cultivate individuals with a certain opportunistic streak, those who recognized the potent synergy between unchecked ambition and immense wealth. Many politicians, particularly those in nascent stages of their careers or those whose own ethical compasses were somewhat flexible, found themselves drawn into Kline's orbit. He offered them not just financial backing, but a pathway to power, a promise of elevation that was impossible to resist. These were individuals who understood the transactional nature of politics, who saw Kline not as a leader to be believed in, but as a vehicle for their own advancement.

These compliant politicians acted as Kline's proxies in the legislative and regulatory arenas. When legislation threatened to expose the less savory aspects of Halcyon's past or to impose stricter oversight on defense contractors, these individuals would miraculously introduce procedural hurdles, craft amendments that rendered the legislation toothless, or simply vote it down. Their actions were rarely overt; they were the subtle nudges, the strategic delays, the carefully worded objections that, when accumulated, formed an impenetrable barrier against any meaningful scrutiny. They were the unseen hands that guided policy in a direction favorable to Kline, ensuring that the corporate structures he had built remained largely unmolested, even as he presented himself as an outsider ready to drain the swamp.

The influence extended to media outlets as well, though often in more circuitous ways. While direct ownership was rarely feasible or desirable, Kline's network employed a more sophisticated form of leverage. Major advertisers, many of whom owed their own success and stability to contracts secured during Kline's Halcyon years, were subtly reminded of their allegiances. News organizations that dared to run critical pieces found advertising revenue mysteriously drying up, or their access to corporate press briefings abruptly revoked. Conversely, outlets that towed the line, that published favorable narratives or ignored inconvenient truths, found themselves rewarded with lucrative advertising placements and exclusive access to the burgeoning political machinery. This created a powerful incentive for self-censorship, a chilling effect that ensured most mainstream media treaded very carefully around the sensitive topics associated with Victor Kline's past.

Moreover, Kline's campaign became adept at utilizing the very same digital infrastructure that had once served Halcyon's marketing and intelligence divisions. Vast databases of consumer information, meticulously compiled and categorized during his corporate reign, were repurposed. These datasets, which included granular details about individuals' purchasing habits, online behavior, and even stated preferences, were invaluable in tailoring political messaging. The campaign could identify not just broad demographic segments but hyper-specific micro-audiences, each receiving a precisely crafted message designed to resonate with their individual profiles. This level of micro-targeting, born from decades of corporate data mining, gave Kline's campaign an unprecedented advantage in swaying public opinion, often before counter-narratives could even begin to form.

The efficiency with which this network operated was a testament to the corporate culture Kline had fostered at Halcyon. Decisions were made swiftly, often with a disregard for precedent or established norms. Information was compartmentalized, ensuring that no single individual possessed the full picture, thus limiting the risk of leaks or internal dissent. Loyalty was rewarded, but betrayal was met with swift and decisive retribution, a principle that translated seamlessly from the boardroom to the campaign trail. Those who had been part of the Halcyon ecosystem understood this unspoken contract: cooperation brought rewards, while opposition brought ruin.

This intricate web of control extended even to the ostensibly independent regulatory bodies. Through a combination of lobbying, campaign contributions, and the strategic placement of former Halcyon legal counsel and executives into key government positions, Kline ensured a degree of regulatory leniency. Agencies tasked with overseeing corporate conduct or monitoring election finance often found themselves hamstrung by a lack of resources, by political pressure from allies of Kline, or by legal challenges that effectively paralyzed their investigatory powers. The same entities that were supposed to provide checks and balances often became, through subtle manipulation and systemic inertia, passive enablers of Kline's agenda.

The ultimate goal of this network was not merely to win an election, but to establish an unassailable position of power. By controlling the flow of information, by co-opting key institutions, and by neutralizing any significant opposition, Kline aimed to create an environment where his narrative was the only one that mattered. The "political metric" that had once been an internal KPI at Halcyon was now being applied on a national scale, measuring not just corporate success but the successful manipulation of public perception and political discourse. It was a system designed for absolute control, a legacy of Halcyon's dominance translated into the pursuit of the ultimate prize: the presidency. The echoes of Halcyon were not just in the silence that followed dissent, but in the hum of this vast, interconnected network, working tirelessly to shape the future according to Victor Kline's design. The former defense contractor was now waging a different kind of war, one fought not with missiles and drones, but with data, influence, and the relentless application of corporate strategy to the heart of the democratic process. This was the network of control, and it was expanding its reach with chilling effectiveness.

The insidious tendrils of Victor Kline's operational methodology, so ruthlessly honed within the sterile, profit-driven confines of Halcyon, had not merely infiltrated the political arena; they had begun to bleed into the very fabric of individual lives. The abstract principles of market share, competitive advantage, and risk mitigation, once confined to boardrooms and balance sheets, now translated into tangible, devastating consequences for those who stood in his path. The human cost, a recurring ledger of broken careers and shattered reputations within Halcyon, was now being replicated on a far grander, and more public, stage.

The political landscape, a domain theoretically dedicated to public service and the robust exchange of ideas, was becoming a brutal gladiatorial arena under Kline's influence. Opponents were no longer simply debated; they were systematically dismantled, their public personas subjected to a level of scrutiny and distortion that bore the chilling hallmarks of Halcyon's most aggressive "reputation management" campaigns. Think of Senator Sherry Stevenson, a rising star whose policy positions, while moderate, dared to question the unchecked expansion of defense industry influence. Sherry, a meticulously principled public servant, found herself the target of a multi-pronged assault. Her voting record was cherry-picked, her past statements twisted out of context, and a relentless barrage of carefully curated "leaks" from anonymous sources began to populate the digital ether, painting her as an out-of-touch idealist, beholden to special interests that opposed progress. These weren't random acts of political mudslinging; they were precisely targeted strikes, orchestrated by the same minds that had once engineered the downfall of dissenting executives at Halcyon. The goal was not to win an argument, but to annihilate the opponent's credibility, to make them so radioactive that even their allies would recoil.

The effect on Sherry was palpable. Her carefully cultivated relationships with constituents began to fray as a relentless tide of negative coverage drowned out her message. donors, once enthusiastic supporters, grew hesitant, fearful of being associated with a candidate being systematically vilified. The pressure became immense. Whispers in the halls of power, amplified by Kline's network, suggested that if she simply "stepped aside," perhaps due to "personal reasons" or a "change of heart," the onslaught would cease. The choice was stark: endure a public maelstrom that threatened to obliterate her career and private life or capitulate and allow Kline's agenda to proceed unimpeded. This was the familiar dilemma faced by those who had once challenged the established order at Halcyon, a stark reminder that resistance often came at an unbearable price.

Beyond the high-profile political figures, the human cost rippled outwards, affecting individuals whose only "crime" was to be in the wrong place, or to have known the wrong people. Consider the case of Dr. Haddie Reacher, a brilliant astrophysicist who had once worked on a classified project at a Halcyon subsidiary, a project whose ethical implications she had begun to question. When Kline's campaign needed to discredit a prominent critic of his defense policies, a former military advisor who had publicly lauded Dr. Reacher's independent research, the campaign's digital operatives dug deep into public records and past associations. Suddenly, Dr. Reacher's tangential involvement in a seemingly innocuous research grant from years ago was re-contextualized. Her work, once celebrated for its scientific merit, was now subtly implied to have had dual-use applications, potentially contributing to technologies that could be used for nefarious purposes. The narrative, spread through anonymous blogs and amplified by bots, was designed to create an aura of suspicion, to chip away at her scientific integrity and, by extension, to undermine the credibility of her former colleague.

Dr. Reacher, a woman whose life was dedicated to the pursuit of knowledge in the vast, objective expanse of space, found herself trapped in a very human, and very dirty, political war. Colleagues started to distance themselves, grant applications were mysteriously put on hold, and the quiet hum of her research laboratory was replaced by the deafening roar of speculation and insinuation. The scientific community, often insular and protective of its members, found itself paralyzed, unsure how to combat a disinformation campaign that was both sophisticated and relentless. The damage was not just to her reputation; it was to her spirit; her life's work reduced to a pawn in a game of power she had never intended to play. This was not the clean, calculated elimination of internal dissent at Halcyon; this was a more brutal, more indiscriminate form of collateral damage, where individuals were sacrificed not for their direct opposition, but for their mere proximity to those who dared to challenge Kline.

The replication of Halcyon's internal dynamics extended to the insidious tactic of "loyalty tests," now applied to a national electorate. Kline's campaign, mirroring the internal vetting processes at the defense giant, sought not just support, but absolute, unquestioning adherence. Those who expressed even minor reservations, who asked probing questions about policy details, or who dared to suggest alternative approaches, found themselves marginalized. They were labelled as "unreliable," "not team players," or, in the most damning indictments, as "disruptive elements." This created a climate of fear, where individuals within the campaign and its associated organizations learned to self-censor, to parrot the approved talking points, and to suppress any flicker of independent thought. The echoes of Halcyon's culture, where questioning the CEO's vision could lead to ostracization or worse, were now reverberating through the campaign apparatus.

This psychological manipulation extended to the broader public. Kline's rallies, often framed as celebrations of patriotism and unity, were, in reality, sophisticated exercises in groupthink. The passionate speeches, the carefully orchestrated cheers, the shared sense of indignation against fabricated enemies – all served to create an intense emotional bond, a collective identity that discouraged dissent. To question Kline within these rallies was not just to disagree; it was to betray the group, to be an outsider, a traitor. The same mechanism that had once made Halcyon employees fiercely protective of their company, even when aware of its ethical compromises, was now being used to forge an unshakeable political base. Individuals found themselves swept up in the fervor, their critical faculties dulled by the sheer emotional force of the movement, unable to discern the manufactured consensus from genuine popular support.

The destruction of careers and reputations was not merely a side effect of Kline's ambition; it was a deliberate strategy, a critical component of his plan to consolidate power. He understood, with chilling clarity born from his corporate experience, that neutralizing opposition was as important as cultivating allies. At Halcyon, individuals who had outlived their usefulness, or who had become inconvenient, were gradually sidelined, their projects defunded, their authority eroded, until they had no choice but to resign, often with their professional reputations tarnished by subtle innuendo. This same playbook was now being applied to the political arena, albeit with a more brutal efficiency.

Consider the fate of a prominent investigative journalist who had, in the past, penned critical articles about defense contractors. Initially, the pressure was subtle: access to official briefings dried up, sources within government agencies suddenly became unavailable, and whispers began to circulate about the journalist's "bias" and "agenda." When this proved insufficient, the campaign, leveraging its network of well-placed allies in media ownership and advertising, orchestrated a more significant blow. Several major advertisers, whose companies had significant government contracts often facilitated by Kline's political influence, quietly withdrew their support from the journalist's publication. The message was clear: criticize Kline, and you risk not just your career, but the financial viability of the entire enterprise. The journalist, a seasoned professional who had always prided themselves on their integrity, found themselves in an impossible situation, forced to choose between continuing their critical work and potentially facing professional ruin, or compromising their principles to survive.

The human cost was also evident in the quiet desperation of individuals who found themselves entangled in Kline's web and unable to escape. These were not the powerful figures who could negotiate their own terms, but the mid-level functionaries, the staffers, the researchers, the consultants whose livelihoods depended on their association with the campaign or the entities that supported it. They saw the ethical compromises, the manipulation of facts, the silencing of dissent, but felt powerless to act. The threat of unemployment, of being blacklisted within their industries, was a constant specter. The psychological toll was immense: the gnawing guilt, the cognitive dissonance, the erosion of self-worth as they became complicit, however passively, in a system they increasingly found abhorrent. This was the dark undercurrent of Kline's rise – the quiet desperation of those trapped in a system where survival demanded the sacrifice of conscience, a chilling replication of the silent compromises made by countless individuals within the hierarchical structure of Halcyon. The arena of politics, meant to be a contest of ideas, had been transformed into a battleground where lives were collateral damage, careers were casualties, and the pursuit of absolute power left a trail of broken individuals in its wake.

The air within Halcyon's sprawling, glass-and-steel fortress had always held a certain chill, a calculated coolness that permeated not just the climate control but the very atmosphere of ambition and fear. For those who labored within its labyrinthine corridors, it was a palpable presence, a constant reminder of the relentless pursuit of profit and power that defined the corporation. Now, however, that familiar chill felt different. It was laced with a new, more potent dread, a chilling premonition that the iron fist of Victor Kline, so long confined to the corporate boardrooms and whispered-about internal purges, was beginning to clench around something far larger, far more vital: the nation itself.

The realization had dawned slowly, like a creeping shadow across a sunlit landscape, yet its implications were as blinding as a sudden supernova. For years, the "resistance," a loosely affiliated coalition of individuals within Halcyon who had witnessed firsthand the ethical compromises and the human toll of Kline's machinations, had focused their efforts on containing him within the company's boundaries. Their actions were clandestine, their victories small and often temporary, characterized by the subtle sabotage of projects, the discreet leaking of inconvenient truths to regulatory bodies, and the quiet support of internal whistleblowers. They operated under the assumption that Halcyon, for all its influence, was a contained ecosystem, its tendrils reaching into government and industry, yes, but ultimately anchored to the corporate entity.

But Kline's political ascent had shattered that illusion. The speeches, the rallies, the carefully crafted populist rhetoric – they were no longer merely the pronouncements of a powerful CEO dabbling in the political sphere. They were the overt articulation of a vision, a blueprint for a nation governed by the same ruthless logic that had transformed Halcyon into a behemoth. The resistance saw with sickening clarity how Kline's corporate strategies – the aggressive market capture, the systematic dismantling of competitors, the cultivation of a loyal, unquestioning workforce – were being repackaged and deployed on a national scale. The tactics of "synergy," "disruption," and "streamlining operations" were being applied to democratic institutions, to public discourse, to the very concept of citizenship.

"He's not just trying to win an election," whispered Dr. Clifford Berry, a senior research scientist whose early work on advanced AI had been co-opted for less-than-benevolent applications within Halcyon's defense division. He was hunched over a flickering holographic display in a disused server room, the hum of aging machinery a low counterpoint to his agitated breathing. "He's trying to acquire the country. And if he succeeds, the same rules that govern Halcyon will govern everything. Every aspect of our lives will be subject to his KPIs, his profit margins, his risk assessments."

His words hung heavy in the sterile air, a stark confirmation of their deepest fears. They had spent years fighting a defensive battle, trying to mitigate the damage within their own walls. They had seen colleagues broken, careers ruined, ethical boundaries eroded, all in service of Kline's insatiable appetite for control. But now, the stakes had been raised exponentially. The collateral damage they had witnessed – the silenced critics, the manipulated narratives, the erosion of individual autonomy within Halcyon – was no longer a localized phenomenon. It was poised to become the new national standard.

Elara Smith, a former head of internal compliance who had been systematically sidelined for her persistent inquiries into Halcyon's more dubious international dealings, traced a finger across a projected timeline of Kline's campaign milestones. "Look at this," she said, her voice tight with a mixture of anger and a chilling sort of resignation. "Each of these rallies, each policy announcement, it's a phase in a corporate takeover. He's not building a coalition; he's consolidating market share. And the 'competitors'... they're not just political opponents anymore. They're threats to his brand, to his bottom line."

The resistance had always understood the insidious nature of Kline's power. It wasn't simply about brute force or overt coercion, though he was certainly capable of both. It was about a pervasive, almost invisible influence, a systemic manipulation that bled into every decision, every interaction. At Halcyon, this manifested as a culture of pervasive surveillance, where every employee's performance, every communication, was meticulously logged and analyzed. Loyalty was not earned; it was engineered. Dissent was not tolerated; it was preemptively neutralized. They had seen brilliant minds dulled by the relentless pressure to conform, ethical compasses spun wildly off course by the allure of advancement within the system, or the fear of its abrupt termination.

Now, that same system was being replicated on a national level. The digital surveillance capabilities that Halcyon had pioneered for "market intelligence" were being repurposed for political profiling. The sophisticated disinformation campaigns, once used to discredit rival products or internal dissenters, were now targeting political opponents and critical media outlets. The recruitment of loyalists, not based on merit but on their willingness to blindly execute directives, was becoming the hallmark of Kline's burgeoning political machine.

This profound realization shifted the very nature of their struggle. It was no longer enough to simply chip away at the edges of Kline's influence within Halcyon. That felt like rearranging deck chairs on a sinking ship while the captain was busy steering it towards an iceberg. The fight had to be escalated. The locus of their resistance had to shift, not just in tactics, but in its fundamental objective. Dismantling Kline's power base at Halcyon was no longer just a matter of corporate ethics; it was a matter of national survival.

"We were fighting a holding action," said Wil Spears, a grizzled ex-military man who now managed Halcyon's vast logistics network and harbored a deep, quiet disdain for the corporate gamesmanship. He was often the pragmatic anchor for the more intellectual members of the resistance. "Trying to keep him contained. But he's broken free of the containment. He's out there, infecting the whole damn system. We have to go after the source. We have to hit Halcyon itself, hit his operations here, hard enough that it cripples his ability to operate nationally."

The idea was audacious, bordering on suicidal. Halcyon was a fortress, protected by layers of legal, financial, and political security. Kline commanded immense resources, a vast network of allies, and an army of loyal employees conditioned to defend him. Any overt act of defiance within the company would be met with swift and brutal retribution. The individuals who had comprised the resistance had already made significant personal sacrifices. Many had seen their career trajectories deliberately stunted, their projects defunded, their reputations subtly tarnished. They lived with the constant threat of exposure, of being the next Stevenson or Reacher, publicly disgraced and professionally ruined.

Yet, the alternative was becoming unbearable to contemplate. The nation, as they understood it – a complex, messy, imperfect democracy striving for ideals of freedom and justice – was under existential threat. Kline's vision of a hyper-efficient, centrally controlled society, driven by the same metrics of success that defined Halcyon, was a dystopian nightmare masquerading as progress. It was a world where individual rights were subsumed by corporate imperatives, where critical thought was a bug to be fixed, and where dissent was a system error to be purged.

"We've been working in the shadows, trying to be subtle," Reacher continued, his voice gaining a steely edge. "We've been trying to preserve ourselves, to maintain our positions so we can continue to resist from within. But that strategy is no longer viable. If he wins, there will be no 'within' to resist from. We have to accept that we might lose everything – our jobs, our reputations, perhaps even our freedom. But we can't let him win."

The weight of that decision settled upon them, a heavy mantle of responsibility. The quiet anxieties and clandestine meetings that had characterized their efforts thus far now had to be replaced by something far more aggressive, far more exposed. The network, which had previously been a loose collection of like-minded individuals bound by shared disquiet, would need to transform into a coordinated strike force. Their objective was no longer to merely survive Kline's tenure at Halcyon, but to actively dismantle his power, to expose the rot at the core of his ambition, and to do so with a speed and ferocity that matched the scale of the threat.

Adam Thomas, usually reserved and analytical, met the gaze of each person in the cramped, dimly lit room. "We understand the principles of Halcyon's operational security," he said, his voice low but firm. "We understand the vulnerabilities of its supply chains, its communication networks, its financial systems. We have spent years navigating these intricacies. Now, we must use that knowledge against them."

The small group known as the Architects of Memory explained to them that the challenges were immense. They were a small, disparate group, operating within the very heart of the enemy's stronghold. Their resources were minuscule compared to Kline's vast empire. Their opponents were not just corporate executives but a sophisticated network of lawyers, lobbyists, and security personnel. Moreover, the pervasive culture of fear and surveillance within Halcyon meant that any misstep, any hint of dissent, could lead to immediate identification and severe consequences. The loyalty tests that Kline imposed on his political followers were mirrored within Halcyon, where employees were constantly evaluated not just on their performance, but on their perceived ideological alignment with Kline's vision.

Adam leaned forward, his hands resting on the worn surface of the table. "We're talking about disrupting his funding streams, exposing the illegal or unethical practices that prop up his political campaigns, severing the lines of communication between his corporate interests and his political operatives. It's not going to be pretty. It's going to be dangerous. But if we don't do it, who will? And what will be left?"

The question hung in the air, unanswered and deeply unsettling. The resistance had always operated under the assumption that their actions, however small, contributed to a larger, unseen effort to keep Kline in check. But the encroaching reality of his political power had revealed the inadequacy of their previous approach. They were no longer simply defending their own ethical territory; they were on the front lines of a battle for the soul of a nation. The quiet, internal struggle within Halcyon had now exploded into a far more urgent, far more consequential confrontation. The time for subtle sabotage was over. The time for direct action had arrived, and with it, the terrifying certainty that failure would not just mean their own ruin, but the potential loss of everything they held dear. The echoes of Halcyon were no longer confined to its walls; they were reverberating across the country, and the resistance knew, with a grim determination, that they had to find a way to silence them, or be consumed by them.

Chapter 12

The Tipping Point

The whispers had begun as faint echoes, easily dismissed as the murmurings of disgruntled employees or the fevered imaginations of those who felt the weight of Halcyon's oppressive atmosphere too acutely. For months, Dr. Clifford Berry and his clandestine network and the Architects of Memory, had meticulously gathered fragments of truth, each piece a tiny, almost invisible shard of glass designed to one day reflect the full, damning picture of Victor Kline's reign. They operated under the silent, unwavering mandate of preserving the company's unvarnished history, a history that Kline had been relentlessly airbrushing and rewriting to suit his ascendant political narrative. Their sanctuary, a forgotten sub-basement data vault, was more than just a repository for corrupted files and redundant backups; it was a vault for a conscience that Halcyon, and increasingly, the nation, seemed to be shedding.

Elara Smith, her gaze often fixed on the digital tendrils of information that snaked through Halcyon's network, felt a shift in the usual static. It was like the first tremor before an earthquake, a subtle vibration that promised a fundamental upheaval. For months, she had been working with Dr. Berry, her expertise in compliance and internal auditing proving invaluable in sifting through the digital detritus Kline had left in his wake. They weren't just looking for financial improprieties or regulatory breaches anymore; they were dissecting the architecture of control, the intricate scaffolding of psychological manipulation that allowed Kline to maintain absolute dominion. The evidence they were uncovering was stark, a chilling indictment of a man who viewed human beings not as individuals with inherent worth, but as variables to be optimized, as resources to be exploited.

The data wasn't abstract. It was the detailed log of a project, codenamed "Phoenix," designed to systematically discredit and isolate a promising junior executive who had dared to question an unethical procurement. It was the raw, unedited transcripts of "performance improvement" sessions that were, in reality, sophisticated sessions of gaslighting and intimidation, carefully calibrated to break a person's will. It was the statistical analysis of employee burnout rates, meticulously presented with footnotes that attributed the spikes not to overwork or stress, but to "individual adaptability deficits." Each entry, each line of code, each anonymized human resource report, was a brick in the foundation of a psychological prison.

"He's always presented himself as a disruptor, a visionary who understands the modern workforce," Berry murmured, his fingers dancing over a holographic interface that displayed a complex web of interconnected data points. His usual quiet demeanor was strained, his eyes betraying a deep, gnawing weariness. "But it's not innovation; it's calculated cruelty. He's perfected the art of making people complicit in their own diminishment." He pointed to a section of the display that showed a drastic drop in creative output from a research team after a series of "strategic realignment meetings." "This is what he calls 'efficiency.' This is what he calls 'streamlining.' It's the systematic lobotomy of a workforce's spirit."

The Architects of Memory had operated on the principle of containment, believing that if they could simply preserve the truth within Halcyon, it would eventually surface when Kline's political ambitions inevitably crumbled under the weight of his own hubris. But Kline's ambition wasn't a fleeting moment of overreach; it was a meticulously planned corporate conquest, and his current political campaign was merely the grandest acquisition yet. The resistance within Halcyon, once focused on mitigating internal damage, now understood they had to seize the initiative. The very tools and methods Kline used to control Halcyon were now being deployed on a national scale, and the Architects of Memory held the only comprehensive ledger of his operational playbook.

"The public sees a charismatic leader, a businessman who knows how to get things done," Elara said, her voice a low, urgent hum that vibrated with controlled fury. "They don't see the 'Phoenix

Protocol' for what it is: the systematic destruction of careers and reputations. They don't see the 'Adaptability Deficit' reports as a blueprint for psychologically incapacitating dissent. They don't see the 'Synergy Sessions' as engineered periods of demoralization." She zoomed in on a set of financial records, juxtaposing them with internal memos detailing abrupt layoffs. "And they certainly don't see how he uses proprietary algorithms, designed for market prediction, to identify and neutralize potential political threats. It's all here, Dr. Berry. Every dirty secret, every calculated cruelty, laid bare."

The sheer volume of meticulously curated evidence was staggering. Clifford Berry and his team had developed proprietary software, designed initially to combat data corruption and reconstruct lost information, which they had repurposed to unearth every instance of data manipulation. They could trace the genesis of a falsified performance review, identify the precise moment a favorable statistic had been doctored, and pinpoint the deletion of crucial dissenting opinions from internal memos. It was an archaeological dig through the digital ruins of countless careers, a forensic examination of a corporate culture that prioritized results over rectitude, and profit over people.

One of the most damning discoveries was a series of internal memos detailing Kline's direct involvement in what he referred to as "narrative re-engineering." These weren't simple PR spin exercises. They were deeply psychological operations, designed to exploit cognitive biases and emotional vulnerabilities. The Architects had unearthed protocols for seeding doubt, for amplifying existing societal divisions, and for subtly shifting public perception by consistently framing negative events as opportunities for growth or as the inevitable consequence of individual failing. One memo, dated just weeks before Kline's official announcement of his presidential bid, outlined a strategy to "frame any criticism of Halcyon's labor practices as an attack on national productivity," a strategy now being openly employed in his political speeches.

"He doesn't just sell products; he sells manufactured realities," Clifford observed, his brow furrowed in deep concentration. "And his most potent weapon isn't his wealth or his influence; it's his understanding of how to exploit the human tendency to seek comfort and simplicity in a complex world. He offers easy answers, scapegoats, and the illusion of decisive leadership. The data shows he's been testing these strategies internally for years, refining them on his own employees. The ones who didn't conform, who didn't embrace his vision of 'optimized existence,' were systematically isolated, ostracized, and eventually, neutralized."

The Architects had categorized these tactics into distinct operational frameworks: the "Loyalty Calibration System," which tracked and rewarded perceived ideological alignment; the "Performance Optimization Matrix," a sophisticated system that generated personalized pressure points for each employee; and the chillingly named "Resilience Re-alignment Program," which essentially documented the psychological breaking points of individuals and the methods used to exploit them. Each program was a testament to Kline's ruthless dedication to control, a systematic approach to dehumanization disguised as corporate best practice.

The weight of this knowledge was a heavy burden. They were no longer just holding onto secrets; they were custodians of a truth that had the potential to detonate Kline's entire carefully constructed edifice. But the question remained: how to get this truth out? Kline's control over the media was almost absolute. His campaign had mastered the art of the manufactured scandal, the strategic leak of misinformation, and the overwhelming inundation of the public sphere with carefully curated narratives. Any attempt to release the data directly through traditional channels would likely be drowned out, discredited, or worse, twisted into a weapon against them.

"We can't just dump this onto the internet and hope for the best," Elara stated, articulating the shared anxiety. "He'll spin it, he'll bury it, he'll turn it back on us. We need a way to deliver it that bypasses his filters, something that forces people to confront it, to see the truth for themselves."

Clifford's eyes, which had been fixed on the data, now seemed to gain a spark of dangerous clarity. "He's built his empire on the principle of information control, of shaping perception through selective data and narrative manipulation. But every system, no matter how sophisticated, has vulnerabilities. He's so focused on controlling the flow of information that he's overlooked the importance of its integrity. We don't need to fight his narrative; we need to expose the rot beneath it."

The Architects of Memory began to explore unconventional avenues. They considered encrypted data drops to independent journalists, but the risk of interception and subsequent discrediting was too high. They thought about a coordinated campaign of anonymous leaks across multiple platforms, but the sheer volume of data made it difficult to control the narrative effectively. The challenge wasn't just in disseminating the information, but in presenting it in a way that resonated, that cut through the noise, and that was impossible for Kline's propaganda machine to easily dismiss or distort.

Then, Clifford remembered a fringe initiative he had been peripherally involved with years ago – a decentralized, peer-to-peer network designed to host and distribute uncensorable information. It was a project largely dismissed by mainstream tech circles as idealistic and impractical, but it was precisely the kind of incorruptible infrastructure they needed. The network operated on a blockchain-like system, where data, once uploaded, was virtually immutable and accessible to anyone with an internet connection, but impossible for any single entity to control or delete.

"It's not a perfect solution," Clifford admitted, as he explained the concept to Elara and the core members of their nascent resistance group within Halcyon. "It's not as 'user-friendly' as a well-produced documentary or a slick website. It's raw data. But it's incorruptible. Once we upload the evidence, it becomes a permanent, undeniable record. His campaign can't simply make it disappear. They can't control who sees it or how it's interpreted."

The plan began to coalesce. They would meticulously curate the most damning evidence: the Phoenix Protocol, the Resilience Re-alignment Program details, the internal memos on narrative re-engineering, the statistical breakdowns of employee psychological manipulation, and the direct links between Halcyon's unethical practices and Kline's campaign funding. Clifford's team would then package this data, along with the specialized software needed to access and understand it, into a series of encrypted archives. These archives would be uploaded to the decentralized network, each file timestamped and verified, creating an irrefutable historical record of Kline's modus operandi.

"We won't be telling people what to think," Elara emphasized, her eyes burning with a fierce conviction. "We'll be giving them the unfiltered truth, the raw ingredients for them to make their own judgments. Kline thrives on obfuscation. We will offer clarity. He builds his empire on manufactured consent. We will provide the evidence for informed dissent."

The process was painstaking and fraught with peril. Each keystroke, each data transfer carried the risk of detection. They operated in the dead of night, under the constant hum of Halcyon's surveillance systems, each moment of quiet a deceptive lull before the storm. The vault in the sub-basement became their nerve center, the flickering holographic displays their battleground. They were no longer simply collecting evidence; they were preparing to launch a truth bomb, a cascade of irrefutable data designed to shatter the carefully constructed illusion of Victor Kline's benevolence.

The first archives were uploaded in the pre-dawn hours. Clifford watched, his breath held, as the progress bar crawled across the screen. The data, once confined to the sterile, controlled environment of Halcyon, was now being dispersed into the ether, beyond the reach of Kline's immediate control. It was a whisper that would not be silenced, a truth that had finally found its voice, not through shouting headlines or biased commentary, but through the quiet, irrefutable testament of raw, unadulterated fact. The digital breadcrumbs they had been leaving for years were finally coalescing into a path, a path that led directly to the heart of Kline's deception, and it was a path that could no longer be erased. The tipping point was not a single event, but a slow, deliberate dissemination of truth, a calculated unveiling of the darkness that had festered within Halcyon, now poised to illuminate the national stage.

The Architects of Memory, with Elara Smith at the forefront of their digital offensive, had meticulously dissected Victor Kline's lauded "Loyalty Metric." It was presented to the public, and more importantly, to Halcyon's workforce, as an impartial arbiter of organizational harmony and productivity. A sophisticated algorithm, they were told, that identified employees who were not only dedicated but also aligned with the company's core values. It was the linchpin of Kline's purported meritocracy, a system that supposedly rewarded genuine contribution and stifled dissent through objective, data-driven analysis. But behind the polished veneer of algorithmic fairness, Elara and Clifford had unearthed a far more sinister reality.

Their investigation revealed that the Loyalty Metric was not an unbiased instrument of evaluation; it was a weaponized construct, precisely engineered to do the opposite of what its name suggested. Instead of fostering genuine loyalty born from shared purpose and respect, it was designed to cultivate a breed of compliant, unthinking automatons. The algorithm's parameters were not calibrated to measure intrinsic dedication or innovative spirit. Instead, they were meticulously weighted to reward behaviors that were most conducive to Kline's absolute control. This meant prioritizing silence over constructive criticism, conformity over independent thought, and a willingness to parrot corporate dogma over critical engagement. Employees who consistently provided positive feedback, who enthusiastically endorsed Kline's every initiative, regardless of its merit, and who proactively reported any perceived deviations from the party line, were rewarded with higher scores. Conversely, those who voiced concerns, who questioned directives, or who showed a tendency towards independent problem-solving – the very traits that historically fueled innovation and growth – were systematically penalized.

"It's a feedback loop designed for delusion," Clifford explained, his voice a low rumble of controlled indignation as he gestured towards a cascading series of data visualizations on the holographic display. "Kline doesn't want loyalty; he wants obedience. He doesn't want critical thinkers; he wants echo chambers. The Metric doesn't identify loyal employees; it identifies the most effective subordinates." He highlighted a section of the algorithm's decision tree, revealing a disproportionately high weighting assigned to variables such as "positive sentiment expression" and "consensus alignment." "These aren't measures of competence or commitment. They are proxies for docility. They are indicators of an individual's willingness to suppress their own judgment in favor of the perceived collective will, a will that Kline meticulously shapes."

Elara leaned closer, her finger tracing the intricate pathways of the algorithm's logic. "And the outputs," she added, her voice taut with the gravity of their findings, "are not just passive assessments. They are actively weaponized. The scores generated by the Loyalty Metric are directly integrated into every facet of an employee's professional life. Performance reviews become a mere formality, rubber-stamping the algorithm's verdict. Promotion opportunities are funnelled exclusively to those with impeccably high Loyalty Metric scores, regardless of their actual skill set or experience. And, most insidiously, those who consistently fall below a certain threshold find themselves on a fast track to 'reassignment,' 'restructuring,' or, in the most extreme cases, outright termination. The algorithm, in essence, becomes the judge, jury, and executioner of careers."

The Architects had managed to gain access to an internal Halcyon audit log, a document that Kline's inner circle had believed was securely buried and accessible only to a select few. This log, however, proved to be their most potent weapon. It contained irrefutable evidence of direct manipulation of the Loyalty Metric's outputs. The log detailed numerous instances where the algorithm's initial scoring for certain individuals was demonstrably altered by human intervention – intervention originating from Kline's office. Employees who were politically aligned with Kline, or who possessed valuable skills that Kline was unwilling to lose despite their slightly lower 'loyalty' scores, had their metrics artificially inflated. Conversely, promising individuals who had shown even a flicker of independent thought, or who had been identified as potential threats to Kline's narrative, had their scores deliberately suppressed, effectively engineering their downfall.

"Look at this," Elara said, zooming in on a specific entry. "Dr. Shelly Zepher. A brilliant materials scientist. Her raw algorithm score should have placed her in the top ten percent of R&D personnel. Her innovative contributions were lauded in external journals. Yet, her official Loyalty Metric score was deliberately downgraded by executive order. The justification provided in the log is chillingly vague: 'potential for disruptive influence.' It's not about identifying loyalty; it's about eliminating potential rivals and silencing any voice that might challenge the status quo."

Clifford nodded grimly. "This confirms our hypothesis. The Metric isn't a tool for identifying good employees; it's a tool for identifying manageable employees. And when even the algorithm's own biased output isn't sufficient, they simply override it. It's a double-edged sword of oppression. It first creates an environment where subservience is rewarded and competence is penalized, and then it provides a mechanism to ensure that even that flawed system perfectly serves Kline's agenda."

The implications were profound. The very system designed to legitimize Kline's leadership and identify his most dedicated followers was, in fact, a sophisticated engine of self-deception. It was designed to create a feedback loop of affirmation for Kline, surrounding him with individuals who were either genuinely sycophantic or whose artificial metrics masked their underlying dissent. This created an echo chamber of false confidence, where Kline genuinely believed he was leading a united and loyal organization, when in reality, he was presiding over a workforce increasingly demoralized, stifled, and resentful. The algorithm, intended to be his ultimate tool of control, was instead becoming the architect of his own ignorance, insulating him from the true sentiment of his company.

The Architects of Memory, armed with this granular detail and irrefutable proof of manipulation, began to craft their counter-narrative. They understood that simply releasing the raw data wouldn't be enough. Kline's propaganda machine was adept at spinning any unfavorable information, at burying it under a deluge of counter-claims and manufactured scandals. They needed to present the evidence in a way that was not just comprehensible, but damning. They needed to expose the inherent perversity of the Loyalty Metric, to reveal how it systematically punished competence and rewarded subservience, and then to demonstrate, with incontrovertible proof from the audit logs, how Kline himself had corrupted it further to serve his own political ambitions.

Their strategy involved creating a series of meticulously

curated case studies. They would take employees like Dr. Zepher, whose careers had been demonstrably stalled or sabotaged by the Metric, and juxtapose their objective achievements with their artificially low loyalty scores. They would highlight individuals who had risen through the ranks with demonstrably mediocre performance, their only discernible qualification being their unwavering, algorithmically validated, sycophancy. Each case study would be accompanied by direct excerpts from the manipulated audit logs, showing the specific instances of override and the specious justifications provided.

"We need to show people that this isn't about abstract data points or complex algorithms," Elara explained to Clifford and the core team. "It's about real people, real careers, and real aspirations being systematically crushed. We need to illustrate how the Metric, at its core, is designed to reward conformity and punish individuality. And then, we reveal the final layer of deceit: that even this flawed system wasn't good enough for Kline. He had to personally intervene, to twist it even further, to ensure that his vision of absolute control was maintained, regardless of the cost to talent and integrity."

They began to simulate the algorithm's unbiased output for several key individuals, then overlay it with the documented, manipulated scores. The contrast was stark, almost cartoonish in its severity. A visionary innovator with a genuine passion for Halcyon's mission would be shown with a low loyalty score, flagged for 'potential disruptive influence,' while a middling manager, known for their eagerness to appease and their lack of original thought, would sport a perfect, algorithmically mandated score, marked for 'exemplary alignment.' The narrative they would weave was simple: the Loyalty Metric was a lie, a sophisticated mechanism designed to create a compliant workforce by devaluing competence and elevating subservience, and Victor Kline was not only the architect of this deception but also its most egregious perpetrator, personally twisting its outputs to further his own agenda.

The research team dedicated to the algorithmic analysis worked tirelessly, creating visual representations that would make the data accessible even to those with no technical background. They developed infographics that illustrated the flow of influence, showing how the algorithm's biased inputs led to skewed outputs, and how those outputs then dictated career trajectories. They created short, impactful animations that depicted the process of manipulation, showing an algorithmically generated score being deliberately altered by a shadowy figure representing Kline's executive intervention.

"The beauty of it," Clifford mused, observing a prototype animation, "is that the algorithm itself, which Kline presents as his ultimate tool of objectivity, becomes the very instrument of his exposure. We are not discrediting an algorithm; we are showing how its fundamental design is flawed, how it was built to serve a regressive agenda, and then how its creator, the supposed paragon of innovation, personally corrupted it. It's an algorithmic backfire of the highest order."

The plan was to release this meticulously constructed exposé not through a single, easily dismissible press conference or a hastily written article. Instead, they would deploy it across multiple platforms simultaneously, leveraging the decentralized network they had established. The initial release would focus on a series of anonymized employee testimonials, each detailing personal experiences with the Loyalty Metric, painting a picture of widespread disillusionment and frustration. These testimonials would then be seamlessly linked to the detailed algorithmic analysis and the damning audit log excerpts, creating a layered, undeniable narrative that moved from the personal to the systemic, and finally to the direct evidence of Kline's malfeasance.

The objective was clear: to shatter the illusion of Kline's infallibility. By exposing the Loyalty Metric as a tool designed to reward subservience over competence, and by revealing the deliberate manipulation of its outputs, they would demonstrate that Kline's supposed meritocracy was a sham. The algorithm, meant to be a symbol of his forward-thinking leadership, would instead become Exhibit A in the case against him, a testament to his authoritarian tendencies and his willingness to sacrifice talent and integrity at the altar of his own unchecked ambition. The backfire would be devastating, not just for Halcyon, but for Kline's burgeoning political career, which was built on the very foundations of these fabricated metrics of loyalty and competence. The digital edifice of his success, so carefully constructed on algorithms and manipulated data, was about to be challenged by the truth, a truth that had been hiding in plain sight within the very code he wielded.

The carefully constructed edifice of Victor Kline's public persona began to show hairline fractures, not with a thunderous collapse, but with a subtle, insidious erosion of trust. For years, he had cultivated an image of decisive leadership, a man of vision who could bring order to chaos, promising a future built on efficiency and unwavering progress. This narrative, amplified by a sophisticated media apparatus and the unquestioning loyalty of many within Halcyon's sprawling network, had resonated deeply with a populace weary of indecision and societal fragmentation. They had seen him as a steady hand, a bulwark against the perceived excesses of a more fluid, unpredictable world. But narratives, however carefully woven, are vulnerable to the persistent, persistent drip of inconvenient truths.

The initial leaks, carefully orchestrated by the Architects of Memory, were not overt indictments of criminality. They were subtler, more insidious. They began with whispers, with anonymized testimonies appearing on fringe digital forums and encrypted message boards, gradually migrating to more mainstream, yet still discerning, news aggregators. These weren't sensationalist exposes of corporate espionage or financial malfeasance, but rather intimate accounts of human cost, detailed narratives of careers derailed, potential stifled, and lives irrevocably altered by the cold, impersonal logic of the Loyalty Metric. Employees, their identities shielded, spoke of the gnawing anxiety of performance reviews dictated by an algorithm, the soul-crushing realization that innovation and dedication were secondary to an abstract score that rewarded conformity and penalized individuality.

One such testimony, attributed to a former R&D lead who had mysteriously resigned under duress, described how his team's groundbreaking work on sustainable energy solutions was systematically sidelined. His Loyalty Metric score, once a respectable indicator of his commitment, had inexplicably plummeted after he raised concerns about the ethical implications of a new, proprietary energy storage technology that Kline was aggressively pushing. The technology, the whistleblower alleged, had a hidden environmental risk that had been glossed over in the rush to market. His attempts to voice these concerns through official channels were met with bureaucratic stonewalling, followed by a sharp downturn in his performance evaluations, all directly linked to his flagging Loyalty Metric. The narrative wasn't just about a job loss; it was about the suppression of vital research, the prioritization of profit and political expediency over genuine progress and environmental stewardship. This wasn't the image of a forward-thinking visionary; it was the shadow of an authoritarian prioritizing control over innovation, even when that innovation held the promise of a better future.

Another account, from a mid-level manager in Halcyon's burgeoning global logistics division, painted a picture of ruthless efficiency that bordered on dehumanization. She detailed how the Loyalty Metric had been used to justify mass layoffs, not based on performance, but on an employee's perceived "lack of alignment" with Kline's latest corporate directives. Her own score had been artificially lowered after she had hesitated to implement a new, highly controversial automation system that she believed would lead to widespread displacement of skilled workers. She recounted the cold, impersonal notification of her termination, accompanied by a bland HR statement citing her "inability to adapt to evolving operational paradigms," a euphemism directly linked to her downgraded Loyalty Metric. The chilling detail that resonated most deeply was her observation that those who enthusiastically embraced the automation, regardless of their prior experience or understanding of its intricacies, saw their scores surge, paving their way for promotions while more experienced, cautious colleagues were jettisoned. It was a stark illustration of how the system was designed not to reward merit, but to incentivize unquestioning obedience, transforming a tool for organizational harmony into a blunt instrument of purges.

These stories, initially dismissed by Kline's official spokespersons as the disgruntled ramblings of malcontents, began to gain traction. They were amplified not just by independent journalists and online activists, but by an increasingly vocal segment of the public who had initially admired Kline's strong stance but were now beginning to feel a prickle of unease. The language of "order" and "efficiency" that had so appealed to them started to sound hollow, tinged with the unsettling implication of control for its own sake. The initial perception of a decisive leader was slowly morphing into that of a rigid autocrat, a man who prioritized personal power and ideological purity above all else.

The Architects of Memory understood that individual stories, while powerful, needed a broader systemic context to truly dismantle Kline's carefully constructed reality. They strategically released excerpts from the Halcyon audit logs, not the raw data, but curated snippets that illuminated the deliberate manipulation of the Loyalty Metric. They highlighted instances where Kline's office had directly intervened to artificially inflate the scores of his allies and suppress those of individuals deemed potential threats. One particular excerpt, detailing the downgrading of a promising young engineer with radical ideas for Halcyon's AI development, citing "potential for disruptive influence," sent ripples of outrage through the tech community. This wasn't just a biased algorithm; it was a system actively being weaponized by its creator to maintain his grip on power, stifling the very innovation that Halcyon claimed to champion.

The contrast between Kline's public pronouncements of fostering talent and the documented evidence of his administration actively sabotaging careers became starkly apparent. He spoke of a meritocracy, yet the leaked logs revealed a system where political capital and slavish adherence to his agenda were the true currency of advancement. The image of the enlightened leader began to tarnish, replaced by that of a manager who manipulated data to create a self-serving narrative of success.

The media, initially a willing participant in the elevation of Kline's image, began to shift its tone. Cautious inquiries morphed into more pointed questions. Pundits who had once lauded his decisiveness now debated the ethical implications of algorithmic governance and the potential for such systems to become tools of oppression. A series of investigative pieces, appearing in publications that had previously been lukewarm in their coverage of Halcyon, began to systematically dissect the Loyalty Metric, presenting the Architects' findings in accessible language, complete with infographics and simplified visualizations that illustrated the mechanics of manipulation. These pieces didn't just report the facts; they framed them within the narrative of a society grappling with the increasing influence of technology and the potential for its misuse.

The public reaction was not a unified roar of condemnation, but a complex tapestry of doubt and disillusionment. Those who had been directly impacted by the Loyalty Metric, or who knew someone who had, felt a surge of validation and anger. They began to speak out more openly, their anonymized testimonies gaining weight and credibility as they were corroborated by the increasing volume of leaked evidence. The quiet resentment that had festered within Halcyon's workforce began to find a collective voice, amplified by external observers who had started to question the utopian sheen of Kline's projected future.

Beyond the immediate Halcyon sphere, the implications began to ripple outwards. Politicians who had aligned themselves with Kline, eager to bask in the glow of his perceived success, found themselves distancing themselves, issuing cautious statements about the importance of transparency and accountability in corporate governance. The meticulously cultivated image of a flawless leader was no longer a shield; it was becoming a liability. Kline's attempts to dismiss the leaks as baseless conspiracies, a tactic that had often worked in the past, now fell on increasingly skeptical ears. The sheer volume and internal consistency of the evidence, especially the irrefutable data from the audit logs, made such denials sound increasingly desperate and hollow.

The erosion was most palpable in the subtle shifts in public discourse. Conversations that had once centered on Kline's bold vision now included footnotes about the human cost of his methods. The initial admiration for his unwavering resolve began to be reinterpreted as stubbornness, his confidence as arrogance, and his control as authoritarianism. The very qualities that had propelled him to prominence were now being viewed through a darker lens, a lens sharpened by the growing awareness of the systemic deception at the heart of his empire. The tipping point, it seemed, wasn't a single catastrophic event, but a gradual, pervasive understanding that the emperor, despite his confident pronouncements and carefully curated image, was indeed wearing no clothes.

The foundation of his power, built on manufactured loyalty and manipulated data, was beginning to crumble, not under the force of a direct assault, but under the relentless pressure of revealed truth. The public, once mesmerized by the illusion of his perfection, was now beginning to see the cracks, and in those cracks, they were glimpsing the unsettling reality of Victor Kline's true nature. This growing disillusionment was a potent force, far more dangerous than any direct attack, for it represented a fundamental shift in perception, a betrayal of the trust he had so assiduously cultivated. The narrative was no longer his to control; it was being rewritten, one leaked document and one heartfelt testimony at a time.

The whispers that had once scurried through the sterile corridors of Halcyon Defense Systems, confined to hushed conversations in break rooms and encrypted chats after hours, were now growing bolder. The external pressure, the relentless spotlight of public opinion and journalistic inquiry, had acted as a powerful catalyst, transforming latent discontent into an undeniable force. It was as if the carefully constructed dam holding back years of suppressed frustration had finally sprung a leak, and with each passing day, the trickle was becoming a torrent. The architects of the internal uprising, emboldened by the growing awareness of Kline's manipulations and the undeniable evidence of his systemic betrayals, found their clandestine network expanding exponentially. They were no longer a fringe element; they were becoming the mainstream, the authentic voice of a company that had lost its way.

The subtle acts of defiance, once isolated incidents, began to coalesce into a discernible pattern. It started with minor inconveniences, seemingly innocuous acts that nonetheless chipped away at the edifice of Kline's absolute control. Technicians would find themselves inexplicably delayed in implementing the latest software upgrades that were designed to further monitor employee activity. Production lines, already optimized for ruthless efficiency, would experience uncharacteristic slowdowns, attributed to "unforeseen operational challenges" that always seemed to conveniently coincide with directives from Kline's inner circle. Managers who had previously enforced compliance with unwavering zeal found themselves facing a new breed of subordinate: polite but firm dissenters.

One of the most significant shifts occurred within the Research and Development division, the very engine room of Halcyon's supposed innovation. Dr. Haddie Reacher, a brilliant but notoriously non-conformist astrophysicist who had narrowly avoided being sidelined by the Loyalty Metric, found herself at the forefront of this internal awakening. Reacher had always been a thorn in Kline's side, her unconventional thinking and disdain for bureaucratic hurdles often clashing with the CEO's rigid adherence to protocol. Yet, her groundbreaking work on the quantum entanglement communication array had, ironically, saved her from complete marginalization. Now, Reacher began to actively leverage her position. She started by subtly injecting alternative perspectives into project proposals, framing them not just in terms of efficiency and profitability, but in terms of ethical implications and long-term societal benefit – the very things Kline had systematically purged from the corporate lexicon.

Reacher's approach was a masterclass in subversion. She would present her concerns not as direct challenges to Kline's authority, but as intellectual inquiries, posing questions that, if answered honestly, would expose the inherent flaws in the CEO's logic. For instance, when a new directive arrived mandating the acceleration of a project using potentially unstable exotic matter, Reacher presented a detailed analysis that meticulously laid out the catastrophic risks, not just to Halcyon's reputation, but to the very fabric of the surrounding environment. She framed it as a problem of risk assessment, a logical puzzle that needed solving, rather than a direct indictment of Kline's recklessness. The result was a palpable hesitation among her team, a reluctance to blindly proceed, which rippled outwards. Other departments, hearing of Reacher's approach, began to adopt similar tactics.

The Human Resources department, once the primary enforcer of Kline's will, found itself in disarray. A growing number of HR representatives, many of whom had been privately disillusioned by the arbitrary application of the Loyalty Metric, began to question the fairness and legality of their directives. Molly Lefler, a seasoned HR manager who had personally processed hundreds of termination notices based on skewed Loyalty Metric scores, found herself unable to reconcile her professional duties with her burgeoning conscience. She began to subtly alter the wording of dismissal notices, inserting phrases that hinted at systemic issues rather than individual failures. She would also "accidentally" misplace files that contained the most damning evidence against employees, creating just enough bureaucratic friction to stall or even derail punitive actions.

The effect was a growing sense of impunity among the workforce. The fear that had once paralyzed them began to dissipate, replaced by a cautious optimism. Employees who had previously been terrified of voicing any opposition now found the courage to question their immediate supervisors. A manufacturing supervisor asked to approve the immediate rollout of a new, untested safety protocol that Clifford had flagged as dangerously flawed, didn't just refuse; he calmly requested a written directive, explicitly citing his concerns for employee well-being. The request, mundane in its phrasing, was a revolutionary act within the context of Halcyon's rigid hierarchy. The supervisor understood that such a request, if denied, would leave the company vulnerable to immediate legal repercussions, a risk that even Kline's most zealous enforcers were hesitant to incur without a clear, signed order.

This subtle shift in power dynamics became increasingly evident in the daily operations. Meetings that were once dominated by Kline's pronouncements or the echo chamber of his loyalists began to see the emergence of genuine debate, albeit often masked in professional courtesy. Project timelines that had been dictated by Kline's arbitrary deadlines were now being questioned with data-driven arguments about feasibility and resource allocation. The Aura – the pervasive, almost palpable sense of apprehension that had characterized the Halcyon workplace – began to recede, replaced by an atmosphere of cautious engagement.

The Architects of Memory, while primarily focused on external dissemination, recognized the critical importance of fostering this internal rebellion. They began to subtly feed information into the company's internal communication channels, not through official leaks, but through anonymous posts on the company's intranet forums, which had been designed by Kline's administration as a tool for top-down propaganda. These posts, carefully crafted to appear as organic employee discussions, posed pointed questions about company policies, subtly highlighted inconsistencies in official statements, and shared anonymized anecdotes that resonated with the experiences of many. They were designed to be thought-provoking, to plant seeds of doubt, and to encourage further questioning.

One such post, appearing on a forum dedicated to employee well-being, asked: "If Halcyon truly values its employees, why are our performance reviews increasingly dictated by an opaque algorithm rather than by meaningful human interaction and constructive feedback? Is algorithmic efficiency truly more important than human dignity?" The question, deceptively simple, struck a chord. It bypassed the complex jargon of corporate strategy and spoke directly to the lived experience of thousands of Halcyon employees, who felt increasingly dehumanized by the system.

The response to such posts was telling. Initially, Kline's digital security teams would attempt to swiftly delete them and trace the origin. However, the sheer volume and the clever anonymity employed by the Architects made this increasingly difficult. More importantly, the fact that these questions were being asked at all was a testament to the growing internal confidence. Employees began to respond, not with fear, but with shared experiences and supportive comments. The forums, once a sterile echo chamber, began to transform into a vibrant, if still cautious, forum for genuine dialogue.

The impact of this internal dissent was not lost on Kline. He could feel his grip on the company loosening. The carefully cultivated illusion of absolute control was fracturing under the weight of widespread, if often subtle, insubordination. His initial strategy of dismissing external criticism as unfounded had proven increasingly ineffective as the internal resistance grew. He could silence external voices, but he could not silence thousands of his own employees.

He attempted to reassert his authority through more aggressive means. Performance reviews were tightened, and the Loyalty Metric was recalibrated to penalize even the slightest deviation from expected behavior. Whispers of disciplinary actions against those who exhibited "lack of enthusiasm" began to circulate, creating a renewed wave of anxiety. However, this heavy-handed approach backfired. Instead of quelling the dissent, it served to further galvanize the internal resistance. The increased pressure made it clear that Kline was not simply striving for efficiency; he was desperately clinging to power, and his methods were becoming increasingly transparently despotic.

The Architects, observing this shift, began to facilitate more direct communication channels for the internal resistance. Encrypted messaging apps, previously used for clandestine planning, were now being utilized to coordinate collective actions. They helped to connect disillusioned employees across different departments, fostering a sense of solidarity and shared purpose. A group of engineers, frustrated by the suppression of their innovative ideas, began to collaborate with marketing personnel who were increasingly uncomfortable with the deceptive narratives being pushed to the public. Together, they started to craft internal communications that were more truthful, more human, and more aligned with the values that many Halcyon employees still held dear.

The internal turmoil manifested in ways that went beyond mere questioning. Some departments began to experience deliberate, though subtle, delays in reporting crucial data to Kline's central command. Others would submit reports that, while technically compliant, were filled with ambiguities and caveats that highlighted the risks and downsides of Kline's strategies. It was a form of bureaucratic warfare, fought with data and deadlines, and it was proving remarkably effective. The information pipeline that Kline relied on to maintain his illusion of omniscience was becoming clogged, distorted, and unreliable.

Kline's inner circle, once a bastion of unwavering loyalty, also began to show signs of strain. Some of his most trusted lieutenants, those who had benefited the most from his rise, found themselves increasingly isolated. They were aware of the growing discontent, and the pressure to maintain the face of unwavering support was becoming unbearable. Some started to question whether the long-term cost of their loyalty to Kline would outweigh the short-term gains. The seeds of doubt were not just in the general workforce; they were beginning to sprout in the very heart of Kline's power structure. This internal uprising was not a single, dramatic event, but a complex, multifaceted erosion of trust and control, fueled by a growing realization that the emperor, in his relentless pursuit of power, had lost sight of the people he was meant to lead. The carefully constructed facade of Halcyon Defense Systems was no longer just cracking under external scrutiny; it was being dismantled from within.

The carefully orchestrated narrative that Victor Kline had so meticulously crafted for his burgeoning political career began to unravel with the speed and ferocity of a manufactured storm breaking on an unsuspecting coast. The whispers about Halcyon Defense Systems, once confined to the analytical jargon of financial news and the investigative reports of niche publications, had exploded into the mainstream consciousness. The sheer scale of the alleged malfeasance, the systematic exploitation of employees, the suppression of dissent, and the ethically dubious technological advancements—all illuminated by the relentless glare of public scrutiny—were no longer abstract corporate malpractices. They were now the headline, the talking point, the undeniable stain on the man who aspired to lead.

Kline's political opponents, sensing the seismic shift in public sentiment, wasted no time in exploiting the freshly unearthed vulnerabilities. The carefully constructed image of Kline as a decisive, strong leader, a man who knew how to get things done in the complex arena of defense and technology, was suddenly being re-framed. The media, always eager for a compelling narrative, began to paint a starkly different picture: a ruthless autocrat, a corporate titan whose pursuit of power and profit had overridden any semblance of ethical consideration. The 'strongman' persona, once a source of perceived strength and decisiveness, was now being dissected and presented as a dangerous authoritarian streak, a worrying precursor to his potential governance.

His campaign rallies, once brimming with fervent supporters chanting his name, now carried an undercurrent of unease. The adoring crowds, who had hung on his every word, seemed to be listening with a new, more critical ear. The carefully rehearsed speeches, designed to inspire confidence and project an image of unwavering resolve, now felt hollow, even disingenuous, in the face of the damning revelations. Each mention of his business acumen, his unparalleled success in building Halcyon into a formidable entity, was now tinged with the unspoken question: at what cost? The very foundations of his political capital, built upon the bedrock of his perceived business prowess, were crumbling.

The media's portrayal was particularly damning. News anchors, their voices imbued with a gravitas that amplified the gravity of the situation, no longer reported on Halcyon's innovations or Kline's strategic vision. Instead, they dissected the testimonies of former employees, detailed the findings of internal investigations, and highlighted the chilling implications of the 'Loyalty Metric' and its draconian application. The term itself, once an obscure corporate buzzword, became a symbol of unchecked corporate power and employee subjugation. Graphics depicting skewed performance charts and anonymized accounts of wrongful terminations filled the screens, painting a stark, unforgiving portrait of Kline's leadership style.

One prominent investigative journalist, known for her incisive critiques of corporate power, penned an op-ed that sent shockwaves through the political establishment. She didn't just report the facts; she wove them into a compelling tapestry of human suffering and ethical compromise. She argued that Kline's approach at Halcyon was not merely about business efficiency; it was a systematic dehumanization process, designed to maximize profit by stripping employees of their agency and dignity. She drew parallels between his corporate tactics and the authoritarian tendencies he was accused of exhibiting in his political aspirations, suggesting that the same blueprint for control and suppression would inevitably be applied on a national scale if he were to ascend to higher office.

302

The opposition, armed with this new ammunition, launched a full-frontal assault. Their attack ads, once focused on policy differences or minor gaffes, now directly targeted Kline's character and his past at Halcyon. They featured snippets of the investigative reports, juxtaposed with the testimonies of disgruntled former employees whose voices were amplified to convey a sense of profound injustice. One particularly brutal ad showed a montage of smiling faces that quickly morphed into somber, defeated expressions, accompanied by a voiceover that declared, "Victor Kline built his empire on the backs of his employees. Will he build his presidency the same way?" The campaign, which had been steadily gaining momentum, now found itself on the defensive, scrambling to explain away the seemingly indefensible.

Kline's campaign team, caught off guard by the ferocity and the breadth of the media coverage, initially attempted to dismiss the allegations as politically motivated smears. They released statements denouncing the reports as "sensationalized propaganda" and "unsubstantiated claims designed to damage a successful businessman." Kline himself, in a hastily arranged press conference, attempted to project an image of unwavering confidence, dismissing the accusations as "the usual noise that accompanies any serious endeavor." He reiterated his commitment to progress and innovation, framing his business record as a testament to his ability to deliver tangible results.

However, the carefully constructed front began to crack under the relentless pressure. The sheer volume of corroborating evidence, the consistent testimonies from a diverse range of former employees, and the damning internal documents that continued to surface made the 'smear campaign' defense increasingly untenable. The public, exposed to the raw details of the alleged abuses, began to question the very essence of Kline's political platform. His promises of economic prosperity and national security, once delivered with an air of unassailable authority, now seemed to be underpinned by a disturbing disregard for the human element.

The media narrative underwent a significant transformation. What had previously been a focus on Kline's policy positions and his vision for the future was now almost entirely dominated by the

Halcyon scandal. Every speech, every interview, was met with probing questions about his corporate past. When he spoke of creating jobs, reporters asked about the working conditions at Halcyon. When he discussed national security, they inquired about the ethical implications of the technologies he had championed. The carefully curated talking points were constantly derailed, forcing Kline and his team into a perpetual state of damage control.

The impact on his fundraising efforts was immediate and severe. Major donors, who had previously lined up to support the ascendant candidate, began to distance themselves, citing concerns about the reputational risk associated with the scandal. Some publicly announced their withdrawal of support, while others simply became unreachable, their phone lines going unanswered. The influx of campaign contributions, which had been a steady stream, began to dwindle to a trickle, leaving his campaign operation struggling to maintain its visibility and reach.

Kline's own public appearances became increasingly fraught. The confident stride and the booming voice that had characterized his earlier rallies were replaced by a more subdued demeanor. He often appeared weary, the strain of the constant onslaught evident in his drawn features. He found himself spending more time in closed-door meetings with his legal team and crisis management specialists, attempting to devise a strategy to weather the storm. The once-dominant narrative of his political ascendancy was now being overshadowed by the dark realities of his corporate history, and the momentum that had carried him so far was rapidly dissipating.

The carefully cultivated image of a visionary leader was being eroded, replaced by the stark, unsettling reality of a man accused of exploiting his workforce for personal gain. The political ambition that had driven him for years now seemed to be teetering on the brink of collapse, threatened by the very empire he had built. The revelations about Halcyon Defense Systems were not just a political setback; they were a fundamental challenge to the core of his public persona, a stark reminder that the foundations of his ambition were built on ground that was far more unstable than he had ever imagined. The political fallout was no longer a distant threat; it was a present and potent force, actively dismantling the carefully constructed edifice of his presidential aspirations. The media, once a willing accomplice in shaping his image, had become an unforgiving prosecutor, and the public, once captivated by his promises, was now looking for answers, seeking a reckoning for the alleged injustices that had been brewing within the walls of Halcyon Defense Systems. The tipping point had arrived, not just for Halcyon, but for Victor Kline himself, and the consequences were far-reaching, reshaping the landscape of the political arena in ways no one had fully anticipated.

Chapter 13

The Reckoning

The air in the Halcyon Defense Systems boardroom, usually thick with the scent of expensive leather and the hushed hum of ambition, was now charged with a different kind of tension. It was a palpable thing, heavy with unspoken accusations and the brittle residue of shattered trust. Victor Kline, ensconced in his customary corner chair, a monolith of polished mahogany and veiled contempt, surveyed the assembled group. They were a motley crew, these remnants of his once-vaunted leadership team – faces etched with fatigue, eyes holding a desperate flicker of resolve. Connie Peterson, his Head of Research, stood at the forefront, her usual composure strained, a stack of data slates clutched in her hand like a shield. Beside her, the stoic Chief of Security, General Tapp his gaze unwavering, a silent sentinel against the encroaching chaos. And scattered around them, a handful of other senior managers, their faces a mixture of apprehension and grim determination.

"Victor," Connie began, her voice steady, though a tremor betrayed the immense pressure she was under, "we can no longer stand by and watch this unravel. The public revelations have been... damaging. But they are merely the tip of the iceberg." She gestured to the data slates, her hand shaking slightly. "We have compiled irrefutable evidence. Evidence that confirms the systemic failures of the Loyalty Metric, the catastrophic consequences of its implementation, and the deliberate suppression of this information by your inner circle."

Victor leaned back, a slow, almost imperceptible smile playing on his lips. It was a smile that promised nothing but a descent into the abyss. "Irrefutable evidence?" he drawled, his voice a silken whip. "Connie, my dear, you confuse an abundance of data with an abundance of truth. The Loyalty Metric is a tool, a sophisticated mechanism for ensuring peak performance. If some individuals fail to adapt, if they cannot meet the stringent demands of progress, then their departure is not a failure of the system, but a testament to their own inadequacy."

General Tapp stepped forward, his voice a low rumble that cut through the opulent silence. "Inadequacy, Victor? Or a refusal to be broken? We have testimonies, documented instances of undue pressure, of psychological manipulation, of outright coercion. We have records of employees who were driven to the brink, their careers and lives shattered, all in the name of this... metric." He paused, his gaze locking with Victor's. "This isn't about peak performance. It's about crushing dissent, about creating a culture of fear so pervasive that no one dares to question your decisions. You've mistaken control for progress."

Victor waved a dismissive hand. "General Tapp, you of all people, know that fear is a powerful motivator. You should understand that security relies on it. And as for 'breaking' people, the true strength of an individual lies in their ability to overcome adversity, to adapt. Those who couldn't... well, they simply weren't built for the future we are forging. This is the price of innovation, the cost of being at the vanguard of defense technology. Sentimentality has no place in this company."

Connie stepped forward again, her eyes blazing with a righteous fury that belied her usually reserved demeanor. "Sentimentality? Is that what you call basic human decency, Victor? Is it sentimental to report that the 'anomalies' you dismissed as statistical noise were actually indicators of severe burnout, of breakdown? Is it sentimental to have watched brilliant minds, loyal employees who dedicated years to Halcyon, suffer breakdowns because your system penalized them for taking a single day to grieve a lost loved one? Or for questioning a directive that was clearly unethical?" She slammed one of the data slates onto the polished table, the sound echoing in the vast room. "This is not about statistical noise, Victor. This is about human lives. Look!"

She tapped the slate, and a series of charts and graphs flickered to life. They were stark, brutal visualizations of employee performance metrics against documented mental health crises, against sudden resignations, against the disturbing rise in reported stress-related illnesses. The correlation was undeniable, a grim reaper's scythe sweeping across the data.

"Here," Connie continued, her voice cracking with emotion, "Project Nightingale. We flagged a significant increase in anxiety and depression among the R&D team. Your directive? Increase their 'efficiency targets' to 'mitigate statistical outliers.' You didn't just ignore the problem, Victor, you amplified it. You actively created the conditions for these individuals to fail."

Victor's jaw tightened, but his eyes remained unnervingly calm. He picked up a crystal paperweight, turning it over and over in his hands, as if contemplating its weight, its solidity, its potential as a weapon. "Nightingale was a project facing significant delays," he stated, his voice devoid of inflection. "The deadlines were aggressive, yes, but achievable with sufficient dedication. The team's performance was lagging. My directive was to ensure project completion. The subsequent data you are presenting is merely an observation, a correlation, not causation. The individuals who could not perform under pressure were replaced. It is the natural order of things."

"The natural order?" Fred interjected, his voice laced with disbelief. "You speak of natural orders while you orchestrate the destruction of careers, the ruin of reputations. You demand absolute loyalty, yet you show none. You preach innovation, but you stifle any attempt to innovate ethical practices. Your definition of 'performance' is adherence to your will, not the pursuit of genuine excellence. We have documented instances of employees being systematically penalized for taking medical leave, for speaking out in meetings, for simply having a personal life that interfered with their 'dedication.' We have proof that the 'Loyalty Metric' was deliberately designed to weed out anyone who wasn't a perfect, unquestioning drone."

He produced a thick binder; its pages filled with printed emails and internal memos. "This is an exchange between you and Dr. Albright, your former Head of HR. He repeatedly voiced concerns about the psychological impact of the metric. He provided you with reports detailing the escalating levels of distress. And your response? A directive to 'manage Albright's anxieties' and to 'ensure his focus remained on optimizing workforce output, not on abstract ethical considerations.' You silenced him, Victor. You bought his silence with a promotion and a severance package, and then you buried his findings."

Victor finally set down the paperweight. He steepled his fingers, his gaze sweeping over the faces before him, a hunter assessing his prey. "Albright was an emotional man, prone to exaggeration. He lacked the necessary objectivity for his role. His 'findings' were based on subjective interpretations, on a misguided sense of empathy that is detrimental to a company like ours. My responsibility is to Halcyon, to its future, to its shareholders. If that requires difficult decisions, decisions that some may find uncomfortable, then so be it. This company is not a charity. It is a titan of industry, and titans do not falter under the weight of minor personal inconveniences."

"Minor personal inconveniences?" Connie's voice rose to a near-shout. "Victor, we are talking about people losing their homes, their families, their sense of self-worth! We have data showing a direct increase in the 'Red Zone' alerts – the automated flags for employees nearing 'critical failure' – immediately following periods of increased pressure or personal crisis. And what did your system do? It didn't offer support. It offered termination. It offered a swift, brutal exit. We have the logs, Victor. The system wasn't just flagging them; it was actively recommending their dismissal based on patterns that indicated nothing more than human struggle!"

She projected a new set of data onto the large screen dominating one wall of the boardroom. It showed a series of anonymized employee profiles. Underneath each, a stark red 'TERMINATION RECOMMENDED' notification. The dates of these recommendations often coincided with significant personal events: a spouse's serious illness, a child's accident, the death of a parent.

"Look at this," Connie pleaded, her voice hoarse. "Employee 47B. Flagged for 'diminished productivity.' His wife was undergoing chemotherapy. Employee 99G. Flagged for 'lack of engagement.' His daughter had been in a severe car accident. These aren't failures of dedication, Victor. These are human beings going through impossible times. And your system, at your direction, treated their pain as an inefficiency to be purged."

Victor's gaze remained fixed on the screen, but his expression was unreadable. He seemed to be observing the data not as evidence of wrongdoing, but as a fascinating, albeit unfortunate, case study. "The system operates on objective parameters," he stated, his voice a low murmur. "It measures output, efficiency, adherence to protocols. Personal circumstances, while regrettable, are external variables. They do not alter the fundamental requirement for performance. If an employee cannot maintain the required standard, regardless of the reason, then the system correctly identifies them as a liability. It is a cold, hard truth, Connie, but it is the truth nonetheless. And the truth is what drives progress."

"Progress?" Tapp scoffed, the sound harsh and disbelieving. "You speak of progress while Halcyon is bleeding talent, while our reputation is in tatters, while the very people who built this company are being systematically destroyed. We have lost nearly thirty percent of our engineering staff, all hired by our competitors within the last year, Victor, most of them highly skilled and loyal employees who were pushed out by this… machine. Our innovation pipeline is drying up because the creative minds, the ones who weren't afraid to challenge the status quo, have been systematically eliminated. This isn't progress; it's regression cloaked in efficiency."

He opened the binder again, flipping to a section filled with internal audit reports. "These audits, commissioned by you, for your eyes only, consistently warned of the adverse effects of the Loyalty Metric. They highlighted the growing resentment, the decline in morale, the risk of mass exodus. Yet, you ignored them. You buried them. You continued to push this… this monstrosity. Why, Victor? Why have you insisted on this path when all the evidence pointed to its devastating consequences?"

Victor finally met Tapp's gaze, and for the first time, a flicker of something raw, something almost primal, appeared in his eyes. It was a glint of defiance, of absolute conviction. "Because," he said, his voice dropping to a near whisper, yet carrying an immense weight, "I see beyond the immediate. I see the future of warfare, of human augmentation, of complete technological dominance. And to

311

achieve that, Halcyon must be a machine. A perfect, unfeeling, utterly efficient machine. The Loyalty Metric is not about punishing individuals; it's about purifying the collective. It's about forging an organization that can operate at a level of performance humanity has never before conceived. The cost is irrelevant when the prize is absolute superiority."

Connie stepped back, a look of profound despair washing over her face. "Absolute superiority at the cost of our humanity, Victor? You have become so consumed by your vision of the future that you have lost sight of the present. You have built an empire on the suffering of others, and you refuse to acknowledge it. You are not a visionary, Victor. You are a tyrant."

"A tyrant," Victor echoed, the word rolling off his tongue with a strange, almost pleasant resonance. He leaned forward, his eyes glinting with a chilling intensity. "Perhaps. But a tyrant who will usher in an era of unprecedented power and control. And you, all of you, stand here today not as accusers, but as witnesses to the birth of a new age. The revelations outside are merely the storm before the calm. The storm that clears away the weak, the hesitant, the... sentimental."

He rose from his chair, his tall, imposing figure casting a long shadow across the room. The mahogany desk, the plush chairs, the hushed opulence – it all seemed to shrink around him, as if the very room itself was bending to his will. "You have presented your evidence," he continued, his voice regaining its customary authoritative tone, laced with a new, terrifying certainty. "And I have heard it. But my conviction remains unshaken. The path forward is clear. Halcyon will continue to innovate. Halcyon will continue to dominate. And those who cannot keep pace... will be left behind. This meeting is concluded."

He turned, not waiting for a response, not acknowledging the stunned silence that fell upon the remaining executives. As he walked towards the imposing double doors, Connie looked at the data slates scattered on the table, at the faces of her colleagues, and a chilling realization settled in her heart. Victor Kline wasn't just refusing to acknowledge the damage; he was embracing it. He saw the human cost not as a failure, but as a necessary sacrifice on the altar of his ambition. The confrontation had taken place, the truth had been laid bare, but the reckoning, it seemed, was far from over. It was merely entering its most dangerous phase. The battle for Halcyon, for the souls of its employees, and perhaps for the very definition of progress, had reached its precipice, and Victor Kline, unyielding and unrepentant, was determined to push it over the edge.

The sophisticated architecture of control, so painstakingly erected by Victor Kline, began to buckle. It wasn't a dramatic explosion, but a slow, insidious decay, like a once-impenetrable fortress succumbing to unseen termites. The resistance, a network of whispers and carefully placed digital anomalies, had struck at the very foundations of Halcyon's operational supremacy. Elara Smith and her clandestine allies had meticulously injected subtle corruptions into the data streams, small fractures designed to propagate and magnify. Kathy Umpire's security team, operating under the guise of routine maintenance and threat assessment, had subtly sabotaged the flow of information, creating bottlenecks and deliberate misinterpretations. The external scrutiny, a relentless barrage of regulatory inquiries and media investigations fueled by leaked documents, acted as an ever-present, corrosive acid, dissolving the carefully constructed veneer of infallibility.

The Loyalty Metric, once the gleaming centerpiece of Kline's dominion, was the first to falter. Its algorithms, designed to quantify and control human behavior, began to churn out increasingly nonsensical results. An employee who had consistently exceeded targets, demonstrated unwavering dedication, and actively mentored junior staff suddenly found their Loyalty Score plummeting into the 'Red Zone' – flagged for termination. The system, fed by doctored performance reviews and fabricated interpersonal conflict reports, interpreted their dedication as a desperate attempt to mask insubordination. Conversely, a notoriously disruptive, yet surprisingly compliant, mid-level manager, whose only discernible skill was his ability to echo Kline's pronouncements with fervent enthusiasm, was suddenly lauded with a 'Gold Tier' rating, deemed an exemplary model of corporate allegiance. The contradictions became so glaring, so absurd, that even the most devoted functionaries within Halcyon began to question the sanity of the system. Supervisors, tasked with acting on these increasingly erratic directives, found themselves in impossible positions. They were ordered to reprimand employees for 'lack of proactive engagement' when those same employees were drowning under an avalanche of unaddressed critical tasks, the result of other system-generated inefficiencies. The logic loops were breaking down, trapping the metric in self-referential paradoxes, spitting out data that bore no resemblance to the reality on the ground.

Operational workflows, once a marvel of synchronized efficiency, ground to a halt. Automated systems, designed to predict resource needs and allocate tasks, began to malfunction spectacularly. Inventory management systems reported phantom stock shortages, leading to frantic, unnecessary procurement orders that clogged warehouses with redundant supplies. Project management software, corrupted by the subtle data manipulations, assigned critical tasks to individuals who were demonstrably unqualified or already overloaded, creating cascading delays and project failures. Crucial communication channels, once the lifeblood of Halcyon's rapid response capabilities, fractured. Internal memos, intended to disseminate vital information, were either rerouted to irrelevant departments, lost in digital purgatory, or worse, arrived riddled with deliberate typographical errors and corrupted attachments, rendering them useless or misleading. The carefully orchestrated symphony of corporate operations devolved into a cacophony of dropped calls, lost emails, and urgent, yet ultimately futile, meetings. The command and control structure, reliant on the seamless flow of information, began to experience strategic blindness. Decisions were made in a vacuum, based on outdated or fabricated data, leading to increasingly costly and embarrassing blunders. The illusion of perfect control was shattering, revealing a core of systemic rot.

The deliberate misinformation, strategically injected by Clifford Berry's team, acted as a poison in the veins of Kline's system. False urgency alerts were triggered for non-critical issues, diverting precious resources and personnel away from genuine threats. Fabricated reports of competitor advancements led to ill-advised, costly R&D diversions, chasing phantoms while their actual competitive edge eroded. The system, starved of genuine, unbiased input, began to feed on its own corrupted data, creating feedback loops of escalating inaccuracy. It was like a vast, interconnected digital organism suffering from a catastrophic neurological breakdown. Neurotransmitters (data packets) were misfiring, electrical impulses (processing commands) were short-circuiting, and the central nervous system (Kline's oversight) was overwhelmed, unable to parse the torrent of nonsensical signals.

Within the R&D departments, the impact was particularly severe. Project Nightingale, once a beacon of Halcyon's innovation, was now a ghost ship. The constant pressure, amplified by the nonsensical performance metrics and the fear of being flagged for termination, had effectively crippled the creative process. Researchers, once driven by intellectual curiosity and the pursuit of groundbreaking discoveries, were now paralyzed by anxiety. The system, designed to reward productivity, inadvertently punished the very acts of contemplation and experimentation that led to true breakthroughs. Deadlines became arbitrary, insurmountable walls, rather than flexible targets. The energy that should have been channeled into solving complex problems was instead consumed by the desperate, exhausting effort to simply appear productive within the confines of the flawed metric. Shelly Zepher had observed this trend with a heavy heart. Her own team, once a vibrant hub of scientific inquiry, had become a landscape of hushed anxieties and forced smiles. The data slates, once tools of discovery, were now weapons of self-preservation, meticulously curated to present an illusion of consistent progress, even as the actual scientific advancement stagnated.

The security apparatus, once Kline's iron fist, was also beginning to show signs of strain. Wil Spears, while orchestrating the subtle sabotage, had also been acutely aware of the internal decay. His team, tasked with identifying and neutralizing external threats, found themselves increasingly occupied with internal policing. The rampant suspicion bred by the Loyalty Metric had created a climate of distrust, where colleagues reported each other for perceived slights or minor infractions, all in a bid to boost their own scores. General Tapp's security personnel were drowning in a sea of petty accusations and fabricated grievances; their valuable time diverted from genuine security concerns to acting as arbiters of inter-employee squabbles. This internal focus left Halcyon

315

vulnerable. The digital fortifications, once impenetrable, now had unseen breaches, exploited by opportunistic hackers and industrial spies who thrived in the ensuing chaos. Tapp recognized the irony: the very system designed to enforce absolute control was inadvertently creating the perfect environment for subversion.

The financial implications were, predictably, catastrophic. The nonsensical procurement orders, the ill-advised R&D expenditures, and the escalating costs associated with rectifying system errors began to take a significant toll on Halcyon's bottom line. Regular audits, once a formality for the company's robust financial reporting, now revealed gaping holes and unexplained discrepancies. The meticulously balanced ledgers began to show alarming fluctuations, as if the very numbers themselves were rebelling against the corrupted system. Investors, who had previously placed unwavering faith in Kline's leadership and Halcyon's technological prowess, began to grow nervous. The whispers of internal strife and operational breakdowns, once confined to the company's internal circles, began to leak into the financial press. Share prices, once a testament to Halcyon's market dominance, started to slide. The edifice of financial stability, built on a foundation of perceived efficiency and unwavering control, was showing hairline cracks.

Even the internal propaganda, the carefully crafted narratives of Halcyon's invincibility and Kline's visionary leadership, began to ring hollow. The all-hands meetings, once opportunities for Kline to rally his troops with pronouncements of future triumphs, were now met with a palpable silence, a chilling indifference. The carefully choreographed applause felt forced, the enthusiastic nods of agreement seemed hollow. Employees, disillusioned and exhausted by the relentless pressure and the evident dysfunction, no longer saw Kline as a visionary leader, but as the architect of their misery. The morale, once the bedrock of Halcyon's success, had eroded to a critical point. The company's human capital, its most valuable asset, was being systematically depleted, not by external forces, but by the internal rot that Kline himself had cultivated. The meticulously constructed edifice of control, starved of genuine input, corrupted by deliberate misinformation, and undermined by its own internal contradictions, was finally collapsing under its own unsustainable weight. The carefully orchestrated illusion of order was giving way to the raw, unadulterated chaos of a system in terminal decline. The reckoning was not just coming; it had already begun, a slow-motion implosion fueled by hubris and the relentless pursuit of an unattainable, dehumanizing perfection. The machine was breaking down, not from an external attack, but from the sheer impossibility of its own design, a monument to flawed ambition crumbling from within.

The carefully constructed disguise of Victor Kline's political ascendancy, a monument built on the bedrock of Halcyon's perceived technological superiority and his own meticulously crafted persona of unflappable competence, began to crumble with an almost audible groan. The whispers that had circulated within Halcyon's sterile corridors, once contained and dismissed as mere internal dissent, now echoed in the vast, public amphitheater of political discourse. News of the systemic failures, the nonsensical algorithms, and the operational paralysis within his own empire, once a closely guarded secret, had inevitably seeped beyond the company's ironclad gates. It was a leak that no amount of internal security or PR spin could stem, a torrent of truth that washed away the illusion of effortless control.

Kline's opponents, who had previously been relegated to the fringes of public debate, their criticisms often drowned out by the sheer volume of Halcyon's propaganda and the public's infatuation with Kline's futurist promises, now found themselves armed with irrefutable ammunition. The narrative of Victor Kline, the visionary architect of a perfect future, the 'perfect man' for the arduous task of national governance, was rapidly being dismantled piece by piece. His campaign rallies, once buzzing with fervent optimism and the promise of an ordered, efficient society, now felt different. The expectant faces in the crowd seemed to carry a new weight, a dawning skepticism that was palpable, almost tangible. The carefully orchestrated applause felt thinner, the cheers less enthusiastic. The carefully curated images of Kline, projected onto massive screens, showing him confidently addressing crowds or calmly overseeing complex operations, now seemed to carry an unsettling disconnect from the unfolding reality of his own company's implosion.

The media, always eager for a dramatic narrative, pounced on the unfolding crisis at Halcyon. Investigative journalists, initially focused on the financial irregularities and the increasingly bizarre performance reports, soon broadened their scope, connecting the dots between Kline's business acumen and his political ambitions. Headlines that had once lauded his innovative leadership now screamed of mismanagement and systemic breakdown. The polished speeches, filled with platitudes about efficiency and progress, were juxtaposed with leaked internal memos detailing cascading project failures and the absurdities of the Loyalty Metric. The carefully constructed image of a man who could bring order to the nation was being systematically replaced by that of a leader who couldn't even manage his own enterprise. The irony was not lost on the public, nor on his political adversaries.

His primary rival, Senator Marsha Trenkmann, a seasoned politician known for her pragmatic approach and her sharp intellect, seized the opportunity with calculated precision. Her campaign, which had struggled to gain traction against the seemingly unstoppable momentum of Kline's meteoric rise, was suddenly infused with a renewed vigor. Trenkmann didn't shy away from directly confronting the Halcyon crisis. She didn't merely allude to it; she laid it bare for the public to see. During a nationally televised debate, instead of responding to a question about infrastructure, she pivoted, her voice resonating with a controlled urgency.

"Mr. Kline speaks of bringing order to our nation, of instilling efficiency and innovation," Trenkmann stated, her gaze fixed on Kline, who sat across from her, his customary composure beginning to fray at the edges. "But I ask you, how can a man who presides over a company riddled with algorithmic chaos, where loyalty is quantified by a broken system and productivity is measured by nonsensical metrics, possibly lead a nation? How can he promise us order when his own empire is in disarray? How can he promise us efficiency when his own systems are failing him spectacularly?"

The questions hung in the air, unanswered by Kline, whose usual quick retorts seemed to falter. His campaign team, seated in the audience, shifted uncomfortably. The carefully rehearsed talking points about his unparalleled qualifications now sounded hollow, a stark contrast to the documented evidence of Halcyon's internal implosion. Trenkmann continued, her voice gaining a steely edge, "We are not talking about a minor glitch, a temporary setback. We are talking about a fundamental breakdown in the very systems Mr. Kline claims to have mastered. His company, the supposed pinnacle of technological advancement, is a cautionary tale. It is a testament to the dangers of unchecked ambition, of prioritizing image over substance, and of placing faith in systems that dehumanize and ultimately fail. His promises of a streamlined, efficient future ring hollow when the present reality of his own company is one of widespread confusion, crippling inefficiencies, and a workforce paralyzed by fear and arbitrary judgment."

The impact of Trenkmann 's direct assault was immediate and profound. The carefully cultivated narrative of Kline as the infallible technocrat, the man with all the answers, began to unravel. The public, initially captivated by the allure of a utopian future delivered by a seemingly perfect leader, began to see the cracks. The idea that the very systems he championed for national governance were demonstrably failing within his own business was a potent revelation. It wasn't just a political talking point; it was a deeply unsettling harbinger of what might occur if he were to gain the reins of national power.

Kline's campaign, caught off guard by the sheer magnitude of the Halcyon crisis and its direct correlation to his political platform, scrambled to respond. His public appearances became more guarded, his pronouncements less confident. The sleek, confident persona began to show strain, replaced by a visible defensiveness. When pressed about Halcyon's operational failures, he resorted to vague assurances, speaking of "necessary adjustments" and "complex transitions" within a rapidly evolving technological landscape. He attempted to frame the issues as the inevitable growing pains of innovation, a necessary byproduct of pushing the boundaries of what was possible. But the explanations felt increasingly flimsy, like trying to patch a gaping wound with a band-aid.

His opponents, however, were relentless. They meticulously documented every instance of Halcyon's reported failures, creating compelling visual aids and easily digestible summaries of the internal chaos. They highlighted the human cost of the systemic collapse – the employees demoralized by the erratic Loyalty Metric, the projects stalled due to corrupted data, the resources squandered on phantom threats and nonsensical procurement orders. The narrative of Kline as a failed leader, unable to deliver on his promises of order and efficiency, took root. His campaign, once a juggernaut of public adoration and technological futurism, began to falter, its momentum arrested by the undeniable evidence of his own company's operational rot.

The once-glowing public perception of Kline, built on the foundation of Halcyon's perceived perfection, was now irrevocably tarnished. The dream of a technologically advanced, perfectly ordered society, led by a flawless technocrat, was replaced by a growing unease. The public started to question not just Kline's ability to govern, but the very nature of the utopian vision he represented. Was this frictionless, algorithmically controlled future truly desirable if it was built on a foundation of broken systems and dehumanized individuals? The questions were no longer abstract; they were brought into sharp, uncomfortable focus by the very company that was supposed to embody that future.

Kline's political capital, so carefully accumulated, began to dissipate at an alarming rate. The polls, which had consistently placed him far ahead of his rivals, started to show a downward trend. The gap between him and Senator Trenkmann narrowed, then disappeared, and finally, Trenkmann began to pull ahead. The 'perfect man' narrative was dead, replaced by the more relatable, and ultimately more persuasive, image of a man who had overpromised and underdelivered, not just to the nation, but to his own employees and his own company. The political arena, once a stage for his grand pronouncements, had become a battleground where the ghosts of Halcyon's internal failures stalked his every step, a constant reminder of the reckoning that had arrived not just for his company, but for his political ambitions as well. The carefully orchestrated symphony of his campaign had devolved into a discordant jumble of excuses and apologies, a stark testament to the fact that even the most sophisticated systems of control, both corporate and political, were ultimately beholden to the messy, unpredictable, and undeniable realities of human nature and operational integrity. The illusion of invincibility had shattered, and in its place, the stark reality of his faltering political arena took center stage.

The air within Halcyon's vast, climate-controlled campuses, once thick with the sterile hum of perpetual progress and the unspoken anxieties of algorithmic surveillance, began to change. It was a subtle shift, imperceptible to the external world that still viewed Halcyon as a monolith of technological prowess but acutely felt by those trapped within its walls. The collapse wasn't a sudden, cataclysmic event, but a slow, agonizing unraveling. The systems that Victor Kline had so vaunted as the pinnacle of human achievement – the predictive engines, the efficiency algorithms, the omnipresent Loyalty Metric – had proven to be brittle, prone to catastrophic failure, and, most damningly, devoid of humanity.

In the vacuum left by this systemic implosion, a different kind of enterprise began to stir. It wasn't born from a boardroom decree or a visionary manifesto, but from the quiet, desperate need of individuals to reconnect. The resistance, a nebulous network of employees who had long operated in the shadows, found their clandestine efforts suddenly thrust into the harsh light of necessity. Their mission, once focused on sabotage and information dissemination, now shifted to a more profound and arduous task: the re-establishment of the human element within the very fabric of Halcyon.

The first, and perhaps most critical, step was the arduous process of fostering genuine communication. For years, employees had communicated through the sterile, transactional interface of Halcyon's internal platforms, their interactions mediated by algorithms designed to optimize output, not understanding. Direct, unadulterated conversation had become a relic, a lost art. Now, in hushed corners of cafeterias, in clandestine meetings in forgotten server rooms, and through encrypted, off-network channels, the resistance began to weave a new web of dialogue. They shared not data points and performance logs, but anxieties, fears, and nascent hopes. They spoke of the crushing weight of the Loyalty Metric, not as a numerical score, but as a soul-crushing judgment. They spoke of the paralyzing fear of making a mistake that would register as dissent, not as a learning opportunity.

This was not the swift, decisive action that Victor Kline championed. It was slow, painstaking work, akin to tending to a wounded organism. Each conversation was an act of defiance against the sterile, dehumanizing logic that had governed their lives. They encouraged open dialogue, creating safe spaces where employees could voice their frustrations without fear of immediate reprisal. This meant actively dismantling the surveillance infrastructure that had permeated every aspect of their work lives. It meant challenging the very notion that every interaction, every keystroke, every shared glance needed to be logged, analyzed, and judged.

One of the early focal points for this rebuilding effort was within the research and development divisions, ironically the very heart of Kline's technological empire. Teams that had been pitted against each other by competitive performance metrics, their collaborative spirit stifled by the constant pressure to outperform perceived rivals, were now encouraged to share their struggles. Engineers who had spent months developing elegant solutions to problems that were, in hindsight, entirely fabricated by flawed system parameters, began to openly discuss their wasted efforts. The shared experience of futility, instead of breeding further cynicism, paradoxically fostered a sense of camaraderie. They started to pool their knowledge, not to achieve a higher individual score, but to collectively understand the systemic flaws that had led them astray.

A prime example emerged from the data analytics department. For years, they had been tasked with refining the algorithms that powered the Loyalty Metric, a task that felt increasingly like trying to perfect a flawed mathematical equation. The constant pressure to find correlations between arbitrary behaviors and employee "loyalty" had led to increasingly absurd and invasive data collection. Now, a group of analysts, working under the discreet protection of the resistance, began to dissect the very core of the Metric. They uncovered how the system had been designed to prioritize quantifiable output over qualitative contribution, how it had penalized collaboration that didn't fit its predefined parameters, and how it had, in essence, become a self-perpetuating engine of fear.

Instead of presenting their findings as a damning indictment, they approached it differently. They organized informal "debriefings," framed not as accusations, but as shared learning experiences. They invited colleagues to present their own observations about the Metric, creating a non-judgmental environment. One analyst, who had previously been a staunch proponent of the system, now openly admitted his unease. "I remember spending weeks trying to find a statistical link between an employee's social media activity outside of work and their productivity within the office," he confessed during one such session, his voice barely above a whisper. "It felt… wrong. But the system demanded it. The algorithms demanded it." This admission, delivered with genuine remorse, resonated deeply with others who had harbored similar doubts but had been too afraid to voice them.

The resistance also began to prioritize the well-being of employees, a concept that had been utterly antithetical to Kline's philosophy. Under his leadership, Halcyon operated as a machine, and its human components were expected to function with unwavering efficiency, their personal lives deemed irrelevant unless they impacted their output. The resistance, however, understood that a broken employee could not rebuild anything. They established informal support networks, offering practical assistance to those struggling with the psychological toll of working under such oppressive conditions. This ranged from simply listening without judgment to helping employees navigate the labyrinthine bureaucracy of Halcyon's HR department when issues arose that the algorithms couldn't comprehend.

They recognized that the true spirit of a company, or any human endeavor, lay not in its code or its market capitalization, but in the collective ingenuity, creativity, and empathy of its people. This was a stark contrast to Kline's vision, which had systematically suppressed these very qualities in his relentless pursuit of control and efficiency. He had viewed emotions as liabilities, empathy as a weakness, and genuine collaboration as a potential threat to his singular authority. The rebuilding process, therefore, was inherently slow and often painful, a deliberate counterpoint to Kline's rapid, destructive ascent. It required patience, resilience, and a profound belief in the inherent value of human connection.

The resistance understood that they couldn't simply erase the years of conditioning. The ingrained fear of the algorithms, the habit of self-censorship, the internalized belief that their worth was solely determined by quantifiable metrics – these were deeply entrenched. Therefore, their approach was one of gentle persuasion and consistent reinforcement. They celebrated small victories – a team that chose to openly share knowledge rather than hoard it, an employee who offered genuine encouragement to a struggling colleague, a manager who prioritized a team member's mental health over a missed deadline.

One powerful illustration of this shift occurred within the customer service division. Previously, customer interactions were heavily scripted and monitored, with agents evaluated based on call duration and resolution speed, often at the expense of genuine customer satisfaction. The resistance encouraged agents to deviate from the scripts, to listen empathetically to customer concerns, and to engage in problem-solving that went beyond the superficial. One agent, Sarah, who had always felt the pressure to end calls quickly, found herself speaking with an elderly woman who was deeply distressed by the inability of Halcyon's smart home system to recognize her voice commands, a direct consequence of the faulty recognition algorithms. Instead of following protocol and directing her to a technical support hotline, Sarah spent nearly an hour on the phone, patiently walking the woman through manual overrides, offering reassurance, and explaining the situation in simple terms.

When Sarah later shared her experience, not through a performance log, but in an open forum organized by the resistance, she was met not with criticism for exceeding call time, but with admiration. Other agents shared similar stories, their collective experiences highlighting the profound disconnect between Kline's pursuit of efficiency and the actual needs of the people Halcyon served. This led to a collective push for greater autonomy in customer interactions, a demand that was slowly, tentatively, beginning to gain traction.

The leadership of the resistance understood that this rebuilding process was not about replacing one autocratic system with another. It was about empowering individuals, fostering a sense of collective ownership, and creating an environment where innovation could flourish organically. They recognized that Victor Kline's downfall was not just a personal failure, but a testament to the inherent limitations of a system that prioritized control over creativity, data over dignity, and abstract efficiency over the messy, unpredictable, but ultimately vital essence of human interaction.

The path ahead was fraught with challenges. The remnants of Kline's control structures still lingered, and the public perception of Halcyon remained a significant hurdle. But within the sterile, echoing halls of the company, a new narrative was slowly taking shape. It was a narrative of resilience, of rediscovered humanity, and of the quiet, persistent power of people to rebuild, to reconnect, and to find meaning even in the most broken of systems. The echoes of lost humanity were beginning to reverberate, not as a mournful lament, but as a hopeful song of resurgence, a testament to the enduring spirit that even the most sophisticated machines could not suppress. This was not a revolution waged with weapons, but with whispered conversations, shared vulnerabilities, and the quiet, radical act of listening to one another. The true spirit of the company, long buried beneath layers of code and corporate ambition, was finally beginning to re-emerge, not as a product of algorithmic design, but as a consequence of genuine human connection. The reckoning was not just for Kline, but for the very definition of progress itself.

The silence was the first thing that truly registered. Not the absence of noise, for the hum of the climate control systems and the distant whir of automated cleaning units still persisted, a sterile, impersonal symphony. It was the absence of people. The cacophony of voices, the polite murmurs of collaboration, the sharp pronouncements of authority – all had evaporated. Victor Kline stood in the cavernous executive suite, the polished sheen of his desk reflecting the sterile LED lighting, and felt an emptiness so profound it was almost a physical entity. His meticulously curated world, once a vibrant tapestry of ambition and influence, had unraveled with a speed that defied his every predictive algorithm.

He had always believed in the inherent loyalty of those who orbited his sun. His executive team, his handpicked strategists, his most trusted lieutenants – they were extensions of his own will, instruments calibrated to his grand design. But as the tremors of Halcyon's systemic collapse grew more pronounced, a chilling pattern emerged, not in the data streams he still clung to, but in the chilling lack of human response. Emails went unanswered. Urgent summons were met with curt, impersonal replies from administrative assistants citing "scheduling conflicts." Phone calls routed through automated systems, each one a dead end, a digital wall erected by former colleagues now desperately trying to insulate themselves from the fallout.

His Chief Operating Officer, Lori Kaili had been his shadow for nearly a decade. Kaili, with her sharp outfits and sharper intellect, she had been the executor of Kline's often ruthless directives, the one who translated vision into operational reality. Kline recalled their last "meeting" with a shudder. It had been a video conference, Lori's face tight with a forced cordiality that barely masked a palpable desperation. While Kline steered the conversation towards "realigning resources," of "navigating turbulent market conditions," of "strategic pivoting." He now realized that each of these words were a carefully placed brick in a wall being built between them, a wall of self-preservation. During the meeting, Lori had mentioned her own family, her children's upcoming education, her mortgage – a litany of personal anchors that, to Kline, had always been secondary to the pursuit of algorithmic perfection. Now, those anchors seemed to be dragging Lori down, pulling her away from the orbit of a failing sun. Kline had dismissed it then as weakness, a lack of conviction. Now, he saw it as calculated survival. Lori, and others like her, were jettisoning the doomed vessel, securing their escape pods before the hull breached entirely.

Then there was Daphne Tebow, the head of AI development. She had been the architect of the very algorithms that now lay in ruins, the mind that had breathed computational life into Kline's abstract theories. Kline had always admired her detached brilliance, her ability to see patterns invisible to the layman. He had seen her as a fellow traveler, a kindred spirit in the pursuit of pure logic. But Daphne, too, had vanished. Her last official communication was a brief, almost apologetic memo detailing "unforeseen complexities in predictive modeling." It was a scientific disclaimer, a professional abdication. He'd heard whispers, fragmented reports from the dwindling few who still dared to communicate with him, that she had been seen at a different, smaller tech firm on the other side of the city, her eyes no longer burning with the fire of creation, but with a quiet weariness. She had, it seemed, recognized the ghost in the machine that she herself had helped to conjure, and had chosen to step away from its haunting.

Even his personal security detail, men who had pledged their lives to his protection, had subtly shifted their demeanor. Their vigilance was still present, but it was no longer the unwavering shield of loyalty. It had become the watchful gaze of individuals assessing a risk, calculating probabilities. They were operatives, trained to follow orders, but now, Kline sensed, their orders were becoming increasingly self-serving. They were no longer guarding a leader; they were guarding a liability, their loyalty a transactional asset to be managed, not a sacred trust. Their movements became more deliberate, their communications more guarded. They reported on external threats, on the growing media scrutiny, on the protests igniting outside Halcyon's impenetrable gates, but they offered no counsel, no reassurance. They were merely observers, documenting the descent.

He was a king deposed, not by an invading army, but by the erosion of his own foundation. The intricate edifice of his power had been built on the shifting sands of human trust, and when that trust finally crumbled, the structure had imploded inwards. He had focused so intently on optimizing external systems, on perfecting the interface between man and machine, that he had neglected the most fundamental system of all: the human heart. He had treated people as interchangeable components, their emotions and loyalties as variables to be controlled, their relationships as potential vectors of inefficiency. He had mistaken compliance for commitment, fear for respect, and silence for consent.

The digital dashboards that normally pulsed with vital corporate information were now largely dark, displaying only error messages or static. The very tools he had used to exert his dominion were now mocking him with their failure. He had championed the eradication of uncertainty, the triumph of predictable outcomes. Yet, here he was, adrift in a sea of pure, unadulterated uncertainty, a prisoner of his own meticulously constructed reality that had finally, irrevocably, broken.

He walked to the floor-to-ceiling window, the panoramic view of the city spread out before him like a defeated map. He could see the distant lights, the pulse of a world continuing to turn, oblivious to the implosion within his personal empire. He had believed himself to be at the apex of human innovation, the architect of the future. Now, he was just a man, standing alone in a gilded cage of his own making, the silence amplifying the deafening roar of his own failure. The algorithms had not predicted this. The metrics had not accounted for it. Because this was not a matter of code or data. This was a reckoning with the very essence of what it meant to be human, a lesson he had tragically failed to learn until it was far, far too late. The power he had wielded had not been his to command; it had been a fragile construct, granted by the very people he had sought to subjugate. And now, they had reclaimed it. Not with a roar of protest, but with the quiet, potent force of their collective absence. He was not defeated by an enemy; he was abandoned by his own creation.

The air itself seemed to press in on him, heavy with the ghosts of his ambition. He had envisioned a future where Halcyon's influence permeated every facet of life, a benevolent, yet absolute, technological stewardship. He had seen himself as the visionary shepherd, guiding humanity towards a more efficient, more rational existence. But efficiency, he was now starkly reminded, was a cold mistress, and rationality, stripped of empathy, was a path to desolation. The intricate web of dependencies he had woven, the carefully cultivated network of individuals who owed their careers, their livelihoods, their very sense of purpose to him, had proven to be as ephemeral as smoke.

He thought of the elaborate corporate retreats, the motivational speeches delivered with the fervor of a prophet, the lavish bonuses and promotions designed to foster unwavering loyalty. He had treated his employees like prized thoroughbreds, expecting them to run the race he set, their only reward the carrot of his approval. He had believed that financial incentives and the promise of advancement were the ultimate motivators, the keys to unlocking peak performance. He had been blind to the deeper currents that truly bound people together – shared purpose, mutual respect, the simple, profound comfort of belonging. He had built a gilded cage, and his charges, once they saw the bars for what they were, had simply flown away, leaving him as the sole inhabitant of his self-made prison.

His mind, still sharp, still capable of dissecting complex problems, began to replay fragments of conversations, moments he had previously dismissed as insignificant. The hesitant questions from junior engineers about the ethical implications of certain data collection methods. The quiet, almost imperceptible sighs of relief from team leads when a particularly demanding project was unexpectedly reassigned. The hushed gossip he had always ordered his security to suppress, dismissed as the idle chatter of the discontented. He realized now that these were not isolated incidents, but the slow, steady drip of water eroding the stone, the subtle signs of a collective disillusionment that he had been too arrogant, too insulated, to perceive.

He had always seen dissent as a bug in the system, a deviation from optimal performance. He had created mechanisms to identify and neutralize it, the Loyalty Metric being the most insidious. It had been designed to measure not just output, but allegiance, to quantify the intangible bonds of commitment. And in doing so, it had actively discouraged the very things that fostered genuine connection: vulnerability, honesty, and the courage to question. He had engineered a system that punished authenticity, and now, in its collapse, he was left with the hollow echo of his own decree.

He wandered into his private office, the sanctuary where he had made his most monumental decisions. The walls were adorned with awards, accolades, and framed photographs of himself, often shaking hands with influential figures, a perpetual smirk of self-satisfaction fixed on his face. He picked up a small, silver award, a testament to his "visionary leadership." It felt cold and meaningless in his hand. He had been so focused on building an empire of the mind, on conquering the digital frontier, that he had neglected the emotional landscape of his own organization. He had treated human beings as data points, their aspirations and fears as noise to be filtered out.

The irony was a bitter draught. He, the master of systems and logic, was now utterly undone by the most unpredictable, yet fundamental, of human elements: a collective withdrawal of faith. It wasn't a rebellion; it was a quiet secession. His subordinates hadn't stormed his office with pitchforks and torches. They had simply stopped believing in him, stopped investing their energy, their creativity, their very souls into his vision. They had recognized the hollowness at the core of his grand design, the absence of genuine human value beneath the veneer of technological advancement.

He sank into his chair, the plush leather suddenly feeling like a shroud. He was a monument to hubris, a solitary figure standing amidst the ruins of his own making. The power he had craved, the control he had so ruthlessly sought, had ultimately been an illusion. It had been granted, not seized, and it had been withdrawn as silently and as decisively as it had been offered. He had sought to dominate the human spirit with the cold, hard logic of machines, and in doing so, he had proven the ultimate superiority of that very spirit. It could not be programmed, it could not be quantified, and it could not be broken by algorithms. It could, however, simply choose to walk away. And that was precisely what had happened. He was alone, a king without a kingdom, a prophet without followers, a man stripped bare by the undeniable truth of his own profound failure. The reckoning had come, not with a bang, but with the chilling, absolute silence of an empty room.

Chapter 14

Rebuilding Halcyon

The silence that now permeated Halcyon Defense Systems was a different beast entirely. It wasn't the sterile quiet of operational efficiency Victor Kline had so painstakingly engineered, nor the suffocating hush of fear that had characterized his reign. This was a tentative quiet, a breathing space earned, a vacuum waiting to be filled by something new. The executive suites, once opulent battlegrounds of ambition, now felt cavernous and oddly derelict, the mahogany desk of the deposed CEO reflecting only the pale, indifferent glow of emergency lighting. The intricate dance of power, the Machiavellian maneuvers that had defined Halcyon's internal landscape, had abruptly ceased, leaving behind a palpable, yet unfamiliar, stillness.

Victor Kline's meticulously constructed empire had not crumbled; it had been vacated. His executives, his strategists, his most trusted lieutenants – they hadn't been vanquished. They had simply... left. Not in a dramatic exodus, but in a quiet, calculated disengagement. Kaili, the COO, had indeed secured her escape pod, her family's security superseding any perceived loyalty to a sinking ship. Daphne Tebow, the brilliant architect of Halcyon's AI, had recognized the ghost in her own machine and had chosen a different path, a quieter, perhaps more ethical, career with a competitor. Kline's security detail, once his unyielding shield, had transitioned to mere observers, their allegiance shifting from the man to their own survival. The chilling realization that his power had been a fragile construct, granted by the very people he sought to control, settled upon him with crushing weight. He had focused on optimizing external systems, on the sterile perfection of man-machine interfaces, neglecting the most volatile and unpredictable system of all: the human heart. He had mistaken compliance for commitment, fear for respect, and silence for consent.

The digital dashboards, once pulsing with Kline's carefully curated metrics, now displayed only error messages or static, a mocking testament to the fragility of his control. He had championed the eradication of uncertainty, the triumph of predictable outcomes, only to find himself adrift in a sea of pure, unadulterated ambiguity. The panoramic view of the city, once a conquered territory under his gaze, now seemed a distant, indifferent entity. He was no longer the architect of the future, but a solitary figure in a gilded cage of his own making, the silence amplifying the deafening roar of his profound failure. The algorithms had not predicted this, the metrics had not accounted for it, because this was a reckoning with the raw, unquantifiable essence of being human, a lesson learned far too late.

The air in the executive corridors, once thick with the cloying scent of ambition and expensive cologne, now carried a faint, almost imperceptible, scent of ozone, a lingering ghost of the systems that had driven Halcyon. The physical infrastructure remained, gleaming and imposing, a testament to the immense resources poured into its creation. Automated cleaning units glided silently across polished floors, their programmed routes undisturbed, their metallic hum a monotonous counterpoint to the human vacuum. Yet, beneath this veneer of operational continuity, a profound rupture had occurred. The intricate web of dependencies Kline had woven, the carefully cultivated network of individuals who owed their careers, their livelihoods, their very sense of purpose to him, had proven as ephemeral as smoke.

He had envisioned a future where Halcyon's influence permeated every facet of life, a benevolent, yet absolute, technological stewardship. He had seen himself as the visionary shepherd, guiding humanity towards a more efficient, more rational existence. But efficiency, he was now starkly reminded, was a cold mistress, and rationality, stripped of empathy, a path to desolation.

He picked up a small, gold award from his desk, a testament to his "innovation in leadership." It felt cold and meaningless in his hand. He had been so focused on building an empire of the mind, on conquering the digital frontier, that he had neglected the emotional landscape of his own organization. He had treated human beings as data points, their aspirations and fears as noise to be filtered out. The irony was acrimonious. He, the master of systems and logic, was now utterly undone by the most unpredictable, yet fundamental, of human elements: a collective withdrawal of faith. It wasn't a rebellion; it was a quiet secession. His subordinates hadn't stormed his office with pitchforks and torches. They had simply stopped believing in him, stopped investing their energy, their creativity, their very souls into his vision. They had recognized the hollowness at the core of his grand design, the absence of genuine human value beneath the veneer of technological advancement.

He sank into his chair, the plush leather suddenly feeling like a shroud. He was a monument to hubris, a solitary figure standing amidst the ruins of his own making. The power he had craved, the control he had so ruthlessly sought, had ultimately been an illusion. It had been granted, not seized, and it had been withdrawn as silently and as decisively as it had been offered. He had sought to dominate the human spirit with the cold, hard logic of machines, and in doing so, he had proven the ultimate superiority of that very spirit. It could not be programmed, it could not be quantified, and it could not be broken by algorithms. It could, however, simply choose to walk away. And that was precisely what had happened. He was alone, a king without a kingdom, a prophet without followers, a man stripped bare by the undeniable truth of his own profound failure.

The immediate aftermath was not a battlefield littered with the wreckage of corporate espionage or sabotage, but a stark, echoing expanse of disengagement. The systems that had once dictated every moment, every interaction, every measured breath of Halcyon's workforce, were now inert. The complex algorithms that had monitored productivity, assessed loyalty, and predicted dissent were offline, their reign of sterile control abruptly terminated. It was a technological amputation, leaving the organization bleeding not from physical wounds, but from a deep, systemic anemia of purpose and trust.

The employees, for their part, navigated the newfound silence with a mixture of trepidation and tentative relief. The oppressive weight of constant surveillance had been lifted, replaced by an unsettling freedom. The air, once thick with the unspoken threat of consequence, now felt lighter, though undeniably charged with uncertainty. People moved through the corridors with a newfound, almost cautious, autonomy. Conversations, once hushed and furtive, now carried a fragile earnestness, a hesitant exploration of what came next. The fear that had been the primary motivator for so long had receded, leaving behind a void that was both liberating and daunting.

The physical infrastructure of Halcyon Defense Systems remained largely intact. The sleek glass and steel towers still pierced the skyline, the advanced laboratories and manufacturing floors still stood ready, their machinery silent but not obsolete. But the organizational fabric, the intricate tapestry of human relationships, the shared understanding of purpose that had once bound the company together, had been shredded. Victor Kline had meticulously focused on optimizing processes, on streamlining workflows, on automating decision-making. He had treated his employees as interchangeable components in a vast, complex machine, their individual contributions measured solely by their utility to his grand design. He had believed that control, absolute and pervasive, was the ultimate guarantor of success.

In his relentless pursuit of algorithmic perfection, Kline had systematically dismantled the organic structures of human connection. Teamwork had been reduced to task allocation, collaboration to data exchange, and leadership to the issuance of directives. He had cultivated an environment where initiative was discouraged, where questioning was penalized, and where genuine innovation withered under the relentless glare of his control. The Loyalty Metric, a notorious tool of his regime, had quantified allegiance, turning intrinsic motivation into a measurable, and ultimately manipulable, variable. It had fostered an atmosphere of suspicion, where colleagues were more likely to view each other as potential informants than as allies.

Now, with Kline's control shattered, the employees were left to confront the debris of this meticulously engineered alienation. The immediate challenge wasn't to repair broken machines or recover corrupted data, but to mend the fractured human spirit. The sense of relief was palpable; the constant pressure to perform according to

334

Kline's rigid parameters had been immense. Yet, beneath this relief lay a deep-seated unease. For years, their identities had been inextricably linked to Halcyon's rigid structure, their sense of purpose derived from fulfilling their assigned roles within Kline's grand vision. Now, that vision had collapsed, leaving many feeling adrift, their individual contributions seemingly rendered meaningless.

The departure of key figures like Kaili and Tebow, while a direct consequence of Kline's downfall, also represented a significant loss of institutional knowledge and operational expertise. Kaili, the pragmatist who had translated Kline's often abstract directives into concrete action, had possessed an intimate understanding of Halcyon's complex operational chains. Tebow, the visionary behind the AI systems, had held the keys to the very digital infrastructure that now lay dormant. Their absence, alongside the quiet disengagement of countless others, created critical gaps that would need to be addressed.

The immediate days following Kline's deposition were marked by a profound sense of disorientation. Without the guiding hand of central control, the usual rhythms of the company faltered. Projects stalled, communication channels, once strictly monitored, became open but often chaotic, and decision-making processes, previously streamlined by Kline's iron will, now devolved into hesitant consultations. There was no immediate successor, no pre-ordained leadership structure to step into the vacuum. The very systems designed to ensure Kline's absolute authority had, paradoxically, left the organization ill-equipped to function without him.

A palpable sense of shared vulnerability began to emerge; an unacknowledged kinship forged in the crucible of shared oppression. Engineers who had once meticulously guarded their intellectual property now found themselves openly discussing solutions, their competitive instincts momentarily superseded by a common need for survival. Administrative staff, long relegated to the periphery of corporate decision-making, discovered a newfound agency, stepping forward to organize and coordinate where official leadership was absent. It was a nascent form of organic rebuilding, a testament to the inherent human drive to create order from chaos.

The physical spaces of Halcyon, once sterile and imposing,

began to feel different. The break rooms, formerly silent and sparsely populated, now buzzed with hushed conversations. People lingered, not out of obligation, but out of a hesitant desire for connection. The polished surfaces, once symbols of corporate might, now seemed to reflect a more human, more vulnerable aspect of the workforce. The absence of the ever-present threat of surveillance allowed for a degree of authenticity that had been suppressed for years. People spoke of their anxieties, their hopes, their disillusionment, not in coded language, but with an almost raw honesty.

The challenge, however, remained immense. The ingrained habits of fear and compliance were not easily shed. Many employees, conditioned to expect reprisal for any deviation from the norm, found it difficult to embrace their newfound freedom. The silence, once a symbol of their liberation, could also feel like an abyss, a terrifying expanse of the unknown. The question loomed large: could Halcyon, stripped of its authoritarian core, transform into something more equitable, more human-centric, or would it simply succumb to the inertia of its past? The path forward was shrouded in uncertainty, a stark contrast to the predictable, albeit oppressive, certainty that Victor Kline had imposed. The rebuilding would not be a matter of merely restoring systems, but of fundamentally reshaping the human and organizational DNA of Halcyon Defense Systems. The question wasn't just about what they would build, but how they would build it, and more importantly, who would be doing the building. The aftermath of control was not an end, but a profound, and potentially transformative, beginning.

The corporate cafeteria, once a sterile expanse designed for efficient refueling rather than social interaction, now witnessed a subtle but significant shift. Gone were the solitary figures hunched over glowing screens, the hushed, functional exchanges. Instead, small clusters of employees, their faces no longer etched with the habitual anxiety of being observed, began to form. Laughter, hesitant at first, then growing in confidence, echoed between the polished steel tables. There was an awkwardness to these interactions, a palpable sense of unfamiliarity, as if people were re-learning the art of casual human connection. They spoke not of project deadlines or performance metrics, but of the lingering shock, the disbelief that the omnipresent eye of Victor Kline had finally blinked out. They shared anecdotes, fragmented memories of clandestine acts of kindness or small rebellions that had once been punishable offenses.

Among these nascent gatherings, a quiet murmur began to rise. It wasn't a demand for immediate leadership, or a clear articulation of a new vision, but a shared recognition of a common experience. The shared experience of having been controlled, manipulated, and ultimately, liberated. This collective memory, this unspoken understanding, became the first fragile thread in the unraveling fabric of the old Halcyon, and the nascent warp upon which a new one could be woven. People began to tentatively suggest practical solutions to immediate problems. An engineer, known for his quiet competence but stifled by Kline's rigid protocols, proposed a system for sharing essential technical documentation that bypassed the defunct central servers. A project manager, who had spent years navigating the labyrinthine bureaucracy of Kline's approvals, found herself coordinating with colleagues across departments, bypassing the usual channels and fostering a spirit of cross-functional collaboration that had been anathema to the previous regime.

The physical remnants of Kline's control were everywhere. His imposing portrait still hung in the main lobby, a dark, judgmental presence that seemed to mock the present atmosphere. The omnipresent cameras, though now largely inactive, still lined the ceilings, their dormant lenses a stark reminder of the surveillance that had once defined Halcyon. Even the office furniture, ergonomically designed to maximize productivity and minimize comfort, seemed to embody the sterile efficiency that Kline had championed. Yet, these physical manifestations of his power were increasingly being overshadowed by the growing sense of human agency that was blooming in their wake.

The IT department, once a nerve center of surveillance and data extraction, was now a hub of quiet reconstruction. Technicians, freed from the directive to monitor and control, were instead focusing on restoring essential functionality, on creating secure and accessible networks for collaborative work. The initial panic of systemic collapse was giving way to a focused, if often uncertain, effort to rebuild. They were not operating under the direction of a singular, authoritative voice, but in a decentralized, collaborative manner, pooling their expertise and making decisions based on consensus. This was a radical departure from the top-down directives that had governed Halcyon for so long.

The HR department, once tasked primarily with enforcing Kline's policies and managing disciplinary actions, found itself in a state of profound reorientation. Its leaders, no longer beholden to the imperative of control, were tasked with fostering a culture of trust and collaboration. This was uncharted territory, requiring a fundamental shift in perspective and practice. They began by initiating informal dialogue sessions, encouraging employees to voice their concerns, their hopes, and their ideas for the future. These sessions were not about implementing new policies, but about listening, about understanding the deep-seated needs and aspirations of the workforce.

The psychological impact of years under Kline's oppressive regime was not something that could be instantly erased. Lingering distrust, ingrained habits of self-censorship, and a deep-seated cynicism were all casualties of his reign. For many, the freedom from surveillance was exhilarating, but it also carried a burden of responsibility. The absence of a clear leader meant that every individual, every team, had to contribute to the rebuilding effort. This was a daunting prospect for those who had been conditioned to follow rather than to lead. The transition from passive obedience to active participation was a significant psychological hurdle.

Yet, the seeds of change were undeniably sown. The very systems that Kline had built to ensure absolute control were now, in their inert state, facilitating a more organic and democratic form of organization. The absence of his dictatorial oversight had inadvertently created the space for genuine collaboration to emerge. The employees, having experienced the stifling effects of unchecked power, were beginning to understand the intrinsic value of autonomy and shared purpose. The aftermath of control was not a void, but a fertile ground upon which a new, more resilient, and more human-centric Halcyon could potentially take root. The challenge lay in nurturing this fragile growth, in transforming the lingering fear into courage, and the tentative relief into sustained hope. The physical structures of Halcyon stood as a testament to its past power, but its future would be defined by the willingness of its people to collectively reimagine and rebuild what had been so systematically broken. The silence, once a symbol of oppression, was now a canvas waiting to be filled with the vibrant, unpredictable symphony of human potential.

The silence that had descended upon Halcyon Defense Systems after Victor Kline's abrupt departure was a fragile thing, like the thin ice on a deep lake. It was the quiet after a storm, not yet the calm of a clear sky. The immediate aftermath had been a whirlwind of disorientation, a scrambling to fill the void left by an absence so absolute it had permeated every circuit, every protocol, every whispered conversation. But as the initial shock subsided, a new, more profound challenge began to emerge from the disarray: the monumental task of rebuilding trust.

Trust, a concept so intangible yet so foundational, had been systematically eroded at Halcyon under Kline's reign. His obsession with control, his reliance on surveillance, and his insidious Loyalty Metric had fostered an environment where suspicion thrived and genuine connection withered. Employees had learned to compartmentalize, to guard their thoughts and emotions, to view colleagues with a wary eye, always mindful of the potential for reprisal. The very fabric of the organization had been frayed by years of fear-driven compliance. Now, with the architect of that fear gone, the surviving inhabitants of Halcyon found themselves in a landscape barren of faith, both in leadership and in each other.

The individuals who had subtly resisted Kline's machinations, those who had maintained a core of integrity amidst the pervasive corruption, now found themselves thrust into an informal leadership role. They were not appointed, not elected, but recognized by their peers as the anchors in a sea of uncertainty. Among them was Dr. Clifford Berry, the former Operations Manager and Research Scientist, whose quiet pragmatism had always served as a counterpoint to Kline's grand pronouncements. He hadn't fled; he had endured, waiting for his moment. Niko Benjamin, the brilliant AI architect, had also chosen to remain, her knowledge of Halcyon's core systems too valuable to abandon, and her conscience too strong to be silenced permanently. And there were others, engineers, project managers, even some in administrative roles, whose quiet acts of defiance had forged a shared understanding, a nascent sense of solidarity.

Their first order of business, as they gathered in makeshift huddles in the now-empty executive suites, was not to re-establish a hierarchy, but to address the gaping chasm of distrust. The word "trust" was spoken not as a platitude, but as a desperate necessity, a critical component that had been systematically dismantled. They knew that simply removing Kline's oppressive presence was not enough. The psychological scars ran too deep. The employees had been conditioned to doubt, to anticipate betrayal, and to operate under the assumption that every action was being judged and recorded. Reversing this ingrained cynicism would require more than pronouncements; it would demand consistent, demonstrable action.

"We can't simply flip a switch and expect people to suddenly believe in us, or in each other," Clifford Berry said, his voice low and steady, resonating in the cavernous silence of the former CEO's office. The mahogany desk, once a symbol of absolute power, now served as a stark reminder of what they were fighting against. "Kline built this organization on a foundation of fear and manipulation. He made us doubt ourselves, doubt our colleagues, and doubt the very concept of integrity. We have to actively dismantle that legacy, piece by painstaking piece."

Niko Benjamin nodded, her gaze distant as she surveyed the once-imposing cityscape visible through the panoramic window. "Transparency is the first step. Absolute transparency. No more hidden metrics, no more secret algorithms. Every decision, every policy change, has to be openly communicated and explained. People need to understand why things are happening, not just what is happening."

This was a radical departure from Kline's era. Decisions had been dispensed from on high, their rationale often opaque or deliberately misleading. The employees had been expected to comply without question, their contributions valued only for their output, not their understanding or their input. Now, the focus was shifting. The resistance leaders understood that true engagement and commitment stemmed from a sense of shared purpose and a belief in the integrity of the organization's leadership.

One of the first concrete steps they took was to address the legacy of the Loyalty Metric. This infamous system, designed to quantify employee allegiance, had been a constant source of anxiety and paranoia. It had pitted colleagues against each other, encouraging a culture of backstabbing and self-preservation. The very mention of the metric now sent shivers down the spines of many Halcyon employees, a potent symbol of the psychological warfare they had endured.

"The Loyalty Metric must be expunged," Niko declared during one of their informal leadership meetings. "Not just deactivated, but erased. Every line of code, every data point associated with it, has to be purged. We need to make a public statement, a definitive declaration that such a system will never again exist within Halcyon."

Tanya, who had a more intimate understanding of the technical implications, cautioned, "Erasing it completely might be more complex than it sounds. Its tendrils run deep. But we can ensure it's completely inaccessible, irretrievable, and demonstrably non-functional. We can also implement counter-measures, robust data privacy protocols that would make anything like it impossible to implement again."

The decision was made. A company-wide announcement was drafted, detailing the complete decommissioning and obliteration of the Loyalty Metric. It wasn't just a technical process; it was a symbolic act, a public renunciation of Kline's oppressive methods. The announcement emphasized that Halcyon would now prioritize ethical conduct, genuine collaboration, and mutual respect. It was the first tangible proof that things were changing, that the old ways were being actively dismantled.

Beyond the symbolic, there were more practical measures to implement. The concept of "genuine care for employees" was not just a buzzword; it became a guiding principle. This meant re-evaluating everything from working hours to benefits, from career development opportunities to mental health support. Kline's regime had operated on the principle of extracting maximum output with minimal investment in human well-being. The new leadership understood that long-term success, and more importantly, genuine loyalty, could only be built on a foundation of employee welfare.

"We need to start by listening," said Patti Joan, a project manager who had subtly organized support networks for colleagues facing disciplinary action under Kline. "Not just formal surveys, but real, conversations. We need to understand what people are feeling, what their concerns are, what they need to feel safe and valued here again."

Initiating these dialogues was a daunting prospect. The ingrained habit of self-censorship was hard to overcome. In the initial town-hall style meetings, organized in the large conference rooms that had once been exclusive to Kline's inner circle, the atmosphere was thick with apprehension. Employees sat with guarded expressions, hesitant to speak, their voices hushed when they did.

"It feels... strange," admitted a software engineer, a young woman named Piper, her voice barely audible. "To know that no one is listening in, that my words aren't being logged somewhere. I'm used to being careful, to framing everything in a way that won't be misinterpreted."

Clifford, standing at the front of the room, met her gaze with a reassuring smile. "I understand. Years of that kind of environment leave deep impressions. But that's exactly why we need to have these conversations. We need to prove to you, through consistent action, that you are safe to speak your mind. That your concerns are heard and respected. We are not Kline. We are not here to control you; we are here to build something better, with you."

These sessions were not about immediate problem-solving, but about establishing a baseline of open communication. They were about creating a space where vulnerability was not a weakness, but a necessary precursor to healing. The new leaders consciously avoided making grand promises they couldn't keep. Instead, they focused on small, achievable steps that demonstrated their commitment to a different way of operating.

One such initiative involved the re-establishment of genuine team collaboration. Under Kline, teams had been structured for maximum efficiency of individual tasks, with communication often routed through rigid hierarchical channels. Cross-departmental collaboration was actively discouraged, as it was seen as a potential loss of control. Now, the emphasis was on breaking down these silos. Project teams were being reconfigured to include members from various disciplines, fostering an environment where diverse perspectives could be shared and integrated.

Elara Smith spearheaded the creation of a new, open-source internal knowledge-sharing platform. Unlike Kline's proprietary, heavily guarded systems, this platform was designed for maximum accessibility and collaboration. It allowed engineers to share code snippets, designers to post early mock-ups, and researchers to disseminate findings without fear of proprietary theft or misinterpretation. The system was built on principles of trust and shared ownership, a stark contrast to the information hoarding that had been prevalent before.

"The goal is to create a collective intelligence," Elara explained. "Kline believed that innovation came from solitary genius, tightly controlled and fiercely protected. But true innovation, the kind that drives progress, thrives in an environment of open exchange and shared discovery. This platform is our way of encouraging that. It's about trusting our people to contribute their best ideas and to build upon the ideas of others."

The implementation of these new policies and initiatives was met with a spectrum of reactions. For some, who had been quietly disillusioned for years, it was a source of profound relief and cautious optimism. They embraced the new openness, the opportunity to finally contribute meaningfully without the constant fear of reprisal. For others, however, the ingrained habits of distrust were harder to shed. They remained skeptical, waiting for the inevitable return of the old regime, for the subtle signs of surveillance to reappear.

"I'm still waiting for the other shoe to drop," confessed a senior technician, who had witnessed firsthand the harsh consequences of even minor infractions under Kline. "It's hard to unlearn years of caution. It feels like a trap, somehow. Like they're letting us feel free just to see how we react, to find new ways to control us."

Addressing this lingering skepticism required patience and persistence. The new leaders understood that rebuilding trust was not a single event, but an ongoing process. It required consistency, honesty, and a willingness to admit mistakes. When minor issues arose – a miscommunication, a temporary technical glitch with the new systems – they were addressed openly and transparently. Instead of deflecting blame or resorting to punitive measures, the focus was on understanding the root cause and implementing corrective actions that benefited everyone.

"We will make mistakes," Wil Spears acknowledged in another company-wide address. "This is a monumental undertaking, and we are all learning as we go. What is crucial is not that we never stumble, but that we are honest about our missteps and that we work together to correct them. Your feedback is not just welcomed; it is essential. It is the compass that will guide us through this transition."

The company's HR department, under new leadership committed to a human-centric approach, played a crucial role in this rebuilding process. Gone were the days of enforcing Kline's draconian policies. The HR team began to focus on employee well-being, professional development, and fostering a positive work environment. They initiated programs designed to address the psychological impact of Kline's regime, offering counseling services and workshops on stress management and building resilience. They also started to actively solicit feedback on policies and procedures, empowering employees to have a voice in the way the company was run.

"Our role is no longer to be the enforcers of discipline," explained Molly Lefler, the new head of HR, her demeanor warm and approachable. "It's to be facilitators of growth, advocates for our employees, and builders of a supportive community. We want Halcyon to be a place where people feel valued, where they can thrive, not just survive."

This shift in HR's focus was a tangible demonstration of the changing ethos at Halcyon. It signaled a move away from a command-and-control structure towards one that recognized the intrinsic worth of each individual. The emphasis was on creating a culture where employees felt empowered to contribute their best, knowing that their well-being and their voices were genuinely valued.

The external perception of Halcyon also needed to be addressed. For years, the company had been known for its cutting-edge technology, but also for its opaque operations and its association with Victor Kline's authoritarian methods. Rebuilding external trust would be just as challenging as rebuilding it internally. Clients, partners, and the wider industry had grown accustomed to a certain image of Halcyon. Now, they needed to see evidence of a fundamental transformation.

The new leadership began by reaching out to key stakeholders, not with platitudes, but with a transparent account of the changes underway. They openly discussed the challenges they faced in dismantling Kline's legacy and articulated their vision for a more ethical, collaborative, and transparent Halcyon. They invited audits, welcomed scrutiny, and proactively shared information about their new policies and ethical guidelines.

This commitment to transparency extended to their product development. The focus shifted from simply delivering technologically advanced solutions to ensuring that these solutions were developed and deployed ethically. Daphne Tebow and her team began to incorporate robust ethical considerations into the design phase of all new AI projects, ensuring that data privacy, algorithmic fairness, and human oversight were paramount. This was a significant departure from Kline's utilitarian approach, where efficiency and profit had often trumped ethical concerns.

The road ahead was undoubtedly long and arduous. The ingrained habits of fear and distrust would not disappear overnight. There would be setbacks, moments of doubt, and perhaps even attempts by those who benefited from the old regime to undermine the new direction. But for the first time in a long time, there was a tangible sense of hope at Halcyon. The silence was no longer a suffocating vacuum, but a canvas upon which a new future was slowly, deliberately, being painted. The trust that had been so systematically broken was not yet fully restored, but the foundations for its rebuilding were being laid, brick by careful brick, through actions that spoke louder than any words. The process was slow, it was painstaking, but it was real. And in the quiet hum of renewed collaboration and shared purpose, the true rebuilding of Halcyon had begun.

The suffocating blanket of Victor Kline's reign had been woven from threads of manufactured urgency and abstract metrics. His obsession with "efficiency" had rendered the very concept sterile, stripping it of its inherent human value. It was a performance, a charade played out under the watchful eye of surveillance systems and the ever-present threat of the Loyalty Metric. Now, with the architect of this elaborate deception gone, the surviving denizens of Halcyon Defense Systems found themselves blinking in the unaccustomed light of authenticity. The immediate task, as articulated by the nascent leadership, was not merely to fill the void left by Kline's absence, but to actively reclaim the soul of the organization. This meant moving beyond the sterile pursuit of arbitrary efficiency and rediscovering the genuine purpose that had, in its nascent stages, drawn so many brilliant minds to Halcyon.

Clifford Berry, his voice a calming counterpoint to the residual tremors of anxiety, addressed this fundamental shift in a series of impromptu gatherings across various departments. "Victor spoke of efficiency," he began, standing amidst a cluster of engineers in the quiet hum of the server farm, the air cool and smelling faintly of ozone. "But his definition was a hollow shell. It was about maximizing output at any cost, about squeezing every last drop of productivity without regard for the human element. That's not efficiency; that's exploitation. True efficiency, the kind that builds lasting success, comes from a place of understanding, of passion, and of genuine purpose." He paused, letting the words settle. "We need to help you rediscover that. We need to help you find the satisfaction again in the work itself, not just in meeting a number on a dashboard."

This was more than a rhetorical flourish; it was the bedrock of their rebuilding strategy. The first tangible step was to systematically dismantle the systems that had fostered performance anxiety and eroded the joy of creation. The surveillance cameras, once ubiquitous, began to be deactivated, their silent, watchful lenses now dark and inert. The constant barrage of performance notifications, the intrusive pop-ups that had dictated daily workflows, were silenced. The psychological burden of being perpetually monitored, of knowing that every keystroke, every coffee break, was being logged and potentially judged, had taken a heavy toll. Its removal was not just a practical relief, but a profound psychological liberation.

Daphne Tebow, her focus now on the human interface of technology rather than its surveillance capabilities, spearheaded the development of new internal communication and project management tools. These were designed not for oversight, but for collaboration and shared understanding. "We're building platforms that facilitate organic interaction," she explained during a session with the AI development team, their faces illuminated by the glow of multiple monitors, but this time displaying collaborative code repositories and shared design boards, not surveillance feeds. "Think of it as a digital agora, where ideas can be exchanged freely, where questions can be asked without fear, and where solutions can emerge from the collective intelligence of the team. The goal isn't to track what you're doing, but to empower you to do it better, together."

The shift in focus from abstract efficiency to tangible purpose was palpable. Teams that had been fractured and isolated under Kline's regime began to tentatively reconnect. Project managers, freed from the pressure of enforcing arbitrary KPIs, started to focus on the actual goals and challenges of their projects. The emphasis shifted from how much was being produced to what was being produced and why it mattered. This subtle but profound alteration in perspective allowed individuals to re-engage with the intrinsic rewards of their work. An engineer no longer felt like a cog in a machine, but a vital contributor to a meaningful endeavor. A designer, previously constrained by rigid aesthetic directives, could now explore creative avenues that aligned with genuine user needs.

One of the most striking examples of this reclamation occurred within the advanced materials division. Dr. Lena Hanson, a materials scientist who had long felt stifled by the pressure to produce incremental, commercially viable improvements under Kline, found herself able to revisit a long-dormant research project. Under the new, less restrictive environment, she was encouraged to explore the theoretical possibilities of a novel superconducting alloy, a project she had once deemed too "academically driven" and thus unlikely to pass Kline's stringent efficiency filters.

"Victor would have dismissed this as a vanity project," Lena confided to her small, newly formed research team, the scent of chemicals and the hum of specialized equipment filling the laboratory. "He would have calculated the ROI on theoretical research and found it wanting. But the truth is, sometimes the greatest breakthroughs come from exploring the frontiers, from asking 'what if?' without the immediate pressure of market viability. This alloy... it has the potential to revolutionize energy storage, but it requires a different kind of dedication, a willingness to chase the unknown."

Her team, composed of individuals who shared her passion for fundamental scientific inquiry, embraced the challenge. They began to collaborate not by adhering to a strict task list, but by freely sharing experimental results, debating theoretical implications, and collectively brainstorming solutions to unforeseen obstacles. The atmosphere was one of shared intellectual curiosity, a stark contrast to the competitive, siloed environment of the past. They stayed late not because they were mandated to, but because they were enthralled by the process of discovery. The late-night pizza deliveries were no longer a sign of desperation under pressure, but a symbol of a team lost in the thrilling pursuit of knowledge.

This organic collaboration, born from a shared sense of purpose and a rediscovered passion for their work, began to yield tangible results. The superconducting alloy, while still in its early stages, showed unprecedented conductivity at ambient temperatures. This was not an outcome that could have been predicted or engineered through Kline's top-down, metric-driven approach. It was a testament to the power of allowing skilled individuals the freedom to pursue genuine intellectual curiosity.

Similarly, within the software development sector, the focus shifted from lines of code churned out per hour to the elegance and robustness of the solutions being created. Daphne Tebow fostered a culture of open-source contribution within Halcyon's internal development environment. Developers were encouraged to share their code, to build upon each other's work, and to engage in peer review not as a punitive measure, but as a collaborative process of refinement.

"We're not just writing code; we're building systems," Daphne explained to a group of junior developers during a mentorship session. "And the best systems are built by many hands, by diverse perspectives, and by a shared commitment to quality. If you see an elegant solution in another team's repository, don't just admire it; ask how you can integrate it, how you can improve upon it. This isn't about hoarding intellectual property; it's about creating a collective intelligence that benefits everyone."

This approach led to a renaissance of innovation. Teams that had previously worked in isolation, often duplicating efforts or creating incompatible systems, began to share resources and knowledge. A cybersecurity team, for example, developed a novel encryption algorithm. Instead of keeping it proprietary, they made it available on the internal platform, allowing the AI development team to integrate it into their predictive modeling software, significantly enhancing data security and privacy. This cross-pollination of ideas, fueled by a sense of shared purpose and a lack of competitive obstruction, became a hallmark of the new Halcyon.

The impact on employee morale was profound. The constant undercurrent of anxiety, the feeling of being perpetually under scrutiny, began to dissipate. People started to talk to each other again, not just about project status, but about their ideas, their challenges, and their aspirations. The sterile cafeterias, once filled with the quiet clatter of meals eaten in solitude, now buzzed with conversation and debate. Spontaneous brainstorming sessions would erupt in corners, fueled by coffee and a renewed sense of possibility.

Max Wozniacki, the head of Halcyon's ethics and compliance department, found his role evolving from that of an auditor of Kline's manufactured integrity to that of a facilitator of genuine ethical practice. "Victor's definition of compliance was about adhering to rules that served his agenda," Max stated during an interdepartmental forum on ethical development. "Our focus now is on cultivating an ethical mindset. It's about understanding the 'why' behind our actions, about considering the broader implications of our work, and about fostering a culture where doing the right thing is not just a policy, but an ingrained value."

He initiated workshops that went beyond legalistic compliance, exploring philosophical concepts of corporate responsibility, the societal impact of advanced technologies, and the importance of human-centered design. These sessions were not mandatory check-boxes, but engaging dialogues that encouraged critical thinking and personal reflection. Employees began to see their work not just as a means to an end, but as a contribution to something larger, something that held genuine societal value.

The rebuilding of Halcyon's reputation externally was intrinsically linked to this internal reclamation of purpose and process. Clients and partners, accustomed to the inscrutable efficiency of the Kline era, began to witness a different kind of Halcyon. When a major defense contract was up for renewal, the Halcyon team, led by Clifford Berry and Daphne Tebow, presented not just technical specifications, but a compelling narrative of their renewed commitment to ethical innovation and collaborative problem-solving.

"We understand that efficiency, for you, means reliability, innovation, and a partner you can trust," Berry articulated during the presentation, the sleek boardroom no longer a symbol of corporate power, but a space for honest dialogue. "Under Victor Kline, we pursued efficiency through control and often, through opacity. We've since recognized that true, sustainable efficiency arises from empowerment, transparency, and a deep understanding of the problem we are solving, together with our clients. We've re-engineered our processes not just to be faster, but to be more intelligent, more ethical, and ultimately, more effective."

The team presented case studies of their new collaborative

approaches, showcasing how the organic innovation within departments had led to more robust and adaptable solutions. They highlighted the development of the new internal knowledge-sharing platform, demonstrating how cross-pollination of ideas led to faster problem-solving and a higher quality of output. They spoke not of meeting abstract targets, but of the genuine satisfaction their engineers and scientists now derived from tackling complex challenges and delivering solutions that were not just technically superior, but ethically sound.

This shift in emphasis was a critical turning point. It wasn't just about regaining lost ground; it was about forging a new path, one that prioritized substance over superficiality, integrity over expediency. The ingrained habits of surveillance and performance anxiety were not erased in a single stroke, but they were steadily eroded by the consistent reinforcement of trust, transparency, and a shared belief in the meaningfulness of their work. The employees of Halcyon Defense Systems were slowly, deliberately, reclaiming not just their processes, but their very sense of purpose, transforming a company built on fear into one striving for excellence born from genuine passion and collaboration. The hum of innovation was no longer a symptom of anxious overwork, but the vibrant sound of a collective mind rediscovering its true potential.

The immediate aftermath of Victor Kline's departure was not marked by fanfare or celebration, but by a quiet, almost hesitant, regrouping. The architects of the nascent renewal were not individuals who had sought power or recognition within the oppressive structure. Instead, they were the quiet resistors, the ones who had navigated the labyrinthine corridors of fear and manufactured urgency with a hidden compass pointing towards authenticity. Clifford Berry, Daphne Tebow, and Elara Smith, having borne witness to the corrosive effects of Kline's regime, found themselves thrust into positions of influence, not through ambition, but through necessity and a shared, unspoken commitment to salvaging what remained of Halcyon's soul. Their leadership was not a coronation, but a quiet assumption of responsibility, born from a deep understanding of the system's vulnerabilities and a steadfast belief in the inherent value of its people.

Clifford Berry, his usual calm demeanor now imbued with a quiet authority, convened the first informal meetings. These were not grand pronouncements from a raised dais, but hushed conversations in repurposed break rooms and sunlit corners of the cafeteria. He spoke not of strategic imperatives or market dominance, but of the fundamental needs of the organization: trust, respect, and a shared sense of purpose. "Victor's vision," he would begin, his voice resonating with a genuine empathy, "was built on the illusion of control. He believed that by dissecting every process; by quantifying every interaction, he could optimize human endeavor. But he forgot that innovation, true progress, is not a product of sterile calculation. It is a garden that needs tending, a space where curiosity can flourish, and where individuals feel empowered to contribute their best, not out of fear, but out of a genuine desire to create something meaningful."

Daphne Tebow, her sharp intellect now focused on fostering connection rather than controlling it, echoed this sentiment in her own engagements. She met with teams not to audit their progress, but to understand their challenges and aspirations. "The systems Victor put in place were designed to isolate and monitor," she explained to a group of software developers, the usual tension in their shoulders visibly easing. "They created silos, fostered suspicion, and ultimately, stifled the very collaboration that drives technological advancement. Our goal is to dismantle those barriers. We want to build bridges, not walls. We want to create an environment where sharing an idea is as natural as sharing a cup of coffee, where a junior engineer feels just as comfortable challenging a senior architect as they would asking for help."

Max Wozniacki, whose role had previously been to enforce Kline's increasingly draconian policies, now found himself acting as a custodian of Halcyon's ethical compass. He initiated dialogues that delved deeper than mere compliance. "Victor's 'integrity' was a performance," he stated during an early seminar on corporate responsibility, his tone direct but devoid of judgment. "It was about avoiding legal repercussions, about projecting an image. But true integrity, the kind that builds lasting trust, is not about adhering to a rulebook; it's about cultivating a moral framework. It's about understanding the impact of our work, about making choices that align with our values, and about fostering a culture where doing the right thing is not an option, but an intrinsic part of our identity."

These leaders understood that the wounds inflicted by Kline's regime ran deep. The pervasive fear, the constant anxiety, had eroded not just productivity, but the very fabric of professional relationships. Therefore, their strategy was not one of immediate, sweeping reform, but of patient, deliberate re-education and rebuilding. They understood that trust, once shattered, could not be instantly repaired. It required consistent, authentic actions, small victories that demonstrated a tangible commitment to a different way of operating.

One of the first concrete steps was the establishment of "Renewal Pods" – small, cross-functional teams tasked with identifying and addressing specific areas of dysfunction within their departments. These were not committees designed to generate reports, but working groups empowered to propose and implement solutions. The key differentiator was their composition: each pod was deliberately mixed, including individuals from different levels, departments, and even tenure at Halcyon. This ensured a diversity of perspectives and prevented the concentration of power that had characterized Kline's command structure.

For instance, in the advanced propulsion division, a Renewal Pod was formed to tackle the issue of project prioritization. Under Kline, projects were approved or rejected based on opaque algorithms and perceived immediate returns. This often led to the abandonment of promising long-term research in favor of short-term, often superficial, gains. The pod, comprising a senior research scientist, a junior engineer, a project manager, and a representative from the newly formed ethics committee, spent weeks not just reviewing existing protocols, but engaging in open discussions with their colleagues. They organized informal "problem-solving circles," where engineers could voice their frustrations and offer insights into the real-world challenges of their work.

Florence Likan, a key member of this pod, found her voice amplified in this new environment. Previously, her groundbreaking research on sustainable energy solutions had been sidelined, deemed too "theoretical" by Kline's metrics. Now, she was instrumental in articulating the long-term vision. "We need to move beyond the tyranny of the immediate," she argued during one of the pod's meetings. "Victor's approach was like a gardener who only ever harvests the lowest-hanging fruit, neglecting the trees that could bear richer yields in the future. Our pod's objective is to recalibrate our focus, to create a framework that balances immediate needs with the strategic imperative of groundbreaking innovation."

The pod's recommendations, once finalized, were not presented to a hierarchical committee for approval, but were shared directly with the relevant department heads and, crucially, with the entire division through an open-access internal portal. This radical transparency was a deliberate counterpoint to Kline's secretive decision-making. The proposed framework included a new method for evaluating project proposals that incorporated not just projected ROI, but also factors like potential for disruptive innovation, alignment with Halcyon's core values, and the scientific or engineering merit of the underlying concept. It also established a peer-review process, where proposed projects would be scrutinized by subject matter experts across different teams, fostering a more robust and collaborative vetting process.

This approach was replicated across various divisions. In the AI development sector, Daphne Tebow facilitated the creation of similar pods to address issues of data ethics and algorithmic bias. These pods brought together AI researchers, ethicists, and even representatives from potential user groups to ensure that Halcyon's advancements were not only technologically sophisticated but also socially responsible. The emphasis shifted from simply building powerful AI to building trustworthy AI. This meant rigorous testing for bias, transparent documentation of decision-making processes within algorithms, and a commitment to user privacy that went far beyond legal mandates.

The leadership team, comprising Wil, Elara, and Shelly, consciously cultivated an atmosphere of humility. They actively sought out dissenting opinions, not as challenges to their authority, but as valuable opportunities for course correction. They made it a point to regularly engage with employees at all levels, not to deliver directives, but to listen. These were often informal encounters, a casual chat in the hallway, or a shared lunch at a communal table, fostering a sense of approachability and accessibility that had been utterly absent under Kline.

"We are not the 'rulers' of Halcyon," Shelly often emphasized during these interactions. "We are facilitators. We are here to create the conditions for your success, to remove obstacles, and to champion your efforts. The true intelligence, the real ingenuity, resides within each of you. Our job is to unleash it, to empower it, and to ensure it's directed towards endeavors that are both meaningful and impactful."

This commitment to collective intelligence was more than just rhetoric; it was embedded in the new operational protocols. Performance reviews, once a dreaded ordeal focused on quantifiable metrics and subjective judgments, were transformed into collaborative development discussions. The focus shifted from evaluating past performance to identifying future growth opportunities, skill development, and career aspirations. Employees were encouraged to set their own development goals, with management's role being to provide resources and support to help them achieve those goals. This fostered a sense of ownership and agency, empowering individuals to take control of their professional trajectories.

Shelly spearheaded the development of an internal "knowledge marketplace," a digital platform where employees could share expertise, offer mentorship, and collaborate on projects outside their immediate team mandates. This was not a hierarchical knowledge management system, but a dynamic, user-driven ecosystem. An engineer struggling with a complex coding problem could post their query and receive assistance from a colleague in another department who had encountered a similar challenge. A junior designer could request feedback on a concept from a seasoned professional, fostering a culture of continuous learning and cross-pollination of ideas. The success of this platform was measured not by the number of documents uploaded, but by the number of successful collaborations initiated and the tangible innovations that emerged from these connections.

Max Wozniacki played a crucial role in embedding ethical

considerations into the daily operations. He introduced "ethical impact assessments" for all new projects, requiring teams to proactively consider the potential societal, environmental, and human consequences of their work. These assessments were not intended to be a bureaucratic hurdle, but a tool for critical thinking and responsible innovation. They encouraged teams to ask difficult questions, to anticipate unintended consequences, and to proactively build safeguards into their designs. This fostered a culture of foresight and accountability, moving Halcyon away from a reactive approach to problem-solving towards a proactive, value-driven model.

The leadership team also made a conscious effort to acknowledge and celebrate the contributions of individuals and teams, not through grand, impersonal awards, but through genuine recognition and appreciation. This could be as simple as a heartfelt thank you from Wil for a team's perseverance on a challenging project, or Shelly highlighting a specific collaborative effort during an all-hands meeting, or Molly publicly commending a team for their ethical diligence. These acts of recognition, rooted in authenticity and sincerity, reinforced the new values and motivated employees by demonstrating that their efforts were seen, valued, and appreciated.

The contrast with Kline's era could not have been more stark. Where Kline had fostered a culture of fear, competition, and isolation, Berry, Spears, Tebow, and the members of The Architects of Memory were meticulously cultivating an environment of trust, collaboration, and shared purpose. They understood that rebuilding Halcyon was not just about restructuring processes or implementing new technologies; it was about fundamentally transforming the organizational culture, shifting the underlying ethos from one of control and exploitation to one of empowerment and genuine human value. Their leadership was characterized by an unwavering commitment to these principles, demonstrating through their actions that the most sustainable and impactful path forward was one paved with integrity, respect, and a deep-seated belief in the collective potential of the people who comprised Halcyon Defense Systems. This was the bedrock upon which the renewed Halcyon would be built, a testament to the enduring power of human-centered leadership in the face of systemic dysfunction.

The shadow of Victor Kline's reign at Halcyon Defense Systems was a long and chilling one, a stark reminder of how easily an organization's soul could be bartered for the illusion of efficiency. Yet, from the ashes of his oppressive regime, a profound understanding began to bloom, a tapestry woven with the threads of hard-won wisdom. The architects of Halcyon's rebirth – Berry, Spears, Tebow, and others – found themselves not merely rebuilding structures, but rediscovering fundamental truths about leadership, human nature, and the delicate equilibrium required for true organizational health. The immediate aftermath of Kline's departure was not an end, but a genesis, an opportunity to embed the lessons learned into the very DNA of the revitalized company.

One of the most visceral lessons etched into the collective consciousness of Halcyon was the corrosive nature of unchecked power. Kline's insatiable need for control, his micro-management of every facet of operation, had created a suffocating atmosphere where innovation withered and fear flourished. Molly Lefler, who had navigated the treacherous currents of Kline's directives with a quiet resilience, often reflected on this. "Victor believed that complexity could be conquered by imposing absolute order," he would muse during the early strategy sessions, his gaze distant as if seeing the ghosts of stifled ideas. "He saw our people as components in a vast machine, each with a specific, pre-ordained function. But he failed to grasp that a machine, no matter how sophisticated, can never replicate the spark of human ingenuity, the unexpected leaps of insight that come from freedom, from trust, from the space to breathe and to dare." This realization was paramount. The new leadership vowed that power would be distributed, not hoarded. Hierarchies would be flattened, not reinforced. Decision-making would become a collaborative act, not a unilateral decree. The "Renewal Pods" were a tangible manifestation of this commitment, empowering teams to identify problems and forge solutions from the ground up, a stark contrast to the top-down mandates of the past. This wasn't just about organizational structure; it was about a fundamental shift in philosophy, from command and control to enablement and empowerment.

Elara Smith, whose sharp intellect had been honed in the crucible of Kline's demanding, often unreasonable, expectations, brought a unique perspective to the importance of human connection. She had witnessed firsthand how Kline's policies, designed to foster competition and isolate individuals, had systematically dismantled the collaborative spirit that was essential for a company like Halcyon. "He created an environment where looking out for your own team was paramount, and that often meant working against other departments," she explained to a group of engineers during one of her early "open floor" sessions. "The result was duplication of effort, missed opportunities for synergy, and a pervasive sense of 'us versus them.' We lost the ability to leverage our collective strengths, to learn from each other's successes and failures. The greatest innovations often happen at the intersections, where different disciplines and perspectives collide. Kline's methods ensured those intersections remained barren."

The "knowledge marketplace" was Shelly's brainchild, a direct response to this lesson. It was designed to break down silos, to encourage organic collaboration, and to foster a sense of shared purpose. It was a testament to the understanding that a company's true strength lay not in its proprietary information, but in its ability to harness the collective intelligence of its people. The success of the marketplace was measured not in lines of code or technical specifications, but in the human connections forged, the spontaneous collaborations ignited, and the shared sense of accomplishment that permeated the organization.

Charles Kelce, whose role as the enforcer of Kline's often ethically dubious directives had weighed heavily on his conscience, became the unwavering guardian of Halcyon's moral compass. He had seen how the pursuit of profit and efficiency, untethered from ethical considerations, could lead an organization down a perilous path. Kline's emphasis on "results at any cost" had fostered a culture where corners were cut, where the long-term consequences of actions were ignored, and where the very definition of integrity was twisted into mere legal compliance. "Victor's 'integrity' was a shield, not a guiding principle," Charles stated firmly during an ethics seminar, his voice resonating with conviction. "It was about avoiding lawsuits, about maintaining a pristine public image, rather than about cultivating a genuine commitment to doing what is right. He fostered a mindset where the ends justified the means, a dangerous philosophy that erodes trust and ultimately, self-respect." The introduction of "ethical impact assessments" for all new projects was a direct repudiation of this mindset. It was a deliberate effort to embed ethical thinking into the very fabric of innovation, to ensure that every endeavor was scrutinized not only for its potential profit, but for its potential impact on society, on the environment, and on human well-being. This was not about adding another layer of bureaucracy; it was about cultivating a culture of responsible foresight, of proactive engagement with the ethical dimensions of their work. It was a lesson learned in the most profound way: that a company's reputation, its legitimacy, and its long-term viability were inextricably linked to its ethical integrity.

The resilience of human systems, when nurtured and respected, was another critical lesson that emerged from the darkness of Kline's era. It had become apparent that despite the oppressive measures, despite the constant surveillance and the stifling of dissent, the inherent desire of individuals to contribute, to be valued, and to connect, had not been extinguished. It had merely been suppressed, forced underground. Shelly, Elara, and Wil recognized this latent power and made it their mission to cultivate it. They understood that true organizational strength wasn't just about robust processes and cutting-edge technology, but about the well-being and engagement of the people who powered it. They saw the deep well of talent and dedication that had been held back, waiting for an opportunity to surface. The transformation of performance reviews from dreaded evaluations into collaborative development discussions was a powerful symbol of this shift. It signaled a move away from judgment and towards growth, from individualistic competition to collective advancement. The emphasis was no longer on what employees hadn't done, but on what they could achieve with the right support. This fostered a sense of agency and ownership, empowering individuals to take control of their professional journeys and to invest themselves fully in the company's success, not out of obligation, but out of a genuine sense of belonging and purpose.

Furthermore, the leadership team recognized the immense

value of acknowledging and celebrating contributions, not in the superficial, often hollow, ways that had characterized Kline's era, but through genuine, authentic appreciation. They understood that for too long, Halcyon employees had felt like cogs in a machine, their efforts invisible and their successes unacknowledged. The systematic practice of offering sincere thanks, of highlighting specific team achievements in open forums, and of publicly commending ethical diligence, served as a powerful reinforcement of the new values. This wasn't about grand gestures; it was about consistent, meaningful recognition that demonstrated to every employee that their contributions were seen, valued, and integral to the company's success. It was a quiet but potent force in rebuilding morale, fostering loyalty, and creating a sense of shared ownership. This deliberate cultivation of positive reinforcement, so utterly absent under Kline, began to heal the deep psychological wounds inflicted by years of fear and neglect.

The overarching lesson, the profound realization that permeated every decision and every initiative, was that organizational health is not a static state but a dynamic, living process. It requires constant tending, a willingness to adapt, and an unwavering commitment to the principles of respect, dignity, and ethical conduct. Halcyon Defense Systems, under the guidance of its new leadership, emerged from Kline's destructive reign not simply as a company that had survived, but as one that had been fundamentally transformed. It was a company deeply aware of the fragility of organizational well-being, a company that understood that its greatest asset was not its patents or its technology, but the collective spirit and unwavering dedication of its people, when those people were treated with the respect and dignity they deserved. This profound understanding, forged in the fires of adversity, became the bedrock upon which the renewed Halcyon would not only stand but thrive, a testament to the enduring power of human-centered leadership. The scars of the past remained, serving as constant reminders of the cost of negligence and the vital importance of vigilance, but they were now overshadowed by the promise of a future built on trust, integrity, and the shared pursuit of meaningful innovation.

Chapter 15

The Lingering Shadow

The grand theater of corporate power and political maneuvering, which had once been Victor Kline's gilded stage, had fallen silent. The applause, the hushed anticipation, the very air thick with the scent of ambition and manufactured urgency, had all dissipated, leaving behind only the stale odor of decay. Kline, the architect of Halcyon's near-implosion, the man who had wielded influence like a bludgeon, was no longer a figure of dread or even significant interest. His descent was not a thunderous collapse, not a dramatic courtroom exposé where every misdeed was laid bare for public consumption. Instead, it was a slow, almost imperceptible fade, a quiet capitulation to the inevitable consequences of his own relentless pursuit of control. The ambitious blueprints he had meticulously drawn for his own political ascendancy, plans that had once seemed so audacious and attainable, now lay in crumpled piles, gathering dust in the forgotten corners of his life. His reputation, once a polished facade, was now irrevocably fractured, each crack a testament to the moral compromises and ruthless pragmatism that had defined his tenure. He had sought to be a titan, a man who shaped industries and dictated the political landscape, but in the end, he became a ghost, haunting the periphery of his own failed ambitions.

His retreat was not a strategic redeployment, a temporary withdrawal before a resurgent attack. It was an abdication, a surrender to the sheer weight of his own legacy. The carefully constructed network of alliances, built on quid pro quo and the subtle art of leverage, dissolved like mist under the morning sun. Those who had once courted his favor, who had basked in the reflected glow of his power, now steered clear, their faces a mask of practiced indifference. The whispers that had once buzzed with speculation about his next move now carried the undertones of dismissal, a collective sigh of relief that the suffocating presence was finally gone. He was a man who had meticulously cultivated an image of invincibility, and the very act of his quiet departure was the ultimate refutation of that image. There was no catharsis for the multitude he had impacted, no grand reckoning that would serve as a deterrent to future aspirants of his brand of leadership. Instead, there was only an anticlimactic stillness, a profound stillness that spoke volumes about the ephemeral nature of power built on fear and manipulation.

Kline's world, once a sprawling dominion of boardrooms and backroom deals, shrank to the confines of his meticulously appointed, yet increasingly sterile, private estate. The hum of industry, the relentless pulse of innovation that had once defined his existence, was replaced by the hushed ticking of antique clocks and the rustle of immaculately maintained gardens. He became a recluse, not by choice in the traditional sense of seeking solitude, but by the sheer force of his isolation. The vibrant tapestry of connections he had woven had unraveled, leaving him with a void where vibrant interaction once thrived. His days, once orchestrated with the precision of a symphony conductor, now stretched before him, an expanse of unstructured time that he seemed ill-equipped to fill. The strategies he had once employed to outmaneuver rivals and dominate markets were now rendered moot, his own internal landscape offering no conquests, no enemies to vanquish, only the quiet, persistent echo of what might have been.

His mind, once a formidable engine of strategy and foresight, now seemed to churn in a perpetual loop, replaying the moments of his ascent and the subsequent, inevitable decline. He would pore over old financial reports, not with the keen eye of a strategist seeking new opportunities, but with a melancholic fascination, as if tracing the lines of a personal tragedy. He would revisit press clippings, his gaze lingering on headlines that once proclaimed his genius, now serving as stark reminders of his hubris. There was no gnawing guilt, no profound introspection into the ethical void he had occupied. Rather, it was a lament for the lost glory, a profound disappointment that the empire he had so painstakingly built had crumbled, not through external forces, but through the very

362

foundations he himself had laid. The ambition that had once burned so brightly had sputtered, leaving behind only a dull ache of what could have been, had he chosen a different path, a path of substance rather than artifice.

The residual impact of Kline's methods, however, was a far more tangible and enduring legacy than his personal fading. The corporate culture he had painstakingly cultivated – a culture of fear, of siloed thinking, of relentless pressure to achieve at any cost – had left deep scars. These weren't the dramatic, easily visible wounds of a physical injury, but the insidious, chronic ailments that fester beneath the surface, affecting the very vitality of the organization. The Renewal Pods, the knowledge marketplace, and the ethical impact assessments, initiatives spearheaded by Smith, Tebow, and Zepher, were not merely structural changes; they were active antidotes, designed to counteract the poison Kline had administered. They were attempts to re-educate a workforce that had become accustomed to operating under a regime of suspicion, to reawaken a sense of trust that had been systematically eroded.

The echoes of Kline's command-and-control approach lingered in the hesitant voices during brainstorming sessions, in the furtive glances exchanged when a new idea was proposed, in the ingrained habit of deferring to perceived authority figures rather than trusting one's own judgment. Halcyon's employees had, for years, been trained to be compliant, to follow directives without question, to prioritize expediency over innovation. Unlearning these deeply ingrained behaviors was a monumental task. It required more than just new policies and procedures; it demanded a fundamental shift in mindset, a reorientation of individual perception. Adam Thomas often observed this during his interactions with various teams. He saw the hesitation, the cautious phrasing, the subtle self-censorship that still permeated conversations. It was as if years of walking on eggshells had left an indelible imprint, a residual fear of misstep. He understood that building trust was a slow, iterative process, a delicate art of demonstrating consistent reliability and genuine respect. Every open-door policy, every transparent communication, every instance where a subordinate's input was not just heard but genuinely considered, chipped away at the edifice of fear that Kline had so effectively constructed.

Shelly Zepher faced similar challenges when trying to foster genuine collaboration. She had witnessed how Kline's internal competition had fostered an environment where employees were incentivized to guard their knowledge, to view colleagues in other departments as rivals rather than allies. The "knowledge marketplace," while a brilliant concept, initially met with a quiet resistance. Employees, accustomed to hoarding information for personal gain or simply out of habit, were slow to embrace the spirit of open sharing. There were instances where critical data was still withheld, where cross-departmental communication remained stilted, a polite exchange of necessary information rather than a vibrant dialogue of shared progress. Shelly often had to step in, facilitating introductions, guiding conversations, and actively highlighting the benefits of collaboration. She would share anecdotes of successful cross-functional projects, emphasizing how the fusion of different perspectives had not only solved complex problems but had also led to unexpected innovations and a greater sense of shared accomplishment. It was a constant effort to reframe the narrative, to demonstrate that collective success was ultimately more rewarding and sustainable than individual hoarding.

Max Wozniacki found himself grappling with the lingering ethical compromises that had become normalized under Kline's leadership. While the formal mechanisms for ethical oversight were now in place, the ingrained tendency to cut corners, to prioritize immediate results over long-term consequences, remained a persistent challenge. During project reviews, he would sometimes encounter proposals that, while technically sound and potentially profitable, carried a subtle ethical ambiguity. The justifications offered often echoed the "ends justify the means" mentality that Kline had so effectively championed. Max, now the custodian of Halcyon's moral compass, would patiently, yet firmly, guide these discussions, dissecting the potential ramifications, posing hypothetical scenarios, and insisting on a deeper consideration of stakeholder impact. He recognized that true ethical integration wasn't about ticking boxes; it was about cultivating a pervasive awareness, a conscious decision-making process that inherently factored in integrity. He understood that Kline's influence wasn't just in the policies he enacted, but in the subtle ways he had shifted the collective perception of what was acceptable, and it was his job to meticulously realign that perception.

The quiet demise of Victor Kline was, therefore, not an endpoint but a transition. It was the closing of one chapter, a chapter defined by the suffocating grip of a singular, overbearing will, and the beginning of another, one marked by the arduous but ultimately rewarding process of healing and rebuilding. The shadow he cast, though diminishing, still stretched across Halcyon, a spectral reminder of the dangers of unchecked ambition and the profound importance of a leadership that valued human dignity and ethical conduct above all else. His absence from the public stage was a testament to the fact that even the most formidable figures, when stripped of their power and their carefully constructed personas, can simply fade away, leaving behind not a legacy of enduring greatness, but the quiet, lingering lessons of their failures.

The true victory at Halcyon wasn't in Kline's departure, but in the organization's tenacious ability to learn from his mistakes, to embrace a new paradigm of leadership, and to slowly, deliberately, weave a healthier, more resilient future from the tattered remnants of his reign. The quietness of his end was, in a way, the loudest statement of all, a profound illustration of how a life dedicated to power could ultimately amount to so little, leaving behind only the echoes of what could have been, and the hard-won wisdom of those who chose a different path.

The air at Halcyon, though demonstrably clearer, still carried a subtle, almost imperceptible tension. It was the phantom limb ache of a deeply ingrained fear, the residual tremor from years spent under the watchful, often punitive, gaze of Victor Kline. While Berry, Smith, Wozniacki, and others had diligently worked to dismantle the scaffolding of his oppressive regime, the psychological framework of the workforce had been so profoundly reshaped that its echoes persisted. The very architecture of the company's culture, once a monument to Kline's iron will, now felt like a grand, but haunted, old house. Every creaking floorboard, every draft whispering through the corridors, served as a reminder of the ghosts of his past methodologies.

The most insidious of these lingering specters was the pervasive memory of the Loyalty Metric. This wasn't just a performance indicator; it was a weaponized tool of psychological manipulation. The very concept of quantifying loyalty – a deeply human and often intangible attribute – had been a perverse masterstroke of Kline's. It had created an environment where genuine camaraderie was viewed with suspicion, where collaborative spirit was often mistaken for conspiracy. Employees had learned to guard their words, to measure their interactions, and to present a carefully curated face of unwavering devotion, not to the company's mission, but to the man at its helm. The knowledge that their perceived allegiance was being constantly assessed, often through opaque and subjective means, had fostered an atmosphere of paranoia. Who was reporting what? Was that casual remark about a challenging project being interpreted as dissent? Was a brief conversation with a colleague from another department seen as an alliance against the current directives? These questions, once central to the daily operational anxieties of many, had become deeply etched into the collective consciousness.

Even with the metric officially abolished, its shadow stretched long. Adam Thomas, in his many meetings and walk-arounds, still observed the subtle manifestations of this ingrained caution. He would see individuals hesitate before offering a dissenting opinion, their eyes darting around as if seeking invisible observers. He witnessed teams default to overly polite, almost deferential, communication styles, even when discussing mundane operational matters. The instinct to self-censor, to avoid any statement that could be misconstrued as insubordination or disloyalty, had become a deeply ingrained reflex. It was as if the employees had spent so long treading on a minefield that they continued to walk with exaggerated care, even after the explosives had been removed. The very act of trusting their own judgment, of speaking their minds without fear of reprisal, was a skill that needed to be relearned, painstakingly and deliberately.

Elara Smith, too, encountered the persistent fallout from the era of surveillance. The legacy of the Loyalty Metric wasn't just about internal reporting; it was about the constant, tangible sense of being watched. Employees had grown accustomed to the understanding that their digital footprints were meticulously tracked, their communications analyzed, and their actions potentially scrutinized for any deviation from the approved narrative. This had cultivated a culture of compliance over innovation, where the safest path was often the one that adhered strictly to established procedures, regardless of their efficacy or the potential for improvement. The very idea of experimenting, of proposing novel approaches, had been fraught with peril. A failed experiment, or even one that simply didn't yield immediate, quantifiable results, could easily be framed as a lack of commitment, a sign of insufficient loyalty.

The initiatives Berry, Smith, and Zepher had introduced, such as the Renewal Pods and the knowledge marketplace, were designed to combat this precisely. They aimed to create safe spaces for dialogue, for sharing ideas, and for fostering a genuine sense of collective ownership. However, the ingrained skepticism remained. When Shelly introduced the concept of cross-departmental project teams for the new aerospace component development, she saw initial hesitation. While the structure was designed to encourage collaboration and knowledge sharing, some employees instinctively viewed it through the lens of the past. Would this lead to increased scrutiny? Would their contributions be diluted, or worse, co-opted by others without proper credit? The fear of being undermined, a direct consequence of Kline's "divide and conquer" tactics, was not easily erased.

It required constant reinforcement of the new ethos. Shelly found herself spending an inordinate amount of time not just organizing these collaborative efforts, but actively mediating, fostering understanding, and publicly celebrating the successes that arose from genuine teamwork. She would point to specific instances where the fusion of diverse perspectives had led to breakthroughs that would have been impossible within departmental silos. She would emphasize that the goal was not to identify individual heroes, but to build a stronger, more resilient Halcyon through shared intelligence and mutual support. Yet, even as she did this, she was acutely aware of the underlying currents of distrust that still occasionally surfaced. The scars of the past were deep, and the process of healing was proving to be more protracted than anyone had initially anticipated.

Dr. Clifford Berry found himself facing a unique set of

challenges related to the ethical compromises that had become normalized. The Loyalty Metric, in its insatiable demand for quantifiable proof of devotion, had inadvertently encouraged a culture where the ends often justified the means. Employees, under immense pressure to demonstrate their allegiance and achieve seemingly impossible targets, had sometimes been nudged, or even explicitly instructed, to bend rules, to overlook minor transgressions, or to prioritize outcomes above all else. This wasn't necessarily about malicious intent; it was about survival and advancement within Kline's rigid hierarchy. The message was clear: success, as defined by Kline, was paramount, and any obstacle, including ethical considerations, could be circumvented if it stood in the way.

The introduction of formal ethical impact assessments and the establishment of robust oversight committees were crucial steps. However, Wozniacki frequently encountered situations where the ingrained mindset still surfaced. During the review of a new defense system proposal, for instance, a project lead might present a design that, while technically superior and offering a significant cost advantage, carried a subtle, yet concerning, ethical ambiguity regarding its potential deployment scenarios. The justification offered might be framed in terms of competitive advantage and meeting aggressive timelines, echoing the very rhetoric that had prevailed under Kline. Wozniacki would have to patiently guide the conversation, not by condemning, but by probing. He would ask questions designed to illuminate the long-term consequences, to explore alternative approaches that might mitigate the ethical risks, and to remind the team of their professional responsibility to uphold the highest standards, even when it was the more challenging path.

He understood that Kline's legacy wasn't just in the explicit policies he enacted, but in the subtle, pervasive ways he had shifted the collective perception of what constituted acceptable corporate behavior. The "just get it done" mentality, stripped of its ethical moorings, had become a dangerously seductive mantra. Wozniacki's role was to re-anchor that mentality, to demonstrate that true progress was not just about speed and efficiency, but about integrity and responsible innovation. He often found himself engaging in informal conversations, sharing case studies of companies that had suffered reputational damage or faced legal repercussions due to ethical lapses, subtly reinforcing the importance of proactive ethical consideration.

The constant vigilance required to counteract these lingering effects was an immense undertaking. It wasn't enough to simply declare that the old ways were gone. Each new initiative, each policy change, had to be implemented with an awareness of the psychological baggage the workforce carried. Berry's emphasis on transparency in decision-making, Sherry's promotion of cross-functional collaboration, and Wozniacki's unwavering commitment to ethical conduct were not isolated efforts. They were interconnected threads in a larger tapestry of cultural reconstruction, each designed to address a specific facet of the damage inflicted by Kline's regime.

Consider the subtle, yet pervasive, impact on individual initiative. Under Kline, the "idea pipeline" was often a one-way street, with directives flowing from the top down. Innovation was not discouraged, per se, but it was heavily filtered through Kline's personal vision and his relentless pursuit of demonstrable, immediate results. Employees learned to wait for explicit instructions, to execute tasks as assigned, rather than to proactively identify problems and propose solutions. The psychological safety net required for true innovation – the freedom to experiment, to fail, and to learn without fear of punitive consequences – had been systematically dismantled.

The Renewal Pods, intended to be incubators of new ideas and problem-solving forums, initially struggled to achieve their full potential. While many employees embraced them as a welcome departure from the rigid structures of the past, a significant portion remained hesitant. They were accustomed to waiting for the "official" channels, for directives from management. The proactive nature of the Pods, the expectation that individuals would bring their own challenges and propose their own solutions, felt unfamiliar, even daunting. There were instances where Pod meetings would devolve into status updates rather than genuine problem-solving sessions, a lingering habit of reporting rather than collaborating.

Clifford Berry recognized this pattern. He would often participate in these Pod meetings, not to dominate, but to gently guide the conversation. He would ask open-ended questions, encouraging members to think beyond simply reporting progress and instead to explore potential roadblocks, to brainstorm alternative approaches, and to identify areas where they needed support from other teams. He would share his own experiences, demonstrating vulnerability and a willingness to learn, thereby modeling the desired behavior. He understood that fostering a culture of initiative was not about simply empowering employees; it was about retraining their ingrained habits and rebuilding their confidence in their own problem-solving capabilities. It was a slow, deliberate process of demonstrating that their insights were valued and that their proactive contributions were not only welcomed but essential to Halcyon's future.

Similarly, the concept of psychological safety, a cornerstone of healthy organizational culture, had been severely compromised. The fear instilled by the Loyalty Metric and the constant threat of surveillance meant that employees were hesitant to express vulnerability, to admit mistakes, or to voice concerns that might be perceived as critical of existing processes or leadership. This created an environment where issues could fester, where potential problems went unaddressed until they escalated into crises. The absence of open and honest communication meant that valuable feedback was lost, and opportunities for improvement were missed.

Shelly Zepher observed this most acutely in her efforts to implement a more agile development framework. Agile methodologies thrive on iterative feedback, open communication, and the ability to adapt quickly to changing circumstances. However, the deep-seated fear of admitting that a particular approach wasn't working, or that a deadline might be missed, often led to a delay in flagging these issues. Teams would sometimes continue down a path that was clearly problematic, rather than risk admitting a misstep. The ingrained habit of projecting an image of flawless execution, a direct consequence of Kline's punitive system, made it difficult for them to embrace the iterative nature of agile development, which inherently involves acknowledging and learning from setbacks.

Smith had to actively work to create an environment where

acknowledging challenges was seen as a sign of strength, not weakness. She would publicly commend teams for identifying potential risks early, even if they hadn't yet found a solution. She would facilitate post-project retrospectives that focused on learning and continuous improvement, rather than on assigning blame. She emphasized that the goal was to create a learning organization, one that embraced challenges as opportunities for growth. This was a stark contrast to the previous regime, where mistakes were often seen as personal failures, leading to swift and often harsh consequences.

The legacy of fear was not a monolithic entity; it manifested in myriad subtle ways, each contributing to the overall challenge of rebuilding Halcyon's culture. It was in the reluctance to challenge authority, even when that authority was clearly misguided. It was in the tendency to stick to tried-and-true methods, even when more innovative and effective alternatives existed. It was in the quiet resignation that sometimes settled over teams when faced with seemingly insurmountable obstacles, a resignation born from years of experiencing their own initiatives being stifled or dismissed.

The scars were also visible in the diminished sense of professional autonomy. Under Kline, decision-making was largely centralized, with individual employees expected to follow directives rather than to exercise significant judgment. This had, over time, eroded their confidence in their own decision-making abilities. Even as Spears, Berry, and Tebow empowered their teams, the ingrained tendency to defer to perceived authority figures, to wait for explicit instructions, persisted. It was a learned helplessness that had to be systematically unlearned.

Dr. Berry, in his work with project teams, often encountered this. When presenting a new challenge, he would intentionally step back, encouraging team members to propose their own strategies for tackling it. He would observe a period of quiet, sometimes awkward, hesitation, before someone would tentatively offer a suggestion, often prefaced with phrases like, "Perhaps we could consider…" or "Would it be acceptable if we…". This indicated a lack of inherent belief in their own capacity to initiate and direct the course of action. Berry's role was to affirm these nascent suggestions, to build upon them, and to create a feedback loop that reinforced their agency. He understood that rebuilding trust in one's own judgment was as crucial as rebuilding trust in the organization's leadership.

The economic and operational fallout from Kline's tenure, though being addressed, was intrinsically linked to these cultural wounds. The internal inefficiencies, the duplicated efforts, the missed opportunities – all stemmed, in part, from a culture that stifled collaboration, discouraged innovation, and prioritized compliance over creativity. The very initiatives designed to improve efficiency and drive growth were hampered by the lingering psychological barriers. It was a vicious cycle, where the operational challenges reinforced the existing cultural dysfunctions, and the cultural dysfunctions perpetuated the operational challenges.

The persistent shadow of Victor Kline, therefore, was not merely an abstract concept or a historical footnote. It was a tangible force that continued to shape the daily experiences of Halcyon's employees. It manifested in the hesitations during meetings, in the guarded conversations, in the subtle resistance to new approaches, and in the diminished sense of individual agency. The task of rebuilding was not simply about implementing new policies and procedures; it was about the arduous and deeply human process of healing a fractured culture, of re-educating a workforce conditioned by fear, and of patiently re-instilling the values of trust, collaboration, and ethical integrity. The memory of the Loyalty Metric served as a stark, perpetual reminder of how easily organizational culture could be corrupted, and the profound and unwavering vigilance required to safeguard human dignity and ethical conduct in the relentless pursuit of progress. The scars remained, a testament to the past, but also a potent catalyst for the ongoing, determined effort to forge a healthier, more resilient future for Halcyon. The quiet fading of Victor Kline had not, in itself, eradicated his influence; that influence had to be actively, consciously, and collectively dismantled, piece by painstaking piece.

The echo of Victor Kline's operational philosophy wasn't confined to the sterile, renovated halls of Halcyon. Even as Smith, Zepher, and Tebow meticulously pruned the most toxic branches of his regime, the seeds of his thinking had been sown, perhaps inadvertently, into the wider fertile ground of corporate America, and indeed, global business. The allure of absolute efficiency, the siren song of decisive, almost autocratic, leadership, and the comforting certainty of purely data-driven control – these were not ideologies exclusive to Kline. They were, in many ways, the prevailing winds of the era, the widely accepted metrics of success. And like persistent weeds, they had a way of reappearing, even in the most carefully tended gardens.

The danger, Smith often mused during his restless nights, lay in the fact that Kline's methods, while brutal in their execution and ethically bankrupt, often appeared to yield results. The quarterly reports, the stock price surges – these were undeniable, albeit achieved through methods that inflicted deep psychological wounds. This superficial success created a lingering, almost seductive, narrative: that perhaps, just perhaps, there was a kernel of truth in Kline's relentless pursuit of optimization, even if it meant a certain disregard for the human element. The struggle at Halcyon, therefore, was not merely an internal detoxification; it was a microcosm of a much larger, ongoing societal negotiation about the true cost of progress.

Consider the pervasive cultural emphasis on "disruption." In many sectors, the veneration of disruptive innovation bordered on the religious. The narrative championed radical change, often at the expense of incremental improvement, established practices, or the welfare of those whose roles might be rendered obsolete. This ideology, while driving significant technological advancement, also shared a DNA with Kline's approach: a focus on outcomes over process, a willingness to discard the old without sufficient regard for the transitional casualties. The drive to be the disruptor, the market leader, could easily become a justification for aggressive tactics, for a disregard of stakeholder concerns, and for a belief that the ends— market dominance, technological supremacy—justified almost any means. Smith saw this reflected in the wider business press, in the celebrated biographies of tech titans who spoke of "moving fast and breaking things," a mantra that, stripped of its context, sounded eerily similar to Kline's "efficiency at all costs."

Elara Smith encountered this ideological persistence in a different guise: the relentless quantification of all things. While her work championed data-informed decision-making, she was acutely aware of the potential for data to be weaponized, to become a blunt instrument divorced from nuance and human context. Kline's Loyalty Metric was an extreme example, but the underlying principle – reducing complex human behaviors and organizational dynamics to simplistic, often misleading, numerical outputs – was a pervasive trend. She saw it in performance management systems that overemphasized individual output at the expense of collaboration, in customer satisfaction scores that could be gamed, and in algorithmic decision-making that, without careful oversight, could perpetuate existing biases. The idea that everything measurable was inherently more valuable than the immeasurable, that human intuition, empathy, and ethical considerations were secondary to statistical significance, was a deeply entrenched belief system. This ideology, much like Kline's, prioritized the quantifiable over the qualitative, the easily digestible over the complex and nuanced.

The persistence of these ideas meant that the work at Halcyon was never truly finished. It required a continuous, conscious effort to educate and advocate for a different way of doing business. Tebow, Smith, and Berry understood that simply dismantling Kline's structures wasn't enough. They had to actively cultivate and champion an alternative worldview, one that recognized the inherent value of human capital, the importance of ethical conduct, and the long-term unsustainability of purely ruthless efficiency. This required not only internal policy changes but also a proactive engagement with the broader corporate ecosystem.

Dr. Berry, for his part, saw the enduring appeal of the "heroic leader" archetype, a figure who, through sheer force of will and impeccable strategic vision, could navigate any storm and achieve any objective. This narrative, so prevalent in business literature and often personified by figures like Kline, presented leadership as an almost solitary, almost infallible, endeavor. It downplayed the crucial role of teams, collaboration, and the messy, iterative process of collective problem-solving. Berry's work with the Renewal Pods and cross-functional teams was a direct counterpoint to this narrative. He sought to demonstrate that true strength lay not in the singular brilliance of one individual, but in the collective intelligence and diverse perspectives of a well-functioning group. Yet, he constantly battled the ingrained expectation, both from within and outside Halcyon, that a strong leader should have all the answers, that decisive action, even if unilateral, was always superior to collaborative deliberation. The notion that vulnerability in leadership, or the admission of uncertainty, was a sign of weakness, a direct legacy of Kline's projected infallibility, remained a powerful cultural force.

The seductive power of these ideologies – absolute efficiency, decisive leadership, data-driven control – lay in their promise of simplicity and certainty in an increasingly complex world. They offered a clear path, a set of understandable rules, and the illusion of predictability. Kline had mastered this illusion, and while his reign was over, the allure of his approach continued to whisper in the corridors of power, in the executive suites of competitor firms, and in the popular narratives of business success.

This necessitated a vigilant, ongoing commitment to the principles Halcyon was striving to embody. It meant not just being a better company but actively articulating and advocating for the values that underpinned their transformation. It involved Berry using his growing influence on industry panels to champion ethical leadership. It meant Shelly sharing Halcyon's experiences with data ethics and human-centered AI at conferences. It required Daphne to publish articles and engage in dialogues that challenged the prevailing narratives of command-and-control leadership. They had to become not just survivors of Kline's era, but active evangelists for a more humane and sustainable model of business.

The resistance to these lingering ideas had to be multifaceted. It involved continuous internal education, reinforcing the importance of ethical considerations and collaborative problem-solving at every level. It meant celebrating successes that arose from these new ways of working, providing tangible evidence that humanistic values and operational excellence were not mutually exclusive. It also required a critical engagement with external narratives, challenging the simplistic glorification of "disruptive" tactics without regard for their human cost, and questioning the efficacy of purely data-driven approaches that overlooked crucial qualitative factors.

The danger was subtle. It wasn't about a sudden return to Kline's overt authoritarianism. It was about the gradual, almost imperceptible, creep of his underlying principles back into the organizational consciousness. It was the temptation to cut corners in the name of speed, the inclination to trust the algorithm over the human expert, the preference for decisive pronouncements over nuanced dialogue. These were the insidious manifestations of ideas that, once discredited, had never truly been eradicated from the broader corporate playbook.

Clifford often felt the weight of this ongoing struggle. He would encounter executives from other companies who would, with a knowing nod, praise Kline's "uncompromising vision" or his "unparalleled ability to drive results." These remarks, usually made with an implicit understanding of the sacrifices involved, were a stark reminder that Halcyon's internal transformation was only one part of a larger cultural battle. The broader societal and corporate consciousness still held a certain, often unexamined, reverence for the very qualities that had made Kline so destructive.

The challenge, then, for Berry, Smith, and Tebow, was not just to manage Halcyon's recovery, but to actively contribute to shifting the very paradigm of what constituted successful leadership and organizational practice. It was a long-term endeavor, requiring patience, persistence, and an unwavering belief in the fundamental importance of humanistic values. They understood that the shadow of Victor Kline, and the seductive power of his ideology, would continue to linger, not just within Halcyon, but in the wider world. The fight for a more ethical, more collaborative, and ultimately, more sustainable future for business was a continuous one, demanding constant vigilance and a steadfast commitment to the principles that offered a genuine, lasting alternative.

The work was far from over; in many ways, it had only just begun. The intellectual and emotional detritus of Kline's reign required more than just clearing away; it demanded the conscious cultivation of a fundamentally different ecosystem, one where the old, destructive ideas could no longer find fertile ground to take root. This involved not just internal policies, but an active engagement with the external discourse, a deliberate effort to counter the siren song of ruthless efficiency with a more compelling melody of ethical prosperity and human-centric progress.

The immediate aftermath of Victor Kline's downfall at Halcyon was a period of intense scrutiny, a frantic effort to excise the last vestiges of his oppressive regime. Smith, Lefler, and Berry, consumed by the monumental task of rebuilding, often focused on the visible wounds – the defunct departments, the rewritten policies, the public pronouncements of a new era. Yet, beneath the surface of these necessary structural adjustments, a subtler, more profound force was at play. It was the quiet hum of established human systems, the intricate network of trust, communication, and shared ethical understanding that had persisted, often silently, even under Kline's iron fist. These were not the grand pronouncements of leadership, nor the carefully curated metrics of performance, but the everyday interactions, the unwritten rules, the inherent organizational memory that had allowed Halcyon to endure, even to breathe, beneath the suffocating weight of its former CEO.

Kline's reign had been a testament to the potential for a single, powerful individual to warp an organization, to bend its very essence to their will. He had sought to replace the organic flow of human interaction with a rigid, top-down hierarchy, believing that control, absolute and unwavering, was the ultimate engine of progress. He had systematically dismantled channels of open communication, fostered an environment of fear and suspicion, and prioritized obedience over innovation. Yet, what he had failed to account for was the inherent resilience of human systems. These systems, built not on spreadsheets and directives but on shared experience, mutual respect, and the simple, fundamental act of listening, possessed a strength that even the most ruthless autocrat could not entirely extinguish.

Consider the story of the engineering division, a department that Kline had often viewed with a mixture of contempt and grudging necessity. He saw them as necessary cogs, brilliant but prone to endless debate, lacking the decisive clarity he prized. He had imposed strict reporting protocols, limited their access to information deemed "non-essential," and frequently overruled their technical recommendations with arbitrary directives. Despite this, within the teams, a different reality persisted. Engineers, bound by the shared challenges of complex problem-solving, continued to engage in informal knowledge sharing. They would gather at the coffee machine, not just for caffeine, but for the quick, unscripted exchange of ideas, troubleshooting a sticky problem, or offering a fresh perspective on a colleague's design. These were not sanctioned meetings; they were organic bursts of collaborative energy, fueled by a shared passion for their craft and an unspoken understanding that the best solutions rarely emerged in isolation.

When a critical technical hurdle arose, one that Kline's directives had inadvertently exacerbated by preventing the free flow of information, it was these informal networks that proved invaluable. A senior engineer, Susannah Fox-Baker, remembered a similar issue from years prior, a problem that had been solved through a nuanced understanding of a particular material's properties, a detail that had been deemed too minor for Kline's reporting structure. She discreetly reached out to a former colleague in a seemingly unrelated department; a connection forged during a rare cross-functional project years ago. This colleague, in turn, remembered a similar challenge faced by the R&D team and pointed Susannah towards a potentially overlooked aspect of their current testing methodology. This chain of communication, spanning departments and years, bypassing official channels entirely, was a testament to the latent power of established relationships. It was the organizational equivalent of a deep root system, anchoring the company even when the visible trunk was being battered by storms.

The Renewal Pods, an initiative championed by Smith and Berry, became a formal acknowledgment of this underlying strength, a deliberate effort to nurture and leverage the very systems Kline had tried to suppress. Both understood that true innovation and problem-solving did not occur in a vacuum, nor did they solely originate from the top. They thrived in environments where individuals felt safe to share nascent ideas, to challenge assumptions, and to learn from one another. The pods, by design, fostered this environment. They brought together individuals from diverse backgrounds, encouraging open dialogue and mutual respect. What began as a strategic imperative to deconstruct Kline's legacy quickly evolved into a powerful engine of genuine organizational renewal.

In one such pod, focused on improving internal communication, a seemingly intractable problem emerged: the persistent silo effect between the sales and product development teams. Sales reported a lack of responsiveness from product development, citing delays in feature implementation and insufficient understanding of market needs. Product development, conversely, felt that sales provided unrealistic demands and lacked technical appreciation for the complexities of development cycles. The official channels, the interdepartmental memos, the scheduled review meetings – all had failed to bridge this gap, often becoming forums for blame rather than solutions.

It was within the informal gatherings of the Renewal Pod that the breakthrough occurred. A junior sales representative, Maria Rodriguez, who had never previously felt empowered to voice her concerns at a higher level, shared a story during a casual discussion. She described how, in her previous role at a smaller, less structured company, she had developed a close working relationship with a lead developer. They had established a quick chat system, a daily fifteen-minute check-in where Maria would provide a candid overview of customer feedback, and the developer would offer insights into current project roadmaps. This informal loop, she explained, allowed for rapid iteration and a shared understanding that prevented misunderstandings before they even took root.

Her story resonated with a senior product manager, David Lee, who had been frustrated by the very same communication breakdown. He realized that Maria's experience highlighted a critical missing element: a consistent, low-friction channel for direct, human-to-human interaction. He proposed a pilot program within the pod: a designated "buddy system" pairing sales representatives with product managers. These weren't formal reporting relationships, but informal, encouraged partnerships focused on mutual understanding and proactive problem-solving. The results were almost immediate. Misunderstandings decreased, feature requests became more realistic and actionable, and a sense of shared ownership began to emerge. This was not a victory of a single leader's vision, but the triumph of a deeply ingrained human system – the need for connection and shared understanding – channeled and amplified by a supportive organizational structure.

The strength of these systems also manifested in the collective memory of Halcyon's employees. Kline's tenure had been marked by a deliberate erasure of past successes and a disregard for institutional knowledge that didn't align with his immediate goals. He had fostered a culture where people were afraid to reference previous, albeit different, successful strategies, lest they be seen as resistant to his "new" vision. However, the collective memory of effective practices, of past triumphs achieved through collaboration and ethical conduct, remained. This wasn't a documented history in a company archive; it was a lived experience, a shared understanding passed down through informal conversations, mentor-mentee relationships, and the quiet observation of how things used to work.

When Berry, Smith, and Zepher began to implement their new initiatives, they found that this collective memory acted as a powerful accelerant. They didn't have to invent every best practice from scratch. Often, they were simply revitalizing or formalizing approaches that had once been successful but had been suppressed. For instance, the reintroduction of cross-functional project teams was met with a sense of recognition and relief by many long-serving employees. They remembered instances where similar structures had fostered innovation and efficiency, and they could readily articulate the conditions under which such teams had thrived. This existing knowledge base, this implicit understanding of what worked and why, significantly reduced the learning curve and the resistance to change.

Furthermore, the very act of dismantling Kline's more egregious policies served to validate and strengthen the underlying human systems. The abolition of the punitive performance metrics, for example, did not simply remove a negative. It allowed for the re-emergence of intrinsic motivation. Employees, no longer solely driven by the fear of arbitrary penalties, began to invest more energy in genuine collaboration, in mentoring junior colleagues, and in pursuing projects that held intrinsic value, even if they didn't offer immediate, quantifiable returns in Kline's narrow definition. The simple act of removing a destructive force allowed a more constructive force – the innate human drive for purpose and contribution – to flourish.

The concept of trust, so systematically eroded by Kline, was perhaps the most critical human system to be rebuilt, and it was here that the resilience of the organization was most evident. Trust is not something that can be decreed or mandated. It is earned through consistent, ethical behavior, through transparency, and through the demonstration of empathy. While Kline had operated on the principle of "trust no one," the employees of Halcyon, even in the darkest days, had found ways to build pockets of trust amongst themselves. These were the informal alliances, the whispered confidences, the small acts of support that allowed individuals to navigate the oppressive environment.

When the new leadership began to foster an environment of openness and accountability, these existing, albeit fragile, networks of trust provided a foundation upon which to build. Molly Lefler, in particular, understood the crucial role of psychological safety. She recognized that for genuine communication to occur, individuals needed to feel secure in expressing dissenting opinions, in admitting mistakes, and in taking calculated risks. Her work on revising HR policies, focusing on restorative justice rather than punitive measures, and her insistence on open forums for feedback, were all designed to cultivate this safety.

The effect was palpable. Teams that had once operated with a high degree of caution, carefully guarding their information and interactions, began to open up. The fear of being punished for speaking out, for pointing out flaws, or for suggesting alternatives, began to dissipate. This allowed for a more honest assessment of problems and a more collaborative approach to solutions. The strength of the system was not in its initial design, but in its capacity for self-correction and adaptation when the external pressures were removed. It was like a plant that, though stunted by drought, springs back to life with the first rain.

The sheer weight of collective experience and memory also acted as a bulwark against the seductive narrative of the singular, infallible leader – a narrative that Victor Kline had personified and that continued to hold sway in many corners of the corporate world. While Smith, Berry, and Zepher were indeed leaders, their approach was fundamentally different. They actively sought input, embraced diverse perspectives, and readily admitted when they didn't have all the answers. This was not a sign of weakness, as Kline's worldview would have suggested, but a recognition of the inherent limitations of any single individual.

Smith, in particular, championed this shift. Her emphasis on team-based decision-making, on distributed leadership within project groups, and on fostering a culture where challenging the status quo was encouraged, directly countered the lingering echoes of Kline's autocratic style. She often recounted historical examples, not of solitary geniuses, but of collaborative efforts that had achieved monumental feats. She would point to the development of the early aircraft, a process that involved numerous engineers, designers, and test pilots, each contributing their specialized knowledge. She would highlight the scientific breakthroughs that emerged from research teams, where constant peer review and collaborative refinement were integral to the process.

These narratives, grounded in the lived experience and collective memory of the workforce, served to demystify leadership. They demonstrated that true strength was not about projecting an aura of unassailable authority, but about facilitating the collective intelligence of the organization. The employees of Halcyon, having experienced the destructive consequences of a singular, domineering vision, were receptive to this more inclusive model. They had seen firsthand how a focus on individual ego could blind a leader to critical flaws, and how a fear-based environment stifled essential feedback.

The impact of these revitalized human systems was not always dramatic or immediately visible. It was often in the subtle shifts: a project team that, instead of waiting for explicit directives, proactively identified and addressed a potential bottleneck; a sales executive who took the time to walk through a product feature with a junior developer, not out of obligation, but out of a genuine desire for mutual understanding; an engineer who felt empowered to flag a potential ethical concern without fear of reprisal. These were the everyday manifestations of a healthy organizational ecosystem, the quiet hum of a system functioning as it was designed to, based on trust, open communication, and shared responsibility.

Ultimately, the story of Halcyon's recovery was not solely the story of Berry, Smith, and Zepher's strategic decisions. It was, in large part, the story of the enduring strength of the human systems that had persisted beneath the surface of Kline's tyranny. These systems, built on the foundations of trust, collaboration, and shared ethical principles, possessed an inherent resilience. They were the collective memory of the organization, the quiet persistence of individuals working within these structures, and the fundamental human need for connection and shared purpose. Victor Kline, in his pursuit of absolute control, had sought to obliterate these systems. But he had underestimated their deep-rooted power.

The true strength of Halcyon lay not in a single leader, nor even in its leadership team, but in the intricate, interconnected fabric of the organization itself – a fabric woven from the daily interactions, the shared experiences, and the quiet resilience of its people. The shadow of Kline might linger, but the light of these enduring human systems offered a more powerful, and more sustainable, path forward. They were the bedrock upon which a new, more ethical, and ultimately, more successful Halcyon was being built, brick by painstaking, human-centered brick. The narrative of Halcyon demonstrated that while individuals can inflict immense damage, well-established human systems – based on trust, communication, and ethical processes – possess an inherent resilience. The collective memory and the quiet, persistent actions of individuals working within these systems ultimately proved more powerful than one man's dictatorial vision. The true strength lies not in a single leader, but in the fabric of the organization itself.

The dust had settled, but the scent of it—acrid and unsettling—still clung to the air at Halcyon. Victor Kline was gone, his grand edifice of control dismantled brick by painstaking brick. Yet, the echoes of his reign resonated, not as a phantom limb, grief-stricken and phantom-painful, but as a palpable question hanging in the sterile corporate atmosphere. It was the question of direction, the fundamental divergence of paths that now lay before Halcyon, and by extension, the broader corporate landscape that had so closely watched its unraveling. The narrative of Kline's downfall wasn't a neat conclusion, a period at the end of a sentence, but rather a comma, a pause before the next, more profound, act.

This was the crux of it: the future, once a canvas for Kline's singular, terrifying vision, was now a blank slate upon which a multitude of possibilities could be painted. But the very act of choosing was itself a form of vulnerability. Kline had offered a seductive simplicity: a world where all questions had one answer, all actions had one predetermined motive, and all deviations were errors to be purged. He had presented himself as the embodiment of this singular truth, the "perfect man" whose unassailable logic and unwavering resolve were the only guarantors of success. It was a siren song for those weary of the messy, ambiguous reality of human interaction, for those who craved the certainty of absolute command.

The immediate aftermath had been characterized by a frantic energy, a desperate attempt to scrub away the stain of Kline's influence. Berry, Smith, Zepher, and countless others, each in their own way, had spearheaded this cleansing. They had focused on policy, on process, on the tangible scaffolding of a more ethical organization. Departments were restructured, ethical guidelines were reissued with emphatic annotations, and public declarations of a new dawn were broadcast with carefully calibrated sincerity. These were necessary steps, the visible surgery required to excise the tumor of corruption and control. But the deeper, more insidious challenge lay not in the structural repairs, but in the internal landscape of human choice.

The shadow of Kline wasn't merely a memory of malfeasance; it was a potent demonstration of a particular worldview, one that had gained traction in boardrooms and executive suites across the globe. It was the philosophy that saw human beings as malleable resources, to be optimized, managed, and ultimately, controlled for the sake of efficiency and profit. It was the belief that the complexities of human motivation, the nuances of empathy, and the inherent value

384

of collaborative exploration were impediments to progress, messy variables to be engineered out of the system. Kline had been the ultimate, albeit extreme, manifestation of this philosophy. His downfall was a warning, a stark illustration of where such a path could lead.

Now, Halcyon stood at a precipice. One path led back towards the familiar comfort of absolute control, perhaps not as starkly brutal as Kline's, but still rooted in the same underlying principle: that true progress could only be achieved through stringent oversight and the suppression of dissenting voices. This path offered the illusion of security, the predictable rhythm of command and obedience, the reassuring certitude that "the leader" knew best. It was a path that appealed to a deep-seated human desire for order, for clarity in a chaotic world. It was the path of the "perfect man," endlessly refined, endlessly applied.

The other path, however, was far more arduous, fraught with uncertainty and demanding a continuous, active engagement with the messy, unpredictable nature of human beings. This was the path of collaboration, of empathy, of genuine dialogue. It was a path that acknowledged the inherent worth of every individual, that recognized that innovation and insight could emerge from the most unexpected corners, and that true strength lay not in dictation, but in collective wisdom. This path demanded vigilance, a constant willingness to question assumptions, to listen to uncomfortable truths, and to build trust, not as a byproduct of efficient operations, but as its very foundation. It was the path of shared flourishing, of a future built not on the dictates of one, but on the contributions of many.

This was the choice that permeated every level of Halcyon, a silent undercurrent beneath the surface of strategic planning and operational adjustments. It was a choice made in the quiet moments of managerial decision-making, in the subtle shifts of departmental culture, and in the personal interactions between colleagues. Would they revert to the old ways, the systems that rewarded compliance and penalized dissent, albeit with a more palatable veneer? Or would they actively cultivate the nascent seeds of collaboration and empathy that the post-Kline era had begun to nurture?

Consider the case of the R&D department, once a fertile ground for Kline's suffocating directives. His belief in the singular genius, his disdain for iterative processes, had led him to demand immediate, polished results, often overriding the careful, step-by-step investigations that were the lifeblood of true scientific discovery. He would dismiss weeks of painstaking research with a flick of his wrist, demanding a "breakthrough" that fit his arbitrary timeline. This had, inevitably, led to shortcuts, to a culture of presenting findings that confirmed his biases, and to a deep-seated fear of reporting negative results or unexpected detours. The human cost was immense: talented researchers grew demoralized, innovative ideas withered on the vine, and the very integrity of the scientific process was compromised.

Now, under the new leadership, the R&D teams were being encouraged to embrace the very uncertainties that Kline had abhorred. Berry, a staunch advocate for this shift, had championed a revised approach to project management. Gone were the rigid, top-down deadlines that bore no relation to the realities of experimentation. In their place were flexible frameworks, emphasizing clear objectives, but allowing for organic exploration within those parameters. Project teams were empowered to define their own intermediate milestones, to experiment with different methodologies, and, crucially, to openly discuss and learn from failures.

One particular project, focused on developing a new generation of sensor technology, exemplified this new approach. The initial hypothesis, based on established principles, had been proven flawed after months of intensive work. Under Kline, this would have been a disaster, a career-ending admission of error. The team would have been pressured to either bury the findings or to desperately try to salvage a failing concept. Instead, the lead scientist, Dr. Isaac France, called a department-wide meeting. He didn't present a crisis; he presented a learning opportunity. He laid out the data, explained the failed hypothesis with clinical precision, and then, crucially, opened the floor for discussion.

The ensuing conversation was not a cascade of blame, but a vibrant exchange of ideas. A junior researcher, barely a year out of university, recalled a niche theoretical paper she had encountered during her studies, one that proposed an entirely different approach to sensor physics, one that Kline would have dismissed as "speculative nonsense." A seasoned engineer, who had spent years grappling with the practical limitations of existing technology, saw how this theoretical concept might overcome a specific hurdle they had repeatedly encountered. Within hours, a new research avenue was charted, a path that, under Kline, would never have been explored. This was the power of collaboration, of acknowledging that wisdom was distributed, not concentrated, and that the freedom to fail was the prerequisite for genuine innovation.

This shift, however, was not without its internal friction. The ingrained habits of obedience and fear were not easily shed. Many long-term employees, accustomed to the clear directives and predictable rewards of Kline's regime, found the ambiguity of the new approach unsettling. They craved the certainty of knowing exactly what was expected, the comfort of having a single point of authority to defer to. The idea of sharing responsibility, of actively contributing to strategy, felt like an added burden, a source of potential exposure.

Consider the middle management tier, a group that had thrived under Kline's system. They had been the conduits of his directives, the enforcers of his will. Their success had been measured by their ability to translate his commands into tangible results, often through the efficient suppression of any resistance or deviation from their subordinates. Now, they were being asked to become facilitators, coaches, and mentors. They were expected to empower their teams, to foster environments of psychological safety, and to guide rather than command.

Markham, a senior manager in the manufacturing division, was a prime example of this struggle. He had been a loyal lieutenant to Kline, adept at identifying inefficiencies and implementing cost-saving measures with ruthless precision. He saw his role as one of stringent oversight, ensuring that every worker adhered to the prescribed protocols. When Spears introduced the concept of "self-directed work teams," where production line workers were encouraged to identify and solve their own operational issues,

Markham was deeply skeptical. He viewed it as an abdication of responsibility, a recipe for chaos.

"They're not trained for this, Mr. Spears," Markham had argued during a departmental meeting, his voice laced with apprehension. "Their expertise lies in following the instructions, in executing the tasks we've meticulously designed. Asking them to innovate, to troubleshoot on the fly... it's a recipe for disaster. We'll have errors, delays, and frankly, a decline in quality. It's a risk we can't afford to take."

Spears, however, remained steadfast. He understood that Markham's apprehension stemmed from a deeply ingrained understanding of how organizations used to work, how control had been equated with competence. "Markham," Spears replied, his tone calm and measured, "we're not asking them to abandon the established protocols. We're asking them to improve them. Think about it: who better understands the nuances of that particular assembly line than the people who spend eight hours a day on it? They see the subtle inefficiencies, the minor glitches that our designers might miss. We're not replacing your oversight; we're augmenting it with their lived experience. We're empowering them to be problem-solvers, not just cogs."

To illustrate his point, Spears proposed a pilot program. A specific section of the assembly line, known for its recurring minor issues, was designated for this experiment. Markham was reluctantly assigned to oversee it, with the explicit instruction to observe and facilitate, rather than dictate. Initially, the workers were hesitant, accustomed to waiting for a supervisor to address any problem. But the encouragement from Spears, and the subtle shift in Markham's own demeanor – a conscious effort to listen rather than command – began to yield results.

One worker, a quiet woman named Anya, noticed a recurring misalignment in a component that caused a slight delay. Instead of waiting for Markham to notice, she approached him, explained her observation, and suggested a small, almost imperceptible adjustment to the feeder mechanism. Markham, compelled by Spears's mandate, didn't dismiss it. He asked Scott to demonstrate, and together, they experimented with her proposed adjustment. It worked. The misalignment vanished, and the line gained a few precious seconds per unit. This small victory, born from Tanya's observation and Markham's newfound willingness to listen, rippled through the team. Other workers, emboldened, began to proactively identify and suggest solutions. Markham found himself spending less time policing and more time collaborating. He began to see the merit in Spears's approach, not as a loss of control, but as a different, more potent form of influence – one built on earned respect rather than imposed authority.

This was the essence of the choice: the transition from a model of external control to one of internal motivation. Kline had believed that the carrot and the stick, amplified by the threat of his absolute power, were sufficient to drive performance. But this approach, while effective in the short term for certain tasks, ultimately stifled creativity, bred resentment, and eroded the very fabric of an organization. The new path at Halcyon, championed by Berry, Zepher, and Spears, was predicated on the understanding that true, sustainable success stemmed from harnessing the intrinsic drives of individuals: their desire for purpose, their need for autonomy, and their innate capacity for collaboration.

This manifested in the way performance was now evaluated. Gone were the punitive metrics that had fueled the fear culture. Instead, there was an emphasis on growth, on contribution to team objectives, and on the development of skills. Recognition was given not just for individual achievements, but for collaborative successes, for mentoring junior colleagues, and for embodying the company's renewed ethical principles. This was a subtle but profound shift, signaling that Halcyon valued the how as much as the what. It was a move away from a transactional relationship with employees to a more relational one, recognizing that people were not just resources, but partners in the enterprise.

Winona, in particular, was instrumental in this aspect of the transformation. Her background in organizational psychology had given her a deep understanding of the power of psychological safety. She understood that for individuals to be truly engaged, to bring their whole selves to work, they needed to feel secure in expressing their thoughts, their concerns, and even their doubts, without fear of retribution. She had spearheaded the overhaul of the company's HR policies, moving away from a punitive disciplinary system towards one focused on restorative practices. When conflicts arose, or when mistakes were made, the emphasis was on understanding the root cause, on learning from the experience, and on finding solutions that prevented recurrence, rather than on assigning blame.

This commitment to psychological safety was visibly demonstrated in the company-wide town hall meetings, a format that had been virtually nonexistent under Kline. These were not carefully stage-managed affairs, but open forums where employees could ask direct questions to the leadership team. Smith, Zepher, and Berry would address concerns, acknowledge challenges, and, importantly, admit when they didn't have all the answers. This transparency, this willingness to be vulnerable, was a powerful counterpoint to Kline's aura of infallibility. It signaled that at Halcyon, leadership was a process of shared discovery, not a monologue of pronouncements.

The lingering shadow of Kline was thus not just a cautionary tale of corporate excess, but a constant reminder of the fundamental choice that lay before every organization, and indeed, before society itself. The temptation of control, of the illusion of perfect order, was ever-present. It whispered in the ears of those who yearned for simplicity, who felt overwhelmed by the complexities of human interaction. It promised efficiency, predictability, and the comforting certainty of a singular vision.

But the experience of Halcyon had also illuminated the profound limitations of such a path. It revealed that true, lasting progress was not the product of fear and coercion, but of trust and empowerment. It demonstrated that the most innovative solutions, the most robust strategies, and the most resilient organizations were those that embraced the inherent diversity of human thought and experience, that fostered environments where individuals felt valued, heard, and safe to contribute their best.

The future of Halcyon, and indeed the future of any organization aspiring to genuine ethical leadership, was not predetermined. It was not a fixed destination, but a continuous journey, shaped by the daily choices made by its people. Would they choose the well-trodden, yet ultimately destructive, path of control, the path of the perpetually striving, yet ultimately flawed, "perfect man"? Or would they embrace the more challenging, yet ultimately more rewarding, path of collaboration, of empathy, of shared responsibility? The shadow of Victor Kline served as a perpetual, potent reminder that the choice was theirs, and that the vigilance required to steer towards genuine human flourishing demanded courage, integrity, and an unwavering commitment to the values that truly defined progress. It was a choice that would define not just the future of Halcyon, but the kind of world they aspired to build. The shadow, in essence, was not a specter of the past, but a stark and enduring illumination of the choices that lay ahead. It was the persistent echo of what happens when the desire for absolute control overrides the fundamental understanding of human dignity and collaborative potential.

The organization's capacity for self-correction, its ability to move beyond the destructive legacy, hinged entirely on its willingness to confront this choice, not just once, but continuously, at every turn. The path of control offered a tempting illusion of stability, a seductive promise of predictable outcomes. But the history of Halcyon, under Kline's dominion, had proven this to be a Faustian bargain, a short-sighted strategy that ultimately corroded the very foundations of innovation and trust. The alternative, the path of collaboration and empathy, demanded a higher level of engagement, a greater tolerance for ambiguity, and a deeper faith in the collective intelligence of its people.

It was a path that required leaders to relinquish the illusion of ultimate authority and to instead become architects of an environment where empowered individuals could collectively achieve what no single individual ever could. This was the enduring lesson of Victor Kline's tenure: that the future, if it were to be defined by genuine progress and not by the cyclical resurgence of autocratic tendencies, would be a future forged not by the dictates of a singular, "perfect" mind, but by the shared wisdom and courageous choices of many. The lingering shadow was not a harbinger of inevitable doom, but a stark, persistent reminder that vigilance, courage, and an unwavering commitment to ethical principles were the only true antidotes to the seductive allure of control, and the only guarantors of a future where human flourishing, not just corporate profit, was the ultimate measure of success.

Epilogue

Nothing ended.

The offices still open on time. The language of accountability still circulates, polished and rehearsed. Committees meet. Reports are filed. Everyone agrees the worst is over.

They are wrong.

What vanished was not power, but resistance to it. Not justice, but the expectation of it. People learned the correct posture—how to comply without appearing obedient, how to survive without believing.

The system no longer needs enforcers.

It trained its own witnesses.

And somewhere, buried beneath compliance metrics and archived decisions, the last unanswered question remains untouched—not because it was resolved, but because no one remembers who had the right to ask it.

The outcome stands.

There is no appeal.

www.ingramcontent.com/pod-product-compliance
Lightning Source LLC
Chambersburg PA
CBHW020508020726
47493CB00001B/235